THE SANTORINI WRITING RETREAT

EVA GLYN

One More Chapter
a division of HarperCollins*Publishers* Ltd
1 London Bridge Street
London SE1 9GF
www.harpercollins.co.uk
HarperCollins*Publishers*
Macken House, 39/40 Mayor Street Upper,
Dublin 1, D01 C9W8
This paperback edition 2025

1

First published in Great Britain in ebook format
by HarperCollins*Publishers* 2025
Copyright © Eva Glyn 2025
Eva Glyn asserts the moral right to be identified
as the author of this work

A catalogue record of this book is available from the British Library
ISBN: 978-0-00-864813-8

This novel is entirely a work of fiction. The names, characters and incidents portrayed in it are the work of the author's imagination. Any resemblance to actual persons, living or dead, events or localities is entirely coincidental.

Without limiting the author's and publisher's exclusive rights, any unauthorised use of this publication to train generative artificial intelligence (AI) technologies is expressly prohibited. HarperCollins also exercise their rights under Article 4(3) of the Digital Single Market Directive 2019/790 and expressly reserve this publication from the text and data mining exception.

Printed and bound in the UK using 100% Renewable Electricity
by CPI Group (UK) Ltd
All rights reserved. No part of this publication may be reproduced, stored in a retrieval system, or transmitted, in any form or by any means, electronic, mechanical, photocopying, recording or otherwise, without the prior permission of the publishers.

For the strangers who became friends during Rosanna Ley's writing retreats at Finca el Cerrillo

Wednesday 30th August

"And above all, don't forget there needs to be a terrible secret at the heart of the story."

Jo closed her agent's email and set her phone on the windowsill, resting her forehead on the glass. *Oh, the irony.* Below her, Curtis the gardener was sweeping hedge trimmings from the broad expanse of the drive. In about half an hour she'd make him a mug of coffee and they'd talk about everything he needed to do while she was away: what daffodil bulbs to buy for the spring, which of the perennials were worth dividing and whether the lawn needed an autumn feed. It would be bliss, losing herself in his enthusiasm. To be able to share your love for something was such a gift.

A gift she didn't possess. However hard she tried, she couldn't love writing. Not anymore. So why the hell had she ever agreed to lead a Kickstart Your Novel retreat, of all things? She needed more than a boot up her arse to put pen to paper herself.

Her chest tightened, her heart thudding ominously. She couldn't do it; she really couldn't. Just the thought of standing in front of people... But she'd committed, so backing out now wasn't an option either.

Slowly Jo lifted her head from the cool glass and gazed out over Wimbledon Common. The grass had faded to its end-of-summer yellowish beige. It would be good to get away. For so many reasons. She just had to keep telling herself that. Every few minutes, if necessary, until she was on that plane and the doors were shut.

Turning, she eyed the suitcases lying open on the dressing room floor. Authoring clothes: palazzo pants in neutral colours; tunic tops, plain or with subtle designs; a sundress or two; a couple of pashminas in case the air-con was aggressive or the nights became cool. Could she get away with flip-flops? Probably. The wide trousers hid a multiple of sins. She gazed down regretfully at her cut-off leggings and hooded sweatshirt. Maybe she'd take some to wear in her room? But no, even on days off she'd still be on duty; she'd still be Jessica Rose.

Perhaps a change of writing attire would do her good. She'd never thought of it before, but maybe sitting in front of her laptop dressed as Jessica would make a difference. God, she was clutching at straws. This whole writing retreat business was one great big frigging straw. No, she couldn't do it. Yes, she had to.

Jo clenched her hands into fists. *Breathe. Breathe and calm down.* This time tomorrow she'd be on Santorini and everything would feel different. From the photos she'd seen online, The Retreat

House was just the oasis of calm she needed. There'd be sun on her back, and a couple of thousand miles between her and Rees. That's why she'd agreed to this craziness really. That and about a bottle and a half of wine inside her when the email inviting her had arrived. Never the best time to make decisions. But putting distance between her and Rees was definitely a good one.

She always struggled to pinpoint exactly when her marriage had gone wrong. Maybe a slightly premature seven-year itch, but it felt like more than that. It had to be. Rees was on at least his second affair and, what was almost worse, she didn't give a damn. She only wished she could escape this gilded prison. *What a frigging cliché.* If one of her students at the retreat wanted to use the phrase, she'd certainly advise them against it.

One of her students. The reality hit home, punching Jo so hard it almost winded her. She sank onto the stool next to the dressing table. Five people had paid a hell of a lot of money for a world-famous, highly talented, best-selling novelist to help them write their books. And she was not that person.

She fumbled with her phone, her mother's number, as ever, at the top of her recent calls list.

"Mum. It's me. I can't do it."

"Oh, darling. Of course you can. This isn't Rees making you doubt yourself, is it? Just because he wants you home to cook his supper."

"No." He rarely came home for supper. But Mum didn't know things had reached that point.

"Then tell me exactly what's bothering you."

Thank goodness for Mum and her knack of breaking every

problem down into bite-sized pieces which were easier to resolve.

"OK, OK... I suppose ... if I'm struggling with my own work... I mean, how can I help anyone else?"

"Because struggling or not, you know your stuff. You have an internationally best-selling novel under your belt and a first class honours in creative writing, and if that doesn't qualify you to lead a retreat, then I don't know what does."

Good point, Mum.

Her degree was something Jo had barely considered; she did know the theory, even if—

"And you're probably fretting over the public-speaking aspect," her mum carried on. "You don't need to tell me that, but it's only five people. No worse than going to a dinner party with strangers. And within a few days you'll get to know them, then you'll wonder what you were so stressed about."

"Thanks, Mum. You always make me feel better."

If nothing else, she'd given her two little life rafts to cling to: her degree, and the dinner party analogy.

"Of course I do. You're my daughter, Jo. I know all your little wrinkles and love you for each and every one of them. Most of the time you just don't realise how talented you are, and I blame Rees for that. He chip, chip, chips away at your confidence, when he should be so proud of all you've achieved."

Except Rees was the only person who knew exactly how little she'd achieved. Just how devastated would her mother be if she ever learnt the truth? The truth – or rather the lie – that lay at the root of everything. The lie that spun out, twisted in, from that one decision. Had it even been a decision? Jo couldn't remember making it – not actively, anyway. Yet neither could she hide from the responsibility, however swept along by events she may or may not have been. There had most definitely been a point, probably multiple points, when she could have said no and nipped this whole charade in the bud.

Mum chatted for a while longer, until Jo remembered Curtis's coffee. She felt calmer now, calmer and a tad more confident. She needed to carry that to Santorini with her. She needed to write her own bloody book. Or at least start it. Her publisher had been more than patient. She hadn't needed to be told the writing – pun intended – was very much on the wall if she didn't deliver.

She jogged down the polished oak staircase and into the hall. The afternoon sun streaming through the windows on either side of the door was like a spotlight on the photograph of her and Rees on the red carpet at the premiere of *Only. Ever. You*. She was sure he'd placed it there deliberately as the first thing anyone coming into the house would see. She hated it. He wasn't even here, so why should she suffer the bloody thing? She laid it flat on its face on the table. That made her feel better as well.

In the gleaming white expanse of the kitchen, she selected Curtis's favourite coffee pod and inserted it into the machine. She'd have tea. And a biscuit. They both loved chocolate digestives. Maybe she'd slip a couple of packets into her case. Or give them to Curtis. And remind him he'd need to bring a flask for the next month.

Tucking the biscuits under her arm and picking up the mugs, she headed outside to find him. He was on his knees, weeding the long cottage-garden border they'd designed together two summers before, and as he heard her approach he stood and stretched, his short, dark curls a halo against the sun.

"Great timing, Jessica. I'm parched."

"I thought you might be."

Every week – no, twice a week – she almost told him that Jessica wasn't her real name, but somehow it seemed too late for that, and she bitterly regretted it. Only those closest to her called her Jo, and she could never pinpoint the moment Curtis had passed from gardener to friend. Her only friend. Even though he couldn't be much more than ten years older than her, his was a solid and reliable presence. A man she could actually talk to and laugh with. Be herself. Or as close as you could be with someone you couldn't even screw up the courage to tell your real name.

Summed up her whole bloody life, really.

"So are you all packed up for the big trip?" He brushed the dirt from his hands on his combats.

"Almost. My passport's in my bag and the taxi's booked for stupid o'clock in the morning." She handed him his mug. "I've made lists of my lists – I'm so scared I'll forget something."

He shrugged. "As long as it isn't your laptop, would it really matter? But I do get it. A month's a long time to be away from home. I reckon it might feel odd."

She looked around her. "I'll miss the garden, for sure. But at least I know it will be well looked after."

"I'll do my job while you do yours. You have a book to finish, if I recall. It would be great if it was out by Christmas.

Copies signed by my favourite client would save me no end of shopping."

"Unfortunately the world of publishing doesn't move that fast." And neither did she. For the last two books, every word had been like pulling teeth. Painful, rotten ones at that.

He grinned at her, easing a biscuit from the pack in her hand.

"Oh well, next Christmas then. Now, have you chosen the bulb varieties you want me to plant while you're away?"

Jo pulled out her phone. "I thought we could decide together."

He stepped closer, leaning over her shoulder. "I was hoping you'd say that."

How Jo had come to adore this garden. At first it had been nothing more than an escape from the house – a displacement activity when she should have been writing. And, if she was brutally honest, a way of delaying her first glass of wine of the day. The wine that took the edge off the guilt, made life just a little more bearable if Rees did come home. But slowly, under Curtis's patient guidance, she'd learnt the difference between annuals and perennials, how to deal with the white fly that plagued her roses, and the frankly mind-boggling number of varieties of the snowdrops she loved so much.

This was in complete contrast to the house. The previous owners had made a thing of the celebrity interiors guy who'd renovated it, but Jo loathed everything about it. Maybe because Rees name-dropped the designer to everyone he invited here to impress, which was basically everyone who stepped through the door. After they'd seen the sodding red-carpet photo, of course. And she'd been wheeled out as his famous wife.

She'd never planned this life. Never wanted it. It felt as though it wasn't even hers. And there was a reason for that. The same reason she couldn't escape it. The secret that only she and Rees shared. The lie that had spawned all the other lies.

She was a fraud. A fake.

And it was far too late to unravel everything now.

Thursday 31st August

Screwing up her nose, Zina Sideris surveyed the courtyard in front of her. She was proud of what she'd achieved. Really proud. Proud and excited and sick, all at the same time. The renovation had filled her every waking hour and Instagram feed for months; now she had to make it work as a business. For so many heartfelt reasons.

The Retreat House surrounded her on three sides: two flat-topped floors in the central portion plus single-storey arms with traditional barrel-vaulted roofs that created a rectangular cobbled courtyard. The clear blue of the sky contrasted gloriously with the freshly painted white walls as they sparkled in the sun. The colours of the Greek flag. Of every Santorini website – and a far cry from the rundown holiday lets that had stood here a year ago.

God, it had been some year. A year she could have never imagined. Tragedies and small triumphs, excitement and uncertainty, sacrifice – yes, sacrifice big time – and now this massive sense of achievement that coursed like adrenalin through her veins. Who would have thought her father's death would lead to all this? A totally new life. Especially as she'd loved her old one so much.

It must have been a day or two after her babá's funeral. Exhausted by everything, darling Mama had fallen asleep in front of the television, so Zina and her husband of five years, Lambros, had stepped onto the farmhouse terrace in the coolness of the autumn dusk. One look at Babá's empty chair had absolutely finished her, releasing the flood of tears she'd been holding inside. Lambros had held her, stroking her hair and rocking her gently in his arms.

Perhaps she'd been the one to suggest the walk, to get away from the sight of that bloody chair, so they'd headed out across the neglected vegetable patch towards the pistachio orchard that stretched up and along the northern slope of the valley, all the way to the winding dirt road which formed the farm's boundary.

The soil beneath their feet was parched, the stiff breeze catching the dust they disturbed, swirling it around in small puffs. The trees, barely taller than Lambros, gave little shelter. Here and there hung ruby-red bunches of nuts, most well beyond picking and destined only to fall to the ground or provide food for the flock of sparrows that chattered in the nearby branches as twilight settled over them.

They'd wandered between the trees, their dried and twisted leaves darkening in the gathering shadows, until they were behind the holiday apartments, unlet this season because with Babá so ill there'd been no one to look after them. The swimming pool lay empty, the land at the bottom of the valley where the campsite normally was, overgrown with weeds. Part of her childhood vanished, alongside the father she'd adored and tried so hard to make proud of her.

"It's sad to see it like this," she'd said with a sigh.

"I know." A silence. A very long silence before Lambros had said, "We could change that, Zi. Bring the farm back to life."

She'd looked up at him, and as the last of the light blushed from orange-pink behind his head she'd realised that for the first time in months hope shone in his eyes, a spark above the dark bruises highlighting his hollow cheekbones. Zina may have loved her life in Athens, but she loved her husband more. Oceans more.

So they'd come. Lambros in December, Zina following in February, having worked her notice but not entirely having worked through her misgivings. Even setting aside how she felt about returning to the island, Lambros had quite a track record of passions that waned after a couple of years at best. Furthermore, he knew nothing about farming; and finally her parents' property hadn't been much of a farm anyway. Her babá had switched into tourism years ago. Right at the budget end.

Released from the stressful job in insurance that had been destroying him piece by piece, Lambros had thrown everything into running the farm. In reviving the abandoned olive trees, vines and pistachios he'd come alive himself. From being constantly withdrawn he'd become animated, from monosyllabic to talkative, from distant to attentive. The threat of a major breakdown had been averted, and that alone had made the move worth it.

It was a thought she'd clung to during those first few

months. That and the fact they were making her mama's life more bearable simply by being here. But what about her? She'd given up so much. She'd adored her job in an Athens marketing agency, relished the challenges and how hectic it was, as well as the social whirl that accompanied it. Rural Santorini was a sleepy backwater she'd left at the age of nineteen, and now she'd returned she needed a project of her own. Even if Lambros was content to be a farmer, she was no farmer's wife. Not in a million years.

The answer was in the old farm buildings her babá had turned into apartments. Lambros had assumed they would do up part of the complex to live in themselves, but Zina had put her foot down. They had to generate extra income; farming alone was too risky. So they'd moved into the farmhouse with her mother and she'd glued herself to her computer researching the latest high-end trends in European holidays.

Three words came up again and again: boutique, retreat and sustainable. *Boutique* certainly had the right vibe, but on its own it was no good; Santorini was awash with boutique hotels, many of them with stunning caldera views, and although here on the low land near Akrotiri they were close to the sea, they were on the wrong side of the island for that. *Retreat* had possibilities, though. Writers, artists, yoga, business reboot breaks. And as she'd mulled it over, wandering around the sad and tatty lino-floored apartments, she had begun to see it as it could be and a wave of enthusiasm had surged through her. Five gorgeous rooms downstairs, together with a suite for the group leader and a studio on the first floor. It could be perfect. Perfect. And it was up to her to make sure it was.

Transformations on this scale cost money. Lots of money.

Zina had always known her parents lived frugally, but her father had left a surprising amount in the bank for someone who habitually lived in holey shirts and trousers shiny in patches with use. Not a fortune, but enough to have a modest budget to restart the farm and upscale the apartments. Sort of. At least, to do one or other of them properly. How best to use the money had become a source of constant bickering between her and Lambros, until her mother had stepped in and said that as the money was hers, she would give them exactly the same amount each, and they'd have to make the best of it.

Any sort of challenge lit a spark in Zina, so she'd dived into sourcing the best value materials, watching online tutorials on interior decorating and filling spreadsheets with her business plans. Trying to find ways to make a bigger profit than Lambros made the whole venture fun and exciting, rather than the frankly scary idea that the farm would never do well enough for them to live any sort of life.

Of course, a little friendly competition didn't mean they hadn't helped each other along the way. Zina would never have finished the house without Lambros turning his hand to mending window catches, putting up mirrors and shelves and pulling chunks of plaster from the walls… And in turn she had tended young tomato plants, harvested grapes and even rounded up those damned goats more times than she cared to remember.

Finally, The Retreat House stood ready. And not a moment too soon, given that her first tutor would arrive at lunchtime, followed by the rest of the guests tomorrow. The slightly sick feeling washed through her again, but she steeled herself against it. Failure was not an option, especially as not everything had gone to plan with the farm. It may have been a good year for the tomatoes, but the first fava crop had failed when, just days before the harvest, the unseasonably hot April had more or less fried the valuable little beans in their pods. Scarily, Lambros had withdrawn into himself again, until her mother, Panora, had persuaded him that these things happened in farming and not to take it personally.

Luckily, the weed-infested mess that remained was a little further down the valley next to the goat enclosure, while the view from the retreat was over the low circlets of vines towards the olive grove. Unfortunately, from ground level the sea was hidden by the gentle rise of the land, but overall the setting gave the impression of being cocooned in nature far from the real world, which was exactly the vibe she'd been hoping to achieve. At least for her guests she'd been able to make a virtue of being this far from civilisation, even if she didn't much like it herself.

The last few days had been an almighty rush of finishing off, and she'd been planting geraniums and fragrant basil into the terracotta pots on the dining terrace until almost midnight last night. It had been so worth it; the splashes of vibrant red and deep pink enticed the eye towards the long communal table, surrounded by comfy director-style chairs in striped blue and white fabric, the matching awning fluttering above. As well as filling the air with their scent, the herbs would keep the annoying flies away. It was no coincidence that pots of basil could be seen on the windowsills of most of the homes on the island.

No coincidence either that hers were so Instagrammable. Zina crouched, snapped, checked and uploaded. Greens, pinks, blues. The rich colours and funky angles her followers expected. Totally on brand. The likes would soon flood in. The likes connecting her to a wider world. A world she knew, and loved, and did not want to forget her.

The picture made the story. Just like celebrity grabbed attention. Which was why she had aimed high for her first tutor, and she could still hardly believe that Jessica Rose, author of best-selling book and movie *Only. Ever. You.* had agreed. Zina had actually, literally, screamed when she'd received Jessica's email, bringing her mother running from the terrace in a total panic. It had been one of the most joyous moments in a long time as they'd danced around the kitchen together. To have made Mama dance again, however briefly, had meant the absolute world.

Zina nibbled what was left of her thumbnail. Would Jessica Rose actually turn up? She had no solution for that particular scenario, and just the idea of a no-show had sent her already high stress levels through the roof. Rather than a triumphant start to brag about, she'd have a total disaster on her hands. She had no Plan B for a tutor; how could she? All the guests would want their money back and the retreat would stand empty for another whole month. There'd be pitifully little in the bank if that happened, and with the tomato season almost over, she could expect nothing from the farm until they were paid for the grapes they'd sold to a local winery.

No, she had to believe. She had absolutely no reason at all to think the woman would let her down – it was just first night nerves. She opened Jessica Rose's website on her phone and looked at her picture. She didn't have a mean face; she had an honest face, as far as you could tell under all that make-up.

Small, even features, pale eyes, a rather hesitant-looking smile. It would be OK. It would. Unfurling her fingers from her phone and slipping it into the pocket of her cut-offs, Zina crossed the courtyard to continue her final tour of inspection.

The heavy wooden double doors that led to the staircase and the bedroom in the central portion of the ground floor were her pride and joy. They were probably as old as the building itself, maybe even older. Her father had painted them blue, but she'd stripped off every last flake, then fed and polished them with beeswax until they'd returned to their deep burnished gold. It had been just the best surprise when Lambros had come home one day with beautiful cast-iron fixtures for them. The fact that he'd thought of it, had thought of *her*, had made her heart sing. The moment she'd known beyond all doubt she had the man she'd married back.

Pushing the doors open, Zina entered the cool terracotta-tiled hall. Most of the materials she'd used were reclaimed; not always the cheapest option, but she was proud of the fact. Over-tourism was becoming a significant issue on Santorini so she'd been determined to keep the retreat's carbon footprint as modest as possible. Water-efficient bathrooms, definitely no hot tubs, and the difficult decision not to revive the swimming pool. After all, even though their land had no direct access to the sea, it wouldn't take her five minutes to run her guests down to Akrotiri beach if they wanted a dip.

Unlike most of the other rooms, the group leader's suite upstairs was completely devoid of original features so it had been the hardest to design. The box-like appearance hadn't mattered for the studio on the opposite side of the landing – that was meant to be functional – but Zina had wanted an ultra-luxe feel to attract the best possible tutors, and she was delighted the result showed the thought, and not just the hours of hard graft, that had gone into it.

For a start, the lounge area could be separated from the bedroom by an opaque glass sliding door, which meant it could double as a private tuition area or breakout room from the studio. Linen-covered sofas flanked a low coffee table, and matching vintage teak bookcases filled the spaces below the windows at either end. She'd been careful to make sure that copies of Jessica Rose's best-selling book in at least three languages graced the shelves. Detail was everything.

She picked up the Greek translation, which was her own copy. She'd never had much time for books, but *Only. Ever. You.* had been such an Instagram sensation she'd felt compelled to read it. She'd been totally swept up into the tragic, aching beauty of Eloise and Anna's secret romance, its vivid descriptions of London – a city Zina loved – in the 80s and 90s, and the undercurrents of male dominance that blighted both their lives in different ways. She hadn't doubted for a moment that the book deserved its accolades, and that Jessica Rose was a rare and special talent.

After a final glance around, Zina ran down the stairs. At the window halfway she stopped. In the drying yard behind, Lambros's dark head was bent as he swept the floor in preparation for the pistachio harvest which he hoped would start soon. His arms were deeply tanned, a million miles from the city pallor that had worried her so much just a year before.

Oh, those muscular arms. Even stronger now than when they'd first caught her attention at the gym. Arms that invited her to climb into them, be held by them, feel cherished in them.

She looked again, thrills spiralling to the pit of her stomach. Oh, what she wouldn't do for half an hour for a little passion beneath the pistachios. That half an hour they never seemed to find.

The spark was still there – of course it was. And it was normal, wasn't it, when they were both working so hard and had little time for each other, that they wouldn't feel quite so close? Normal, and temporary. Surely it was temporary? Zina nibbled the quick of her thumb. These last months had been harder than hard and while there'd been plenty of laughs and moments of joy, there'd been more than enough niggles too. Living with her mother didn't help either because they had no time alone, but what choice did they have?

Lambros looked up and, seeing her there, blew her a kiss. She sent one in return then, filled with a happy glow, set off to inspect the bedroom below. A movement in the courtyard caught her eye through the open door. *Putana!* No! Two furry heads were munching contentedly on her geraniums. The geraniums she'd been up until midnight planting.

"Lambros! Lambros!" she screamed, running at them. "Get your arse over here! Your *bástardos* goats are eating my plants."

If he dared to laugh, she would absolutely – *absolutely* – kill him.

Friday 1st September

As soon as she realised Santorini was coming into view, Professor Karmela Simic grabbed her suitcase and headed onto the small deck at the back of the ferry, gratefully gulping the sea air that ruffled her short, dark hair. Why, oh why, had she not flown directly here, instead of taking a couple of days to see the historical sites of Athens on the way?

The journey had been an absolute nightmare, even in her VIP seat well away from the noisy mass of humanity filling the boat. Not that she was a VIP, but the extra twenty-euro price tag had seemed worth it when she booked. She had envisaged getting some writing done, or just the bliss of reading, but no, she had felt sick as a dog all the way.

She had sat, alternately hot and cold, sipping water whenever she dared in a futile attempt to keep her surging stomach at bay. The long haul from Piraeus to Mykonos had taken all morning, the boat pitching and tossing so much she had barely been able to open her eyes. It had calmed a little between Paros and Naxos and now, finally, at three o'clock, they were heading into Santorini's famous caldera.

The outdoor space at the back of the ferry was tiny and the tang of cigarette smoke hung in the spray created by the plume of water frothing behind them. Holding her breath, Karmela worked her way through the groups of people to the rail, then leant on it, her legs strangely weak. In the distance behind them were the hazy humps of small islands, the thrumming beat of the engines slowing as they entered the egg-shaped archipelago which had once formed the volcano's crater. Looking up to her right she spotted a mass of white-painted buildings perched on top of steep black and terracotta cliffs, in stunning contrast to the deep blue backdrop of sky.

So this was Santorini… It looked every bit as beautiful as the pictures she had seen online. Beautiful, and no doubt crowded, but only last year she had lived through a summer in Dubrovnik so she was sure she could cope. A city girl at heart, this was not where she would have chosen herself, but now she was here she was going to make the most of it. Her nausea retreating, excitement surged through her, making her grin wildly too. A whole month to focus on her historical novel.

She had been beyond surprised – genuinely beyond surprised – when, on the Sunday after her forty-third birthday, her mother had handed her an envelope with the booking for the Kickstart Your Novel retreat.

"There you are, Karmela," she had said. "You need to stop talking about this book of yours and start writing it. And this fits in perfectly before your university term starts." Unfortunately it did not; it would be an awful rush when she got home at the end of the month, but she had spent the last few weeks preparing her lectures like a woman possessed, so now she was free to write, and nothing else, for the whole of September.

For most of her life, Karmela's relationship with her mother had been distant, if not a little troubled – at no time more so than over the last year when she had been desperately trying to put that right. She had no doubt in her mind that they had both been damaged by their experiences as refugees fleeing from Sarajevo during the Balkan war, but her mother dismissed the idea as nonsense.

Karmela understood her denial all too well. For most of her adult life she had told herself that being a refugee had made her an outsider, and that it suited her well. But newly forged friendships she had made in Dubrovnik had shown her how much she had been missing. Her carefully constructed defences had come crashing down, buried emotions bubbling up to meet them and washing the last of the bricks away. The joy that letting people into her life and finding her place in theirs had given her had been truly life-changing, and forging new friendships was something she now embraced wholeheartedly wherever she went.

More than anything she wanted her mother to acknowledge the hurt and reconnect with her own emotions. Mama being so distant and cold had become more than painful – both to see and to experience – when she herself had moved into a world so full of feeling.

With the zeal of the newly converted, Karmela had set about trying to convince her mother it was the only way. Looking back, it was hardly surprising it had quickly become a source of friction between them. Useless friction at that, because her mother would not even talk about the subject, and for a while Karmela had been at a loss over what to do. Especially as her mother claimed she lived a very full life, so clearly nothing was wrong. It broke Karmela's heart that she could not see that what she lacked was emotional connection, even with her only child.

Eventually, Karmela had decided her best option was to be herself. Her new self. When she had first started sharing feelings, rather than opinions backed by objective facts, her mother had almost visibly flinched. But she had persevered, and these days Mama seemed to have become a little more used to it. At least she did not change the subject quite so rapidly, and the gift of the retreat had shown a depth of understanding of her daughter that Karmela found not only surprising, but which filled her with hope. Mama may not have been able to say as much, but she had shown she cared about her in no uncertain terms.

Her mother had seen what Karmela herself had barely recognised: that without an external impetus she would have kept researching the historical aspects of her novel and kept making copious notes without ever leaving her academic comfort zone and putting pen to paper. Here on Santorini, she would have to do it. Especially because when Mama had dropped her at the airport for her flight to Athens she had actually hugged her and told her to get the damn book written because she wanted to read it. It was the first real hug they had shared in years.

Karmela jumped as something cold and wet nudged her leg. Looking down, she met the amber eyes of an almost silver greyhound, which was gazing up at her with an adoring expression. Without thinking, she reached to stroke its head.

"*Hej ti,*" she murmured softly.

A male voice came from above, slightly overloud and English. "I am so sorry." He spoke slowly and left a gap between each word.

"It is OK," she told him. "I speak your language."

"Then I'm sorry again."

She unbent from the dog to find herself standing next to a tall man with a frighteningly short haircut and the most arresting green eyes she had ever seen. His nose had a slight bump but his smile radiated warmth, and she could not help but grin back. Despite the hair, he was surprisingly attractive.

"There is no need. I spoke to your dog in Croatian, after all. It is a rather endearing creature."

"Doesn't she know it? She's a rescue dog, a former racing greyhound, and I'm afraid she can be a little bit naughty."

"And with those eyes of course you forgive her anything."

His laugh was as warm as his smile. "Got it in one."

He leant on the rail next to her, while the dog rested her head against his knee. Behind them the hilltop village was slipping away, and Karmela could see that as well as the houses on top, a huddle of buildings fringed the shore, tucked beneath the honeycomb of russet-grey cliffs. She guessed the varied palette of colour in the rocks was to do with the island's volcanic origins, and it gave the caldera an almost otherworldly feel. In places they were blacker than black but in others, layers of red, ochre, gold and cream sparkled in the sun. It was almost the moonscape of her imagination, but surrounded by sea.

Her new companion interrupted her thoughts. "I don't think we can be long from docking."

"Which is something of a relief. I have just discovered I am not the best of sailors. Zagreb is a long way from any ocean."

"Are you all right now? Is there anything I can get you?"

"That is kind, but no. I feel better for being outside, and I am being met at the port."

"OK. Just thought I'd ask." He looked at her for a long moment, before turning back to the view.

Ships passing in the night. On a ship at that.

She smiled to herself as she gazed at nature's majestic walls rising up from the sea, fringed white with the buildings on top like icing on a cake. Should she grasp the nettle and ask if he was staying on the island long? Should she grab this potential opportunity with eager hands? But she had a book to write and she could do without the distraction, especially as Mama had paid for the retreat. She needed to repay that belief.

Even as she was pondering the question, an announcement came over the Tannoy, first in Greek and then in English, asking drivers to return to their vehicles.

He straightened, grasping the greyhound's lead.

"Right. That's us. Have a great holiday."

"You too."

If nothing else, it had been a pleasant way to pass ten minutes. She had to tell herself that was all it was, but oh, those eyes, that look... She had probably imagined the look. What did she know about flirting anyway? Laughing quietly at herself, she leant back on the rail to enjoy the ferry's final approach to Santorini's bustling quayside.

Jo leant on the Juliet balcony and gazed over the patchwork of fields towards the dazzling strip of sea that at this distance danced with sequinned light. How she longed to dive in and stretch her tired arms and legs, but when she'd asked Zina if she could walk to the nearest beach her host had shaken her head and told Jo she only had to ask and she'd give her a lift. But that seemed like too much of an imposition, so Jo decided tomorrow she'd find out about hiring a car.

The view was not how she'd pictured Santorini, but was glorious all the same – far better than the shiny white urban sprawl around the airport, which had sent her heart plummeting to her sandals. Rather than being perched on the caldera, The Retreat House was on the island's gentler slopes, away from the dramatic expanse of water which had once been the volcano's heart. Below her were olive groves, vineyards and empty fields of cracked earth, dusty grey in some places and almost red in others in striking contrast to the silver green of the trees. The hum of cicadas filled the air, punctuated now and then by the bleats of the goats who wandered between the low mounds of russet-fringed vines. How idyllic was this?

Closer to hand, the courtyard blazed with pots full of colourful flowers and scented herbs that made her heart sing. Nearer still, the richly coloured bougainvilleas which were beginning to wind their way around her balcony rails fluttered in the gentlest of breezes like so many butterflies. Leaning over, Jo snapped a picture of the unusual orange one with her phone to send to Curtis. She knew he'd love to see it.

Reluctantly she dragged herself away. Her bedroom was

light and airy, the walls, wardrobe doors, floorboards and the crisp linen on the bed were white – or rather whites, if you looked carefully enough. It was the perfect backdrop for a whole palette of blues; on cushions, the inviting easy chair by the window. She'd spent much of her day here, book in hand, peeping out from behind the gauzy curtains as her charges arrived, knowing in her heart of hearts she should go down to greet them if only she weren't crippled by shyness. Her first epic fail.

It had, however, helped that she'd had lunch with the first arrivals, an American couple who she guessed were in their early fifties: Susan, with straight blonde hair and huge pink plastic glasses, wanted to write a family history, while Ellen was an artist who'd come with her to sketch. Despite restricting herself to one small glass of wine, Jo had almost relaxed as Susan regaled her with tales of her work as a librarian in a small town called Alpena on the shores of Lake Huron. Her enthusiasm for her work, and books in general, bubbled into a constant stream of delightful chatter. Jo really, really hoped that everyone would be as nice.

Shortly after lunch, Zina had collected two friends, Diana and Sophie, from the airport, and from the safety of her window Jo had watched her show them into adjacent rooms on the opposite side of the courtyard to the dining terrace. Zina's energy and enthusiasm had been palpable, her ponytail of shiny black hair bouncing behind her slim shoulders. Oh to be that confident with people you'd met only half an hour before.

Nothing about their appearance gave Jo any clue which of the friends was which. Both appeared to be in their mid to late sixties, both were shorter than Zina, and one almost painfully thin. Her angular features were made all the more pronounced by her choppy haircut, her hair almost certainly dyed a subtle shade of bronze, while her companion had embraced her natural grey. From the little Jo could see, it suited her, as did the calf-length floral skirt and pale blue T-shirt she was wearing. She was a woman who looked more than comfortable in her own skin.

Curious, Jo checked the lever-arch file Zina had prepared for her. Reading their sign-up forms one after the other, Jo was surprised to see Sophie's said that since their schooldays the women had dreamt about writing a romance together and now they were both free of caring responsibilities they were determined to do it. Meanwhile, Diana claimed Sophie had broached the idea of coming to the retreat recently, and she'd readily agreed, especially as Sophie's friend's husband was in a care home with dementia and no longer knew her, so she needed a distracting break. Given their circumstances, perhaps the over-thin, slightly fraught-looking woman was Sophie. Only time would tell.

Returning to the folder, Jo noticed that the fourth participant was a professor of Medieval History from Zagreb University. Perhaps it should come as no surprise she wanted to write an historical novel set in medieval Dubrovnik, and such was her level of organisation she had attached a detailed scene-by-scene plan. Jo could only hope that this was evidence of commitment and enthusiasm and not that she was an inflexible control freak. The thought of having a professional teacher scrutinise her every move was bad enough. What if she turned out to be a fraud as both a writer *and* a tutor?

She couldn't do this. Really she couldn't.

Jo took one deep breath, and then another.

Remember the life raft. Her degree. And anyway, she wasn't teaching, she was tutoring, mentoring… A voice from long ago echoed around her head. Some snarky girl at school. *"Those who can, do; those who can't, teach."*

Well she couldn't *do*. So maybe she could teach?

A car pulling into the parking spaces beyond the courtyard distracted her. A man with an incredibly short haircut jumped out, no doubt to quell the cacophony of barking from the rear of the hatchback. Ekaterini, the cook, bustled across the terrace to meet him. He reached to shake her hand before opening the boot and releasing a greyhound, which cavorted around him as though it had been trapped in the car for hours. This must be Iain. He'd cut it fine, but presumably he'd come on the ferry from which Zina was collecting the professor.

Locking her room behind her, Jo crossed the beeswax-scented landing to the studio, her flip-flops sinking into the softness of the ever-so-slightly worn cream and blue rug. Jo loved the shabby-chic vibe of the retreat – so fresh and relaxing, so understated. Maybe she could try it at home and make that awful house more like hers. But was it really worth the aggro she'd get from Rees if she did?

The studio was laid out exactly as she'd asked Zina, with four glossy white trestle tables pushed together to form one large workspace with six chairs around it, one at either end and two on each of the longer sides. Two more tables were set against the walls, providing space for anyone who preferred not to work in their rooms, and a fridge hummed in the corner. Jo peeped inside to find it well stocked with soft drinks and a jug of fresh milk for the coffee machine that sat on top of it.

At either end of the studio, windows flooded the space with light, reflecting off the white-painted floorboards and walls. Everything about it oozed brightness and energy, and a ray of hope sparked through Jo. Could she perhaps do this after all? Did she actually know enough to help other people write wonderful books? Even if she singularly failed to do so herself?

Perching on the edge of the table nearest the inland-facing window, she gazed up the hill and over the pistachio trees towards the back of the caldera ridge.

She could do this, she could.

She'd visualised the next half hour so many times, imagined herself greeting the participants as they arrived one by one, then once everyone was here, getting them to talk about themselves and their writing ambitions. How hard could that be?

Very soon the pieces of paper in the file she was clutching so tightly it bit into her fingers would begin to flesh out into real people, rather like characters who grew from a single page and went on to fill a whole book. Jo liked the analogy and decided she might even use it. It would at least make her sound like a proper writer.

Not that the first session would require any knowledge at all. After the introductions, all Jo planned to do was explain how the retreat would run: an hour or so each morning for some tuition and exercises, and for everyone to share their objectives for the day; then writing time until late afternoon when they would come back together to discuss their progress and share their work. Added to that, Jo would offer each of them a one-to-one session every few days to help them hone their manuscripts.

It wasn't complicated … and yet it was. So much depended on how well the group gelled together, and she was the one who needed to make that happen, even though she was well aware that one awkward person could derail everything. She just had to keep her fingers firmly crossed it didn't happen because she rated her chances of managing someone with a strong personality at about zero. Just look at her and Rees.

With the benefit of hindsight, she had a strong suspicion that Rees's dominant personality had been part of the initial attraction. She'd liked that he demanded so little of her. She'd never had to worry about deciding where to go on dates, for weekends away… She'd let him take responsibility for everything, which had probably become a habit for them both – and not a good one from her point of view, not now. But he'd been an absolute rock when she'd needed him and she'd been so damned grateful that she'd somehow fallen into the trap of thinking her dependence was love.

So when had that changed? She couldn't be sure. Had it been when she quit her day job to write, so that apart from official author stuff she couldn't wriggle out of she saw no one but him? When they moved out to Wimbledon? When he stopped coming home every night? She could remember no single moment, and what shocked her most of all was that she'd never much cared. Surely your husband's infidelity was meant to hurt? In the end she concluded she'd never really loved him at all.

Her musings were interrupted by the sound of footsteps on the stairs. A wave of crippling shyness washed through her, leaving her gulping for air. She had nowhere to run, nowhere to hide. One by one she unfurled her fingers from the folder, then stood.

Breathe, Jo, breathe. Breathe and smile.

Zina was paying her to be Jessica Rose, and she could not let her down.

Zina looked around the winter dining area, which doubled as the honesty bar. Champagne flutes polished, check. Santo Sparkling on ice, check. Non-alcoholic fruit punch in the fridge, check.

"Ekaterini!" The singing in the kitchen stopped. "I'm heading home for a quick break, unless there's anything you need me to do."

"Nothing at all. Without you under my feet I can finish the meze at my own pace."

The guests all seemed nice enough, Zina thought as she set off down the track towards the farmhouse, although it had been hard to tell with poor Karmela. She'd gone very quiet in the car as they'd climbed the hairpin bends from the harbour, her skin taking on a greenish-grey hue as she explained that her motion sickness, which had started on the boat, had returned. So Zina had taken every turn extra-slowly, praying that Karmela wouldn't actually throw up, and within minutes of arriving at The Retreat House she'd been tucked up in bed with a jug of iced water beside her to sleep it off.

Zina scanned the parched landscape for Lambros, but he was nowhere to be seen; not in the lower reaches of the pistachio orchard or the vegetable garden to her right, nor ahead of her, leaning into the enclosure to talk to his precious goats. What had he said he was doing this afternoon? *Skatá!* She didn't know. She really should listen to him more carefully, but the retreat was occupying her every waking moment. It was hardly surprising as today was its most important day.

A few hundred yards down the valley stood her childhood home, screened from The Retreat House by one end of the small forest of pistachio trees her father had planted a few years before he gave up farming for good. The farmhouse had grown generation by generation, but had never run to a second floor, even though the rusting iron rods to build one stuck out from the flat roof of the extension her parents had added not long before she was born.

The earlier parts of the house were barrel-roofed in the traditional manner, and in desperate need of a lick of paint – or at least a jet wash to remove the grey-brown dust covering them. The windows, however, sparkled – kept that way by her mother – and behind them were the kitchen and living area, and a lean-to utility to one side. From this angle Zina couldn't see the rattan-covered terrace, but it stretched along the far side of the house giving views towards Akrotiri's famous archaeological site and beyond it, the sea.

Even before she opened the flyscreen which served as a kitchen door for most months of the year, Zina could hear her mother's favourite radio station playing softly, and smell the heady mixture of onions, rabbit and cinnamon which meant she was cooking *stifádo*. The comforting sounds and aromas of childhood wrapped themselves around her, their magic loosening her knotted shoulders. Whatever the stresses and strains of moving back in with a parent, she still enjoyed coming home and sharing her day with her mother, just like they had when she'd been at school. It had been a precious time, just the two of them, before Babá came home and her mother's focus turned to him.

"Mama! I'm taking a break. Where are you?"

"On the terrace, *agápi mou*. There's a lovely breeze."

Her mother sat in her favourite seat – one of a pair of old leather armchairs, Zina's father's looking awfully empty beside her. The loss of her husband had taken a physical toll as well as a mental one on her mother; she looked far older than her fifty-nine years, her hair definitely more salt than pepper in a long, loose plait that hung over the shoulder of her plain navy T-shirt. It broke Zina's heart; Mama had always loved vibrant colours and now she didn't wear them at all, and her face, once heart-shaped like Zina's, now sagged, the sparkle almost entirely absent from her dark eyes. Oh, how Zina longed to see that sparkle again.

Mama patted the chair beside her. "*Ela!* So tell me about your first guests."

"Five women and one man, so he may feel a little outnumbered. He's brought his dog, and even she's female."

"Well we must hope he doesn't mind too much. Is he young? Old?"

Zina screwed up her nose. "Somewhere in between – about fifty? He's been in the English air force and he's using this as a break before finding another job. He's not retired like the other English people."

"So he's the youngest as well?"

Zina shook her head. "That's the professor from Zagreb.

She was so seasick on the ferry that she went straight to bed to sleep it off."

"Poor woman. You must tell her to take ginger for the return trip. Now what about the—?"

Before Mama could finish her question, Lambros appeared around the side of the house and jumped onto the terrace, heeling off his dirty boots then flinging himself onto an old rattan chair, which creaked in protest at his muscular bulk.

"What a day! Exhausting, but good all the same."

Panora stood. "Then let me fetch you a beer. Zina, would you like anything?"

This was so typical of her mother, doing the things she used to do for her own husband for her daughter's. If Zina let it, it might niggle her, although she wasn't entirely sure why, but the important thing was it most likely brought Mama some comfort.

She glanced at the clock on her phone, then called over her shoulder, "I need to get back to work soon, but a sour cherry soda would be nice."

Lambros reached out and took Zina's hand. "It all went well today?"

"Yes. I was just telling Mama about the guests. But while she's fixing the drinks, what have you been up to?" She still felt guilty that she couldn't remember.

He raised an eyebrow. "The pistachios?"

"Of course. The pistachios. I'm sorry."

"It was an important day for you too."

"Are they ready to harvest yet?" She knew this first crop from her father's rather neglected trees should have been ripe by now, and they couldn't afford to lose them. Lambros and Yiannis, a local farmer who'd been mentoring him, had plans to dry them naturally in the sun to fully develop their flavours so they could be sold at a premium.

"Almost. Yiannis thinks they are ripening in September because the male trees were late producing pollen, most likely because of the harsh pruning they needed. I just hope to god he's right, but his knowledge hasn't let me down so far. I owe him so much."

Zina nodded. "The farming community have been good to you."

"Because I am trying to reverse the trend and make tourist land productive again; bring back some of the island's traditional way of life before it is completely lost and everywhere flat is covered with buildings." He could go on about this for hours if she let him. Best nip it in the bud.

"And what do they think of your wicked, wicked wife, encouraging more people to come here?" She put her hand on his thigh.

He laughed, leaning in to kiss her. "They don't know how wicked you are."

Zina's lips responded to his, the tingles from his tongue pirouetting right to the pit of her stomach. *Skatá!* This was by far the biggest downside of moving back here: no slipping off for a quickie, no privacy for these intimate moments. Especially as the beads across the open door rattled, heralding her mother's return with the drinks and a dish of their own small black olives.

Lambros sat back, mouthing the word "later", but she was

pretty sure by the time she finished serving the guests, then washed the glasses and stacked the dishwasher, he'd be fast asleep. But at least the spark was alive, even if it had been pushed to the back burner for the moment. She grinned at him, a warm glow spreading through her.

Her mother set the tray on the table and poured herself a generous measure from the bottle of ouzo. "So, Lambros," she said, "tell us about your day."

Hadn't they been talking about hers? But Zina knew her mother meant nothing by it; it was a generational thing, putting the man first. It had been the story of her childhood. Much as she'd loved her father and he'd loved her, the only way to get him to pay her any attention at all had been to come top in something, or at very least to be on the winning basketball team. Luckily, she'd been very good at basketball.

As Zina sipped her soda, half listening to Lambros explaining in minute detail everything Yiannis had told him, her mind drifted back to The Retreat House. She had a good feeling about this month. Jessica Rose was adorable – the very last sort of person to be a demanding diva; full of smiles yet reserved to the point of shyness. If Zina could only break through, they might even become friends. Imagine … being friends with a famous writer. Not everyone could claim that.

She missed her friends in Athens. Of course they had all promised to visit, but they had such busy lives and there just wasn't the money for Zina to go back to see them. Especially as they spent it like water on nights out. And anyway, she couldn't exactly invite them to the farm. Maybe when The Retreat House was quieter in the winter – then there'd be something worth showing them.

It wasn't as though she didn't know anyone on the island, but these days she had little in common with the girls she'd grown up with, even her former best friend Resi who tried her best to involve her in their plans. Resi was on maternity leave and must have time on her hands. Not that Zina was a snob, but her schoolmates worked in shops or as waitresses, had hordes of children, and she wasn't particularly interested in tales of sore nipples or rude cruise passengers. Just as well she was too busy to be lonely.

She downed her soda and, taking a couple of olives from the dish, stood. "Right, I'll just freshen up then get back to the retreat. See you both later." Although they looked up from their conversation and nodded, Zina had the feeling they'd hardly notice she was gone.

Wrong. She wasn't fifty metres up the path before she heard Lambros calling her name.

"Zi! Wait up!"

She bit her lip as she turned. His day may be over, but she needed to get back to work. Hopefully whatever he wanted wouldn't take too long.

"Today's a special one, and I want to mark it. I will never, ever forget that you came here to stop me falling apart, that you agreed to something you maybe weren't sure about … so I bought you these."

As he held out his gift, she noticed his hand was trembling. She took it between both of hers.

"You're all right?"

"Of course I am – thanks to you. I'm just sorry they're not real gold, but one day…"

Zina opened the box to reveal a pair of stud earrings in the shape of roses. Roses for love. It didn't matter at all that they were coloured metal; what meant so much was his desire to make her special day even more wonderful, and a happy glow spread through her.

"They're beautiful, Lambros. They don't need to be gold. I have everything I need now I've got my husband back."

His eyes filled with tears. "Oh, Zi … that's the most wonderful thing you've ever said to me. Here on Santorini, I am back. I really am. With you at the centre of my world."

Oh god, she loved this man so much. Despite all the niggles along the way, despite his terrible timing now, she loved him and she wanted to stay right here in his arms. She hated that she had to go, even for the retreat's opening night. But go she must.

She fiddled with the diamond studs she was wearing. "Come on, quickly. Help me put them in, then I'll carry a little bit of you with me all evening."

Annoyed as she was to have missed the introductory session, Karmela knew she had needed to sleep and at least she had woken an hour later completely refreshed. Refreshed, and rather hungry. Checking her watch, she leapt out of bed, stripped off her sweaty clothes and hopped into the shower, delighted when the enormous square head gushed copious amounts of warm water. Warm, slightly salty water, and she remembered reading in a guidebook it was the same all over the island. But nevertheless it felt good on her skin, and along with the zesty body wash brought her senses fully to life.

Already she could hear conversation from the courtyard outside, so she searched her suitcase for her plain beige shift dress and sandals, an outfit she had bought for teaching but had discovered was perfect for any situation when she was unsure what to wear.

Her room was directly opposite the dining terrace and the moment she closed the door behind her, Zina rushed over, a tray of delicious-looking meze in one hand.

"How are you feeling?" she asked anxiously.

"So much better, thanks to your kindness, and really rather hungry."

Zina took the hint and held the tray in front of her. "Grab a couple of these *spanakópita*," she said. "Then I'll get you a drink and introduce you to everyone."

As Karmela looked around, her gaze was drawn by the only man in the group, who looked more than familiar.

She gazed at him, motionless and trying not to gape, until he stepped towards her, grinning. "Well this is a pleasant surprise. Seasickness got the better of you in the end?"

She rolled her eyes. "It became car sickness, and I have never been car sick in my life. But I had a sleep, and I must be better because now I am starving." To emphasise the point, she popped one of the triangles of filo pastry into her mouth, an explosion of feta cheese and mint assaulting her taste buds.

"You know each other?" Zina asked.

"We met on the ferry, but we haven't been properly introduced."

Karmela was grateful he had replied, as she chewed and swallowed rapidly.

"Karmela Simic, this is Iain Sinclair," said Zina. "And now I must take Karmela to meet everyone else."

After a whirlwind of introductions fuelled by some excellent sparkling wine, Karmela found herself with the two Americans, who were clearly a couple.

"I am so sorry," she apologised. "Zina went so fast I could not work out who is the writer and who is the artist."

Susan, blonde with glasses, and the shorter of the two, smiled warmly. "I'm neither. I'm a librarian and I'm here to research my family history."

"I thought being on a retreat might encourage her to write it too," added Ellen, a striking, serious-faced woman with an impressive collection of stylised flower and butterfly tattoos on her left arm. "And there was no way I was going to let her come to Europe on her own; I'd have been insanely jealous."

"We've only been once before and that was years ago," Susan added. "London, Amsterdam, Paris – for the art galleries."

"Not to mention the Fawcett Society Conference in London. That was certainly the highlight of my trip."

"The Fawcett Society?" Karmela frowned at the unfamiliar name.

"The cradle of feminism, still fighting for women's rights." Ellen snorted. "As if we should need to in this day and age."

"But unfortunately we do," Karmela agreed, earning herself an approving look from Ellen's coal-black eyes.

At that moment Zina clapped her hands together, then asked them to take their seats for dinner. The long table was decorated with jars of fragrant herbs, and Karmela was delighted when Iain sat down next to her.

"Where is your dog?" she asked.

"Sybil's in my room. Her table manners aren't the best so I fed her first. I expect she'll be fast asleep by now."

"Not whining and pining for you?" Karmela teased.

"I hope not. And thankfully she isn't a chewer, either. When my sister Jen's dog was a puppy she had to put all the books in the bookcase the wrong way around or the dog would pull them out and have a go at them. The little devil started with the recipe books when she was shut in the kitchen. Chewed right through a vegetarian healthy eating one, apparently. Perhaps it was a protest."

Karmela laughed so much she almost spat out her wine. "Oh, I am sorry," she said, wiping her mouth with her napkin, "but that was so funny."

"It's fine," he replied. "In fact, I'm going to take it as a compliment."

Iain had such an easy manner about him and those eyes, oh, those eyes. She had not known eyes could be that green, and with such a sparkle too. A sparkle that made it hard for her to tear her own gaze away.

"As you missed the 'getting to know each other' session earlier, why don't you tell us a little about yourself?" he suggested.

"Yes, please do," added Sophie, the thin English lady with high cheekbones and a rather excellent haircut who was sitting opposite.

"You said on the boat you live in Zagreb?" Iain prompted as Karmela gulped her wine. Why did people always ask a question when her mouth was full?

"Yes. There is not much to tell, really. I am a professor of

Medieval History at the university there. My specialist subject is the Ragusan period and I recently spent almost a year in Dubrovnik studying the women of the time." She could not help but smile. "I had the best year of my life; I made so many friends. And it is where the inspiration for my book comes from. I am going to write an historical novel about them."

"That sounds wonderful," said Sophie. "I do admire the amount of research in that sort of thing. My friend Diana and I are here to write a romance, but we've decided on contemporary for that very reason. Mind you, a lot of people would say that in our late sixties we're rather too old to be first-time writers anyway."

"That's hardly positive thinking," said Susan from the other side of Iain. "What about Anne Youngson? And Bonnie Garmus? Not to mention your British Mary Wesley. I loved *The Camomile Lawn* so much."

"They just happen to be supremely talented," Sophie snapped, although she immediately apologised for her tone, explaining she was tired.

"I do not expect anyone will want a late night after travelling. And I guess we have an early start tomorrow," said Karmela, looking at Jessica who had so far contributed nothing to the conversation. Her skilful mask of make-up made her appear doubly remote; her almond-shaped grey eyes were smoky at the edges, thin lips stained perfectly the palest apricot. It would be unfortunate if she was going to be standoffish.

But then she smiled and her face lit up. "Nine o'clock. A little earlier if you want longer for free writing. How about you and I take ten minutes after dinner, Karmela, and I can explain the timetable? I'm so glad you're feeling better now."

"Thank you, that would be great."

Jessica sat back, and Karmela did the same, allowing the conversation to flow around her, trying not to look at Iain more than she did the others. But it was hard; he had a handsome profile and the terribly short haircut accentuated it, making something deep inside her fizz with attraction. He turned and glanced at her, grinning as their eyes met.

Before she could think of anything to say the food arrived, and as she picked up her knife and fork to cut into the chicken, which was topped with a foamy lemon-scented sauce, she wondered if they had just shared a moment of intimacy, as perhaps they had done on the boat. With so little experience of anything close to dating, she could not be sure, but whatever it was it felt fresh and new and exciting.

Not to mention potentially disruptive to the business of writing, and she was here to write, after all, especially with her mother having paid for the retreat. But surely she could dream a little? There was no harm in dreaming, and even though love was a total stranger, there was a tiny part of her, a part liberated by her experiences in Dubrovnik, that longed to abandon herself to passion in all its forms.

But the larger part was still sensible Karmela. Karmela who analysed everything logically, broke problems down, then built an entirely rational solution. Karmela who still, despite everything, thought first and felt afterwards, and was perhaps just a little scared of putting herself out there – in a romantic sense, at least.

Her train of thought was broken by Susan eulogising about the chicken, and Zina asking if she wanted a second helping. Oh, she should be enjoying the here and now, getting to know these people, not thinking about herself. So she turned to Diana, sitting on her left, and asked her what book she was currently reading.

Saturday 2nd September

"OK, everyone. Please put your pens down. I hope you all enjoyed your first free writing session."

To Jo's surprise, her voice sounded less shaky than she'd expected. She looked around the table. Everyone was nodding except Iain, who was staring at the screen of his tablet.

"Any issues? Or comments?" Jo didn't want to single him out and was glad when he looked up at her.

"I don't think I get it. Everyone else was scribbling away, but I only have two or three lines. And I'm not even sure those make sense. They're certainly not great prose."

"Honestly, Iain, they don't have to be. Let me see if I can explain free writing better. Some people would say that writing is like a muscle, that the more you exercise it the stronger it gets. And free writing is just that – an exercise. I had a tutor once who even made us throw away what we'd written, but personally I don't think that's necessarily a good thing because sometimes it sparks an idea."

"So you just write anything on the topic that comes to mind, and that's good enough?"

"Yes. Nobody else is ever going to look at these pieces. They're just for you."

"Mine reads more like word association than anything else," Susan chipped in, "but my creative brain does feel a little more awake now. It needed to after all that wine and glorious food last night."

"I'm glad I wasn't the only one incapable of putting together a sentence," said Iain, who was looking happier by the minute.

It was time to move on to the main business of the day: her first tutorial. Beneath the table, Jo knotted her fingers together, then unknotted them, before standing and walking to the whiteboard on the wall opposite the door.

"OK," she said. "I guess it's obvious why I chose 'beginnings' as the writing prompt, but it's also our topic for the day. Every novel has to start somewhere, so shall we brainstorm a few ideas about what makes a good opening?"

Silence. Oh god, were they not going to interact? Were they expecting her to spout knowledge at them for an hour?

After what felt like an age, Karmela spoke. "It has to grab the reader. Make them want to carry on."

Susan nodded. "Even better when it tells you something about the main character too. Like *The Curious Incident of the Dog in the Night-Time*. It sets up that there's a mystery, but also that the narrator has quite a specific world view."

"Or a beginning that reveals something about where the book's going," added Iain. "Like in *1984* with the clocks striking thirteen."

"Perhaps *Pride and Prejudice* too," said Diana, "but I'm not really sure. I know it's often listed as a classic opening and it certainly sets up the book, but it doesn't exactly grab the reader. Maybe that wasn't as important when Austen was writing."

"You have a very good point there," said Jo. "There were far fewer books, and people who could read had more time to read them. Now novels compete with all sorts of other leisure activities."

"I had not thought of that." Karmela frowned. "My students only read what they need to for the course; for leisure they watch films or television." She shrugged. "It is their loss. But there are still plenty of people who do love books. And plenty of books for them to love. Maybe too many. If you are thinking of books in English, on Amazon for example, there must be thousands to choose from."

"Millions, actually," said Jo. Should she have said that? She certainly didn't want to discourage anybody. "But the first and most important thing is to write the best book you can. Whether you're writing for your own satisfaction or with a view to publication. So, let's get back to what makes a great, reader-grabbing beginning. Let's think practically and specifically."

"Like two people meeting in unusual circumstances?"

Jo wrote Diana's idea on the board.

"Or there being a mystery to solve. That works in just about any type of book." Karmela sounded excited, and Jo could almost see the possibilities whirring around in her head.

"I guess some of this is genre specific," said Susan, "like action sequences in thrillers." She frowned. "I don't mean they have to be fast and furious, just tense, like Lee Child's *Echo Burning*. I couldn't put that one down from start to finish. Or C. L. Taylor's *Every Move You Make*. Subverting what should have been ordinary was just the most brilliant way to start a book."

Soon the whiteboard was covered with ideas. While Karmela had contributed the most, she hadn't hogged the conversation, for which Jo was grateful. There'd been a moment when she'd worried the professor would be the dominant personality she'd dreaded, and being a teacher as well, it could have been a nightmare. In fact, the only one who was worrying her was Sophie, who'd said nothing at all, although she had scribbled a few notes on her pad. Perhaps she was simply shy, a feeling Jo knew all too well.

Iain interrupted her thoughts. "Jessica, we've come up with some great ideas, but how do we put them into practice?"

Jo started. The use of her pseudonym jarred, although she wasn't sure why. Fixing a smile on her face, she said, "I'm very glad you asked that, because now we're going to try it for ourselves with a little exercise in two groups. Karmela, Sophie and Iain, you're going to start with action. Diana and Susan, with dialogue. I'm not expecting great prose, but I'd like you to make me want to read on, if you can. I'll be on hand to assist."

As she sat down, Jo realised that far from being terrified, she felt excited. Excited for the group and their different aspirations; excited to see what they could produce, not just today, but by the end of the month. If she could help each and every one of them improve their writing, it would be a job well done. Her mother was right – in less than twenty-four hours these people were no longer really strangers, and they certainly weren't scary. That crippling fear had been in her own head, and nowhere else.

Could her other fears be dealt with so easily? Now that was a question to start a book with. Perhaps she should try it herself. Once the page was no longer blank, surely her words would begin to flow? Of course, in her own real life there were no easy answers. No answers at all. But right now she couldn't let the thought drag her down. Here on Santorini, she was beginning to feel she might have left at least some of the mind-draining awfulness at home. Maybe, just maybe, she really could write her book.

Karmela watched as Iain disappeared into the blackness, Sybil straining at her lead, no doubt excited by the endless possibilities of her last walk of the night. Opposite her, Jessica was toying with her almost empty wine glass. It was just the two of them left, and Karmela wondered if, now they were alone, she would have an opportunity to try to bring her out of herself and begin to get to know her. Although Jessica smiled and nodded a lot, she seemed to have little to say outside the confines of the classroom.

The sweet night air drifted around them in an almost imperceptible breeze, the heavy scent of geraniums tickling Karmela's nose. The sky was inky black, the moon no more than a silver ball perching on top of the hillside behind The Retreat House.

"It is so very peaceful here," she said. "So calm."

Jessica nodded. "I wondered how it would be. I didn't dare to hope…"

"A top-up for either of you?" Zina emerged from the bar area, bottle in hand. Jessica held out her glass, but Karmela shook her head.

"I feel bad now," Jessica faltered.

Zina sat down next to her. "It's fine. I won't let you drink alone."

There was a moment of silence before Karmela resorted to the most obvious conversational gambit, asking what had made Zina decide to start the retreat.

"When I came back to the island, I wanted to do something different, something worthwhile. Despite all the talk of over-tourism on Santorini, here we are away from the crowds, and I wanted to capitalise on that. Show the other face, if you like. Support the rural economy with something that would work alongside the farm."

"So do you use your own produce in the kitchen?" Karmela asked.

"Where we can, or we showcase other farmers. I want my guests to experience Santorini with all their senses. Our tomatoes, for example, are not grown anywhere other than the island. And the wild capers, we don't even have to cultivate, just pick them. In authentic local cookery you will barely find a dish without them."

"It must be wonderful to be able to follow your dream," Jessica said.

"I'm privileged, that is for sure. But surely writing is a dream career too?"

"Oh, yes. I am lucky." Jessica sipped her wine but to

Karmela her face seemed closed. Suddenly she looked up. "Karmela, is writing where you see your future?"

"I do not think I would ever give up lecturing. I love my subject too much and I really enjoy the interaction with students, especially the ones who are as passionate about medieval history as I am. Sadly they are few and far between, but if I can inspire just a handful more, then my working life is already worthwhile. And anyway, I have barely started my book, let alone finished it."

"So what is it really like, being a famous author?" Zina asked Jessica, leaning forwards eagerly. "I imagine you go to lots of events – launches, parties, that sort of thing."

Jessica grimaced. "Some authors do, but mostly it's sitting at a desk." She played with the stem of her glass. "You may have noticed I'm pretty shy. I find the social side ... difficult."

"And yet you stand up in a classroom," said Karmela.

"No, I couldn't do that. Not in a million years. The five of you is about my limit and I was perfectly terrified before the first session. You see, I've never done this before."

"It did not show."

Jessica smiled. "Thank you, Karmela. I have seen how easy you find it to chat to people, and you too Zina, and I'm filled with admiration."

"I can't really imagine being any other way," said Zina. "Before I came back here I worked in marketing in Athens so I was constantly putting myself out there, and I loved every minute."

"So why did you come back?" Karmela asked.

Zina raised her hand to her mouth, as if pondering her

answer, then shrugged. "The time felt right. My father died last year and my mother needed my support."

"That is such a lovely thing to do," said Jessica. "So selfless. You must be close to your mother to do that. I have to say, my mum is my absolute rock and I'd do anything for her too."

"Then that's something we have in common." Zina beamed.

Oh, these women were lucky to have such warm relationships with their mothers, but Karmela did at least have something to add to the conversation. "My mother gave me the retreat as a gift. She said I needed to get out of my comfort zone and actually write my book."

"I love a new challenge," said Zina, rubbing her hands.

"I have to say, I am looking forward to this one," Karmela agreed. "The retreat is giving me the freedom to do something entirely new. Perhaps, Jessica, it is the same for you if you have not led one before."

"Perhaps." She looked down into her glass, swirling the last of the wine around, before gulping it down. "Anyway, I think it is probably past my bedtime."

"Mine too," said Zina, standing as well.

Karmela looked up at both of them. "I have really enjoyed our chat. A great way to wind down at the end of the day."

Zina nodded. "One thing ... the one thing I have missed since I've been here, is talking to like-minded women. Women with careers, opinions—" She ground to a halt, biting her lip.

"Then we must do it again," said Karmela.

Jessica stopped a few feet away from the table. "I think I would like that as well."

They went their separate ways, Karmela pausing in the

courtyard, listening to Zina's footsteps on the track. Yes, there was potential here, potential for real friendship, but she had the strangest impression that the other women were holding something of themselves back. With Jessica it was shyness, for sure, but Zina? She could not quite put her finger on it. Was she seeing something that wasn't there because not eighteen months before she had been the one in that position?

Only time would tell, but for the moment she was already looking forward to their next conversation.

Sunday 3rd September

Sweat soaking into the back of her T-shirt, Zina held the piece of wood in place while Lambros hammered in the nails. Inside the rough pasture of the enclosure, the goats watched them with their own particular brand of detached curiosity. This was such a waste of time. The *bástardos* creatures would be out again before they knew it. No doubt aided and abetted by Iain's dog. Why on earth had she ever let him bring it? It was bad enough it left silvery hairs all over the bedroom – hairs she had to clean up.

She was beginning to realise just how mind-numbing the everyday grind of actually running the retreat really was. How come it hadn't occurred to her before? She felt like such a fool, and she hated feeling foolish. Not for a single moment had she envisaged how fast she'd morph from Instagrammable entrepreneur to domestic drudge. Yesterday there had been nothing at all to upload to her feed and today looked like being very much the same. Her friends in Athens, normally such avid followers, would wonder if she'd fallen off the face of the earth. Perhaps she had.

Last night Zina had joined the others in the courtyard with the express intention of asking Jessica for a selfie to post, but when she'd said how shy she was, it hadn't seemed like the right thing to do at all. And she couldn't have left Karmela out of the photo either – even though it wouldn't have had the same impact with a third person in it. Karmela was a guest too. Just not a famous one.

Perhaps there would be other chances. In fact, Zina was sure there would be, given the others' enthusiasm for more late-night conversation. Zina had meant it when she'd said she missed the company of career women like herself, and they had been so interested in her and why she had started the retreat that she had really enjoyed herself.

She looked at the goats and the goats looked back at her. They were kind of cute, especially the russet-coloured one with the long, floppy ears. Glancing down, she saw Lambros's tanned and muscled arms. His chiselled jawline with its hint of stubble was sexiness personified too. Cute with hunky was a winning combination for social media. Could she manage to get both into a shot?

He stood back to admire his handiwork. "Right, that should hold. On to the next one."

"Can we do a couple of photos first? For my Insta?"

"What, now? Do we have to? I've got a lot to get through this afternoon."

Did he honestly think she had time to stand here all day holding planks? She bit back the words. What she needed was to persuade him, not make him even more irritable.

"If you're too busy I could just snap a few of the goats, but it will tell so much more of a story if I show you mending the fence as well. And not just for today; they'll make great library shots for when we're promoting your yoghurt and *chloró* cheese next year."

More than anything, Lambros wanted some sort of deli farm shop like Yiannis had to sell his produce direct to holidaymakers and locals. Of course, being him, he hadn't worked out the details yet, but Zina had to admit the idea was pretty cool.

"OK, but quickly. And don't fiddle about uploading them now either." His voice brooked no argument, but at least she'd got most of what she wanted.

"Thank you," she kissed him lightly on the lips. "If you weren't so hot I wouldn't want you in the pictures."

"Then let's get on with it." At least he was almost smiling.

Frustratingly, it took longer than Zina had expected and Lambros was once again glowering by the time she'd finished. She checked her watch. She needed to be back in the kitchen soon to cook supper as it was Ekaterini's day off, and she definitely had to shower first.

"How many more bits do we need to mend?" she asked.

"Three."

"God, Lambros, I don't have time."

"You had time to mess around with those photos."

"Social media presence is important."

"Couldn't you have just snapped the bougainvillea or something?"

"No, because I've already done that. Nor do I have time to

set anything up. I'm on my own today, remember, cooking *and* waiting tables."

He sighed. "OK, Zi, off you go."

She bit her lip. "I'll help you with one more bit, then I really will need to run, and I don't want you moaning about it."

"If that's the best you can offer, I'll take it."

It was a full twenty minutes later when Zina set her phone on the bathroom windowsill and saw her schoolfriend Resi's message.

Reunion on Wednesday night? Know you're busy, but Georgiou Kallitsis is back for a holiday – from New York!

Followed by a string of yellow taxi emojis.

New York? What was her high school sweetheart doing there? Well for himself, presumably. Zina gazed at the pile of grubby clothing on the tiled floor. If she'd still been working in Athens, she might have flown in for the party and made quite a splash... Thankfully she had an excuse.

Quickly she typed: *Sorry, no. I'll be working. But have some fun for me.*

As if. Three rolling eyes emojis. *With a six-month-old baby feeding.*

Zina stepped into the shower. Would Georgiou miss her, or would he not even notice she wasn't there? When she was sixteen and he was seventeen, they'd seemed made for each other – the girls' basketball captain and the boys' football captain, united by their desire to win at all costs. And the school had won every sporting trophy going that year and they'd basked in each other's glory, smiling, glamorous, successful. Like something out of an American high school prom movie.

Behind the scenes, Georgiou had spent most of the time they were together trying to persuade her to have sex with him. He figured they'd done everything else – and they had, oh, they had – but holding out became something of a game for Zina. The harder he tried, the more she resisted. And the more she resisted, the harder he tried... Until he dumped her without even telling her when he went away to Thessaly University on the mainland, leaving her to complete her last year at school alone.

At the time it had hurt like hell, but by Christmas she'd been dating again, and within a year of finishing school had left the island herself for a job with the national tourist board – Athens, then London, back to Athens, then headhunted by the agency. Little wonder that even before she met Lambros, she'd almost completely forgotten about Georgiou. And she certainly didn't have time to run off to see him now.

Monday 4th September

Even ensconced between the velvet curtains of her palanquin, Filipa Menčetić recognised the moment her bearers turned into Dubrovnik's port. The archway through the city's thick walls muffled every sound but the stench of rotting fish and human waste grew stronger, causing her to reach for her lavender-scented handkerchief and hold it over her nose.

But within moments the air freshened and she could sense the particular light of the winter sun reflecting from the sea. She took a deep breath then settled back into the cushioned seat, clutching her leather-bound account book between her hands. She did not have to inspect her late husband's ships herself but she enjoyed the bustle of the quayside. And the barely veiled disapproval of the merchants around her that she, a mere woman, dared to run a business empire, much less actually leave her house to do so.

The swaying movement beneath her stopped and her steward Vincenti drew back the curtain.

"Madam, we have arrived."

As she held out her hand ready to be helped down, a flash of colour caught her eye. It was the finest green silk, shimmering and shining in the pale sunlight, better than anything she herself could import. But below the hem of the swirling skirt she glimpsed a pair of old shoes, the leather cracked and one seam bursting apart.

She leant forwards, whispering to Vincenti, "Who is that woman?"

"Cvijeta Zuzorić. Her husband is a merchant from Florence and they have rented a palazzo on Prijeko Ulica."

Filipa nodded. Those shoes intrigued her more than the silk. She would have to find out more.

Karmela sat back and stretched, raising her arms above her head and locking her fingers together with a satisfying crack. That was a reasonable start to her day's work and the scene had been made far more interesting by the writing prompt Jessica had put on the whiteboard this morning: *the old shoe*. She had no idea yet how Cvijeta's shoes fitted into the story, but she was sure she could work it out. She had been after a really strong reason for Filipa to take an interest in her, and now she had one.

The daily writing prompts were fun, and Karmela made sure she arrived in the studio as early as she could to make the most of them. She felt the freedom and the joy of simply letting words flow; the magic of creation at the tips of her fingers.

There was nothing about the retreat that Karmela did not love. Jessica was an excellent teacher, and so far each topic had made a hugely positive impact on Karmela's work. She was learning so much, and she was so damn grateful her mother had sent her here. In fact she had become quite emotional when she had called her to tell her so.

Naturally her mother had been embarrassed. In Mama's world, unlike Karmela's, feelings were not to be shared. Other people's emotions were not her business. But Karmela's book was. Her mother had made it so with her generous gift, which Karmela would repay by finishing the first draft while she was here. She had planned it out; it was tight, but possible. Definitely possible.

Of course this was not just for her mother; she was writing the story for other people she cared about too. Her friends from the book club in Dubrovnik who had suggested it in the first place, and for her childhood friend Nejla in Sarajevo, who she had lost but who had been found for her again, and in memory of Emina, who had died in the war. Precious friends, each and every one of them.

So the book she was writing was about friendship, but it had a love story woven into it too. That had not been her original intention, but it was necessary for the plot and also true to the historical record. As far as she could, she wanted to be faithful to that, despite the fact she had moved the enigmatic Cvijeta from a different century, and was feeling rather guilty about it.

Karmela stood and began to pace the room. It was not that the fully adjustable office chair at her desk was uncomfortable – far from it – but she needed to move. It was all too easy to become glued to her desk, making her neck and shoulders stiff. And besides, the rhythm of her steps made it easier to think.

She stopped to admire one of the botanical prints that

graced the wall, deep in thought. She could write about friendship because she knew about friendship, but what about love? Something inside her, something long buried, was more than curious. Oh, that sounded so cold, and that was not how it felt, especially as she had been thinking about relationships a great deal over the last six months. Forty-three and single was fine, of course it was, but a part of her yearned – absolutely *yearned* – for a special someone in her life. To at least try. It had been the longest time since she had had anything even approximating a boyfriend – only a date or two as a student, largely because she had been inquisitive about sex.

Back in the spring she had joined an internet dating site for professional people in Zagreb, but with little success. Neither of the men she had actually met had lit any sort of spark, and most likely it had been the same for them, although one had proved fairly persistent. Oh, she knew she was not beautiful, with her pale complexion and sharp nose and chin, but she also knew that if looks were a man's only yardstick then he was of no interest to her.

So the question remained: could she write love without knowing love? Experienced authors would be able to portray any feeling they wanted to, she knew, but she was an absolute novice. Maybe empathy and understanding were all it took. Maybe research. Find some blogs. Some online agony aunts perhaps. Talk to married people like Jessica and Zina. Somehow she had to be able to make her characters' emotions real.

Of course she was familiar with the tingle of attraction, not least when she saw Iain, and she was having to be extremely careful not to let it become an obsession. Yes, he was kind to her, but then he was kind to everyone. But sometimes those looks that passed between them sent shivers down her spine – melting shivers that went as far as her stomach, if not even further.

What was even better was that she liked him as a person. Although he could act the fool, he obviously had a keen intelligence and a wicked sense of humour. He clearly adored Sybil too, however naughty she could be.

Iain ticked any number of boxes, but they had been thrown together for a month and it would be downright embarrassing to make a move if he was not interested. And even if he was, getting together might upset the dynamic of the group. There were so many reasons not to pursue this. Logical reasons, reasons above and beyond her need to focus on her book. But there was nothing logical about the way she felt, nothing at all. Oh, it was not love. It could not be so quickly, but it was full of thrilling potential all the same.

She turned sharply away from the picture and thumped down onto her chair. This would not do. Not at all. She should remember her priorities. Not least that she had a one-to-one session with Jessica later, and she needed to get this scene finished first.

Turning up the air-con in her room, Jo opened her laptop. Apart from the gentle hum, the retreat around her was silent. That wasn't surprising; the morning session had ended well over an hour before, and everyone was in their rooms writing. Which meant, despite her pointless faffing around ever since, she couldn't put off her own work any longer. No more prevarication.

Arse on seat and get some words down.

She told herself rather sharply that as she was somewhere completely different and writing something completely different, there was no reason at all not to embrace her new project. Cosy crime was a total departure for her but she was convinced that her characters – an Edwardian dowager duchess and her butler, who had first appeared in a Christmas short story she'd sold to a women's magazine years ago – were interesting and sympathetic enough to appeal to readers.

It wasn't as though she'd never written a book before. She had. More than once. But they hadn't exactly been very good. Jo stood up again and walked around the room, her hands interlaced in front of her in a vice-like grip. Through the arch to the bathroom, her heart thudding in her chest as air spilled from her lungs. If she wasn't careful her head would start to spin...

She thumped her palms onto the smooth rim of the honey-coloured stone wash basin. This had to stop happening. Had to. Especially here. She had to get over it and write. Channel that positivity she felt when she was with the group. She ran her wrists under the tap for the longest time, then dried them carefully on the fluffy cream towel. Averting her eyes from the wine she'd bought at the taverna on the way back from her swim, she fetched a carton of peach juice from the fridge and held it against her forehead. *Cool. Calm.* The moment had passed. Time to try again.

But instead, Jo perched on the edge of the bed, eyeing her laptop as though any moment it would leap off the desk and bite her. She knew why these mini-panic attacks plagued her, but she was powerless to stop them. Seeking professional help was completely out of the question, because it would mean telling a stranger the truth.

The truth that she wasn't about to embark on her fourth book; it was her third. And that so-called difficult second novel, which had all but disappeared under a welter of three-star reviews, had actually been her first.

The familiar, overwhelming *how did it come to this* feeling washed over her, but here at the retreat she had no option of hiding from it in a wine bottle. Certainly not at eleven o'clock in the morning. That was not what she was being paid for. More than not. And she really, really didn't want to mess this up, especially as she was beginning to enjoy it.

Was enjoy too strong a word? Now her perspective was returning, she didn't think so. In the main, the little group was delightful, and over the last couple of days had thrown themselves into the morning writing exercises with gusto. Only Sophie was less than enthusiastic, but Diana was good at jollying her along and at least they had begun to write their story together.

So far in the late afternoon feedback sessions Jo had let them off sharing their own work, instead inviting them to read an extract from a favourite book so they could learn to critique kindly and constructively. Tonight that would change, and she was looking forward to seeing what each of them would come up with.

But all this positivity didn't alter the fact that Jo desperately needed to write something herself, and she hadn't. Not so much as a sentence. Maybe she should ease herself into the book through another short story? She could still manage those without panic descending. After all, it was where she had started. It was her thing. Deep down she knew it would be a displacement activity, but a comforting one. One which would take her back to a happier time and place.

Was that when she'd been happiest, living with Pam in her terraced house in Putney? It certainly felt that way and a shard of grief cut through her, bringing tears to her eyes. Grief, guilt, and god only knows what else.

Pamela Collins had been her mother's best friend, so when Jo's first job as a new graduate had been in London it had made sense for her to move in with her, at least temporarily, while she found her feet. But the place she'd found them had been with Pam, not a flat share with girls of her own age. For a start, she didn't know any; the few friends she'd made at university had been scattered across the globe and had pretty soon drifted apart. In the first few weeks of her new job, out of a sense of duty and after some gentle nagging from her mum, she'd tagged along to after work drinks, but she quickly gave up, figuring it was better than having her colleagues stop asking her because she was so boring.

She'd known Pam all her life. She liked being with Pam in Putney and Pam had liked having Jo there. Pam's own career as a high-ranking Whitehall civil servant was demanding, and her social life limited by the fact she'd never come out to more than a handful of people, adamant it would blight her chances of further promotion. Jo may have grown up seeing Pam as a favourite auntie, but living together they'd become good friends.

The best times of all were when Jo's mother Caroline could

join them for a weekend. They'd visit museums and art galleries, shop at Fortnum's for picnics to eat in their pyjamas sprawled on Pam's sofas and talking into the small hours about everything and nothing. At first Jo had worried she'd be a bit of a spare wheel, but Mum had explained that was not the case because a three-legged friendship was like a three-legged stool – the most stable and strongest of all.

Thinking of Mum reminded Jo that she needed to phone her. They'd messaged since she'd arrived – of course they had – but she'd promised her an actual conversation once she settled in. But she so, so wanted to be able to tell her mother she'd started the book... And anyway, now would be absolutely the worst time to talk, because the memories of Pam were making her teary and the sound of Mum's voice would most likely tip her over the edge.

For god's sake, Jo.

This was getting her nowhere; sending her backwards, in fact. Perhaps she should just let herself wallow and get it over with, then write this afternoon. Curl up on the bed and imagine herself back in the time before, when life had been simple, and peaceful, and fun. When the only fly in the ointment had been her mother's gentle suggestions, echoed by Pam, that she should maybe, just maybe, get out a little more.

Pam and Caroline had certainly lived it up in London when they were new graduates, going to theatres, clubbing and gigs. Their attitude had been to work hard and play hard, the have-it-all mentality of the time. Then Caroline had been offered a promotion which meant moving to Cheltenham, met Jo's father and settled down. She'd always assumed her daughter would do the same, but living with Pam taught Jo she didn't need a man to be happy. Didn't need many people at all. When Pam went out, Jo was content with her own company and anyway, she could always lose herself in a book.

The man part was bloody ironic too, considering how miserable being with Rees made her. But when they'd met on the tube of all places and he'd got off at her stop and asked her out, once she was over the shock she'd realised it might just get her mum off her back. Rees wasn't bad looking, and he was sophisticated and so much older. She wondered what he could possibly want with her? But despite the whole thing being vaguely puzzling, she'd quite enjoyed their conversation because he'd done most of the talking.

Dating had disrupted her peaceful life with Pam, so she'd almost stopped before the relationship had started, but Mum had been so excited Jo finally had a boyfriend that she'd thought she ought to give it a decent go. Despite the stresses and strains of thinking about what to wear, what to say, and remembering to put condoms in her bag. God, she should have trusted her instincts and run for the hills. Everything would have been different if she had. But no, that wasn't fair. Not everything. There was one thing that nothing she'd done could have changed: the perfectly ordinary Thursday morning when she'd woken up to find Pam not in the kitchen making tea and toast, but dead in her bed.

Heart attack, they'd said, and most likely she'd have known nothing about it, for which Jo had been incredibly grateful. And she'd also been more than glad that they'd spent what turned out to be Pam's last evening companionably writing on either side of the dining room table, Jo working on a short story to sell to a magazine and Pam on her novel.

Pam had never said what the novel was about, but she'd read Jo extracts and it became clear it was an achingly beautiful love story, full of emotions that Jo hadn't even known existed, let alone had the prose to describe. Pam often asked her advice on phrases and words, even though it seemed to Jo that she didn't need it. Every snippet she shared was wonderful, but when Jo had asked if she was going to look for an agent she'd shaken her head and told her the story was far too personal to ever be published. Not even Caroline knew of its existence.

Which was all the more reason why Jo should never have done what she did.

Pam's book was *Only. Ever. You.*

Wednesday 6th September

Balancing the pile of fresh towels on the arm of the sofa, Zina took a moment to look around. Diana's was perhaps the room she loved most of all. In the middle of the eastern arm of the courtyard in the oldest part of the building, the arch beneath the barrel roof was rugged and uneven, and just the right size for the bed to slide almost a metre into it. In the mini-cave created by the archway, she'd carefully applied subtle glow-in-the-dark dolphin decals, and elsewhere in the room had stripped back the second-hand furniture to make it look like driftwood. Sandy neutrals and blues in the fabrics were the finishing touch in creating a relaxing beach vibe. The pictures had received more likes than just about anything on her Instagram feed, so she must have got it right. Could she get away with repeating one today? There was sod all else to upload.

In one of the niches cut into either side of the arch Diana had placed a photograph of her late husband. Two years he'd been gone, she'd told Zina, and although she obviously missed him, she was getting on with her life. Unlike Zina's mother, who never went anywhere. It was such a worry, seeing Mama's life closed down so much, and Zina wanted nothing more than to help her to move on.

Panora had plenty of friends, but she never made an effort to see them. When Zina asked her why, she said it was because they still had their husbands. And when Zina reminded Mama that Calandra was widowed too, she said they would just make each other miserable. And that anyway, she was happy looking after the house and cooking the meals, especially with Lambros and Zina working so hard.

Which made the problem all the trickier to deal with. Zina could never say, never even hint, that if Mama was always there, she and Lambros had no time alone. Mama would be mortified and hurt, and Zina would hate to be the cause of even more anguish. But three days ago a glimmer of progress had been made. When Mama had gone to the pharmacy, some of her friends had been having coffee outside the bakery next door and she had at least joined them for a while. Now Zina was hatching another plan to get her out and about on the island.

She opened the patio doors to the terrace to let in some air then headed for the bathroom. Diana was the exact opposite of her friend Sophie, whose possessions covered every surface of her room next door. The only thing Zina had to move before cleaning the sink here was the handwash dispenser, which she set to one side to refill.

Of all the jobs designed to make Zina grumpy as hell, top of the list was cleaning other people's loos. Making beds she'd come to terms with because they looked so fresh and inviting afterwards, sweeping and dusting she could tolerate at a stretch, but this ... every time she picked up the brush she wanted to heave. Every day in every room it had to be done. The sooner she could afford a chambermaid the better.

Stretching her rubber gloves as far as they'd go up her arms, she squirted disinfectant and, holding her breath, grabbed the brush and leant over the bowl. It wasn't as though it was even dirty, but—

"Zi! Zi!" She jerked up to see Lambros standing at the bathroom door. Why now, of all times, when she was doing something so demeaning?

"What are you doing in here?"

He took half a step back. "It's OK, I left my boots outside. I'm having a Coke break and saw the doors were open so wondered if you'd like one too."

"As if. I need to get the rooms done before they finish their morning session."

"Can I help?"

His words lifted her mood a fraction; it really was sweet of him to offer, so the least she could do was make an effort, if only for a few minutes. Peeling off her gloves, she shook her head. "I can take five, though." Diana's toilet was clean enough.

"That's great. There's this totally hilarious video on YouTube I want to show you."

YouTube? No wonder he had time to offer to help.

She must have failed to hide her scowl because he carried on, "Honestly, I haven't just been scrolling. It's to do with the farm."

Did he think that made it better? She hadn't agreed to stop

work – which would put her behind – to watch some farming video. She'd expected them to talk. And not about his precious pistachios or whatever it was. Sighing inwardly, she followed him outside.

As he angled his phone screen towards her she couldn't help but notice the video was way more than five minutes long, but thankfully he quickly forwarded it to a part showing goats wobbling around on a less-than-steady pile of pallets. What a total waste of time. As if he didn't have his own goats to look at.

"Very cute," she told him and started back towards the room.

"I'm not watching it because it's cute." A note of frustration crept into his voice. "I think the reason the goats keep escaping is because they lack mental stimulation, and this sort of thing keeps them entertained. Old pallets are cheap enough and…"

Mental stimulation for the goats? What about *her* mental stimulation? He'd made her come here, and now she was no more than a frigging drudge, washing dishes and cleaning *bástardos* toilets. To cap it all, now he was more worried about his goats. Goats!

She stopped. Turned to face him. "Lambros, don't you ever get bored with the farm?"

He looked up from tying his boot laces, genuinely puzzled. "No. There's always something new to learn – like this sort of stuff. Who'd have thought that goats—"

"Well I do." She put her hands on her hips and glared at him.

"Oh, so you want me to bugger off, is that it? Not disturb

you while you're doing something important." He waved in the direction of the duster tucked into her waistband.

"What's more important than the guests coming back to beautiful, clean rooms?" She stamped her foot. That always riled him. Wound him up something proper.

But this time, rather than bite back, he shook his head before standing smartly and walking off in the direction of the drying yard.

"Lambros! Lambros!" she called after him furiously.

He didn't even break his stride. Zina dropped onto Diana's sunbed, head in her hands. He'd changed, oh yes, he'd changed. Now he couldn't even be bothered to argue with her, much less pay her any other sort of attention, *bástardos* man.

Back in Athens he used to love a good row; they both had. She remembered one Saturday night they'd had a bit to drink and fallen out over whether a particular word was allowed in Scrabble. They'd been nose to nose, screaming at each other, but the making-up afterwards had been magnificent. They hadn't got out of bed until the middle of Sunday afternoon. Fat chance of that happening now.

Zina sighed, stood and stretched. Time was getting on. She needed to make Diana's bed then get her arse into Karmela's room. Such was her life these days. Trapped in a cycle of boring, boring tasks with her boring, boring husband. A small voice inside told her she was being unfair to Lambros, but she dismissed it. If he thought the goats deserved more excitement in their lives than she did, her sympathies were misplaced.

Thursday 7th September

Karmela stood at her window, towel wrapped around her, sipping an espresso. It did not matter that she was barely dressed because as her room overlooked the farm track Zina had fitted privacy glass. It was an absolutely genius idea and Karmela had hardly closed her curtains since she arrived.

Now she watched Iain stroll past, Sybil dancing around his legs. She saw them set off most mornings and yesterday had begun to wonder about joining them; it would be nice to take a little exercise in the cool of the day – it was far too hot later on. Oh, who was she kidding? She wanted to get to know Iain better, that was the truth of it. On a one-to-one basis.

The man and his dog crossed in front of her, the pale light around them beginning to bleed colour into the olive grove beyond the low mounds of the vines. Iain was smiling to himself as he glanced towards her terrace, the almost involuntary movement making up her mind. She would sling on her clothes and head out. If their paths were to cross, then so be it.

The first faint rays of the sun were glimmering over the hills behind her as she cut the corner of the vineyard to the path between the nut trees and an empty field, the grass and weeds scorched almost brown by the summer heat. The continuity of agriculture throughout the ages never ceased to amaze Karmela; the Ragusan women in her story would also have known vines, olives, pistachios. It somehow made her, a city woman through and through, feel closer to the land. As she skirted the orchard she admired the trees. Only a foot or so taller than she was, their low-crowned broad canopies and curled oval leaves sheltered generous bunches of nuts which appeared pinkish-purple in the low morning light.

At the far end of the pistachios, the track passed the farmhouse. Lights shone from almost every window and faint strains of traditional Greek music reached her. She had seen lights in The Retreat House kitchen too, so she guessed Zina was already preparing breakfast. God, it was hard work running a place like this and Karmela had every admiration, not only for her host's vision but also for the endless commitment required to make it a reality.

From the conversations they now shared most evenings she knew how tiring it was too, but Zina remained relentlessly cheerful. She liked nothing more than to talk about The Retreat House and when Jo had asked about the interior designs, she had fallen over herself to share her resources and every detail of how she had achieved the look. The conversation had not interested Karmela particularly, but it had been wonderful to see the others bond over a shared passion.

The goats began to bleat as Karmela passed their enclosure, and in the broad gully ahead she caught sight of Iain and

Sybil. Showing her full greyhound turn of speed, the dog was racing up and down the dirt track with Iain in pursuit, pretending to try to catch her as she flew past him time and time again, his breathless laughter carrying on the still morning air.

Karmela did not speak until she was a few yards behind him.

"That looks like fun." He swivelled around as Sybil raced past his legs, barking in delight as she skidded to a halt in front of Karmela, raising a small cloud of dust.

"D'you want to take over for a while? She's worn me out."

Karmela crouched to fondle the dog's ears. "Well she is used to racing."

"She's meant to be retired. When I got her from the rescue they told me that very often former racing dogs get lazy, but not this one. Although to be fair, she does sleep for most of the day."

"It is not too boring for her, being here?" She looked up at him and could not help but notice that unshaven and in the low early light, his features appeared more rugged, and a fizz of attraction shot through her.

Iain shrugged. "It isn't too different to my last posting. We got up, went for a walk, then into the office where she snoozed in her basket next to my desk. I couldn't leave her at home after she pulled up the carpet behind the front door and jammed it completely. Would you believe I had to borrow a crowbar to get in?"

"Oh, Sybil, did you?" Her tail wagged enthusiastically, thumping into Karmela's legs. "I thought you were in the air force, not an office?"

"Flying a desk. All my eyes were good for in recent years, I'm afraid."

She gazed up at him, admiring that unusual green for what was about the hundredth time in a week. "They look all right to me."

"They're not bad, but they need to be twenty-twenty to fly. Especially at high speed."

"I guess they do." So he had not risen to her rather clumsy attempt at flirtation. But as she stood and stretched she noticed him glance at the strip of midriff she had unwittingly revealed then look quickly away.

What the hell did that mean?

Oh, she was so useless at this.

He pointed down the track. "We're heading along the gully for another few minutes. Care to join us?"

"I would love to. It is far too hot to walk later on. I did not think it would be at this time of year. I know I am here to write, but I miss walking to and from work every day. It is my only exercise."

"You're no gym bunny then?"

Karmela laughed. "What a wonderful turn of phrase – I must remember it. Although it has made me picture girls on running machines with white fluffy tails pinned to their arses."

Iain snorted. "I've never thought of it like that, but now I'm having trouble getting the image out of my mind. We used to go to this night club in Hong Kong…" He shook his head, pausing for a moment. "I suppose English is a rather strange language."

"I think all languages are; we each have our peculiarities. It is fascinating."

"Is that fascination why you want to write?"

"Oh no, I never had any desire to. But when I spent my year in Dubrovnik researching the republic's medieval women, their stories were so wonderful, and I made friends too, and one of those new friends suggested I make them into a novel. Jessica is very encouraging, but I am still not sure I can do it." She had barely admitted that to herself, but it had been so very easy to tell Iain.

"The piece you read out last night was so evocative. It was as though I really was on the harbourside with Filipa."

"Thank you. I found the same when I was writing it. How are you getting on?"

Iain screwed up his face. "Struggling a bit, to be honest. I've had all these wonderful characters and stories in my head for years, but when I try to write them down they turn into wooden blocks. Still, I have a one-to-one today, and I'm sure Jessica will have some ideas about how I can animate the buggers."

A skitter of rocks tumbled down the gravel-strewn slope above them, and Sybil's ears pricked dangerously before she dashed upwards. As they swivelled around, Karmela saw the white face of a goat appear over the lip.

"Oh no. She has form with that creature," Iain groaned, then started yelling after Sybil who paid him not a blind bit of notice.

The gully rose too steeply to scramble up and chase the dog so there was only one thing for it. Praying she would have more luck than Iain, Karmela put her thumb and index finger to her mouth and whistled as loudly as she possibly could. Sybil stopped in her tracks and turned, shook herself out, then half ran, half tumbled down the slope, landing at Karmela's feet.

Thank god for that.

She crouched and fussed Sybil's ears, murmuring what a good girl she was.

"Where did you learn that?" Iain asked. "Do you have a dog yourself?"

"No, and not long ago a dog would have been way out of my comfort zone, but a colleague has a spaniel and walking her is great fun." She grinned at him, then stood, grabbing Sybil's collar. "But maybe put her back on her lead? It might not work a second time."

He nodded a little ruefully. "You've shown me up good and proper."

Karmela shrugged. Most men she knew would not have admitted it and she very much liked that he had.

"Come on," she told him. "It must be almost breakfast time and I am starving."

When Jo arrived in the studio she wasn't surprised to see Karmela hard at work scribbling in her notebook. Her glossy helmet of hair obscured her face, but when she looked up her serious, dark eyes were alive with creativity. Already she was so much further advanced than the others, not just because she had prepared a detailed plan, but because she had an innate understanding of how words should flow. The raw talent in her writing shone through, which was very exciting.

Not only that, but Jo liked Karmela as a person very much

and looked forward to their late-night chats, with Zina as well. She just wished she was able to give a little more of herself, but how could she? There was so much she could never share, not with anyone, and her shyness was a more than convenient mask to hide behind.

As Jo set out her notes for the morning's session on narrative voice, Sophie followed Diana into the room, as usual sitting on opposite sides of the table. Sophie was a bit of a worry for Jo. She didn't seem to be gelling as well as the others, although she wouldn't go as far as to call her difficult. Yes, she questioned things more, but that wasn't a bad thing if it enriched everyone's understanding. She was just, oh, Jo didn't know, a little cold? No, that wasn't quite right either and it niggled her that she couldn't put her finger on it.

It was the only niggle though and Jo was not only enjoying working with this lively and thoughtful group of people, but was becoming increasingly confident. Already they were so supportive of each other. Nobody was backwards in coming forwards with their opinions, but they all listened respectfully to everyone else's too. The main issue so far had been getting everyone apart from Karmela to critique the others' work constructively rather than just pick out the positives.

It took courage and trust to share your work with others. The group had reached that point surprisingly quickly, with everyone other than Sophie happy to share their writing hopes and fears as well as their words. Trust made this the perfect environment for everyone to flourish. And Jo was increasingly uncomfortable about an important piece of information that she herself was holding back.

At precisely two minutes to nine, Iain's arrival interrupted her thoughts. Honestly, you could set a clock by that man. Jo assumed it was his background in the forces. After nodding in her direction, he attached his tablet to its keyboard and started to tap slowly away. She knew he was struggling with his novel, but at least he had managed to make a start, and she hoped yesterday afternoon's one-to-one had helped him to see the wood from the trees.

Unusually, Susan didn't appear. Jo decided to give it until the end of free writing time, then go and knock on her door. She needed them all here this morning to hear what she had to say. Before she lost her nerve. Because if she left it any longer it would be too late and the words would remain stuck inside her head forever.

Jo flicked through her notes. Not that anything there would help. As she'd thought about it last night, she'd realised this was something she had never actually told anyone before. So why now? And it had to be now. Now, now. If Susan was much longer, Jo was terrified she wouldn't do it. But she didn't want to feel any more of a fraud than she had to. Not here, not with these people.

Footsteps hurried up the wooden stairs, and Susan rushed in, her cheeks almost as pink as her glasses.

"Sorry, Jessica. I was reading. Ellen went out sketching early and I thought, you know, just one more chapter." She shrugged. "You know how it is."

"Don't worry. Free writing is something you can catch up with on your own if you want to."

Now or never. Clenching and unclenching her hands under the table, Jo took a deep breath.

"Right everyone, finish your sentence." Iain's tapping stopped, and one after the other, three pens were put down. "There's something I want to tell you. A little confession, if you like. My real name isn't Jessica. It's Jo, and I'd like you to use it." Her laugh sounded forced. "I thought if I left it any longer I wouldn't ever tell you, but it feels as though there's a lot of trust between us. The thing is, it's a secret alias; most people think I really am called Jessica Rose, so I'd rather you didn't mention it to anyone outside the retreat."

Sophie's head jerked up, her eyes fixed firmly on Jo, when normally she avoided her gaze. Her mouth opened, but Karmela spoke first.

"Thank you so much for sharing that with us, Jo," she said. "It feels like such a privilege. Do you mind me asking why you chose to use a pseudonym in the first place?"

Jo was wrong-footed, not only by Karmela's question but by Sophie's stare. Her skin tingled, the colour rising up her neck as she struggled to find an appropriate answer. "I think it was my husband's idea," she said eventually. Karmela was still looking at her expectantly. "He knows how shy I am, you see, and my privacy is important." That, at least, was the truth.

"And we will all respect it," said Diana. "I feel honoured you've chosen to tell us, Jo." Diana looked around the table. "We really are lucky to have such a lovely close-knit group. We were strangers just a week ago, and I already feel we've known each other forever."

There was a murmur of agreement, although Jo couldn't be sure that Sophie joined in. But the warmth from the others felt almost like a hug and she basked in it for a moment. Sophie was just being Sophie, after all. Karmela's question had been perfectly valid and Diana's words heartfelt. It was going to be all right.

Saturday 9th September

Zina watched from the kitchen window as Karmela and Iain strolled up the track. Something was going on between those two. If their body language didn't scream intimacy, then she didn't know what did – the angle of their heads as they talked, the closeness of their shoulders. She bet when she cleaned their rooms that one bed or other wouldn't have been slept in.

Karmela, certainly, had that glow of a new relationship, lucky cow. Oh, she shouldn't be bitchy. She really shouldn't. Karmela was a lovely person who deserved all the happiness she could get. Besides, Zina knew full well why she was feeling sore, and it was nothing – *nothing* – to do with Karmela at all.

It was Lambros's fault, keeping her awake all night with his snorting and snuffling. If he'd actually snored she could have elbowed him in the ribs and been done with it, but he couldn't even do that properly. Just long stretches of silence, then a sudden sound like a pig. Staring into the darkness, all sorts of stupid worries had popped into Zina's head, going round and round and round, making sleep impossible. Everything from whether she'd ordered enough pasta flour from the cash and carry, to if she should open for special solo traveller retreats over Christmas and New Year, to the perilously small amount of money in their bank account.

This morning, as usual, Lambros had rolled over and kissed her on the lips, telling her he loved her before padding off to the bathroom. Just as if he'd done nothing wrong. She'd curled into a ball of exhaustion, watching the minutes click over on the alarm clock until she couldn't lie in bed a moment longer. Ekaterini didn't start work until ten, so she had to get up to make breakfast for her guests, however frigging shattered she felt.

Maybe venting by slamming a few pots and pans around would help. But she couldn't because Susan and Ellen's bathroom was next door, and because Karmela would turn up on the terrace any minute, demanding coffee.

What was she like this morning? She'd never known Karmela demand anything; she was one of the most courteous and even-tempered people Zina had met. It wasn't her fault she preferred Greek coffee, which Zina had to make on the stove in a *bríki*. Sophie and Diana's endless cappuccinos were just as much faff. Not to mention Jo's tea. In a pot.

Zina stirred the freshly ground coffee into the cold water and set a gentle heat under it before taking a basket of freshly warmed croissants to the buffet table, where Karmela was helping herself to fruit and yoghurt.

"Good morning, Zina. How are you today?"

How would you be after a sleepless night, then having to

get up to make the perfect breakfast? But she couldn't say it. Of course she couldn't. Even though there was a tiny part of her that felt Karmela might just understand.

"Fine, thank you, and your coffee is on the stove."

"It is so kind of you to make it specially."

Zina turned back to the kitchen before Karmela could see the tears welling in her eyes. What the frigging hell was wrong with her? Emotional, stroppy, jealous even – just because she was the one making the breakfast, not the one sitting on the terrace eating it. She needed to get over herself.

Right now there was nothing she wouldn't give to be back in Athens. One of her favourite clients had been a large hotel chain whose flagship property had stunning views of the Acropolis from its rooftop dining area. Very often she'd taken journalists and influencers there in the coolness of the morning and eaten delicious food served by wonderfully attentive uniformed waiters. It had been a brilliant way to network; even in the digital age it was meeting face to face that really built long-term business relationships. And it had all been such fun as well.

In the courtyard, a chair scraped against the cobbles, followed by a murmur of conversation. Jo. Super-successful Jo. No doubt the book she was working on would take her career to new heights, while her own had been consigned to the rubbish bin. And Karmela and Jo seemed to be becoming such good friends as well.

Zina stopped short. Could she be part of that? She wanted to be part of that, and they both seemed to enjoy her company. Tears pricked her eyes again; she was so frigging lonely, especially as her Athens girls obviously thought it was funny she was making beds and cleaning bathrooms for a living now. They'd even – even – called her a drama queen for complaining about it. Led by Kassandra who couldn't even pick up after her chihuahua without squealing about how yucky it was.

She couldn't see Jo and Karmela being so mean, but neither could she tell them how she felt. They were her guests, and that in itself was the problem. She could never be completely open with them; it would be so unprofessional. Anyway, they'd be gone in three weeks, then she'd be alone all over again. Alone, miserable and bored out of her mind.

No, no, no! This would not do. Zina slammed her palm on the reclaimed pine table, making the milk carton jump and causing liquid to splatter across the surface. *Skatá!* Everything about the retreat had to be perfect, so she'd better buck up her attitude. It needed to be successful, to make money. More money than Lambros, but that shouldn't be hard. Not only would she win the profit game, they might at least be able to have some sort of life.

With enough cash in the bank, she could at least employ a cleaner. Unless, of course, the farm sucked up every last euro. Zina wrung the dishcloth she was using to wipe up the milk between her hands, silently screaming in frustration. No. She had to think about the reasons they'd come here. About Lambros's mental health, about how much better he was. About Mama and how they were making her widowhood just a little bit less lonely. But she doubted either of them recognised the massive sacrifice she'd had to make.

Resisting the temptation to slam the frying pan onto the hob, she placed it there gently, ready for Ellen's easy-over eggs.

Then she poured Karmela's coffee into its tiny cup and filled a glass with iced water from the fridge. These negative thoughts were getting her nowhere. It was what it was. There was nothing she could do but get on with it. And make a very strong coffee for herself, paste on a smile, then dredge up some positive vibes from somewhere.

Picking up the tray, she went onto the terrace. Already the day was warm, and bees buzzed in the nearby bougainvillea. A couple of sparrows hopped hopefully around the table.

Karmela thanked her as she put her coffee down. "We were just talking about the jukebox game tonight. I am looking forward to it."

"Have you put your secret song in the box?" Zina asked. "I seem to be a couple short and there are so few of us to play. Perhaps you could remind everyone, Jo. I need them by lunchtime at the latest to find all the music."

"Sure," said Jo, returning to her cereal.

"If we are so few," mused Karmela, "you should perhaps play as well. Especially as the idea is we get to know each other better through our choices."

What a lovely suggestion. Karmela was indeed an absolute gem, and Zina's spirits lifted a fraction. "Do you know what? I think I will. But there are so many songs I could choose."

"I did not have that luxury," Karmela replied. "I think people mainly discover music as teenagers, and I was a refugee at that time."

"A refugee?" Pictures of tented camps sprang into Zina's mind and she sat down with a thud.

"I was born in Sarajevo," Karmela explained, "and when the war came my parents left. We ended up in Berlin and I had little of the language and none of the culture. It was impossible to make friends and fit in."

"But that's awful!" said Jo.

Karmela nodded. "It was at the time, and if I am honest with myself, I was damaged for a long while afterwards too. It is the reason friends are so very precious to me now."

Zina nodded. "Friends are important. I know it's nowhere near the same, but I miss my friends in Athens."

"I expect you do." There was warmth in Karmela's eyes, and compassion. "I know we have WhatsApp and everything these days, but there is nothing quite like a heartfelt hug from someone who cares about you. Nothing like talking face to face."

A heartfelt hug? In her Athens gang they sort of wrapped arms across shoulders as they kissed each other's cheeks. Carefully, so as not to smudge their make-up. A heartfelt hug sounded like just what Zina needed right now.

The door in the corner of the courtyard opened and Sophie emerged. Zina stood.

"It's been lovely to chat, but I need to get on."

"You will choose a song for tonight, won't you?" Jo asked.

"Of course." And she would. One that would reveal something of herself too. Nothing like Karmela's shocking story, but something real all the same. These wonderful women deserved it.

Jo sat back, swilling the sweet, golden Vinsanto wine around her glass as Zina brought coffee, tea and tiny squares of *baklavá*, *kataífi* and *melekoúni* to the table. The honey aromas of the pastries mingled with the scent of night-blooming jasmine, old-fashioned carriage lamps casting pools of light across the courtyard. It was a moment of calm she wished she could bottle but instead it was about to be shattered.

When Zina had suggested the jukebox game a week ago, Jo had been privately doubtful but had gone along with it as Zina had been so enthusiastic. Maybe it was everyone's choice of song being a closely guarded secret making her uncomfortable. Secrets had a nasty way of tying you up in knots.

The group fell silent as Zina positioned herself at the end of the table. "OK, this is how it works. There is a piece of music from each of you, but because we are a small number of people I have added one of my own. I've shuffled them on my app, so I don't know which order they'll come out, and your job is to guess who chose which song. Then the person whose selection it is needs to say why. It's a great way to get to know a little more about each other and have some fun at the same time."

Oh god, they had to explain the reason they'd chosen it. Why hadn't Zina said? If Jo had known she definitely would have picked something different. Something less personal, less … emotive. She took a gulp of wine. Perhaps she should fetch another glass. She really wanted another glass but it didn't feel right when Zina had gone to all the trouble of bringing her tea. She just had to hope her song wasn't first.

Take That's "Shine" burst from the smart speaker Zina had set in the centre of the table.

Oh, thank god.

It gave her time to work out a plausible story for her own choice. Tweak the truth, perhaps? She didn't want to perpetuate any more lies than she had to. Yes, that was it. It was simple now she'd stopped panicking. She could say it was her mother's favourite song.

The music faded. "Any guesses?" Zina asked.

"Hmmm … Take That?" said Diana. "I reckon age-wise it could be Jo."

"Not me."

"Zina?" She shook her head.

Diana looked deflated. "Oh. I don't know then."

Susan said, "I'm not altogether familiar with the song, but the lyrics sound very positive. Karmela?"

Karmela grinned. "It is me. And it is the lyrics. A little over a year ago I had never heard it, but just before I left Dubrovnik there was a party and my friend Claire said it made her think of me, and how much I had come out of my shell. But when I listened to it properly later I realised it speaks to anyone who does not live their life to the full, for whatever reason. And that is really quite wonderful."

"Thank you, Karmela," said Zina. "Now, who's next, I wonder?"

The mood in the courtyard shifted down a gear as Ella Fitzgerald's voice filled the air. Jo tipped her head back and gazed at the pinprick stars high above, but even so found herself whisked away to New York. It was a short song, and Zina allowed it to play to the last trembling note.

"That was beautiful," Susan sighed, as Diana wiped a tear from the corner of her eye. It had to be hers, but Jo didn't want to be the one to rumble her. Not until she'd pulled herself together a little anyway.

"Was it yours, Susan?" asked Iain, but she shook her head.

"Well, we can't use the age thing because jazz is timeless. But sophisticated. Sophie?"

"Not me."

"Ellen?"

"No."

After a brief silence Zina suggested whoever chose the song should confess, and Diana put up a tentative hand.

"Peter and I went to New York for our honeymoon, and we found a wonderful little jazz club off Broadway, and 'Manhattan' sort of became our song. And yes, in case you're wondering, we did go to the zoo and ate baloney in Coney." Another tear slid down her cheek, but she did nothing to hide it.

"Are you OK?" Karmela mouthed across the table, and Diana nodded as Zina started to play the next tune, the techno beat of Lady Gaga's "Born This Way" blaring from the speaker.

With the song's political overtones and status as a queer anthem, Ellen was the obvious candidate, but in fact the choice was Susan's.

"The title is the name of the singer's charitable foundation, which inspires young people to build a kinder world. Not everyone was very kind to a bookish, overweight lesbian when I was growing up so it definitely strikes a chord."

Next they lurched from one end of the musical spectrum to the other, with a Mozart piano sonata, which Ellen correctly guessed was Sophie's choice.

"Because we had to learn to play it when we were schoolgirls," she explained. "I expect Diana remembers."

Her friend nodded. "Which was why I didn't think I should say."

Sophie had shown nothing of herself, even with her choice of music. Given she would be doing the same, Jo could hardly be critical. But the others had each revealed something personal, and her own white lie was making her feel increasingly uneasy.

Jo didn't know the next song, and by the looks around the table, she wasn't the only one.

"I think it is Iain's," said Karmela with some conviction. "If you listen to the lyrics they are about flying."

Iain's face was positively glowing as he turned to her. "Great spot! It's actually one of the lesser-known songs from *Top Gun*. It's called 'Mighty Wings'. And I thought it wouldn't be quite as obvious as 'Love Me Love My Dog'."

Karmela wrinkled her nose. "A little, I suppose."

For the first time Jo sensed a chemistry between them, but this wasn't a classroom setting and everyone was relaxed. Was she imagining something that wasn't there? Or had Zina been right when she'd said the game was a great way to get to know people? She picked up her wine glass, realised it was empty, and put it down again. What if her own choice gave too much away? But no, no, it wouldn't. Not unless she let it.

The Spice Girls' "Mama" came next. "We don't have many choices left," said Diana, who unlike Sophie, was really getting into the game. "Jo, Ellen, or Zina. And my money isn't on Ellen."

"Nor mine," said Iain.

Ellen grinned. "Then you'd be wrong. I loved dancing around my bedroom to The Spice Girls when I was younger. I was a massive fan. Of this song especially, because it wasn't about a girl and a boy falling in love."

"I'm surprised," said Diana slowly, "that you didn't choose one of their girl power anthems."

"If anything," added Iain, "I would have thought you'd have chosen Lady Gaga, and Susan was the Spice Girls fan. Just goes to show…" He tailed off as Susan began to giggle.

"We really should tell them," she spluttered. "I'm so sorry, but we did swap songs. Just to make it a bit more challenging. I chose 'Mama' because family is so precious to me. I've lost both my parents now, so trying to find my Greek relatives is even more important."

"I knew it!" Iain thumped the table, and everyone laughed.

With the mood so light, Jo desperately hoped her choice would be next, but instead Bruno Mars's "Just The Way You Are" filled the night air. Zina's song. Jo looked up at her, swaying gently to the music, expecting her face to look blissful but instead it appeared troubled, and Jo had to look away.

Given the stage of the game, Zina suggested a vote which was split down the middle. "That was my song, and it means a great deal to me. A few years ago, Lambros took me all the way to Budapest to see Bruno Mars in concert."

"Sounds like he's a keeper," said Ellen with a wink, "for a man, anyway."

"Charming," teased Iain, rolling his eyes, but Zina moved quickly on.

"So, Jo, as this is your song, would you like to explain why you chose it, then we can all enjoy it."

Truth or lie? Lie or truth? Jo looked around the table at their eager faces. The faces of people who had almost all decided to share something of themselves tonight.

OK, here goes.

"Not my favourite, but someone else's." She took a deep breath. "A friend who died."

As the laid-back guitar introduction sounded, Jo tried to relax into it. It was a song, just a song, that Pam had played over and again as part of The Style Council's *Café Bleu* album. But Jo knew it had been her favourite and hearing it again, she began to well up.

At the other end of the table, Sophie stood suddenly. "As we've finished, I'll say goodnight." Briskly she turned and stalked across the courtyard.

"Hey, that's a bit rude," Ellen called after her.

Diana looked down. "I'm sorry. She's not herself. I think she's finding it hard to switch off from worrying about her husband. I'm sure she didn't mean to cause offence."

"None taken," said Jo, but all the same she wasn't entirely sure Sophie's action hadn't been deliberate. She turned to Ellen. "I think in the writing group we're used to Sophie being a bit ... blunt."

Ellen looked uncertain. "Well, as long as you don't mind."

To be honest, Jo didn't. It had proved a welcome distraction, giving her time to pull herself together. The song filled the still night air. The song that Jo had come to realise Pam had loved so much because it had been special to her and her Eloise. Because Jo knew, without a doubt, that Eloise had been the best thing that had ever happened to Pam. And Pam to Eloise.

The song wasn't about a perfect relationship; it recognised there might be more to be gained elsewhere, but what would be the point when you already had the person who was best for you in your life? Eloise may have been married to a bullying brute, which she couldn't change because of her children, but as long as she had Pam lighting up her days there was more right than wrong in her world, as well as in Pam's.

Tears misted Jo's eyes. Tears of remembering, tears of loneliness. She looked around the table. At least she wasn't lonely here. That had to count for something, didn't it?

Sunday 10th September

Karmela selected some bread, two slices of locally cured cinnamon and herb *apóchti* and a handful of the farm's own sweet, oval-shaped cherry tomatoes. On Sundays, breakfast was a cold buffet to give Zina more time off, but still she was running around making coffees and teas for everyone. That girl never stopped.

As Karmela returned to the table, the others were discussing their plans for the free day. She herself wanted to visit the famous Akrotiri archaeological site she had glimpsed on her morning walks with Iain and Sybil. It was such a shame he could not come too, but it was hardly likely to be dog friendly.

"Susan wants to get on with her family research," said Ellen, "so this afternoon we're heading to a village called Megalochori where we think her grandmother came from. Zina's volunteered her mother to take us, which is so sweet of her, and I guess we might need her help to translate if we do find any long-lost uncles and aunts."

"That sounds really interesting," Diana replied. "Sophie and I are going to be lazy. We've booked ourselves a spa day at a beach club up the coast. This is meant to be a holiday, after all."

"Everyone's worked hard this week," said Jo. "Today's your time, although I have put a free writing prompt on the board if anyone fancies it."

As the others drifted away, only Karmela and Jo were left at the table. "So what are you up to?" Karmela asked. "Writing?"

She could have sworn that for a split second Jo looked startled, but then she said, "Actually, I'm interested in seeing Akrotiri as well, if I wouldn't be imposing."

"Of course not. I would love your company. I was thinking of doing some work first, then going later this afternoon, once the cruise ship passengers have moved on. Besides, I talk to my mother every Sunday morning. She is always keen to check on my progress."

"Mums are so important, aren't they?" A smile lit Jo's face. "I think I said how amazing mine is. She's my best friend as well."

"I cannot imagine my mother being that. Let us say we have a different sort of relationship."

Jo looked down at her plate and chased a croissant crumb across it. "I know how lucky I am." A pause. "Anyway, how about we go for a swim and have some supper at a taverna on the beach after we visit the archaeological site? I know it's not far, but it's hot and I'm happy to drive."

Karmela grinned back at her. "I will leave the swimming to you, but supper sounds good." It would be a real treat to spend more time with Jo, to get to know her better. Perhaps getting her to talk about her mother would be a good place to start winkling her out of her shell.

When they reached the site entrance just before four o'clock, it was as quiet as Karmela had hoped. The clerk in the ticket office was reading his book, and the cobbled walkway towards the entrance deserted. A trickle of people was leaving, with others enjoying a quiet drink in the terrace café. Two dogs lazed in the shade close to the doors to the building which sheltered the remains. Just as well Sybil was not there – it was far too hot to rush around containing the havoc she would have surely created in wanting to play with them.

The excavated part of the ancient city was enclosed by attractive local stone walls in every shade of ochre and black, and protected from the elements by what was proudly described on the information panels as a bioclimatic roof. Strips of daylight filtered between the wooden slats, illuminating the excavated buildings as far as the eye could see – a mere fragment of what would have been here before the volcano erupted. Half closing her eyes, Karmela imagined the street set out below them filled with people bustling to and fro, in and out of the houses, stopping to talk and shop on the way.

"Oh, wow," breathed Jo as they surveyed the scene in front of them, and Karmela could only agree. Broad wooden walkways stretched around the edges of the site, the ruins beneath two or three storeys high in places, all buried by volcanic ash millennia ago. No wonder people called this place the Pompeii of Greece.

They had hired audio guides so wandered around in silence, trying to take everything in. Karmela could barely believe the degree of preservation. The walls of whole houses were clearly visible, with square-lintel doors and tiny windows, in places still emerging as excavations carried on, through layers of ash tens of metres deep. But although the scale was impressive, the whole place lacked the soul of other sites Karmela had visited; the wall paintings had been removed, and only a handful of storage jars remained; the whole human story as lost as the city once had been. It was a crying shame, and Karmela felt the loss keenly.

"I do not know if it is me," she said, "but it feels a little ... sterile. If I have the right English word."

"It's exactly that. Incredible preservation of what we've seen, but I read there were once wall paintings and beautiful artefacts."

"They are all in the museum in Fira, but with this fancy roof you would have thought they could have kept them here. I keep trying to imagine the daily lives of the people, but it is so hard."

Jo smiled. "Yes. To picture the women of the houses, the rich ones being pampered, the slaves busy at their work, the conversations..."

"The alliances and friendships. But I suppose imagine is all we can do. As writers – if I can call myself that – I suppose it is what we do."

"You can certainly call yourself a writer," said Jo, her words filling Karmela with warmth.

Out in the sunshine again, they walked down the road towards the shore. While Jo headed for the sea, Karmela stopped to browse the tiny shop that raised money for the excavation and bought a book about ancient Akrotiri's discovery. She planned to start reading in one of the beachfront tavernas that clung to the narrow strip of land between the sea and the hillside behind.

Much as Jo had been the perfect companion with whom to visit the site, over a beer Iain would have come into his own. He always had something diverting to say, perhaps a funny story about Sybil or his time in the forces, told in his typically British self-deprecating manner. As well as being entertaining, Karmela found it rather endearing. As was the way he drew conversation out of others, even Jo who was gradually beginning to lose her shyness.

Karmela was loving her morning walks with Iain too. Flirting was definitely not the order of the day, although they did find plenty to laugh about. And when he spoke of his indecision over what his future might be career-wise, about finding a forever home for him and Sybil, she felt especially close to him. And not just because that was when the long looks returned.

Karmela settled at a table above the narrow black pebble beach and watched Jo swim around the short concrete jetty, her head bobbing up and down between the gentle waves. Once her beer arrived she opened her book, but it proved impossible to put Iain out of her mind. If she had met him at home in Zagreb she would have had no compunction about asking him out, but here things were different. They were colleagues, almost, for the rest of the month, and perhaps dating colleagues was not a good idea. Although now she came to think of it, she had watched at least two long-term relationships unfold in the staffroom of the history faculty with barely a ripple, so maybe…

No doubt it would be a risk, but she had taken risks with

her feelings before. Or had she? No, not actively, not consciously, she had not. From the distance of eighteen months she could see that now. She had become part of the other book club members' lives in Dubrovnik so easily she had hardly realised what was happening, but she had certainly not sought it out. So, given she had stumbled blindly into the most wonderful friendships of her adult life, could she find love in the same random way? Maybe this time she should reach out and grab that chance of happiness. Or maybe she should get over herself and concentrate on her book.

Oh, she was overthinking this, intellectualising it as usual. How did she feel? The smile playing around her lips was a bit of a giveaway, as was the unfamiliar sensation in the pit of her stomach when Iain looked at her. *Sranje!* She really, really, liked the guy. But what could she actually do about it?

Jo emerged from the water not far from where Karmela was sitting and looked around. Karmela waved and, smiling, Jo picked up her towel, wrapping it sarong-like across her chest.

"Fancy a beer?" Karmela called.

"Yes please. I just need to dry off a bit first."

She was a pretty woman, Karmela thought, especially now the thick make-up she normally wore had been washed off by the sea. She had a glow about her, fresh from her exertion. Although in her bikini she had looked painfully thin, her smile was as natural as Karmela had ever seen it.

"You look really happy," she told Jo when she joined her at the table.

Jo considered this for a moment. "Know what? I am."

"You sound surprised. Have you been missing home? Your husband? A month is a long time away."

Jo looked down at her glass, then back at Karmela. "I don't want to lie to you. I wanted to get away. Rees and I … we kind of live separate lives. Maybe it will do us good to be apart."

"That sounds tough. How long have you been married?"

"Not that long… About a year after *Only. Ever. You.* came out." She laughed. "Everything happened at once, and probably far too quickly. How about you?"

"I have always been single. My experiences as a refugee meant I had no desire to date, and it took me years to get my head around friendships even. I left two good friends behind in Sarajevo and one of them was killed in a bombing raid, so perhaps, somewhere deep inside, I was frightened of being hurt again."

Jo nodded. "Like I said last night, I lost a very good friend too. I don't know if you ever get over it."

They sat in silence for a while, listening to the wash and draw of the waves over the pebbles, the low music from the bar next door. Karmela thought about suggesting they raise their glasses to lost friends, but Jo's face was closed. Clearly that part of the conversation was over.

For once the farmhouse was silent around Zina as she stretched out on the sofa and closed her eyes, sinking into the comfortable faded red cushions of her childhood. She couldn't remember the last time she'd been alone here, but she'd managed to persuade Mama to take Susan and Ellen to Megalochori, and they'd gone for at least a couple of hours. Although it felt strange here without her, Zina had been heartened by the fact that her mother had at least put on a little make-up. Surely that was progress towards a more normal life too.

Even though it was Zina's day off, Lambros was somewhere on the farm. Somewhere. Doing something. No doubt she should go and find him to see if he needed any help, but now Zina was settled she had no enthusiasm at all for moving. Even picking up her phone was too much effort. A third of the way through the retreat's first month, and already she was exhausted, if not by the hard work, then by the endless monotony of her days.

She hadn't planned to take Sundays off, but thanks to the group's kindness she had at least some downtime. Obviously she couldn't ask Ekaterini to work seven days a week, so she'd been expecting to have to do everything herself. When last week she'd explained Sunday's meals were rather simpler because of it, her guests had decided that after breakfast they would fend for themselves so that Zina could have a break too. But the brief respite it gave her still wouldn't be a patch on the lazy weekends she and Lambros had shared in Athens.

After a hectic week at work, they'd normally slept late on Saturday mornings before heading out for lunch with friends, then maybe to the cinema, or more often than not snuggling on their very own sofa to watch a movie with a bottle of wine and meze from the deli. Oh, the bliss of it. Just the two of them, not having to worry about anyone else. She so wanted that part of their life back; surely, surely it would ease the niggles between them? The niggles which were becoming increasingly regular.

Zina was almost asleep – or at the very least, dozing into a daydream where she and Lambros were enjoying a romantic dinner at her favourite marina-side restaurant in Piraeus – when she heard the screen door from the terrace open and close. She opened her eyes, blinking.

"It's hot out there," Lambros said, fanning himself with his sun hat.

"Cool in here though."

"You look very comfortable."

"Care to join me?"

"God, yes. But I'm more than a little sweaty."

"I don't care." She sat up and swivelled around to make space, stretching her legs in front of her and wriggling her toes. "Would you like a drink?"

He nodded. "You stay there; I'll get them." He disappeared into the kitchen, then called, "Where's your mum?"

"I got her to drive some of my guests to Megalochori for the afternoon."

"That must have taken some doing! But why didn't you tell me? Clearing the last of the tomatoes could have probably waited."

Zina smiled to herself at the "probably". In other circumstances it might have riled her, but after her snooze she felt pretty chilled, and anyway, she didn't want to break the moment. Especially when Lambros came back with a bottle of Assyrtiko wine from the local co-operative.

"Just like old times," he said, opening it with a single twist of the corkscrew. God, he was strong these days and those new muscles of his were seriously hot. She grinned lazily up at him, then he settled next to her, putting a glass in her hand.

"To peace and quiet." The rims chinked. "And to us."

"Yes, to us," Zina murmured, snuggling closer as he put his

arm around her shoulder. He was right; he did whiff a bit, but she didn't mind. It was his scent – familiar, comforting. And she had him all to herself.

"So the tomato plants are all pulled?"

"Yes. I need to be sure I'm ready for the pistachio harvest. Yiannis said it could be any day now."

"Are there lots of nuts?"

"Thankfully, yes. I've borrowed his machine for removing the husks and the drying yard is ready. Hopefully by the end of the month the money will start rolling in."

"Then I'll need a few more bookings to beat you."

"No competition, Zi. Not today. Let's just chill. Even if I don't miss Athens, I do miss our lazy weekends."

"Me too." For once they were on exactly the same page, and the thought gave Zina a spark of hope that with a bit more money, and a bit more time, they could go back to being the way they'd always been. Just having Lambros's arm around her shoulder made her wonder if she'd been worrying unnecessarily. They were both so busy, both so stressed, and a few hours of togetherness like this would make all the difference.

Zina took another sip of wine, its citrus dryness tingling on her tongue. Mama should be gone at least another hour, so they had time to enjoy this moment. Her thoughts were already turning to the bedroom, but today they didn't have to dive straight in for a silent, fumbled quickie. They had time, real time, to sit together and share the wine and their thoughts. For a little while longer at least.

Her phone buzzed in her pocket, and she groaned.

"Can't you just leave it?" Lambros asked, pulling back her hair and kissing the sensitive skin behind her ear.

"What if it's Mama, saying she's coming home early? Honestly, Lambros, if it isn't I'll just let it ring."

But it wasn't her mother. It was Iain. They looked at the tiny screen together, and when Zina picked up, Lambros shifted away from her with a sigh. But how could she not answer it? The call was from a guest.

"Zina, I'm so sorry to disturb your afternoon off, but there's a guy who's turned up saying he's Jo's husband. She isn't here and, well, he's none too happy. He's calling the retreat all the names under the sun for not having twenty-four seven reception."

Jo's husband? Zina couldn't afford to have him badmouth her business. "Tell him I'm on my way."

She stood, but Lambros stayed on the sofa, looking up at her accusingly. "Can't he just phone his wife? Why do you have to get involved?"

"Because it's my retreat house."

"And your afternoon off. Our time together. Our only time."

Zina sighed. "And if the call had been to say your precious goats had escaped, what would you have done?" Lambros shrugged, but she knew he couldn't argue. "I'll be as quick as I can."

She all but jogged up the path, stopping only in the shade of the building to brush the dust from her denim skirt and retie her hair in its ponytail. She needed to appear at least fractionally professional, even if she'd had no time to change into her work clothes.

As she rounded the corner, Iain was nowhere to be seen so presumably he'd beat a hasty retreat as soon as he knew she was on her way. The stocky man with a face screwed up like a chicken's arse was sitting at the table with a bottle of her best Chianti in front of him, and didn't even stand to greet her. How could lovely Jo be married to someone like that?

"Oh, so you're here. At last."

Despite his attitude, Zina crossed the courtyard and reached down to shake his hand, holding hers in front of him until he could ignore it no longer. "I'm Zina Sideris, the owner. How can I help?"

"You can find my wife. I come all this way to surprise her, and she's not even here."

"I believe Jo wanted to see the archaeological site at Akrotiri. Have you tried calling her?"

"She isn't answering her phone. Honestly, she's such an airhead. She probably hasn't even taken it with her."

Zina gritted her teeth and smiled. "I think it closes soon. I'm sure she won't be long." Actually, she wasn't sure of that at all; Jo and Karmela had definitely spoken about having dinner on the beach, but as well as his general demeanour, the dismissive way he'd spoken about Jo put Zina on her guard. "I see you've found the honesty bar. Is there anything else I can get you while I'm here?"

"Something to eat. It was a four-hour flight and the best they could serve was a poor excuse for a panini. I'm starving."

"The kitchen's closed, but perhaps I could rustle something up for you."

"Closed? I thought you provided food?"

"It's Sunday." She said it as though it explained everything.

"How long have you worked in hospitality?" he snapped.

No, she wasn't having that, but neither could she be rude. However much she was struggling with the idea, this man was Jo's husband. She had to put her instant loathing of the guy and her niggling doubts that all was not well to one side and be professional.

"I'll be as quick as I can," she told him. "In the meantime, enjoy the wine."

"Shit. Shit, shit, shit." Jo couldn't help herself as she stared in horror at the lock screen of her phone as she pulled it from the glove compartment. Kicking herself for the outburst, she apologised to Karmela.

"Do not worry. Most Croatians swear all the time. Is something wrong?"

No point in lying. "Rees, my husband, he's at the retreat."

Karmela's neat eyebrows disappeared into her fringe. "Oh."

"Oh" just about summed it up. "We'd better get going. He's been there a couple of hours and he's not the most patient of men."

Which was a massive understatement, given the increasing fury of the messages she'd glanced at. Jo put the little hire car into gear and turned onto the road, gripping the steering wheel tightly. Why was he even here?

"You had no idea he was coming?" Karmela's voice was gentle.

"No." The word sounded slightly choked. What more could

she say? For a moment she regretted telling Karmela even that little bit about her and Rees, but it was hard to lie to someone you liked so much. And she'd seemed to understand, despite never having been in a relationship herself.

Jo just hoped Karmela didn't seek to prolong their conversation because she needed to think. What could she do? What would she say to Rees? She didn't want him here, she really didn't. This was *her* time, *her* space, and she was terrified his arrival would turn her dream into a nightmare. He had to go. Had to. But would she be able to pluck up the courage to tell him? Away from the horrible atmosphere of that prison of a house, it was possible, but it would take just about everything she had when she saw him face to face. She glanced at the woman in the passenger seat; she was pretty sure Karmela wouldn't take shit from anyone.

They were bumping down the farm track between the pistachio trees, dust billowing around them, when Karmela spoke.

"Jo, I have to ask. Are you scared of Rees?"

Did it show that badly? Of course she was scared of the man who could blow her world apart, but she could hardly tell Karmela that. "No," she replied, trying to make her voice sound more like her own. "Of course not. I'm just wound-up that he's here."

"So you do not need moral support when we get there?"

She did. She so badly did. But she couldn't accept it. For so many reasons. Yet somehow just knowing Karmela was prepared to back her gave her confidence a little boost. It almost felt as though she had a friend.

"No, it's fine. Honestly. But thank you."

The moment they arrived in front of the courtyard she saw Rees sitting at one of the tables, a bottle of wine at his elbow. So he'd found the honesty bar. That hadn't taken him long. But she doubted it would make him any sweeter.

As she walked towards him, Jo's legs were shaking and she forced herself to take long, deep breaths. She needed to be strong. Very strong.

"Where the hell have you been?" Part sullen, part angry. She'd become adept at gauging his moods – so much depended on it.

"To the archaeological site at Akrotiri, then for a swim, then for some supper."

"You're meant to be writing that bloody book, not having a holiday."

He always knew which buttons to push, sod him.

Strength, Jo, strength.

"I needed a break. I've been working hard." She had. On the retreat workshops and with her students at least, but the half-truth sent her resolve into a downward spiral. She needed to get on the offensive before it disappeared completely. Be forthright. Channel Karmela. "Why are you here?"

"To see you, of course. Why else? When I arrived the place was like the frigging *Marie Celeste*. And you wouldn't answer your phone."

"I left it in the car when I went swimming. It's not like I was expecting a call. You haven't phoned since I've been here."

"You only left me one message."

"And I suppose you want me to beg?" Jo folded her arms. The anger bubbling inside her was unexpected, and she had to be careful. She had to use it but not go too far. "Anyway," she said, indicating the wine bottle and his empty plate and bread basket. "I see you've been looked after."

"If you call a rubbery omelette being looked after. And I was here more than twenty minutes before some guy with a dog appeared and phoned the woman who's supposedly running this place."

"It's Sunday. It's Zina's day off. Or it's meant to be."

Rees shrugged, a flicker of something dark in his eyes and his voice beyond cold when he said, "Glass of wine, Jo? I know how fond of a little drinkie you are, and I suspect that's what led to your error of judgement. Honestly, telling these people your real name? How do you know you can trust them?"

But it was her name, her choice. "Why are you here?" she repeated.

"I fancied a few days in the sun. I hope our room's better than the food."

Their room? *No. No way.* She wasn't having that. "*Our* room? You haven't been near our room at home in months. Not that I'm complaining."

"Careful, Jo. I bet voices carry in this courtyard and you don't want your dirty little secret coming out, do you? I bet you don't trust these wannabes who're paying to leech off a *best-selling* author that much."

Every barb. He knew just where to land them, but his threats were rarely as open as this. Why was he attacking her now? Was it just his anger at being left to wait? Or was he trying to soften her up because he wanted something? Was he trying to make her so desperate to get rid of him she'd agree to just about anything? With distance, she could see it, but whether she could hold out against him was another matter.

She turned away. "Follow me." He'd get as far as the living room of her suite and no further. At least there they could talk in private so she had half a chance of getting to the bottom of this.

She was aware of him grumbling behind her as he hauled his suitcase up the stairs. She was tempted to say he could leave it in the hall, seeing as he wouldn't be unpacking it, but why should she save him the trouble? Racing inside, she closed the glass partition to the sleeping area as he followed her into the room.

They glared at each other over the coffee table, although it was all Jo could do to hold his angry gaze.

"Where am I supposed to sleep?" he shot at her. "On the sofa?"

"Not even there. But before you go, now that we're in private, you can tell me why you really came."

He at least had the decency to look mildly embarrassed. For about ten seconds.

"I need you to sign something."

"Oh?" Jo folded her arms. To stop herself from trembling more than anything. Did he want a divorce? *Oh please, let it be that*. And then she'd be free. With a start she realised how much she wanted it.

"We need to remortgage the house."

"Why?"

"A little local difficulty with one of my investments, and I need some cash to pay into my pension. You know I plan to retire at fifty, which isn't that many years away."

His pension. One of *his* investments. She hadn't been so stupid as to leave the financial side of everything to him, but she couldn't say she'd taken a lot of interest in it either. Now it looked like that might have been a mistake, but they'd always seemed to have plenty, and her needs weren't half as extravagant as his. Not a quarter.

"If we really don't have any money anywhere else, which I struggle to believe, why don't we sell up and buy somewhere smaller?" *Or two somewheres smaller*. But she didn't dare say it. He knew too bloody much. It always, always came back to this, and the tiny thread of confidence she'd been clinging onto snapped.

What he knew. What she'd done. It could do so much damage.

Even divorced, she'd never be free. Tears scalded the backs of her eyes.

"Come on, Jo. There's no need to upset yourself over this. It's no big deal. Not in the grand scheme of things." He sighed. "If you really don't want me to stay then just sign the papers and I'll be on my way."

There was a time when this sudden gentler offer would have persuaded her, but in a moment of clarity she glimpsed more behind this visit than just the remortgage; something more insidious, something about control. Something that meant, like Eloise's husband in *Only. Ever. You.*, that he'd never let her go, even if he didn't want her.

Deep inside her gut she knew she had to make a stand. But could she? Could she do it? Jo was really shaking now, so she stepped away from Rees, closer to the window, but he followed her. She had to get him out of here. She couldn't bear him being in the same room. But that was what he was relying on, wasn't it?

"Leave me the papers and I'll look at them."

"How about you do it while I unpack?"

Strength, Jo, strength. "Because you're not unpacking. You're not staying here."

"Are you sure about that, Jo? Really sure?"

She folded her arms again and drew herself up to her full height.

"Yes. Those are my terms. You leave – I'll even call you a taxi – then I'll read the mortgage papers. Consider them. A few days won't matter. Not if it's *no big deal*."

"*Terms!*" She flinched as his spittle hit her cheek. "You're in no position to dictate terms! I can ruin you, Jo. Ruin you with just a few words. Even your precious mother will never forgive you for what you've done, and you damn well know it."

She turned her back on him. There was nothing more to be said. He knew he'd win in the end, but as long as he left right now she was beyond caring. He'd invaded her sanctuary, wormed his way back inside her head, just when she was trying so hard not to think about the past so she could write that sodding book. But how could she ever forget? The tightness rose in her chest, choking her, making it hard to breathe. She'd die here in front of him, and then he could do what he frigging well wanted and he wouldn't care a jot.

Calm down, Jo, calm down. She wasn't dying. This was just another stupid panic attack. Rees's hand landed on her shoulder and she shrank away.

"Please, darling, just sign it."

"I will. Later. If you go."

He sighed. "I don't appear to have a choice, so you'd better get me that taxi. You can courier the documents to my office tomorrow. Because you *will* sign them, darling. You know it makes sense."

Jo very nearly crumbled at his tone of voice, hiding her face as she fumbled in her bag for her phone and called the taxi firm. Twenty minutes. Maybe a bit more. She needed him out of here now. One more push. She had to do it.

"You can wait in the courtyard," she told him. "Finish that wine if you like."

"I'm helping myself to the best whisky they have and it'll be on your tab."

Jo shrugged. Even if he downed the whole bottle it would be worth it to get rid of him.

She didn't move when he left. She stood like a statue, listening as he dragged his suitcase down the stairs. Finally, the heavy wooden doors of the hallway slammed behind him and his footsteps crossed the courtyard, his case rumbling over the cobbles.

There was a whine from Sybil in the room below. Then silence. Blessed silence.

Only then did she sink onto the arm of the settee and weep.

Once the voices in the courtyard faded, Karmela curled her feet under her on the sofa and picked up her notebook. The time had come to write the first love scene of her story, and how to approach it was troubling her greatly.

It needed to be a moment of maximum tension, when Agnez ran to her secret boyfriend Miho to tell him her father was forcing her into the Convent of St Clare so they would never see each other again. Dramatic in itself, but also because the rest of the plot revolved around the older women's – Karmela's main characters' – attempts to free the teenager from this injustice.

The problem exercising Karmela at the moment was whether the couple should kiss. A modern audience would expect it but the city's historical record was silent on such matters. Of course, ideas of courtly love would be well understood by the Ragusan nobility, and kissing in the romantic sense was mentioned in Chaucer's *Canterbury Tales*, so it should be safe to assume it would be a possibility between the couple, even if outside the social mores of the age. But given they had broken all the rules to be together anyway...

In the era she was writing, casual kissing was outside the norm because a kiss had a quite specific meaning. It was a seal, a pact, a sign of homage, and as such most often performed between men. But what about a kiss of passion? Was such a kiss instinctive? Would the young lovers kiss this way, or in the courtly manner of Agnez bestowing the greatest gift she could to young Miho? What would that kiss feel like? How would it come about?

The knock on her door made Karmela jump. Immediately Jo came to mind, but no, Iain stood in front of her, a frown creasing his forehead, while Sybil leapt up, barking with joy, as though she had not seen Karmela for weeks.

"I hope I'm not disturbing you," he said, "but I'm worried about Jo."

This was unexpected, but she nodded. "So am I. Is her husband causing trouble?"

"Thankfully he left in a taxi a few minutes ago. But before

that they had an almighty row. At least, he was the one doing the shouting. I didn't mean to overhear but I was on my terrace and it was pretty hard not to. He was trying to bully her into signing something. She held her ground, but she sounded pretty shaky, and once he left she was sobbing fit to break your heart." He looked down at Sybil, who was standing between them. "I knocked on her door to see if she was OK, but she said she was and sent me away."

"She might just need to cry, you know, get it out of her system." Karmela understood that feeling well, but it was hard to articulate to a pragmatist like Iain. Then inspiration struck. "Besides, from a woman's point of view, well, have you ever seen Jo less than perfectly presented? She might not want anyone to see her looking a blotchy mess."

"I hadn't thought of that."

"I would not expect you to."

"Well, if you're sure she'll be all right."

"Not really, but I do think she would rather be alone." Iain nodded but seemed reluctant to leave. As reluctant as Karmela was to let him. "Would you like to come in?" she asked.

"How about I head over to the bar first, grab a bottle and some glasses. Red or white?"

"I rather like the white with the funky blue label. It is called Aidani, I think."

"I know the one. You take Sybil; I won't be a moment."

She glanced around, but her space was, as ever, perfectly tidy, so she settled back onto her favourite end of the sofa, Sybil jumping up next to her and rather endearingly resting her head on her thigh. Sharing a bottle of wine would be an unexpected pleasure, even if it was driven by Jo's misfortune.

But she had already seen that Jo was a very private person, had refused her offer of support earlier, as well as sending Iain away. No, there was nothing they could do. Tonight, at least.

After closing the door behind him, Iain set the bottle and glasses on the low table and poured them each a generous measure before joining her on the sofa. Sybil did not move. Clearly at this moment her master was very much second best.

Iain raised his wine to Karmela's in a sort of salute. "You said you were worried about Jo too, but I didn't think the row was loud enough to reach you here."

"It was not. But I saw her reaction when she picked up her phone and realised Rees was here. It looked very much like fear to me, although she denied it."

"Sadly, I think you're right. He's holding something over her; he said something about a secret that even her mother would never forgive her for."

Jo? Surely not. "I cannot imagine her…"

"Me neither. But everyone makes mistakes, don't they? And people change over time. They grow up. If something happened when she was younger, that might explain it. I remember having an officer under my command who was a total pisshead and found himself in serious trouble more than once. It got as far as him being suspended and that shocked him into turning his life around. He ended up as my boss, and he was brilliant."

"Of course you are right. Listen, Iain, just between us, Jo told me their marriage is not very good anyway, and this was before she knew Rees was here. But from what you heard it sounds as if it is worse than that; as if he is trying to control her. I have a friend… He was in an abusive relationship, and he is still dealing with the scars. She needs to get out."

"Do you think you could talk to her?"

Karmela frowned. "I could try, but I am hardly qualified to give relationship advice, having never been in one."

"You haven't?" Iain looked genuinely surprised.

"For a long time it was through choice, but since that changed I have not found the right person." Was it time to grasp the nettle? The thought made her heart jump in her chest, but she was going to do it. "How about you?"

"Similar really. I've moved around so much on different postings that it didn't seem fair. That was rather brought home to me in my twenties; I was engaged for a while but she broke it off, and I completely saw her point so I didn't bother again. It's not just the moving… I've been on active service and obviously that's dangerous. When you've seen men shot down, men you care about, and then you have to write to their families…" His face twisted in anguish.

Karmela could not help but reach out to him, his arm warm beneath her hand.

"Dealing with bereaved families. That must be so hard."

He did not pull away. In fact, his eyes met hers and she saw genuine pain in them. Gone was the conversationalist, the joker. Here was the man's soul stripped bare.

"Worst part of the job. By a mile. But it doesn't do to dwell. I'm out of it now and ready for a new life in all sorts of ways."

He put his free hand on hers and patted it. Slowly, rhythmically, almost as though he was not sure how to, their eyes still locked together. The room felt stuffy, despite the air conditioning, the wine heady, even though she could normally take her drink. Perhaps it was not the wine. Perhaps it was him. Perhaps even, because he was leaning in to kiss her, his lips gently touching hers. He tasted of wine, and salt, and something she could not identify but it was good, so good.

After a few moments he pulled away. "Was that … all right?"

Karmela laughed. "I did not slap your face, did I?"

He grinned. "Which was something of a relief, knowing my luck. Not that I make a habit of kissing women I hardly know." Colour rose up his neck beneath his evening stubble. "I'm making a hash of this, aren't I?"

"Of course not. I enjoyed it."

"It was nice, wasn't it?"

Not the word she would have used, but she knew English reserve when she heard it, so she nodded, wondering if he would try again, or if the second kiss was up to her. Tempting as the idea was, she really wanted to know where they were going with this. If he was after a one-night stand that was definitely not happening. She wanted more than a casual fling with this man.

Where the hell had that thought come from?

"So now what?" she asked.

He cleared his throat. Was he going to back-pedal? Was it just about sex? But looking at his expression, she did not think so.

"I'd like to take this further. Get to know you better as more than a friend, but there's a lot we need to think about too. The impact on the group in particular."

Karmela tried not to let her relief show. He shared her concerns, which was a wonderful thing in itself. "I think we are on the same page with this. Even before tonight I was coming to the conclusion it might be worth mentioning I find you attractive because we are both mature enough to put it behind us if you did not feel the same about me."

He smiled, and wrapped his arm back around her shoulder, pulling her closer across Sybil's prone body. "I'm flattered … so flattered … and really glad you've been thinking the same. Tell you what, why don't I take you out to dinner? A proper date." He paused. "I know. I'll book somewhere really nice in Oia for next Sunday so we can watch the sunset."

"That sounds very romantic." Even though it was a whole week away.

He grinned down at her. "I'm no good at this, but I'm trying my best."

First their noses, then their lips touched, this time Karmela taking the initiative. A date was all very well, but no way was she waiting all that time for another kiss.

"Well, *agápi mou*, it's bedtime for me," Zina's mama said as she stood and stretched, turning off the television. "You too, given how tired you look."

"Thanks, Mama. I won't be long." She watched her mother cross the room. "And I'm so very pleased you had such a good time with Susan and Ellen."

Mama nodded. "It stretched my English, but they are good company. I'm already looking forward to taking them out again."

Once again the house was silent. Lambros had absented

himself onto the terrace straight after supper, during which he'd returned to his monosyllabic Athens self. At first she'd been annoyed at his childish behaviour, but as she'd been sitting with her mother, barely concentrating on the television, she began to wonder whether he was in a low place. If Santorini hadn't made him better after all, what had been the point? But no, that was an awful thought. A heartless one. And even though she was a little bit cross with him, she knew she didn't mean it.

Her phone bleated like a goat. Lambros. He'd set up the novelty ringtone for them both when his little herd had arrived. At first it had been funny; now it irritated her every time she heard it, especially after his comment about his goats needing mental stimulation. That still stung every time she thought of it.

She read his message: *Can we talk?*

Of course they could, but she hesitated, suddenly worried about what he was going to say. Something felt out of kilter. He didn't normally stew like this; usually they rowed with a passion, made up with a passion, and then it was over and done with. But to do that they needed their own time and space, neither of which they'd had this evening. They never did. Apart from this afternoon, and Jo's bloody husband had messed that up royally.

Zina stood, sighed, and slipped her phone into her pocket. Crossing the lounge, she opened the screen door and stepped into the darkness, the only light a sharp bright rectangle from her mother's room, extinguished with a creak as Mama closed the shutters. Even here they would have no privacy, and the thought made her suddenly angry.

"Yes?" Her voice sounded harsher than she'd intended. It wasn't Mama's fault. She needed to get a grip.

Lambros inhaled sharply. "I was going to apologise, but you're not making it easy."

Tears stung her eyes. "Nothing is easy, Lambros. Not at the moment."

"Tell me about it." He sounded so defeated, and Zina could not let that happen.

She sat down next to him on the rattan sofa, the warm velvet of the night closing around them. As her eyes adjusted, she began to make out pinpricks of light from the riding stables across the valley, and a soft yellow-white glow from the cluster of buildings that edged the bay. She remembered Lambros saying how hard he'd found the darkness when he first came here, but for her it had always been comforting. Except right now it wasn't enough. She needed his comfort too.

"We will be all right though, won't we?" she ventured. "We do love each other."

"Of course we do, Zi." But he didn't move towards her as she'd hoped, even though he dropped his voice to a whisper she struggled to hear. "I just think that living with your mother adds to the pressure, that's all. If we had our own home..."

"And just how would we pay for it?" Honestly, what choice did they have? And they weren't going anywhere until she was sure Mama no longer needed them either. But as soon as the words were out, she regretted them. "Sorry," she murmured.

He reached out and patted her arm. "So am I. I meant one day. Something to aim for."

She nodded, then after a moment or two slid closer to him, gripping his hand in hers. "A dream we can share."

He turned to her, his voice as urgent as it was low. "We need that, Zina, we really do. Not something that's yours, or mine, but something that's ours."

What did he mean, yours or mine? Zina didn't understand, and his words sounded loaded. Dangerously loaded. She was too tired, though, to start down that track. He'd apologised after all. And he must have been upset when she had to go off to the retreat like that. But she'd had no choice.

She rested her head on his shoulder. "I'm sorry Jo's husband messed up our afternoon."

"I'm sorry I ruined our evening by behaving like a child."

"Sounds like we're quits."

He pulled her close, and together their breathing settled into a regular pattern, the soft rhythm binding them into peace of sorts.

For the moment, it was enough.

Monday 11th September

It was not when Karmela saw the prompt on the whiteboard that it struck her, nor when she began to write. She was alone in the studio, with Jo nowhere to be seen, although she had turned up at breakfast maybe a fraction quieter than usual, and certainly with more make-up around her eyes.

Karmela knew there were extra bags under her own as well. She had had an almost surreal night, drifting off to sleep in a wine-fuelled fug of contentment after Iain left, reliving his gentle kisses, the solid strength of his arm around her shoulder. That was all they had done, cuddle and kiss and talk, but it had been enough – especially now she knew there was more to come.

Then, at three in the morning, she had woken with a start, worrying about Jo and feeling terribly guilty she and Iain had not even tried to reach any conclusion about what they might be able to do to help her.

Lying wide awake in the darkness, Karmela had run

through what Iain had told her about the overheard row and come to the conclusion that if Jo was harbouring a secret that even her mother would find hard to forgive, she was unlikely to share it. But clearly her relationship with Rees was not just distant, as she had told her at the taverna, but actually toxic. She had seen the damage a controlling relationship could do and witnessed how hard it was to move on. She had to persuade Jo to get out, and quickly. But how?

Round and round her thoughts had chased, so she had been glad to get up early, shower, then sit on her terrace with an espresso, watching the sunrise flood the low hill between the retreat and the sea with a deep band of orange light, the fingers of the dawn stretching between the olive trees beyond the vineyard as colours came to life and the shadows around their trunks became goats.

The presence of the escaped goats to the south side of the retreat meant that the best place to release Sybil was in the pistachio orchard to the north. Karmela had been delighted that as they wandered between the trees, watching the greyhound sniff and run, their hands had somehow wound together. She could not be sure which one of them had initiated it, and it had felt completely natural. If this was being in a relationship ... wow ... she wanted more. More tingling lips and fingers, more ... what was the word? Oneness?

By unspoken consent they had separated when they came in sight of the farmhouse to return towards the retreat. While Karmela had no wish for their affair to be clandestine, she had the distinct impression that for Iain the watershed would be their date, and logic told her he was right; it was better to get to know each other a little more in private first.

Dragging herself from her thoughts, she looked at the prompt again. *Childhood*. Write the first thing that came into your head, that was the idea.

> *My childhood ended the night we left Sarajevo for good, our car crammed with our most precious possessions and the necessities of life.*

Sophie and Diana arrived, and Karmela nodded to them, before bending over her notebook again, smiling to herself. Eighteen months ago she never would have been able to write those words, her painful past locked away in a box. Just a year ago, she had never returned to Sarajevo, even though her father had died there after separating from her mother at the end of the war. But she had loved growing up in the pre-war city, and now she would write a letter of praise to it.

> *For too many years I left my memories behind in the house where I grew up. Perhaps tucked in the drawer of my grandmother's ornately carved hallstand, along with keys, stamps, loose change... Or maybe they were hidden beneath my bed, or between the pages of the books on the shelf, in the room where Emina, Nejla and I played with my doll's house, then later wrote our stories, shared our hopes and dreams.*

Karmela sat back for a moment. Letting the hidden past in still felt as liberating as when she had first realised she could do it. Back then there had been copious tears – of happiness and of grief – but now it simply filled her with joy that her life was so much better for being able to embrace it.

She glanced at the clock. Five to nine. She heard Jo's door close and footsteps cross the landing. Jo smiled at Karmela, but it was a small, tight thing. And as Karmela lowered her head to continue writing it hit her: her story was Jo's too. She had to confront her past to be free as well. Whatever the secret was, she needed to exorcise it, or it would drag her down forever. Karmela had wasted thirty years in a half-life and she could not let Jo do the same. Could not and would not.

She had an idea about how to get her message across, but was she a good enough writer to pull it off? There was only one way to find out.

Tuesday 12th September

Playing truant by leaving Ekaterini to clear up after lunch only added to Zina's excitement. She had warned her cook that she had a surprise for Lambros, and the moment her mother collected Susan and Ellen for another family-finding mission across the island, it was time to act. This afternoon was her very last chance; the long-awaited pistachio harvest would start tomorrow, and then her chances of getting her husband's attention were practically nil.

Ever since their conversation on the terrace on Sunday night, Zina had become increasingly determined to make it up to Lambros. He'd seemed so sad about the lost opportunity of their afternoon and it had touched her heart deeply. Now she was going to put it right by recreating the broken moment, but with all the added romance she could muster. In the cool bag over her shoulder was a half bottle of real champagne and she was wearing her best black silk undies – the ones Lambros had bought her. The soft fabric next to her skin sent a thrill of anticipation through her.

Now all she had to do was find Lambros, but normally his first stop after lunch was to check on the goats and she reckoned he'd still be there. Oh, they were going to have just the best afternoon together, reconnecting in every way imaginable. They needed it so badly, and having arranged for her mother to be out for a few hours, Zina was determined to make the most of their privacy.

Even from halfway down the track she could see Lambros wasn't at the goat pen, but then she caught sight of him rounding the side of the farmhouse. Rather than head in her direction, he unlocked her father's battered old truck which he used around the farm. She hailed him, waving.

They walked towards each other. "I'm just heading over to give Yiannis a hand," Lambros said. "His ATV's slipped down a ravine and he needs help hauling it out."

She put her arms around his neck. "Don't go now," she breathed. "Go later. Mama's out so I've taken a couple of hours off."

He didn't look at her, just continued looking over her shoulder. "I have to. I said I would."

Zina stepped back. This couldn't be happening. She'd planned it all so carefully. He couldn't … just go. Not because of some ATV. "You're not serious."

"Yes, Zi, I am. Chrysto's already on his way and he needs us both. I mean, if you'd said…"

"I wanted it to be a surprise." Tears burnt the backs of her eyes.

"I'm really sorry. Any other time…"

But there wouldn't be another time. Not for weeks. Weeks!

"*Bástardos, bástardos* man!" Zina stamped her foot. "We need this! We need time together."

He closed his eyes briefly before raising them to the heavens. "I don't disagree. Just not now." He clenched his fist around his car keys. "I can't stay now. Yiannis—"

"Fuck Yiannis!" Zina screamed. "How dare you put your friends before me? You put everything before me and I've had enough."

"You can talk, after Sunday." Anger flashed in his eyes, darker and more dangerous than she had ever seen, but boy, was she angry too.

"I had to go. It was work." Didn't he get it?

"And I have to go now. Think of all the help Yiannis has given me. I can't let him down."

Oh, but he could let her down all right. "You put him first! You frigging well put him first! It's never me. What about letting *me* down? Are you fed up with me already? Like you got fed up with your mountain bike, with your gym membership, even with your proper job?"

"What the hell are you talking about?"

"You know what I mean! One minute you're all over something like a rash and then within about a millisecond, poof! You're off to the next big thing. You're unstable, Lambros, unstable. You're like a frigging butterfly! I suppose I'm lucky I've lasted this long."

"Zina—" Her name rasped from his throat.

"And now the farm. Everything's the farm." She pressed her face close to his, to make sure he understood. "I've given up my life for your sodding farm, and you can't even give me one afternoon."

He looked at the sky again, took a deep breath, then spoke slowly and deliberately. "There are clearly things we need to discuss if you're so unhappy. I'll be an hour, an hour and a half at most, then we can talk about this properly."

"I don't want to wait," she wailed. "I don't want your empty promises. I don't want to spend my life cleaning toilets to prop up your bloody farm!"

His arms cartwheeled as he yelled at her. "Don't try to tell me the retreat's for my benefit. You just want to beat me, Zina. You want to rub my face in my failures and punish me for bringing you back here. *Skatá!* Why didn't I see it before?"

"That is just so much crap, Lambros. Yes, you made me come here, but I did it for your frigging mental health. And this is the thanks I get. God, I wish I was back in Athens. But even that wouldn't be far enough from you."

She pushed past him and ran into the house, slamming doors behind her and throwing herself onto their bed, beating his pillows in rage. Outside, the engine started and wheels screamed in the dust. Good frigging riddance.

She pummelled and cried until her anger was spent, then rather shakily sat back on her knees. Silence. No radio. Nothing. The cool bag with the champagne was on the bedroom floor, and red-hot tears trickled down her cheeks. Her marriage was over. Perhaps not today, but this was the beginning of the end. Lambros had made his priorities crystal clear, and Zina wasn't prepared to be at the bottom of anyone's list. No frigging way, after all she'd done for him.

She wiped her eyes on her sleeve and stood up. If this was the end, she was going to make him pay. Make him hurt like she was hurting right now. Hell, yes, she was. She would shut him out like he'd done to her, and see how he liked it.

Standing in front of the mirror, Jo carefully reapplied her eyeliner with a shaky hand. An extra glass of wine after lunch had done her no good at all, except that she'd actually slept for a couple of hours. Then woke dry-mouthed with a thumping headache, which thankfully some painkillers and the longest of showers took the edge off, enabling her to function.

So now she was in the process of becoming Jessica. Eyeliner, then mascara, then concealer smudged over her shopping-bag-sized dark circles. Except to the group she wasn't Jessica, she was Jo. Was Rees right? Had it been a mistake? No, he couldn't be. She liked that they used her proper name. It was Rees's fault she felt so vulnerable and exposed, and him messaging her three times a day to ask if she'd signed the mortgage papers didn't help. He was wearing her out. Wearing her down. Chip, chip, chipping away, like her mum said.

Only if you let him. But she couldn't help it. Oh, she'd been brave enough at the time, but his coming here had rammed it home that she'd never really be free. There might be battles she could win, but he held all the aces. She'd always be tied to him, because he knew. And he used what he knew. *Don't be a frigging drama queen.* Her lipstick wobbled in her hand. But right now the walls were closing in around her, suffocating every possible spark of creativity and life.

Part of her wanted to agree to the remortgage to get rid of

him. Another part, perhaps the bigger part, didn't want to give him an easy win. She wanted to make him sweat, at least. Underneath everything, a flicker of anger remained, although she didn't know how long she'd be able to hold out if he threatened her again. He didn't even have to tell the world, just her mother. He'd been right about that at least; Mum would never forgive her for what she'd done, and Mum was the very best thing about her wretched life.

Her hand trembled as she picked up her blusher. *FFS, Jo.* She had ten minutes – ten minutes until this afternoon's feedback session, with Karmela reading first. That, at least, was something to look forward to. *Channel Karmela. Sensible, unflappable Karmela.*

Voices from the stairs told her the group was assembling, so she picked up her notebook and crossed the landing, helping herself to a cola from the fridge before sitting down. Susan puffed and panted up the stairs, just back from her trip out with Panora, and Iain arrived last. Jo couldn't look at him. How much had he heard? She hadn't remembered the back window was open until he'd knocked on her door, and his terrace was right below it. He could know ... well, not quite everything, but enough. More than enough.

"Right then." Her voice sounded a little unlike her own. "It's Karmela first. I know we're all looking forward to our next trip to Ragusan Dubrovnik."

Karmela shook her head. "I am taking you somewhere else today. It is a piece I have written about the city where I was born, and why I left it far too long to go back." She cleared her throat, then her low, measured voice filled the room.

"My childhood ended the night we left Sarajevo for good,

our car crammed with our most precious possessions and the necessities of life.

"For too many years I left my memories behind in the house where I grew up. Perhaps tucked in the drawer of my grandmother's ornately carved hallstand, along with keys, stamps, loose change… Or maybe they were hidden beneath my bed, or between the pages of the books on the shelf, in the room where Emina, Nejla and I played with my doll's house, then later wrote our stories, shared our hopes and dreams.

"From the first day at kindergarten we were constants in each other's lives. A bond too precious for a child to understand, until it was broken. And then I was no longer a child.

"Sarajevo was our playground, a city of beauty, culture, harmony. All the things we took for granted until war ripped them away: tree-lined avenues, red and cream trams, the river icy from the mountains; domed roofs of the mosques cheek by jowl with the towers of the churches; bazaars and department stores; east meeting west, easy as breathing.

"Until it was not. The desperate anguish of home, friends, ripped away. Irreplaceable. The pain locked inside. The secret of it was my defence against the world – or so I thought for the longest time. Instead it became a slow, powerful poison, the poison of war. A war I had no right to grieve over, because my parents had run away.

"The war ripped out the heart of Sarajevo with its mortars, snipers and bombs. Emina was killed by a bomb, right at the end of the siege. I did not go back. I did not witness the city begin to heal. I did not heal myself. I closed myself off from the world and hid in another time.

"Secrets fester. They blight your life. Thirty years later I met two men whose sacrifices in that war made mine seem small. Yet they were not just living, they were truly alive. They were filled with love, and courage, and pain. So I borrowed some courage, and for the first time in years the word 'Sarajevo' crossed my lips, the names of my friends on an ocean of tears. And finally, finally, I went back."

A stunned silence filled the room. Jo had stopped making notes just moments before, when a slow realisation had struck her. What Karmela's piece was really about. Karmela knew. She *knew*. Iain must have told her.

Shit.

Susan took off her glasses and wiped a tear from her eye. "Oh my, Karmela. That is so ... raw."

Karmela nodded. "It is, yes. But every time I share my story, it becomes easier."

Jo had to pull herself together. She had to move away from the personal and steer this back to the critique.

"That was beautifully written, Karmela, an excellent and engaging stream of consciousness." God, her voice sounded prissy. "I think a little more detail in the descriptions of your childhood in Sarajevo would strengthen it. Maybe show the readers how you experienced the city with your friends, to build the link between the two ideas. What does everyone else think?"

"It is, perhaps, almost uncomfortably personal," said Sophie. "But that is obviously just my reaction. Susan and I often find ourselves at different ends of the spectrum with this sort of thing."

"Maybe it needed to be that intimate? Descriptions alone

wouldn't have pulled us in in quite the same way," suggested Diana. "And I was pulled in, completely."

The conversation was taking on a life of its own, with Karmela listening to their comments and scribbling notes on the paper from which she'd been reading. But Jo knew that she had no intention of rewriting or improving her piece in any way. Its job was done, because Jo had heard the message loud and clear. And that message made her want to run away and hide. Karmela knew what Rees had said, knew that Jo had a terrible secret. How could she look her in the eye again?

But Karmela was looking at her, and she was smiling. Perhaps, perhaps, she was reading this wrong. She was panicking again; thinking the worst. Could it be that Karmela had put her heart and soul onto the page and relived those painful memories because she cared? Now that she was thinking clearly, Jo knew that from everything she had seen of Karmela, that was the only explanation. Once again she found herself wondering whether, in Karmela, she might just have found a friend. A warm tingle of something close to strength ran through her, and finally, finally, she smiled back.

Around her, the discussion of Karmela's piece was finally petering out.

Come on, Jo, get your head out of your arse and do your job. Diana was reading next and normally needed every encouragement.

"OK, everyone. Time to move on. Are you ready, Diana? Is there anything in particular you'd like our feedback on?"

It was late when Zina turned on the dishwasher for its final load, then checked the list for the cash and carry Ekaterini had left on the kitchen table. Karmela and Jo were still on the terrace, but she was far too wrung-out to feel sociable, and far too distracted by what she might find when she got home. On the other hand, they were her guests and she could not ignore them. Besides, a glass of wine would put off the evil moment a little longer.

Decision made, she took the bottle of Karmela's favourite Aidani from the fridge. Outside, she heard Jo saying goodnight. A slightly slurred goodnight. She hadn't seen her drink that much, but yesterday morning she'd noticed a bottle of wine peeking out from Jo's swimming bag when she was cleaning her room. She'd told herself it was none of her business, that perhaps Jo had bought it as a gift, or prize, for one of the group. But now she doubted that was the case. *Skatá!* Much as she liked Jo, she couldn't cope with her problems as well as her own.

Picking up a glass for herself, she took the Aidani outside.

"Do you fancy a top-up?" she asked Karmela.

"Just a tiny one, please, then I need my bed. But it will be nice to unwind. Today has been rather tense."

Zina sat down next to her. "Do you mind me asking why?"

"Of course not. It's Jo. I worry about her and her husband. To me, it seems like an abusive relationship and she has not been herself since his visit." Zina wondered if she should mention the wine or not? But Karmela carried on. "Not that I have first-hand experience of this sort of thing myself, and I do not suppose you do either, Lambros being such a lovely man."

Lovely? Selfish shit, more like. But what could Zina say? It seemed that everywhere lay conversational traps; nothing was safe. There was no way she could tell a guest how bad things were between her and her husband. She couldn't tell anyone – the way he'd treated her this afternoon was far too humiliating. Tears smarted in her eyes again, angry tears. And worse, Karmela seemed to be waiting for an answer.

"I suppose some men do like to control their wives, but Lambros is not one of them."

"And no woman should ever be controlled. No human being, come to that. In fact, the one time I have seen this before, it was the girlfriend doing the controlling. Jo needs to get out, but I have no idea how to even broach the subject."

At least Zina could be truthful here. "Me neither."

"Well if you do think of something…"

"Of course."

There was a long, uncomfortable silence, then Karmela tipped back her head, pointing upwards and beyond The Retreat House. "Look, is that Cassiopeia up there? The night sky here is wonderful. There is far too much light pollution at home."

"When I was a little girl, Mama used to sit me on her lap on the terrace before bed and point out all the stars." They sat for a moment, gazing at the pinpricks of light in the velvet blackness, then Zina drained her glass and stood. "Talking of Mama, if you don't mind I'd like to get back in time to find out how she got on with Susan and Ellen this afternoon."

Karmela smiled. "Given the conversation over supper it was a triumph but I will not spoil it for you. Goodnight, Zina."

Walking down the track, Zina was not thinking about Mama at all but replaying the argument with Lambros over and over in her head. The way he hadn't even considered staying with her for a moment. Not even one moment. It had been all about frigging Yiannis and she hadn't come into it at all. Although her anger had faded in the hours since, replaced with unease about what he might say when she got home, now it was back with a vengeance.

And she had been oh so vengeful. She had known just the right button to push.

She'd done something similar in Athens years ago, although she couldn't remember exactly why. She'd made up a bed for him on the sofa and he'd gone absolutely ballistic when he'd come home from a night out with the boys, so much so that they hadn't made up for a whole twenty-four hours. Living with Mama, the best she'd been able to do was to place a wall of bolsters down the centre of the bed, and pin a note on his pillow with those cheap rose earrings he'd bought her, telling him to stick to his own side because she couldn't bear to be anywhere near him.

She'd been so mad, and he'd hurt her so much, that her actions had felt entirely justified. Anyway, how else was she meant to get his attention when he'd sodded off? Now there was no way he could ignore how furious he'd made her. His choice this afternoon was symptomatic of everything wrong with their marriage. His choice. Not hers. So although she may have made the bed in a physical sense, metaphorically at least it was his to lie on. All the same, as she approached the kitchen door, Zina couldn't help feeling just a little sick about what his response might be.

Mama was in the kitchen washing pans, the rich aroma of

pastitsio emanating from the half-empty dish on the table. Automatically Zina picked up a tea towel.

"Haven't you had enough of that at the retreat?"

"A few more won't hurt. How did it go today with Susan and Ellen?"

Mama's eyes shone in a way Zina hadn't seen for a very long time.

"It was wonderful. We went back to Megalochori to see the elderly lady the café owner told us about on Sunday. She lived there before the earthquake and she was delightful, offering us coffee and *baklavá* on her terrace. She told us she'd married a village boy, and when the rebuilding started they'd come back to her parents' old home. So I asked her if she remembered the Liatsou family and she did, and she thought they had gone to Kamari and stayed there.

"Of course, it's a huge place now with the tourism, so as soon as we came back I phoned the *papás*, and he said yes, he knew them. He called me later to say he'd spoken to one of them who could even remember his father buying lottery tickets so he could visit his aunt in America. He was so excited to meet Susan and we're heading over there tomorrow."

Zina gave her mother a hug. "That sounds wonderful, and you are quite the sleuth."

Mama laughed. "Not at all, but there is a new British detective drama I want to watch, and it starts in five minutes."

"Off you go. I'll finish here then go to bed."

"Lambros has already turned in. He looked exhausted when he came back, poor man."

Zina dried the last pot, then put it back on the shelf above the range.

Would he be asleep, or only pretending to be? Or awake and spoiling for another fight? Albeit a furiously whispered one so Mama wouldn't hear.

But one thing was for sure: if he'd moved those bolsters she'd damn well put them back. For a couple of nights at least. Just to make sure he understood how very wrong he'd been.

But in the bedroom there was no sign of Lambros. Or his pillows. The bolsters were still in place, although the note was on her side now, her words scrawled over with an equally angry message. Coward! Frigging, frigging, coward. Red-hot anger burst through Zina again. If that was how he felt, why not stay and fight? God knows where he was sleeping, but she didn't much care. She wouldn't give in to him, she just wouldn't. If this turned out to be their very last argument, it was all the more important to win it.

Wednesday 13th September

After towel-drying her hair, Karmela ran her comb through it and headed back into her bedroom. Outside, the pre-dawn grey was slowly leaching towards colour and the birds were beginning to sing. Otherwise, silence. And time for the quickest of coffees before her morning walk with Iain.

As she popped a capsule into the machine she noticed the note pushed under her door, so she strolled across and picked it up.

Dear Karmela,

I know I'm being a coward writing to you but I've thought long and hard about this and come to the conclusion that it would be better not to take things further between us. I have every respect for you and hope we can continue to be friends. Iain

Oh. Oh.

She stood stock still. Had he been cowardly? Certainly if the boot had been on the other foot, she would have come right out and said it, but now she thought about it, that might have been wrong. It was definitely easier to read Iain's words of rejection than to have to listen to him saying them. For a start, she had time to work out how to react.

Slowly she let the feeling in. She had to manage this, or else it could overwhelm her. Each thought, each unfamiliar emotion, one at a time. It was a logical, rational way of dealing with it. What she always did.

First, disappointment. Deep disappointment. And hurt. Hurt for what might have been. Hurt so sharp it took a gargantuan effort to push it away and refocus. There was something else too, something she could not pinpoint. Something that remained beyond her grasp. She frowned, trying to give the idea a name, but instead a crippling anguish rushed unbidden through her. Why had he decided to do this? Everything had been going so well. Or at least, she had thought so until about two minutes ago.

On the last couple of mornings they had not only held hands on their walks, but shared the occasional kiss as well. And they had talked so much more about the things that mattered: his indecision over his future, the friends in Dubrovnik that meant so much to her; and Jo, of course, and what they might do to help her. Had he pulled away because she had not told him about her plan to read out that piece yesterday? It was such a very small thing, and he did not seem the type to sulk. No, that could not be it.

Had he decided she was not attractive enough? He had not

struck her as that superficial, but she did not really have the experience to tell. She picked up her coffee cup and set it on the drip tray. Whatever his reasons, the result was the same, and there was nothing she could, or even should, do. Had she not said that if it did not work out they were both mature enough to put it behind them? She should not question it, just accept it for what it was. Goodness, it had only been a matter of days. She was being so silly. Everything would be fine once she had time to get used to the idea.

Karmela pressed the button on the machine and the scent of strong coffee filled her nose. It was a shame, that was all. For the first time in her life she had been part of a couple, and it had felt good. Very good. She hugged her arms around her ribs. What you did not know could not hurt you, but when you did know … when you had even just tasted… That felt entirely different.

It was not as if she was a stranger to rejection. Not as if it was the first time. It was a lesson she had learnt as a teenage refugee in Berlin and she had allowed it to blight her life. This business with Iain was a blip, a temporary setback, and it could not be permitted to do the same.

Karmela looked at her watch. If she hurried she could catch him and Sybil on their walk. Throwing on shorts and a T-shirt she raced from the room, looking left and right when she reached the track. In the distance she could see they had barely passed the farmhouse so she began to jog after them.

Iain turned when she was about a hundred or so metres away, and Sybil gambolled towards her, long legs a flurry of canine joy. Somehow having the dog around made this less uncomfortable, and Karmela managed to paste on a grin.

"You could have waited." His face was a picture of uncertainty, his bottom lip sucked slightly in. She walked up to him, resting her hand briefly on his arm.

"It is fine, you know. Friends is fine."

His exhalation was visible.

"Thank you. Thank you for making it easy."

She shrugged. "It is what friends do." Then clicking her fingers at the greyhound she started to run, calling, "Come on Sybil, shall we race him?"

There was no point standing around talking when there was nothing to be said. Just as there was no point drowning in the inevitable hurt. What she needed to do was get on with her day, focus on her writing, then later, when she felt more ready, she could work out how best to deal with the emotional fallout.

Thursday 14th September

Jo squinted at the lock screen of her phone. It was fuzzy and blurred, much like she was feeling. But not so much that she couldn't make out two messages. One from her mother and one from Rees. Neither of which was she sufficiently sober to answer. No point thinking now that she should have stopped drinking after dinner. No point acknowledging that she should have stayed at the table in the courtyard where she could still hear voices. Sipping tea, instead of creeping away to down more wine from the secret supply she'd bought from the taverna after her swim.

God, this needed to stop.

This morning she'd barely been able to engage with the group through the crippling fug of her hangover. "Show not frigging well tell" was hard enough to explain at the best of times, but luckily she'd had plenty of examples in her notes. At one point she'd felt so rough she had almost pleaded a migraine, but Karmela and Iain at least would have known the truth. Karmela, who for a few precious moments had felt like a friend, but who would surely hate her if she knew what she'd done.

It was damned hard work being a secret drinker away from home. She'd used so much mouthwash she'd felt as though her tongue was on fire, so was pretty sure the boozy aura hadn't followed her into the studio. And she'd flung the windows of her room wide so Zina wouldn't catch a whiff when she went in to clean.

Drinking was a frigging waste of time too. It didn't help her to write. Which was another reason she had to stop. Right now. But she'd only just opened a new bottle. Jo stood, shakily, from the sofa and walked back into her bedroom towards the fridge, glass in hand. A slight stagger left her almost sprawling on the bed, but she righted herself, swayed a little, then slumped onto the edge of the mattress.

She had two choices. There were always choices. Life was just one frigging great— What were those weird charts with lozenges and arrows called? Yes, that was it, decision trees. Or something like that, anyway. You stood in the lozenge and decided which arrow to take. Then another, and another, and another. Except one branch was always short and simple, and right now anything convoluted was beyond her.

What the frigging hell are you on about, Jo?

Good point. Very good point.

But choices were important. She was bad at them. Badder than bad. So she could do with a road map. Try – try – to be logical. Choice one: drink, sleep, wake up with hangover, repeat. Easy. Choice two: throw out the rest of the bottle, take painkillers – or just plain suffer and serve her right – not sleep very well – or enough painkillers to knock herself out – wake up, or not wake up… No, that was silly.

Wake up, go to breakfast, do what you're being paid to do.

Outside in the courtyard she could hear voices. Diana, Susan, Ellen … and Zina. Zina must have finished work and joined them. They were asking her about the fireworks tomorrow night. Iain couldn't go because of the dog. A girls' trip out. That was it, she'd got it, she'd offer to drive, and then she couldn't have so much as a glass. Not tomorrow, at least.

Even this drunk, Jo knew what was right. Right was taking the difficult path and pouring the rest of the wine down the sink. It had to be that way because otherwise it would be there, tempting her, even when she inevitably woke at four in the morning. Especially at four in the morning. She set her glass on the desk.

Jo, this has to stop.

Now, before it gets out of hand.

It might numb the pain a little, but it wouldn't make her problems go away. Even the small ones, like Rees and his sodding remortgage. So if it was small, why was she holding out? Let him do it; get him off her back. But somewhere under the fug, a sober Jo was angry. Angry that every decision in her life came down to his insidious bullying. What had Mum said? He chip, chip, chipped away at her. The trouble was that he could. Because he knew.

Oh, Mum.

She wanted to talk to her mother, but she couldn't. Not like this. Another reason to sober up. Picking up her phone, she very carefully typed a message, promising to call tomorrow, checking it three or four times before sending it. At least now her mum thought she was OK. She worried about her. Their shared grief over Pam had brought them even closer together, but her mum had never understood why Jo couldn't bear to talk about Pam now the rawness of loss had passed. Because Mum didn't know.

Her mother thought it was because Jo had found Pam's body and she had once or twice suggested counselling to help her process the traumatic event. Or if not counselling, to at least write it out of her system. But it hadn't been traumatic. It had been a huge shock of course, had felt completely unreal, but Pam had looked so peaceful, and the paramedics had been wonderful.

She remembered it vividly, even holding Pam's cold hand and talking to her until help arrived, but the next few days had always remained a blur. Pam had no family, so Jo's parents had arrived and made all the arrangements. Jo's mum had been Pam's executor and the main beneficiary of her will, and she'd promised to make the house over to Jo as soon as she could so she didn't lose her home as well.

It had taken Jo about a month to venture back into Pam's room, on a Sunday morning when Rees was playing golf. Back then he'd been marvellous, always there when she needed him, and she wondered at it now. Had his love been real at first at least? Maybe. He hadn't known about the house or the manuscript, so it couldn't have been money. Not then.

The manuscript had been one of the first things Jo had found when she opened Pam's laptop and wiped the dust from the keyboard. She'd borrowed it once or twice so she knew the password, and her task for the morning was checking through Pam's inbox to make sure nothing needed dealing with, and that all Pam's email contacts knew about her death.

But there on the desktop was a file labelled "Only. Ever. You." She'd gazed at it for a while. Pam had said the story was personal, so perhaps she should have deleted it, but Jo had wanted to read it first. She'd been missing Pam so desperately that it was impossible to think of destroying this important part of her. This last part of her. Impossible not to crave spending a few hours in her company again.

Jo had taken the laptop downstairs to the lounge, made herself a pot of tea, then opened the document. And there it was, Pam's secret life laid bare in the most wonderful prose: a forbidden affair with the wife of a high-profile MP spanning two decades. No wonder Pam hadn't come out at work; pretending to be something she wasn't had given her and her lover added protection. Especially as the husband in the piece wasn't the nicest of men. But the women had planned their escape; when the children were grown-up, when Pam could take early retirement.

They'd so very nearly made it too. And somewhere a woman had been grieving more than anyone for Pam, yet couldn't let it show. Little wonder that when Rees had rung the doorbell some hours later Jo had been in floods of tears, and of course he'd asked her why. And rather than keep Pam's secret, she'd been in such a mess that she'd told him.

Her first big mistake. The biggest. With a sudden flash of clarity Jo knew this, right now, was not the moment to make another. She couldn't quite fathom why, but she recognised an important decision when she saw one. She stood, waited until she stopped swaying, and tugged the wine bottle from the fridge. She tipped the contents down the sink, watching until the very last drop had swirled away.

She would not buy another. She would not pop into the taverna on her way back from tomorrow's swim, "just in case". But what the hell would she do instead? A voice in her head told her she could solve this problem for once and for all.

Break it down into pieces. Take a first step.

It was her mother's voice. Or was it Karmela's?

Karmela who, now her head was clearing just a little, Jo knew would support her. Karmela who knew about her row with Rees. Which meant … which meant … this small part of her problem need not be a secret. But could she trust her? Rees said she couldn't trust anyone. But why would she believe him anymore?

Friday 15th September

"No, *agápi mou*, let me drive," Zina's mother said, picking up the car keys. "You work so hard. It will be good for you to relax this evening and have a few drinks."

How typically thoughtful of Mama, and anyway, Zina was too mentally exhausted to argue, so she settled into the passenger seat while they bumped along the track to collect Ellen and Susan.

When Zina had mentioned the plan for a girls' night out to see Santorini's annual firework display, Panora had swung into action, arranging for them to watch from the roof terrace of her cousin Eleni's house in Firostefani on the rim of the caldera. Zina had been doubly pleased because as far as she knew, this was the first contact Mama had made with her family since her husband's funeral. Maybe, just maybe, The Retreat House was doing her mother some good. If that was indeed the case, it was the one bright spot in Zina's life at the moment.

Once they were on their way, with Jo following behind in her hire car, Zina snuggled down in her seat and closed her eyes. Under normal conditions the drive would take half an hour, but they'd left early because of the crowds that would doubtless be gathering in the cliffside towns and villages to watch the display.

Zina just hoped it would be enough time to get her head into party mode. This business with Lambros was tougher than tough. She'd never expected him to huff off and sleep on the terrace – and worse, stay there. She was sure it wouldn't be long before her mother realised what was going on, and she couldn't bear the questions and the minute analysis of her marriage that would surely follow. Especially as she was completely without answers.

She'd thought she knew her husband inside out, but this was an entirely new reaction. His temper had always been a match for hers, but he'd never been one to keep an argument going, and she realised, a little guiltily, she'd been relying on that. Relying on him to make the first move towards reconciliation, which she could graciously accept, as long as he promised never to put the farm ahead of her again. *Skatá!* He'd married *her*, not *it*. She had every right to be the most important thing in his life.

Lambros apologising would be a win, but right now she'd take a temporary truce. Breathing space from her tangled emotions. But Lambros was keeping out of her way. It wasn't hard, given she was working all hours and so was he, but when he'd rounded the corner and seen her on the farm track he'd rammed that stupid sun hat of his down on his head and walked in the other direction, the message loud and clear.

"So what do you think, Zina?" Ellen asked, making her jump in her seat.

"Sorry, I was miles away. Having a little doze if I'm honest."

"If an early buffet supper every Friday would give you and Ekaterini more time off?"

Right at this moment, more time in the farmhouse with Lambros and her mother was the last thing Zina wanted. Best be non-committal. "I'll ask Ekaterini what she thinks."

After squeezing both cars into the parking lot in front of Eleni's husband's bakery, the small party walked up the slope to the village square, the setting sun colouring the walls of Agios Gerasimos church a warm ochre. The Greek flag on its blue and white striped pole rippled overhead, largely ignored by the noisy crowds heading for the terrace looking over the caldera.

Trying not to lose each other in the mass of humanity, they threaded their way up the narrow street past restaurants and bars buzzing with music and light, the aroma of freshly grilled meat filling the air. Every table was full, with people queuing outside in the vain hope of a seat, and Zina was more than relieved to reach the wrought-iron gates of Cousin Eleni's house.

After introductions in the terracotta-tiled living area, Eleni led them to the roof, just as the last of the light drained from the sky, the faintest orange glow a smudge on the horizon. Fairy lights were wrapped around the potted palms, and hung from the fringes of the rattan awning, which rustled gently in the warm breeze. It was the perfect vantage point, with a clear view of the caldera over the single-storey building across the street. Zina snapped a few pictures for her Instagram. If she got some of the fireworks as well she could eke them out over the next week or so. It was hard to feel particularly enthusiastic about it at the moment, but she couldn't let it drift completely.

A buffet table was laden with sweet and savoury treats of every kind, and Zina was glad they had brought so much wine. The pastries had most likely come from Savvas's bakery, but their generosity was eye-watering. There was enough to feed twenty, not just the small party from the retreat. When Zina thanked Eleni, she gave her a hug, saying how wonderful it was to see Panora again after all these months.

With that she rushed downstairs to make iced coffees for the drivers, and Zina made her way towards Diana, who was standing alone gazing out over the caldera.

"It's so beautiful, isn't it?" Diana said. "All the little boats on the water are like fireflies. Thank you so much for bringing us here."

"This is my mother's doing, and I'm doubly glad because she hasn't seen her cousin since Babá's funeral last autumn."

Diana nodded. "It is hard, getting out and about again, but I think everyone finds their own way. Eventually. I do worry about Sophie when the time comes. Lawrence was a larger-than-life personality when he was well; he was a Member of Parliament for years and he's gone downhill so fast. But at least she finally seems more settled here. She's stopped snipping at people, anyway."

"Snipping?" Zina wasn't entirely sure what Diana meant.

"Being a bit short-tempered. You know, almost rude, but not quite. I felt like I spent the whole of the first week apologising for her, and it's great that she's beginning to relax. You've created something really special, Zina."

Jo joined them, carrying a tall glass of iced coffee which

was thick with cream-coloured foam. "I totally agree. The retreat is a brilliant environment to work in. It's so calm and beautiful – not to mention the food. The whole place has … I don't know, a generosity of spirit that reflects your personality."

Zina felt quite choked by Jo's words. To hear them from someone as genuine as her meant the world. "That's just the loveliest thing to say. Thank you. I wanted to make it special and I'm so glad it's hit the mark."

"It's the perfect size too. Just perfect. Everyone can get to know each other and for me, well, I think I'd have found a larger group a bit too daunting."

"But don't you have to speak at launches and the like?" Diana asked.

"Not if I can help it. I don't know how Karmela stands up in front of a room full of students every day."

Karmela wandered over. "Did I hear my name?"

"Only in praise and wonder," Diana said with a laugh. "How you have the confidence to lecture."

"It is not confidence. It is knowing your subject inside out, then you are ready for anything. Much like you do, Jo. And you have a great way of putting your knowledge across, making it relevant to each of us, and that is a real gift."

Jo's smile seemed to light her face from the inside out. Much as her words had made Zina feel. She liked everyone staying at The Retreat House right now, but their habit of chatting most nights made her feel a little closer to Karmela and Jo. How could you not like Karmela, with her natural warmth and interest in other people? And Jo had such a sweet personality… If only, if only, they weren't her guests, then she could confide in them about Lambros. It was so very lonely not having anyone to share the awfulness with. Certainly not her so-called friends in Athens. They'd probably just tell her she was being a drama queen again.

Forcing her mind back to the conversation, Zina feigned interest as Karmela asked Diana whether she had finished the tricky scene on which she had sought the group's advice, nodding enthusiastically as Diana outlined her progress.

Once she had finished speaking, Zina turned to Jo. "How is your new book going?"

For a split second it seemed that Jo gripped her coffee a little more tightly, but then she smiled and said, "Fine, thank you." It wasn't Jo's normal smile, but perhaps Zina was imagining it. Had she seen a slipping mask because she herself was wearing one?

Eleni bustled up. "It's almost time. Fill your glasses, everyone."

The little group broke up, leaving Zina alone for a moment before her mother joined her, wrapping an arm over her shoulder.

"I have to tell you, Zina, I'm having a wonderful evening. For the first time without your father… Perhaps … perhaps the worst is over?"

Zina squeezed her back. "I hope so, Mama. I really do." This was wonderful, wonderful, but instead of being filled with joy, Zina found herself awash with her own misery. This would not do. Mama's newfound happiness deserved better.

"I don't want you to think…" Her mother hesitated. "I mean, I still miss him terribly and some days I feel so wretched

I can't even bear to leave the house. But on others, well, I think I need to make more of them. Yes?"

"Definitely yes."

"I also know … much as it is wonderful having you and Lambros living with me, it won't be forever. Things between you…"

An explosion of light and sound filled the sky, huge starbursts vibrant and shimmering as they cascaded towards the water far below. Gold, green, red … so many colours. Then massive sparkling balls appeared from nowhere against the velvet backdrop of the night, overlapping silver circles mimicking full moons. Some burst a distance from them, others close enough to illuminate their upturned faces.

The lights dancing across the night were magical, and in Zina they stirred a memory: watching the Athens New Year fireworks over the Acropolis with Lambros, not long after they'd started going out. Drunk from wine and from love, their faces lit by cascading sparkles and stars had been wreathed in more happiness than she had thought she would ever know. The moment was made even more perfect when he'd bent his head and whispered, "I'm so glad I found you, Zi. You make me complete."

She couldn't let her mother see her tears so she slipped from under her arm and went to refill her glass. She watched from the dark shadows at the back of the terrace as the display reached its crescendo down in the caldera itself, the fireworks imitating the volcanic eruption that had formed the island's unique geography. Shooting flames coloured the smoke an eerie red and rivulets of flickering light appeared to flow like lava. A terrible, terrible beauty indeed. Zina bit her lip, stifling a sob.

A voice beside her: "Are you all right?"

Karmela. What could Zina say?

"Sure. Happy tears. My mother just told me this is the first time she's enjoyed an evening out since my dad passed away. Isn't that wonderful?"

Karmela nodded. "I am so pleased. For you both."

She had to buy a little time to pull herself together. "You have mentioned your mother but not your father?"

"He died more than twenty-five years ago, but my parents were already separated by then. It made it easier for her, I think. But I am guessing, because sadly she is not one to share her emotions."

Right now, Zina got that. She didn't want to share hers either. She nudged Karmela. "Shall we top up our glasses? And I don't know why I'm hungry, but those *hortópita* look delicious."

Jo joined them. "I didn't know eating your greens could taste so good! But I suspect it's to do with the herbs, and the quality of the olive oil in the filo."

Karmela nudged Jo. "It is good to see you eating. I noticed you hardly took anything from the buffet at supper."

Jo looked down. "I guess … I guess … Rees's visit unnerved me. I know you know about our row, Karmela, and it wasn't pretty."

"I have to say, Jo, I didn't warm to your husband," Zina told her. "If I had known his visit would upset you I'd have told him to go."

Jo put her hand on Zina's arm. "Thank you, that's really

kind. You two ... you really are..." She took a deep breath. "Karmela offered me moral support on the night but I turned it down. I've learnt how to manage him a bit over the years..." Suddenly she grinned. "At least this time I didn't give in and let him have what he wanted. Something about being here gave me the strength."

"I'm so glad, really I am." Tears pooled in Zina's eyes again. She wanted to return the confidence and tell her about the row with Lambros, if only to share their stories of men at their worst. She was sure they would have both felt better afterwards, but she couldn't, just couldn't. Instead, she popped the *hortópita* she was holding into her mouth and excused herself, going in search of another drink.

Over the course of the evening there were more than a few top-ups of wine, and Zina wasn't the only one reeling when they more or less fell out of the cars at the retreat's courtyard. There was talk of a night cap, but after very carefully setting out some glasses for Jo, Ellen and Susan, Zina made her way back down the path to the farmhouse.

It was late, and the tiniest sliver of new moon was no use to guide her, but she knew this track like the back of her hand. Every rustle from the pistachio trees was familiar as she trotted along, keen to fall into bed. Alone, without Lambros. She stopped. Put her hand over her mouth. She missed him. So much. Was she drunk enough to head out onto the terrace to talk to him? Or would he just be mad that she was tipsy? He'd told her often enough he'd never take her seriously when she was hammered so best not. Really best not. She didn't want to make things worse.

As she approached the house she noticed the light was on

in their bedroom window. She shouldn't allow herself to hope he might be waiting for her – that would be foolish – but even so, she quickened her pace, almost falling up the steps into the kitchen.

The house was silent; Mama must have gone straight to bed. Turning out the lights behind her, Zina made her way to their bedroom. Please, please, let Lambros be there, holding his arms open to welcome her home.

She peeped around the door. He was there all right, but fast asleep on top of the sheet, a tanned arm flung over his head, his T-shirt riding up and his mouth so relaxed she could almost imagine he was smiling. As she gazed at his beautiful, familiar face, relief flooded through her, weakening her knees. He'd come back. The argument was over. They'd wake together in the morning, and he'd roll over and kiss her like he always did, and everything would be fine.

Silently she stripped off her clothes right where she was standing, then, praying the switch wouldn't click too loudly, extinguished the lamp and slid under the sheet. It was hard to resist the temptation to cuddle up but she didn't want to wake him. In any case, lying on her back might just stop the room from spinning. As would closing her eyes.

Within seconds Zina was dead to the world.

Saturday 16th September

It was definitely not the morning to have to try, and fail, to round up a goat, Karmela thought bitterly as she followed Iain and Sybil up the track, her legs stinging from scratches earnt in the scrub, while her hungover brain rattled noisily around in her under-sized skull.

Sybil had of course caused the problem by running after the creature in the first place. Somehow Iain had managed to grab her collar, the dog pulling him to the ground in the process and enveloping them both in a cloud of dust. Now Iain was limping very slightly while Sybil's tail hung lower than Karmela had ever seen it. Master and hound made a sorry pair this morning, and Karmela would definitely need another shower before breakfast, not to mention some painkillers.

Iain stopped a hundred or so metres short of the courtyard, waiting for her.

"I'm so sorry."

"It was not the best start to my morning, I must admit, but I think both Sybil and the goat need to take some responsibility."

He smiled a kind of half-smile. "I'd like to make it up to you. Take you out, except..." He looked down at his trainers.

Karmela sighed. "Except you would not want me to think it was a date. I know. Your simple apology will do nicely."

He was still looking down. Maybe she had been a little abrupt, but it was hard not to be. Why, oh why, did he have to rub it in? It was bad enough that he had changed his mind about her, without having to remind her in this way. Especially when she had the hangover from hell, which was definitely making her grouchy. Then Sybil stepped forwards, her elegant head nudging Karmela's hand, so she crouched and fondled her ears.

"It is all right, beautiful girl. I forgive you."

After taking her painkillers, Karmela stood under the shower for the longest time. She did not care if she missed breakfast because she was not hungry, and there were plenty of coffee pods in her room. Neither did she want company, but missing the morning session was unthinkable. She was here to write. To write and nothing else, and if it took every last gram of mental strength she had left, she would do it. They were already a little over halfway through the month. Unfortunately, she was not halfway through her story, but if she really got her head down over the next couple of days, then the target of finishing her first draft was not impossible. That and that alone must be her focus.

Thankfully Jo suggested a relatively short morning session, given that most of them were hardly bright-eyed and bushy-tailed after the night before.

"I thought I'd tell you a little about the publishing process," she said, "then all you have to do is sit back and listen. Although I do appreciate not all of you are aiming in that direction." She smiled at Susan.

"Oh, but it will be so interesting," Susan replied. "When we have authors visit the library they're always asked about their path to publication."

"Mine was a little unusual," said Jo. "So I'm going to keep things quite general, and I've prepared a handout too – some simple advice about approaching agents and publishers, and dealing with the inevitable rejections."

"I don't really understand how agents fit into it, and whether you have to have one," said Diana.

"That's as good a place to start as any," Jo replied, and began to explain.

Karmela pulled out her notebook. The process might not be quite the same in Croatia, but the basic principles probably were. With not even half of the very first draft of a book complete, publication seemed so far away that she had given the practicalities of it little thought. But of course she had dreamt about bringing the Ragusan women's story to the widest possible audience, and making her mother proud.

By the time Jo finished talking, Karmela had filled a couple of pages with hurried script, so she sat back, shaking out her fingers while Jo asked if there were any questions.

Sophie leant forwards. "You said the way you were published was unusual. Can you tell us about it?"

Jo nodded slowly. "Of course. It's simple and I was very lucky. My husband had a friend who worked in the business and he asked him to look at the manuscript. He liked it and wanted to acquire it."

"Well of course he did," added Susan. "It's a wonderful book – one of my favourites. And from a lesbian viewpoint it was marvellous to see such mainstream success for a queer romance."

"That's something I wondered about when I was reading it for my book club," said Sophie, "how you, as a straight woman, came to write that particular story." Something about her tone of voice, and the way she folded her arms once she had finished speaking, put Karmela on her guard and had her antennae twitching. When a student asked a question that way either there was some sort of agenda behind it or they expected to be able to score a point.

But Jo was smiling. "It's something I'm often asked, and the answer is that love is love."

"No, but why write that particular story? What inspired you?"

A shadow passed across Jo's face, there and gone in a flash. "I didn't plan the book, so it's hard to say. It took years to write as well. Which reminds me, the length of time from putting the first word on paper to publication – even from acquisition to publication – can be surprisingly long."

Sophie looked set to open her mouth again, but Iain cut in with a long-winded and tortuous question about cover design. Whether it was a deliberate ploy, Karmela could not be sure. Jo had hardly missed a beat, and yet ... perhaps they had both noticed? Or maybe, knowing Jo was keeping a big secret, they were both looking too hard for something that was not there.

Either way, the last thing Karmela wanted was to waste her time discussing it with Iain.

The Ragusan Republic was calling. Her happy place. Her safe place. And then she realised she had not looked at it in quite that way for over a year. For a moment the thought shocked her; escaping there was something the old Karmela had done.

No, this was nonsense. She was not escaping. She needed to go there to write her book. But what else did the old Karmela do? She buried pain and pretended it did not matter. The thought made her more than uneasy, but now was not the time for distractions. If nothing else, she needed to up her word count before speaking to her mother tomorrow.

Sunday 17th September

Zina carefully dried the *bríki* she used to make Karmela's coffee and set it on the shelf next to Ekaterini's gleaming pans. Everyone had plans for Sunday except her. Even her mother was going out later, taking Susan and Ellen to meet more members of their extended family in Kamari. Zina didn't even have rooms to clean, which was not a bad thing, not really, and the day yawned emptily ahead.

Maybe she should try to catch up on some sleep? She still needed to recover from her drunken stupor on Friday, as well as yesterday's restless night. When she'd woken with a blinding hangover on Saturday morning, Lambros had already been up and about, presumably in the pistachio orchard. But foolishly as it turned out, she hadn't been worried, instead spending the day fantasising that in bed that night, even if nothing was said, at least they might touch, ever so casually. A thread to hold on to that would pull them back together.

But when she'd rushed home as soon as Ekaterini left, he'd been nowhere to be seen. Worse, his pillows had gone again.

She'd peeped onto the terrace, but he wasn't there. Only the closed door of the office giving any clue to his whereabouts. Clearly their row wasn't over after all.

How dare he play cat and mouse with her, coming back into her bed one night and buggering off again the next? Then avoiding her all day, spending every waking hour picking those frigging pistachios. But at some point in the smallest hours of the night, indignation had flickered into fear. Fear this was never going to come right. Then what the hell would she do?

Already it was something of a miracle her mama hadn't noticed anything was wrong, but it was only a matter of time. She needed at least a truce before that happened and with every day that passed it looked less likely Lambros would even think of brokering one. She'd never known him be so stubborn. It looked like it was down to her. She was the one who would have to give in this time. Oh, it was so unfair, but this had gone on long enough. Best get it over and done with before she changed her mind.

Full of determination, she set off in the direction of the pistachio orchard, then stopped. At breakfast she'd overheard Iain say he was planning to help with the harvest. No way could she bear the humiliation if Lambros ignored her – or worse – in front of one of her guests.

One of her guests. A guest she should look after. That was the answer. Obvious, now she thought about it. She'd just stroll up there and ask if they wanted a cold drink. It was neutral ground and her offer would be a kind and thoughtful thing to do. Then when Lambros said yes, she would perhaps bring a soda for herself. Then she'd ask him how the harvest was going, and he'd tell her. He could never resist talking about the farm. Somewhere along the line he'd realise how much he loved her and all would be well.

Decision made, Zina hurried along the side of the retreat and into the pistachio orchard. This low down the valley the trees had been stripped of their nuts, which were now lying in the drying yard behind the building. She glanced in as she passed; there were plenty of them, so that must be good. It would hopefully put Lambros in a positive frame of mind.

Her father's old truck was parked on the edge of the orchard about two hundred metres away, and she quickened her pace, the heat of the morning burning into her back. With any luck, in just a few minutes this whole sorry mess would begin to be over, and she couldn't wait to see him smile when he realised how nice she was being.

But Lambros didn't smile. In fact, he positively scowled when he saw her. He and Iain were working on adjacent trees, wearing long, thick gloves to carefully twist the bunches of nuts from the branches then put them in wooden boxes to carry to the truck. Iain gave her a cheery wave, but Lambros ignored her until he had finished what he was doing.

He walked slowly towards her, a box of pistachios in his arms. Zina's mouth went dry. This was so not what she had expected.

Quick! Get the words out.

"I wondered if you guys would like a cold drink?"

"We have plenty of water. Whatever you may think, I am not so stupid as to come out for a day's work without any." He had barely broken his stride to say it.

She couldn't look in Iain's direction. Couldn't speak

because the dust from the dry, grey earth felt as though it was clogging her throat. She cleared it with a small cough.

"No worries," she said brightly and loudly enough for Iain to hear. "Just thought I'd ask."

Zina forced herself to stroll back through the trees, stopping now and then to look at an imagined something between their branches. At first she had wanted to run and find somewhere to weep, but now the slow burn of anger was building inside her, fuelled by humiliation. How dare Lambros treat her like that? There was every chance that Iain had heard him. How would she look him in the eye again? She'd tried so hard to keep their rift private, but clearly Lambros didn't care. He'd made it perfectly obvious he had no intention of putting this right, so why should he keep it a secret? He'd never even considered how it would look to her guests. Never considered her at all.

God, she hated him! *Hated* him! It took every last reserve she had not to kick at the aubergines and winter potatoes he'd planted in the vegetable patch as she passed, but now she was nearing the house she had to calm down. Mama's car was still parked outside and although a part of her longed for her comfort, she still wasn't ready to share what had happened.

Mama was in the kitchen, tending a pan on the stove, the rich aromas of tomatoes, mint and oregano filling the air as she fried one of the island's traditional snacks.

"I thought I'd make some *tomatokeftédes* for your lunch. For Lambros and Iain too, if they come in, although he took a couple of beers and some leftover *pitarákia* from Friday night with him. He said they might well work through and he can never resist anything with cheese in, can he?" She turned from gently easing the fritters around the pan, looking over her shoulder as she continued. "Are you going to help them? I'm sure they could do with another pair of hands."

Zina shook her head, her throat too thick to speak. Even if she knew what the hell she could say.

Her mother sighed. "Zina, what's wrong between you and Lambros?"

"Nothing." It came out as a squeak.

"That doesn't sound like nothing. Certainly not when he was sleeping on the terrace last week. And now he's borrowed a blow-up mattress from Yiannis and put it in the study."

Skatá! "You knew…"

Even frigging Yiannis knew, by the sounds of it. Why hide their differences anymore, when clearly Lambros didn't care? Tears scratched the backs of her eyes.

"Of course I knew. For a start, I could hear him outside all night, shifting around. And much as I don't want to interfere if you don't want to tell me, I won't be taken for an idiot in my own home."

Zina felt about nine years old. "I'm sorry, Mama," she whispered.

Her mother crossed the room and wrapped her in a hug. "More than anything, I hate to see you hurting."

"Oh, Mama…" Zina started to sob, the tears she'd dammed up on Friday night flowing freely now, while her mother rocked her slowly, keeping her tight in her arms.

Eventually she calmed down enough to look up. "We had a row on Tuesday. I mean, everyone argues, don't they? But this one's going on forever."

"And why do you think that is?"

"I don't know." Zina sniffed, and her mother pulled a large white handkerchief from her pocket and gave it to her.

"Do you want to tell me about it?" she asked. "You don't have to, but talking things through sometimes helps."

"You mustn't tell Lambros you know."

"If he asks me, I won't lie, but I have no intention of getting involved. You're almost thirty, Zina, your marriage is your own affair. Even though it's hard to keep it that way when we're all living in the same house."

"That was my point. That's what started it. When you were out on Tuesday afternoon I thought we could spend some time together, just the two of us. But he chose to go to help Yiannis instead."

Mama frowned. "I thought it was something of an emergency."

"Not that much of one. Yiannis has other friends, and it could have waited."

"Lambros is a loyal man, you know that."

"Not to me."

Mama sat down at the kitchen table and Zina followed suit. "In what way, exactly?"

"It's always the farm this, the farm that…"

"Life on the land can be like that," said Mama. "Trust me, when I was a young bride … but that's by the by… And hospitality is just the same. Animals, nature, guests; they're all demanding. I can remember being so excited when your father and I traded the pigs and the crops for the apartments and campsite, but it didn't get any better, especially not in the season. And you and Lambros have both. You haven't chosen an easy path."

Zina crossed her arms. "I didn't choose it."

"I know. You never wanted to stay on the island and I was proud I had a daughter whose world would be bigger than mine. But I was also proud when you gave up so much for your husband. And for me."

Zina began to cry again. "At least you understand what I sacrificed. Unlike Lambros. If only he'd just say—"

Mama held her hand across the table. "It seems to me that perhaps this row is less about Tuesday afternoon and more about resentment on both sides simmering over. You have a lot to think about, *agápi mou*. Really big questions about what you want from life, and what's most important to you, because from where I'm sitting it may not be possible to have it all."

"Lambros has no reason to be resentful. He's got everything he wanted."

"That's not for me to second guess. You either need to ask him, or think it through for yourself, because there must be a reason he's holding out. To me, it does not seem in his nature."

As if Zina knew what her husband's true nature was anymore. But how could she, when he deliberately put barriers between them? She had every right to feel resentful, not him. He'd shut her out. He'd clearly tired of her like he did everything else, and that was that.

Mama stood. "I'm sorry, Zina, but I need to get ready for the big reunion. My interpretation services will definitely be needed today."

"Sure, sure." She picked up her phone and began to scroll. Everyone's frigging perfect lives on Instagram. Mariam in Athens on her father-in-law's yacht; an interior designer she followed holidaying in the cutest cottage in England; even Resi was at Balos Beach. It was only at her father's taverna, and the margarita in front of her was virgin, not a real one, but still…

Of course, she could go to see Resi. It wouldn't be the most exciting of afternoons, but it would stop her nagging to visit the baby. She could have a bit of a chat with her old friend, coo over tiny fingers and toes, then take a dip in the water. It was hardly cocktails in the Plaka like the old days with her Athens gang, but it was better than being here on her own. She might even be able to engineer the odd photo for her Instagram feed and pull at least one positive from this frigging awful day.

Zina quickly changed into her bikini and slipped a short floral-print sundress over the top. After digging out her underused beach bag from the bottom of the wardrobe she added a towel and some sunscreen. She didn't need anything else. Resi's dad's hospitality to his daughter's friends was legendary, and she was determined to put herself into the mindset to enjoy it.

Despite Balos Beach being such a tiny ledge of concrete and shingle at the base of the caldera's cliffs, the parking area was almost full, so Zina had to leave her car at the very far end. Dust and gravel caught in her sandals as she walked, but the water looked blue and inviting, dotted with small white boats belonging to the dive school.

She spotted Resi as she approached, sitting under the rattan shelter that covered the taverna's terrace nursing her baby daughter. Low music mixed with the wash and draw of the waves on the shingle, just centimetres away.

Resi waved. "Zina! Over here! It's great to see you. Where's Lambros?"

Zina set down her beach bag and sat opposite her friend. "Harvesting pistachios."

Resi rolled her eyes. "Good for you for escaping. We can catch up on our news before the boys get back and start talking about football. Again."

"Boys?"

"Vasilis and Georgiou – they're taking a quick dip. I don't suppose you remember they're cousins?"

Zina shook her head. The size of Vasilis's family was mind-boggling and she'd never bothered to make the connections. But Georgiou? She'd kind of assumed he'd be gone by now. Well, she would have assumed it if she'd given him a thought.

"You don't mind, do you?" Resi asked.

"*Skatá*, no. We were kids when we were together. It'll be fun to see him again."

"That's all right then. Now tell me, how's your new business going? Your photos on Insta are amazing. They cheer me up no end when I'm elbow deep in nappies."

Zina sat back and told Resi about all the good things that were happening, feeling just a little guilty when she saw the look of longing in her friend's eyes. Before her maternity leave, Resi had been head receptionist at the island's swankiest boutique hotel and clearly she missed her job. Who wouldn't? Zina thought. Babies that tiny, however cute, must be so very boring.

"Will you go back to work next season?" she asked her.

"I might... Look, here come the guys." She swivelled in her seat, turning towards the kitchen. "Babá! You can bring the meze now. I'm starving." She looked at Zina, giggling. "I always am. God knows how I'll ever lose my baby bulge."

"You will when you're ready."

"Zina! Good to see you!" Vasilis called. "I won't hug you or I'd soak your dress." Zina stood to greet him. Half a step behind was Georgiou. My god, he'd matured well. He'd been good-looking enough as a teenager, but now he had a neatly trimmed beard, and the way his wavy hair was slicked back from his high forehead accentuated his perfectly straight eyebrows and pale grey eyes.

"Now this is a pleasant surprise." He grasped her hand, holding it just a fraction too long, making her fingers tingle.

"It's good to see you too, Georgiou."

"George. Everyone calls me George these days. It's so much easier now I'm working in New York."

Show off. But then, he always had been. She'd spent their time together torn between wanting to take him down a peg or two and feeling smug that she was the girl on the arm of the most desirable boy in school.

Resi rolled her eyes and Zina thought it was becoming quite a habit. "Georgiou. You're in Greece now, remember."

He shrugged his muscled shoulders, drops of water running down his chest as he reached for his towel. "In truth I answer to just about anything."

"You work in New York? That must be exciting," Zina said. God, she sounded like a blushing schoolgirl. Not that she'd been particularly blushing when they'd dated. For a split second she wondered how he saw her now, compared to those American girls. But at least her sundress was a Christina Kontova, not some cheap tat from a tourist shop on the island.

He smiled at her, right to his eyes. "It has its moments. But tell me, what are you doing these days? I don't see any babies attached to your hip."

"Until recently I was account director at a marketing agency in Athens, but when my father died I came home, and I've just opened a high-end retreat house on the island."

"Retreat? As in religious? That doesn't sound like the Zina I knew."

"No," Zina laughed. "Creative. I have a group of writers there at the moment, led by Jessica Rose who wrote *Only. Ever. You.* You've probably seen the movie. But also for things like yoga, and businesses, if they need to get away for strategic planning and the like. Small and exclusive. That's the vibe."

"What a great idea. Do you have a card?"

"Not on the beach. I only came down to see Resi and have a quick swim."

He almost pouted. Almost, but not quite. Just enough to be sexy but not ridiculous. "You didn't come to see me?"

"Sorry, no."

Resi looked up. "You will join us for meze though?"

"Yes, please do," Georgiou added. "You can tell me more about this business of yours. If it wouldn't be an imposition on your afternoon off."

"I don't want to bore everyone else…"

"Then don't," said Vasilis, ruffling her hair as though she were ten years old. "Let's just chill."

"I don't remember Zina being boring," said Georgiou.

"You're kidding!" Resi exclaimed. "When she was basketball captain everything was win, win, win. And if we dared to lose it was never her fault. Even that time she missed the basket in the last two minutes in the Cyclades semi-finals. She was no fun at all."

"Why play unless it's to beat the hell out of the opposition?" Georgiou draped his towel over the back of the chair next to Zina's and sat down on it, picking up a beer. "If I remember rightly, while I was whipping the most successful football team the school ever had into shape, you were doing the same for basketball. Natural winners, both of us. Dragged the others up to our standard."

It was Vasilis's turn to roll his eyes. "Oh, please. Without my speed midfield you'd have been stuffed."

"I always thought you wanted to turn professional?" Zina asked Georgiou.

"Injury," he replied.

"You only ever had one trial!" said Vasilis.

"Because I was injured. But enough of me. I want to hear all about Zina." He turned to face her and chinked his beer glass against her iced coffee. "It is so very lovely to see you again."

The conversation flowed along with the drinks and the plates of meze which appeared every so often: *tomatokeftédes*, of course, but also thick homemade *tzatzíki* burning with garlic, and plates of *dolmádes*. Reluctant as she was to leave the table, Zina knew the reason for her visit would lose all credibility if she didn't swim. It would be mortifying if Georgiou thought she had really come to see him. His ego was still as healthy as it had always been, but with his success in the corporate world that was hardly surprising, and good for him too.

She stood, pleased she'd kept her figure as she pulled her sundress over her head. "Swim time for me."

"I'm ready for another dip too," Georgiou said as he looked up at her admiringly. "Want some company?"

"That would be good." And it would be. They had history swimming off this very beach that if Zina were a different sort of woman she might blush to remember. But Georgiou knew she wouldn't be up for that sort of thing anymore. Inevitably Lambros had cropped up now and then as they'd talked. But just for a little while it would be good to spend time with someone who was paying her an awful lot of attention and who made her remember all the good things about herself. Yes, after the week she'd had, she definitely deserved a little fun.

Jo clambered out of the car, following Karmela who'd leapt from her seat and was already gazing at the huddle of white houses spreading down the gentle slope below. The parched hillside rose in front of her with villas and farms dotted here and there under the deepest blue sky.

"Well, this is pretty," Karmela said as they started into the village. A wall built of black volcanic stone edged the street on one side, a deep red bougainvillea and white stars of jasmine reaching over the top and tumbling towards them. The jasmine in particular was exquisite, and Jo stopped to take a photo to send to Curtis later. Opposite, a man chipped plaster from the wall of an older property, stopping as they passed so as not to envelop them in dust.

A little further on, the doors of a workshop stood open, the enticing almost salty smell of leather issuing from it. Hanging outside were a dozen or so bags, one a laptop-sized rucksack with subtle gold chasing that was so gorgeous Jo stopped to finger it. More suede than leather, it was soft to the touch but hopelessly impractical for rainy London. Though London, despite Rees's increasingly furious messages, seemed a million miles away.

"Shall we find a cold drink first?" she asked. "Then explore before supper?"

Karmela nodded. "I think the square is at the end of this street."

As they continued to walk, Jo glanced up, her eyes drawn to a dark blue dome with a cross on top. Beyond it stood a church, and in front of them, built across the road, was an elaborate bell tower like so many white wedding cake pillars, the bells themselves arranged in decreasing tiers. No wonder a group of Japanese tourists was waiting patiently to take selfies under its arch.

"Megalochori is rather lovely," she said.

"It is also an interesting place," Karmela replied. "I read up about it a little when you suggested we come here. The village was almost completely destroyed in the earthquake of 1956 and left empty until the 1990s when there was finally the money and the will to rebuild it. But when you look online there are still a few hidden corners that have been left as they were."

"Imagine! Losing everything like those poor people did."

Karmela nodded. "And in minutes, too."

They continued down the narrow street which was bordered on both sides by whitewashed walls that were punctuated by wooden gates painted every shade of blue. Had Karmela lost everything in minutes too? Jo wondered. From the piece she had written, it sounded that way, and Jo was burning to ask her. Burning to hear her whole story, to understand… It was one of the reasons she'd been so delighted when Karmela had suggested they have supper together today. But where such a conversation might lead terrified her.

If Karmela knew the truth about what she'd done, she wouldn't want anything to do with her. She was such an honest and forthright person, not to mention a talented writer. If nothing else, she'd be asking herself what right Jo had to try to teach her anything. But on the other hand, what was friendship without honesty? And Jo really wanted her friendship with Karmela to grow.

The square was blessed with a number of cafés and restaurants, drowsing through the lull between lunch and dinner. To their right was an open space surrounded by oleanders and bougainvilleas in bright orange and pink, and even some small olive trees beneath which local cats were hungrily feeding on food some kind soul had left out for them.

Opposite was an art gallery and an ice cream parlour, but just beyond they found an inviting-looking taverna. A handful of tourists were dotted around under a sea of square umbrellas, and a group of people, all dressed in their Sunday best, was leaving, their continuing conversation voluble as they rounded up small children then headed down the street.

Jo and Karmela chose a table with a bright green painted top next to an equally colourful ceramic fountain. Now the terrace was quiet, the only sounds the click of backgammon counters as two men played near the steps to the dark interior, and birdsong from a nearby tree.

A waiter bustled over, notebook in hand. Karmela ordered

a beer, but Jo prevaricated. She should really have an iced coffee, but ... alcohol would help. Or should she be brave, and try to do this sober? But would that lead to yet another failure?

Stop overthinking it, Jo.

"One small beer will not hurt, even with the car," said Karmela, as if reading her mind. "I imagine we will be here for some hours yet."

"Go on, then." Once again, she'd let someone else make the decision for her. It had become so engrained: her agent with the sort of book she should write; Curtis with the garden – although to be fair he did go out of his way to involve her; and Rees with ... everything else. But not the remortgage. She'd messaged him to say she was consulting a financial advisor, so he'd have to wait. He'd called her back and blown a fuse on a voicemail she'd deleted halfway through. Had that been a win? The thought made her just a little more confident. Perhaps it was time for another one.

"Karmela, I wanted to ask you about your Sarajevo piece."

Her words were all but drowned out by a cacophony of firecrackers that caused a ginger cat balancing on the edge of the fountain to slip, then leap to the floor, shaking its damp fur in disgust. A waiter rushed up to them, pointing at the bell tower at the bottom of the square.

"A wedding!" he cried. "A village wedding! You must see."

It seemed rude not to abandon their table and stand to watch the procession pass under the arch, led by a violinist and a bouzouki player dressed in colourfully embroidered waistcoats. Next came the bride in an elegant cream silk dress, her handsome face covered in more make-up than even Jo would consider wearing. Both she and her groom looked tense, and Jo hoped that only the pressure of the occasion, and not the prospect of marriage, made them appear this way.

And pressure there was, as most of the village appeared to be following them, the women in colourful dresses and bright silk trouser suits and tiny flower girls like miniature replicas of the bride. Music and laughter filled the air as the couple turned into the church, the sun gleaming from its bright blue dome, just half a shade lighter than the sky above.

As the procession disappeared inside, the women returned to their table. Maybe fate had intervened to save Jo from a difficult conversation. Or maybe not.

"You asked me about Sarajevo?"

She had no escape now. Jo fiddled with the ashtray. "Your love for your home and your friends shone through in your piece. Yet after the war you didn't go back? Even though you wrote that you'd shut yourself off from hurt and pain, I'm not quite sure I understood and I'd like to know more." Sweat pooled in her armpits. What had she started? She couldn't be sure, but whatever happened, this was a conversation she needed to have in order to break the habit of a lifetime. If she could.

"In practical terms, I did not go back because once the war was over my parents separated and my father returned to Sarajevo. Before we left he had been a university lecturer like me, but once we were in Berlin he started to drink. My mother worked all hours helping other refugees and as I was unable to make friends at school, I was stuck in our tiny apartment with this man we had once loved who became increasingly unpredictable. Neither of us wanted to be anywhere near him after that. It was a relief when the war ended and he left."

"It must have been awful."

Karmela shrugged. "I guess he had his own problems. Maybe he felt guilty about not staying to fight? But it certainly made me put up the walls faster than I might otherwise have done. I was bullied at school for not belonging and had no one to turn to at home. Once the war was over, I decided to go back to the former Yugoslavia to university and ended up in Zagreb. The Germans wanted the refugees gone, so it made sense for my mother to come too.

"But even there I was an outsider; the others had suffered the war, but we had run away. It set me apart. Or rather, I thought it did. So I stayed apart for the longest time and, without me even noticing, it became a habit. I missed out on so much."

So Karmela knew what it was to be lonely and friendless, isolated in her own home. They had more in common than Jo had ever imagined. But it would be impossible to base a friendship on lies, especially when Karmela was so open about her own life and experiences.

Jo fingered the metal tray the waiter had left with the bill. *Here goes nothing.* "So there wasn't a secret?" she asked. "Your piece talks about keeping a secret."

Karmela looked at her, her dark eyes sharp yet soft at the same time. "Then perhaps it was clumsy. My lack of skill. But there was something hidden, something buried, that was blighting my life. Like secrets do. But I think you know that."

Play for time.

Jo picked up her glass, sipped, then put it down.

"How did you find out? Iain, was it?"

Karmela nodded. "He could not help overhearing your row

with Rees, and when you sent him away he came to me." She reached across and lightly touched Jo's hand. "He did not understand that perhaps you did not want to be seen all red and blotchy. Or that perhaps you just needed time to cry. He was worried about you."

Jo nodded, saying nothing. At the ice cream parlour across the square, a young man tried, and largely failed, to stop the two small children with him bouncing up and down with excitement. She watched as he checked the contents of his wallet before ordering two small cones. He looked more like a local than a well-healed tourist and she leapt up, ran across, and pressed a twenty euro note into his hand, walking swiftly back to the taverna before he had time to argue.

"You like children?" Karmela asked.

"Yes, but I wouldn't bring one into my marriage."

"If you were not married to Rees?"

Jo shrugged. Having kids wasn't something she allowed herself to think about too much. "But I am."

Karmela sat forwards. "Jo, you cannot live a half-life. I was guilty of that, and I wasted years. I cut myself off from so much that matters, because I had no idea that it did."

"You don't understand—"

"I cannot if you do not tell me."

"I can't tell anyone."

"Then perhaps you should."

Jo drained her drink, then stuffed another twenty euro note under the tray with the bill.

"Come on, let's walk."

They crossed an open space with a memorial of some sort, then joined a curved path lined with the smooth white walls so typical of the village, overhung by a beautiful red bougainvillea. Turning left up the hill, they passed a house with dirty cream walls, the paint cracked and peeling away. The iron grills on the windows were rusted, in contrast to the pots of pink and white geraniums on the sills, which looked well cared for. Something about the contrast stuck in Jo's throat and a wave of unbearable sadness washed over her.

The father scrabbling for loose change to treat his children had made her feel the same. She could only imagine how much he must have wanted to buy them the biggest ice cream possible to make them smile. All around her, small but important human emotions were playing out; people everywhere were striving to gather every scrap of happiness they could. She may have money, but they were richer than her in so many ways.

Every scrap of happiness. She thought about her garden at home and the photos Curtis was sending her. And the ones she was sending him... She thought about the progress her little group at the retreat was making. She thought about the brave woman standing next to her, who'd been through so much, but hadn't been afraid to change when she'd understood what she was missing.

In silence they turned up a side alley, the cobbles that graced the more important streets replaced by shiny, patched concrete. Here the houses were all single storey, some neat cubes of white and others no more than rough walls with random remnants of plaster clinging to them and padlocked wooden doors. One, with an official-looking notice taped to the peeling blue paint, had trees so tall inside they were visible from the street.

They were nearing the edge of the village now. Jo could see the last of the houses and the vineyards beyond. She stopped in front of a property that was no more than a ruin. Clearly, here, no one had come back. Perhaps they had all died – lives wasted in an instant as the earth shook beneath them. She gazed at the collapsed wall, at the gate hanging off its hinges, at the tumbledown shack with weeds growing from cracks in the plaster, and at the concrete staircase leading to nowhere but the sky. Would her life go to waste as well, because of just one moment? Could she allow that to happen?

Karmela stood silently beside her. Silent and strong. Karmela, who had been through so much. Jo clenched her hands into fists.

Now.

Now.

Now.

"What would you think," she said slowly, "if I told you I didn't write *Only. Ever. You.*?"

Karmela turned to her. There was no sharp intake of breath, no horror in her eyes, only something that might have been compassion.

"I would think you had been really brave to tell me."

"It would be a brave thing to do, wouldn't it?"

"It would. Especially as I do not think you have ever told anyone. My guess is that the reason Rees knows is because he was involved in whatever happened too."

Jo nodded. "Yes. And it would be easy to say that it was his idea, but the reality is I could have stopped it so many times. But I didn't."

"Do you want to tell me who did write it?"

Jo nodded. "Remember I said I had a friend who died? It was her book."

"And you wanted her memory to live on?"

"No … no … it wasn't like that at all. Karmela, it was an awful thing to do … awful."

Jo closed her eyes, but it didn't stop the tears or the flood of indescribable emotions washing through her: grief, shame, anguish, fear. Fear of what would happen now that someone else knew. She covered her face with her hands and sobbed, Karmela's comforting arm around her shoulder.

What now? What the fuck now?

Monday 18th September

Sleep was not Karmela's friend tonight.

Sighing, she plumped her already plump pillows for what she was sure was the twentieth time. But how had she even expected a good night, given the magnitude of Jo's confession? The secret was out, albeit in a small way, and although that had the power to change Jo's life for the better, Karmela knew all too well how disturbing the start of that journey felt.

After their brief conversation outside the ruined house, Jo had given no further explanation, but Karmela had a shrewd idea that Rees was behind the deception and was using it to bind Jo into a toxic relationship. The more she had thought about it yesterday evening, the angrier she had become, but when she had tried to raise the subject again as she and Jo ate dinner in Megalochori, Jo had shaken her head and told her she was too wrung-out to talk about it anymore. Karmela had nodded and told her that her door was always open. And that her mouth was firmly closed.

Was she still angry now? No. Just troubled in a way she could not put her finger on. And very, very tired. Beyond tired. She pummelled her pillows again, rolled onto on her back, and started to count imaginary goats.

In her dream, Karmela knew she was in the flat in Berlin because of the smell of cigarettes and stale alcohol. And because of the heat burning through the kitchen windows, only partly shielded by the broken blind with its orange and brown zigzag design. But then, it could not be the flat because there was no space in the room for her; her parents, sitting on either side of the Formica-covered table, were filling it completely. So she went onto the landing then down the stairs, knocking on every door she passed, but not one of them opened. Running faster and faster. Her heart thudding in her chest. All the while knowing that no one would let her in.

She lay in the soft darkness of her room, feeling slightly disoriented, with the tang of smoke lodged at the top of her nose. But it could not be, not in real life. Not when she breathed in normally. It was just a remnant of the dream and, reassured that the retreat was not burning down, she turned over to go back to sleep.

Except that she could not, because the dream stayed with her, an intense sorrow she half recognised, pressing into her forehead. A feeling she would forever associate with Berlin. A feeling she had never wanted to feel again and against which she had guarded herself so carefully for most of her life. But that was the trouble. Let down those walls, and not only the joy came in, but the pain did as well. And although her head knew it was a price worth paying, at three in the morning it was hard for her battered heart to be completely convinced.

She sat up and hugged her knees. She was hurting. She could not set the feeling aside for one more moment; the dam had burst. She was hurting, hurting so very much, and coping with it as an adult was a new experience. In the past she had been so successful at shielding herself but now she was confronted by this she had no clear idea what to do. When she had first let her memories flow, the pain had been awful, of course it had, but it had been a good pain, a cathartic one. A pain from which, ultimately, she had learnt and which had made her life so much better.

This hurt was entirely different. It was bitter and dark, and backwards looking, not forwards, but could she learn from it too? She could not return to a life of avoiding pain; she had promised herself that she would be open to experiencing everything – both good and bad. She had vowed that she would live life to the full and grab every opportunity it gave her with both hands. Surely what she needed to do was learn how to handle the bad stuff better?

Her analytic brain began kicking in and she decided to break the problem down. If hurt was the effect, what was the cause? Iain's rejection, of course. So rejection was the real enemy. It was hard enough to put yourself out there, let alone get knocked back once you had.

Was that why she had dreamt about Berlin? The school where no one had wanted to know her. Coming home to that dingy apartment with her father mired in drink, and her mother never there. Karmela's only way of coping had been to shut herself off from her emotions, and everyone else as well. But shutting herself off was not an option now, she had come too far. She needed a different strategy.

Sleep would be impossible until she had written down these thoughts that were bubbling up, one after another in an impossible tangle. Slipping out of bed, she picked up her notebook from the desk, then curled her legs under her in her favourite position on the sofa.

There, on the page in front of her, were Jo's notes on dealing with rejection as a writer:

1) *It will happen so you need to prepare yourself mentally.*

2) *Build a support group of other writers around you to share the pain as well as the joy. They'll all have been there.*

3) *Mostly you will not be given a reason for a rejection, but if you are and a pattern emerges, you need to consider what is being said.*

4) *Remember even the most successful authors, like JoJo Moyes and J. K. Rowling, were rejected many times before their stories found the right homes.*

5) *Allow yourself to experience the emotion: curse, cry, sigh, eat chocolate – rejection only hurts because you care, and caring is good. Feel it, then move on.*

Karmela frowned then read them again, and again, reshaping them away from writing but keeping the meaning. *Rejection only hurts because you care, and caring is good.* That was true enough, so perhaps the rest of Jo's wise words would help her as well.

One thing was for sure, it would not hurt to try.

If Jo didn't do it now, she never would. And she needed to.

"Karmela, do you have a moment?"

Karmela tucked her notebook under her arm. "Sure."

Jo waited until the others were on their way downstairs then crossed the landing to her room with Karmela following. By the time she reached the sofa her legs were well and truly shaking, and she more or less buckled onto it, leaving Karmela to shut the door behind them.

Jo glanced at the windows. They were both closed too, the air conditioning unit humming gently to keep the heat of the morning at bay. Karmela sat opposite, her eyes dark above smudged bruises. It looked as though she had lost sleep as well. She deserved to know the truth. But more than that, Jo needed to tell it, because otherwise she would hide in a wine bottle again, and she couldn't do that. She couldn't let Zina and the group down. However much this felt like free fall, the reality was that she'd already jumped. Now it was time to see if her parachute would open.

"I want to finish what I started yesterday." Jo had expected her voice to sound strangled, but instead it was strangely calm, almost as though someone else was speaking.

Karmela nodded. "I would like to hear what happened, and to help if I can."

"Help?" Jo shook her head. "No. There's nothing that can be done, but your piece made me think. It's crippling me, no one else knowing. I haven't written a single word of my new book. I don't think I can."

"Oh, Jo."

"No. No sympathy, because I don't deserve it. Pam was a dear friend – my mother's best friend, actually – but I lodged with her when I left uni and we became close as well. She used to read me the tiniest snippets of her book, so I knew full well that it was never meant to be published. That it was too damned personal."

"You mean that wonderful love story is true?"

"Yes. The forbidden love, the secrecy that had to surround it, the Whitehall civil servant and the politician's wife. All those years of Pam knowing she was the other woman, that they would probably never truly be together." Karmela's eyes were huge, but Jo ploughed on. "So you see, it was an awful thing to do. I should have destroyed the file the moment I found it on Pam's computer, but I couldn't bear to. It was the last piece of her I had and I so wanted to read it."

Karmela nodded. "I get that."

"And reading it would have been OK, except I told Rees about it. Things were different between us then. He supported me so much when Pam died. I trusted him... But he showed it to a friend in publishing."

"So I was right. It was him who—"

"No! He may have started the process, but I could have stopped it at any time. Could have and should have. I just ... I don't know… He convinced me it was a good idea. Said if we changed the names of the characters, because we couldn't be sure whether Pam had or not … then the publisher suggested we set it all twenty years earlier so it would be more credible anyway. Credible! When it was the absolute truth all along. But of course they didn't know that, because they thought *I* wrote it."

Jo bit down on her lip, the metallic taste of blood in her mouth. It had seemed like a travesty at the time, but also protection for Pam and her lover, so Jo had worked painstakingly through the manuscript, dug into old newspapers, convinced herself that her careful work made publishing the book all right.

"So you did write some of it," Karmela said. "I wondered, knowing how Rees is, if any of Eloise's experiences were yours."

"No, back then things between us were good. Or at least I thought they were. It was only later … and then … I don't know. Perhaps what Eloise went through almost normalised Rees's controlling ways for me." She shrugged. "It took me so long to wake up to what was really happening, Karmela. To wake up to anything, really. Including doing the right thing and stopping the process in its tracks. Instead, I actively colluded."

"How long after Pam died were you working on the book?"

"Four, five months."

"You must have been reeling with grief!"

Jo shook her head. "It's not an excuse."

"No, but it is a reason."

Was it? Was it?

Or was she just so grateful for any crumb of absolution she'd clutch at the tiniest semantic straw?

Jo took a deep breath and straightened her phone on the coffee table. "The biggest problem of all ... the biggest problem ... is that my mum doesn't know the truth. She was so excited when Rees told her I had a book deal. She kept saying how proud I'd made her. I just ... I couldn't ... tell her."

"So she did not know Pam was writing?"

"No." Jo's throat felt so thick she could barely speak. She took a deep breath, coughed, then carried on. "She'll feel so betrayed, not only that I lied to everyone, but that the book belonged to her best friend, a woman we both loved. Mum and I have always been so close. She's my rock. She understands about Rees and me ... everything. Well, everything else. I can't be without that support." Her voice had thinned to little more than a squeak, like a mouse. She even sounded like a frigging mouse.

Karmela reached across the table and held Jo's hand. "So the one thing you really should do is tell her."

"No!"

"Yes. Because if she knows how Rees is, she will see the story as I do. How culpable he is in all this." She put her head on one side. "Tell me, did he ask you to marry him before or after the film deal?"

"As soon as it was optioned," Jo whispered. "He thought it would be a good way to celebrate."

"He knew how much money was at stake, more like." Karmela's voice was steely. "He likes money, does he?" Jo nodded. "Then you can forget any threats he makes about telling your secret to the world. *Only. Ever. You.* is the goose that laid the golden egg. He is not going to kill it."

It took a few moments for what Karmela was saying to sink in.

"Oh," said Jo.

She ripped her hand from Karmela's and buried her face in her palms.

"Oh, god, you'll think I'm such an idiot. I *am* such an idiot. That never even occurred to me."

"No, because I bet he has bullied and belittled you so much that you cannot think straight around him. I had a friend who was in an abusive relationship. It was exactly the same; first she isolated him, then shredded his confidence piece by piece. It took something cataclysmic for him to even half realise. That is what happens. That is how they retain their control over you. So no, you are not an idiot."

"I feel like … like my eyes are slowly opening." She shook her head from one side to the other. "I always blamed my shyness for not having any friends, but that's only part of the story. Now you've said it out loud I can see how he exploited my weakness to make sure I had no one to turn to. He insisted I used my writing name in real life too … as if the real me had actually ceased to exist."

"She does exist, though," said Karmela. "She is here in front of me and she is a wonderful, brave person who has the opportunity to stop existing and to start living."

"Thank you." Jo rested her hand on Karmela's. "But all that changes absolutely nothing. Even if Rees would never tell the world, all he has to do is tell Mum."

"Then you know how to take that power from him."

"It's no good—"

"I know this is new, and strange, and you will need thinking time. There is no rush to act. But just one thing, one thing, I would ask you to do. Try to imagine this from your mother's point of view. Yes, she will be shocked. And most likely hurt. But I would bet a great deal of money she would also walk to hell and back to release that horrible man's hold over her precious daughter."

Jo nodded, but her chest was tight, the panic only just below the surface. She needed to breathe, breathe, breathe. Then run her wrists under cold water and breathe again. And she couldn't do that with Karmela here. Karmela, who was so assured. Karmela who knew the answer to everything – or at least thought she did. Even if this time she was wrong.

"Thank you, Karmela. I've kept you too long from your work."

Karmela stood. "Friends are more important than word count." She placed her hand on Jo's shoulder. "See you at lunch."

"Yes."

The door closed behind her and Jo sat rigid, gazing at the polished grain of the wood. Then slowly, very slowly, she took two enormous breaths before spinning her phone on the table, watching it illuminate. Karmela was wrong. She had to be. But it wouldn't hurt to do what she'd suggested and imagine this from her mother's point of view. It wouldn't hurt to imagine, even, what it might feel like telling her. Jo waited for the breathlessness to choke her again, but it didn't happen.

Something else had taken its place. Something undefinable. But it was there.

She had two hours until lunch. Two hours to get her shit together after one of the most intense conversations of her life.

She couldn't do it.

But maybe she could. If she really, really tried. While she was every bit as wrung-out as an old rag, the something new was taking shape and growing. And it was tough and shiny, like steel.

Slowly she walked to her desk and turned on her laptop. Two hours to make a start. If not on her book, on something even more important. A letter to her mother, telling her the truth. She'd probably never have the courage to send it, but once it was written...

Well, you never knew.

Zina read the message from George, as he now called himself, for a second time. It had come, like any other business enquiry, through her Instagram account. And it *was* a business enquiry, but she'd been toying with the idea of inviting him to see The Retreat House anyway and this would make it a hell of a lot easier to explain to Mama what her ex-boyfriend was doing here.

Hi Zina. Good to see you again yesterday. I've spoken to our European HR director in Frankfurt and she could be interested in sending the exec team to your retreat. She's asked me to take a look, so how are you fixed this morning?

This morning was a definite no; it wouldn't do for

Georgiou to see her in the old shorts and T-shirt she wore for cleaning. Then there was lunch service … but this afternoon? That could work.

She looked again at his profile. George, not Georgiou. Which should it be? Would calling him George be pandering to his ego? Or would it simply mark that they had a different relationship now? A mature one. It somehow separated the attentive and attractive man from the boy who'd left her behind without a word or a backward glance all those years ago. Not that she had any intention of rekindling more than friendship. Obviously.

Let's say 3pm.

Even if Ellen and Susan lingered on the terrace over coffee as they often did, a business meeting was a valid excuse to leave them to it. But she didn't want to be all hot and sweaty when he arrived; that would be disrespectful and make it look as though she didn't care. About winning his business. So before pressing send she changed the three to a four.

Having explained to Mama that George now worked for a multinational financial services company that might use the retreat, Zina opened her wardrobe doors wide, looking for inspiration. Her work clothes from Athens were mostly packed away in boxes, and anyway, they'd make it look as though she was trying too hard. But she had a beautiful cream silk sleeveless shirt she could team with a short denim skirt that would achieve exactly the look she wanted.

Zina strolled back to the courtyard with ten minutes to spare. Would George come? He hadn't replied to her message, but he didn't need to. This was a business arrangement, nothing more. No doubt it was the prospect of high-level executives filling The Retreat House that was making her so nervous and excited. Nothing to do with the messenger.

But why had he done this for her? People didn't normally call their colleagues while they were on holiday. Not if they didn't have to. Certainly not someone in a different office. He really had put himself out, which was kind of sweet.

It was also sweet that he arrived carrying a box of expensive chocolate truffles and took her hand between both of his as he shook it.

Then rather confusingly, he looked into her eyes and said, "So beautiful." He held her gaze for a fraction too long, then glanced around the courtyard. "What you have created here is so beautiful."

Oh, so he wanted to flirt, did he? Her stomach clenched, but not in an unpleasant way. What would be the downside of playing along? If Lambros caught a glimpse of George being super-attentive, it might just make him stop sulking and end their stupid row.

"Well yes. I do like things to be easy on the eye." She half raised an eyebrow before bending to pluck a shrivelled basil leaf from the otherwise perfect pot. Glancing over her shoulder she explained that she wanted the overall vibe to be one of serenity; conducive to creative thinking.

He laughed. "I think even I could be creative here. Are you going to show me around?"

"We can't go into the bedrooms because they're occupied, but we can look at the studio and other communal spaces."

"Shame about the bedrooms." It would have been crass if he'd winked, but he didn't. He was classier than that and clearly knew his game. Time to put the brakes on a little. Back to business.

"Especially the group leader's, but I know Jessica will be working on her next bestseller. The lounge area of her suite is designed to double as a breakout area. My own idea, and it works really well. Of course everything in the rooms is high-end. Shabby chic, but quality all the way."

"That must have been quite an investment. You'll get it back, I presume?"

God, she hoped she would. "People pay for luxury and exclusivity. And confidentiality, of course."

He nodded. "Too often, people aim too low, or fail to differentiate. But of course, you know all these things, having been a marketing director." Or close enough. Zina didn't correct him. She was pleased he'd remembered and that he recognised her as a fellow professional, as well as an attractive woman. Both made a welcome change from "domestic drudge".

Seeing the retreat through George's eyes was a joy. He exclaimed at the highly polished antique furniture in the indoor bar and dining area and the carefully chosen cushions on the cracked leather sofas; he commented on the shade of blue she'd chosen to paint the shutters around the courtyard and the modern art on the staircase. Things barely anyone else had even noticed. Zina's heart swelled with pride.

In the studio she explained that the room could be laid out to the group leader's exact requirements. "Not just tables," she told him. "Next month it will be yoga mats, and we have easels as well for the artists. The space is designed to be as flexible as possible."

"It's businesslike yet relaxing at the same time. And the light from both ends is spectacular." He strolled towards the window that looked across the orchard and up the hillside. "Oh, such a wonderful contrast to New York," he sighed.

"You like it there though?"

"It will do for the moment. It's important to gain international experience so I can push my career to the highest level, but Greece will always be home."

"Really?"

"Yes, really. Just perhaps not Santorini. Far too many of my family around for a start, and it can get a bit claustrophobic. It's why I've taken an apartment above the beach, rather than stay with my folks. They weren't best pleased, but I have my privacy there, if you get what I mean." He flashed her a quick grin. "Anyway, enough about me. Tell me, Zina, do you prefer it here or in Athens?"

"Athens for sure." The words were out before she'd had time to think about them.

"Then if you don't mind me asking, why did you come back? I know you said your father died, but is that really a reason? And to create something so wonderful here ... I assumed you wanted to stay."

How could she answer? How could she tell him the truth? How could she expose the reason for Lambros's rapid exit from the corporate world to someone as successful as George? No way on god's earth could she do that.

"It's complicated and I won't bore you with it, but obviously I wanted to support Mama in her grief. She sends her regards, by the way." She hadn't but it was the right thing to say. "Now, can I offer you a beer, or some coffee? Then, if you think the retreat may be of interest to your company, I can go through how the pricing works."

A half-smile played at his lips. "Of course." He turned back to the window, pointing. "Is that your husband?"

She joined him and together they watched a shirtless Lambros unloading a box of nuts from the back of his truck, his tanned body dripping with sweat, made faintly ridiculous by that stupid sun hat of his.

"Yes," she told George. "I think I mentioned it's the pistachio harvest."

"Personally, I prefer an air-conditioned gym to work my muscles but I guess it takes all sorts."

His hand was in the small of her back. A gentle touch. A brief one, but a sure one. In the moment before she moved away, Lambros glanced up at the window, his face showing not a flicker of emotion. She couldn't even be sure he'd noticed her, damn the man.

Zina stepped back into the room, straightening a chair under the table. George's footsteps followed her, but she couldn't look at him, although she wasn't quite sure why. Something inside her was stirring, something above and beyond her harmless flirtation. Something she shouldn't want, and it added a layer of complexity she didn't need. She'd only been playing, after all.

"A beer would be nice, if you can spare the time. And Zina, the way you said 'complicated' back there… I get what that can mean. I really do. And although I respect the fact your personal business is personal, we were close once, weren't we?" His hand rested on the top of her arm. "You can trust me, you know."

The man was definitely kinder than the boy. Sensitive. Caring. The look in his eyes only for her.

"Yes, we were."

Fleetingly she returned his touch, before setting off smartly down the stairs. There was nothing she could tell him, of course. But it made her feel so much better he'd noticed and wanted to help.

Tuesday 19th September

Unbelievable. Frigging unbelievable. Jo's hand trembled as she gripped her phone. Even for Rees, this was… Words failed her. Tears scalded the backs of her eyes, but they were angry tears. God, she was furious and she would not let him do this.

I've sacked Curtis. We can't afford a gardener if we don't remortgage.

Not only was it a lie, but it was also out and out manipulation. But was that really anything new? Now she was beginning to truly understand that it had always been about power. He hadn't chosen a much younger girlfriend to flatter his ego; he'd picked her for her naïvety. Had she ever said no to him, even in those early days? She couldn't remember. It hadn't been important. She hadn't even wanted a boyfriend all that much.

She hadn't wanted him until she'd needed him. Rees had propped her up so completely in the weeks and months following Pam's death not just emotionally, but with all the practical things too – the practical things that had seemed almost impossible, like getting up for work, or cooking a meal, or paying the bills. At the time he'd been her rock. Now she saw him as a spider, weaving a web around her, taking away every last shred of independence she'd had.

Not that there'd been much to take. Timid little Jo. He must have sensed it right from the start. But she didn't feel timid anymore. In her head, at least, she'd been rebelling against Rees for quite some time. At first it had seemed like a useless fantasy, but now she wondered if she had, in fact, been building her reserves of emotional strength. Waiting until she was brave enough to act.

First things first: Curtis.

Ignore Rees. No way are you sacked.

A wait. A very short one.

Don't worry. If he says anything I'll tell him I don't take instructions from him.

So he hadn't even ... but then, he was a coward. Now she thought about it, no way would he want to get into any sort of confrontation with six feet of well-honed muscle. The tosser!

She typed again: *So sorry. Misunderstanding on my part.*

Jessica, is everything OK?

Jo pictured the concern in his deep brown eyes. She didn't want to lie, but what could she say? Nothing. Nothing at all. Except...

Thanks for your understanding, it means a lot.

Cool. A pause. *Hey – have a virtual hug if you need one.*

Jo wrapped her arms around herself. Curtis cared. Karmela cared. Her mum certainly cared. But how could the bond between her and her mother ever be the same if she told her what she'd done? She'd betrayed her, lied to her – stolen from her, even, given that Mum had been the sole beneficiary of Pam's will. Telling her was just too awful to contemplate.

But not telling her was worse. Karmela had shown her that. She had shown her that the only way to escape from Rees was to remove the hold he had over her. Well, either that, or murder him, which she really wanted to do after this morning's antics. It wasn't fair to drag Curtis into the crossfire but he'd made her do it. Manipulated her, yet again. Would it be for the very last time?

Jo pushed the chair back from the desk and stood at the window, gazing out over the courtyard. She could leave Rees; she knew she could. But she'd need her mother's support, and that had to be based on the truth. Regardless of whether Rees would ever really spill the beans, her future couldn't be built on a lie. She'd had enough of those. If she was going to move forwards, the skeleton needed to be out of the closet first.

Before she could change her mind, Jo grabbed her phone and called her mother. She may have written the most eloquent piece she'd managed in years yesterday, but some things needed to be said out loud.

Jo was relieved that when her mother answered the call she was in the conservatory at home, lounging in her favourite chair in front of the delicate pale purple flowers of the plumbago which was her pride and joy.

"Darling! How lovely to see your face."

"Mum, I have something to tell you."

Her mother sat up straighter. "What is it? Are you OK?"

"Yes, yes … I'm fine, but there's something I should have

told you ... or rather ... something I should never have done, but I did ... and ... oh, god, it's such a horrendous mess..."

"Calm down, Jo. Breathe. Speak slowly."

"And you'll listen? Right to the end? Then you can get mad as hell, but please, first, hear me out."

"Of course I will." Mum's voice was gentle and encouraging, but that wouldn't last once she knew. Jo could only try to imagine how her mother might feel, what she might say, how angry she'd be. But already she'd gone beyond the point of no return. This had to be done.

"OK, OK. I didn't write *Only. Ever. You.* Pam did."

Her mother's mouth hung open for a split second, but then it snapped shut and she nodded. "Go on."

So Jo did, stating the facts, much as she'd told them to Karmela the morning before, all the time watching her mother's impassive face all those miles away in Gloucestershire. What was she thinking? What was she going to say? Finally, Jo petered to a halt.

"There's a lot to take in, I know," she finished. "And saying I'm sorry, well, it doesn't feel adequate."

Mum nodded slowly. "I've always assumed that Pam influenced the book, and probably even helped you with the setting and characterisation. Maybe I should have seen it went further than that but I never knew Pam was in love. She was my best friend and she didn't tell me, and right now that hurts more than anything."

"I'm so sorry, Mum."

"It isn't your fault. And I know, once I get used to the idea, I'll be grateful and glad that she found her special someone."

"You don't seem ... angry?" Jo ventured.

"No, not angry. Sad though, more than sad, that both of you kept secrets from me in your own way. Was it something I said or did? Did you not trust me?"

"Of course I trust you! Oh, Mum, I was just so ashamed of what I'd done, and Rees said—"

"Pah! Rees! If I'd known how he's been holding this over you I would have put a gun to his head years ago ... provided your father hadn't beaten me to it. But what will make me angry is if you go back to him. Don't get me wrong, I know all about how coercive control works, but you've shown such courage this morning and I won't have you backsliding."

"He has no hold over me anymore. Not now you know the truth. But I think it will take me a while to get used to the idea." Jo blinked. The free fall feeling had stopped but she still had the sense of floating some distance above the ground. Like nothing was real. Forty-eight hours ago she'd had no intention ... no idea that the truth would ever come out.

"Maybe don't tell him just yet. You need to make this *your* narrative, Jo. *Your* story. The way *you* tell it to the world."

"To the world...?" Jo whispered. "I can't... What about Pam? What about her lover? She's probably still alive and there aren't that many MPs' wives..."

"*Only. Ever. You.* is a work of fiction, Jo. At least as far as most people are concerned."

"But Rees knows the truth. He could still make this bloody. He could sell his version of events even."

"That man would sell his own mother, and he really won't like the money from the book drying up when I remind him it's mine. I mean, not that I'd take anything from you, darling, but we can sort out the legal side of things once you've divorced."

Jo was free falling again, trying to keep up with her mother's train of thought. These new ideas, this very conversation, had seemed impossible just a short while before. Everything was new and scary. And shiny. And desirable.

"Mum, please, slow down."

"I'm sorry. Perhaps I'm thinking too far ahead. This is all such a shock. I've quite lost my cool." Her mother laughed. "So much for my mantra of breaking a problem down logically, and it's important that we do. One step at a time. You've taken the first one, the biggest one, and I'm so very proud of you."

"You shouldn't be. I've made such a wretched mess of everything."

"Oh, Jo. The hardest thing is going to be building up your self-belief again after what that man's done."

Jo frowned. "No, I don't think so. Being here ... it's helped no end. I know I'm doing a good job, and I've made a really good friend. I've even stood up to Rees more than once. That has to count for something."

"It counts for a great deal. But all the same, do you want me to come? To support you?"

"Honestly, it's fine. I have good people around me. In fact, it was Karmela who persuaded me to tell you. That woman's a total rock. And I'll need you more when I get home."

"In which case, I'll stay put. And I'll go and tell your father, although I might need to hide his car keys first in case he takes it into his head to go after Rees with his golf clubs."

Jo giggled. It was the last thing her mild mannered dad would do, but she appreciated the sentiment. She felt so loved, so supported. She supposed she would never know how much she had hurt her parents by what she had done, because her mum and dad would always put her feelings first. What an incredible love, and she was more than blessed to have it. How she had thought anything could change it, she did not know. But deep inside she did. Rees. His manipulation of her. His control.

Jo set her phone down on the desk and gazed out of the window. In the courtyard below, Ekaterini was setting the table for lunch, and beyond the track to the farmhouse a lone goat nibbled around the brownish mounds of the dying vines. Life went on. No earthquakes. No volcanic eruption. But the shape of her world was completely different.

A bleep behind her made her jump, and she picked up her mobile.

I love you, darling girl, and never forget it.

Jo clasped her phone to her chest. For once in her life, she'd done the right thing.

Skatá, skatá, skatá! Opening the drinks fridge, Zina could see Ekaterini was right; there were only two cans left of the upmarket tonic water Sophie preferred, and the gin bottles had taken quite a hit as well. How come she was so off the ball all of a sudden? She'd completely forgotten to do her weekly stocktake and book her delivery yesterday, so now she'd have to go to the cash and carry herself.

Scribbling a note on her pad, she sat back on her heels. The tiled floor of the bar was cool beneath her bare legs, and a part of her longed to stay there, drinking in the mixed aromas of beeswax, and of garlic and herbs from the kitchen, where Ekaterini was already preparing the sauce for dinner. It felt comforting and safe in a world that was becoming increasingly uncertain.

For the last twenty-four hours George had been clouding everything. She knew she was being stupid, she honestly did. He'd be gone again within days. But it was so nice to be noticed, to be appreciated for who she was. Especially with Lambros being such a frigging arsehole. If he'd put as much effort into their relationship as he was into prolonging their rift, they wouldn't be in this sorry state in the first place.

Oh, she could so do without this. She didn't want to be obsessing over George, but she couldn't help it. He made her feel so damned good and clearly he was no longer the boy who'd dumped her. The one who, let's face it, could occasionally have a bit of a vindictive streak when he didn't get his own way. Grown-up he was kind, considerate, successful – the ultimate fantasy. And fantasies didn't hurt, did they?

Zina scrambled to her feet. None of this would solve the immediate problem of the drinks cabinet. The cash and carry was on the main road towards Fira, so if she got her skates on she'd have time to run down to Balos beach for a swim as well. Why not? She'd be passing the turning anyway. And George might be there.

It shouldn't matter. But it did. She shouldn't go. But she would. She just couldn't help herself. It wasn't as though they'd do anything other than swim.

Zina finished her shopping list in double quick time, then

all but ran to the farmhouse to change. Her beach towel and bikini were still on the airer on the terrace, and as she grabbed them Mama looked up from her book.

"Going swimming, Zina?"

"Just a quick dip on my way back from the cash and carry. To clear my head."

"The cash and carry? Where are you planning to swim?"

"Balos."

Mama raised her eyebrows.

"So I can leave my car keys with Resi's dad."

"Oh well, if you're going that way anyway, that does make sense. As does clearing your head. I don't suppose you and Lambros have made any progress?"

"No." Zina saw no reason to elaborate. After all, on Sunday her mother had said she wanted to stay out of it.

"Someone's got to give, Zina. Be the bigger person. It's your future we're talking about here. All our futures, in fact."

All their futures? But of course, what happened to her marriage affected Mama too. If she went back to Athens... But how could she? Even if Lambros wanted out, Zina had The Retreat House now. She had bookings, commitments, some of them into next season. Even if and when Mama made enough progress to cope without her being here, she was trapped. Well and truly. Stuck in this backwater when, like George, her career could have taken her anywhere. The thought made her want to weep with frustration.

She gave her mother a quick kiss on the forehead. "I'll think about it while I swim."

Almost as soon as she stepped out of her car, Zina spied George at one of the taverna tables, scrolling on his phone with a beer to one side. Should she pretend not to notice him? Play it cool? But given the position of the terrace that was hardly possible. And it would be rude. And not what she wanted, anyway.

The decision was made for her because as she approached he looked up, then stood to greet her. "This is a lovely surprise. To what do I owe the pleasure?"

"I'm afraid once again the main attraction is the sea," she said with a laugh, pulling off her scrunchie and shaking out her hair. "I've come for a swim."

He put his hand on his heart. "You know how to wound a man."

"Or at least wound his pride."

"I am not all pride, Zina, you should know that." His eyes held hers, then he broke away, glancing towards the bar. "Can I offer you a drink first?"

She really wanted to, but there'd been a queue at the cash and carry and she was already running late. Even if she put the tonics in the freezer, they'd need enough time to chill before anyone came looking for a refreshing G&T. She bit her lip. "Maybe afterwards. I'm quite tight for time."

"I can't persuade you?"

"Business before pleasure, I'm afraid."

"Well I'm very glad I'm in the latter category."

Oh, he was still a little arrogant but in a way that was scarily attractive. Arrogant and infuriating, because before she could formulate a suitable reply, George leapt up and stripped off his T-shirt, kicking his leather flip-flops from his feet and jumping down onto the shingle.

"Race you in!"

Putana! He'd given her no warning at all. Ripping her sundress over her head, Zina fumbled with her sandals before running after him, failing to catch him until he stopped to wait for her, thigh deep in water.

"I won!" he crowed.

"You cheated! You didn't give me any—"

Her words were cut short as his strong hands enveloped her waist, catching her off balance. He tipped her under the water, the crackle and wash filling her ears. She was still bobbing up and spluttering when he called, "Out around the boats to the far buoy. If you're good enough you can get even."

Right. That was it. Zina stuck her head down and ploughed through the swell, her heart pounding with exertion. He had a head start but she wouldn't let him beat her a second time. She passed one of the dive school's white launches, then another. George was passing the third but she cut around behind it to reach the buoy seconds before him.

"You cheated! You didn't go around all the boats."

She brushed her wet hair from her face. "You said boats. Not all the boats."

"Oh, you little minx." He was laughing. "God, Zina, we had so much fun, didn't we?"

She grinned at him. "Mostly."

He raised his eyebrows. "Only mostly?"

"You don't remember what you did to me right here on my birthday?"

A slow smile spread right to his eyes. "I do. Because you

disappointed me then, as well. I stole your bikini bottoms as a punishment. I could do it again, if you want me to. Resi isn't here to rescue you now. You'd be completely at my mercy."

His pupils were dark as he gazed at her, his hand reaching towards her, stroking the curve of her hip, just below the surface of the water. Oh, this was wrong, so wrong, but the sensual part of the memory turned her stomach to liquid. He'd had such an electric touch she'd let him do anything. Well, almost anything. And when she'd refused his pleading he'd swum away and left her there. Practically naked. Humiliated. With all their friends on the beach and him waving the scrap of fabric around like a trophy.

His hand was travelling lower now, and Zina backed away, stumbling on the pebbles beneath her feet.

How the hell…

How the frigging merry hell had she almost allowed herself to fall for his games? She was a fool. A fool! The realisation slipped through her like ice. He'd only wanted one thing then, and it was all he wanted now.

"If you're not up for a bit of fun," he said, folding his arms across his chest, "why flirt with me?"

To make her husband jealous? That would certainly burst Georgiou's balloon, but it would also expose the cracks in her marriage. That was the very last thing she wanted to do. She'd have to brazen this out.

"Flirt? You've been reading too much into it. I was just being friendly. You know I'm married."

"There's married … and there's married. Come on, Zina. I know you want to, and your husband need never find out."

The absolute cheek of the man! He wasn't better than the boy; he was *worse*. Twenty times worse. And he'd reeled her in, like a fish on a line.

"I'd never cheat on Lambros. I love him," she told him tartly.

The thought was like a thump in her solar plexus. She did love him. She really did. What ... what ... had she almost done? For a moment Zina thought she was going to throw up, and she backed away further, the anchor rope of a nearby boat rough beneath her gripping fingers.

"You haven't changed, have you? You always were a cocktease – not that it bothers me. You're not that desirable, Zina. You're not that special."

Arrogant shit! He frigging beggared belief. "Luckily my husband thinks I am," she told him, before diving into the waves and striking out for the concrete platform on the shore.

As she was rubbing herself down with a towel, hidden from the taverna by the trees lining the car park, she began to consider her words. She'd told Georgiou she loved Lambros, and it was true. He'd never in a million years behave in that disgraceful manner; he'd never been disrespectful, or dishonest. Her love for him was alive. It may have been buried so far beneath her anger at his continuing distance that she'd all but forgotten about it, but it was there all right. And it was beginning to hurt.

She got into the car and gripped the steering wheel. She could succumb to that pain and weep for a year, or she could use it. She could admit to herself her whole focus had been wrong. Her whole energy.

She needed to stop playing stupid games and do something to try to reach Lambros. Before it really was too late to save her marriage.

Wednesday 20th September

Standing at the patio doors, Karmela sipped her espresso, watching the orange-red of the sunrise fade to golden streaks across the pearl-grey sky. She was missing her morning walks with Iain and Sybil, but after Saturday's awkwardness she had made the excuse that she was getting behind with her book and needed all the time she could muster. At least that much was true, even if the real reason was the R word looming large in her thoughts.

She had been thinking a great deal about the first item on Jo's list of manuscript rejection hacks: prepare yourself mentally. But how? In terms of the publishing process, she understood how that might work. She had read a blog written by an agent, revealing the number of submissions she received and how few were accepted, so statistically speaking, obviously rejections would happen.

Karmela sipped her coffee again, cradling the small cup in her hands. Like anything, the more you were rejected the easier it became. Practice makes perfect. And you could set your expectations accordingly. But did that mean you had to go into every new relationship expecting it to fail, just so it was easier when it happened? With that mindset, why would you even bother? To her, that sounded a whole lot like the old Karmela, the one who expected nothing from the world, and it was a place to which she would not return.

Her recent life experience did not support that either. Since Dubrovnik, people had not rejected her; in fact the exact opposite was true, which was still a thing of wonder. Here at the retreat, she got on with everyone perfectly well and in Jo, Karmela felt she had made a new friend. Zina, too, although on the last couple of evenings…

So was it a numbers game? You could have many friends, but only one significant other. But was that thought even helpful? Oh, she had to … had to … find a way of managing this awful feeling, of stopping it from dragging her down and overwhelming her. Because at times it did, and then she felt as though she was drowning, with no possible foothold to reach for the shore.

Should she just give up on the idea of dating and save herself the trouble? Lots of people remained happily single and she was sure she could be one of them. Her life was pretty busy as it was, with her full-on job, her frequent trips to Dubrovnik and Sarajevo and her increasingly hectic social life.

But was being busy actually living life to the full, as she had promised herself she would? Her mother was always busy, and Karmela had a strong suspicion she used it as a shield against emotional involvement. So busyness in itself was not the answer. The range of experiences was important, and damn it, she wanted to feel love. Real, all-encompassing love. Passionate love. She was forty-three. She had to at least try. But the cautious Karmela was still sufficiently close to the surface to want to minimise the potential for hurt. Obsess over it, even. Was that cheating in some way? Or just common sense?

Oh, she was getting nowhere – nowhere – and wasting so much time. She turned to the second point on Jo's list; build a support group around you – they will all have been there. Well, not where she had been, exactly. Did that matter? Her experiences of war had been very different to her neighbour's in Dubrovnik, but they had bonded over them in the end, and more than anyone he had helped her to crawl out from her protective shell when it broke.

Was there support here in Santorini? There was Jo, of course. It sounded as though her marriage had been one long catalogue of rejection though she must have loved Rees at some point so that must have hurt. Karmela was sure she would have coping strategies she could share, but right now she had far too much shit of her own to deal with.

Then of course there was Zina who was younger than her but who had been married for a number of years. That had to bring its challenges, did it not? Experiences from which she could perhaps benefit? But Karmela had the strangest feeling that all was not well in Zina's world either. Last night especially, she had been so withdrawn – polite and helpful when serving dinner, of course, but rushing off straight afterwards with barely a word.

Oh, she knew support amongst friends worked both ways, but at times it was just not possible. Which was most likely why Jo's advice had been a group. Like the book club in

Dubrovnik. There had been four of them in the inner circle, as they had jokingly called it, and that had been perfect. Back in Sarajevo, she and Nejla and Emina had made three. So here? Was there anyone else? Lovely as they all were, Karmela just did not feel close enough to any of them to burden them with her troubles.

Resolutely, she turned to the next piece of advice on Jo's list: to watch for a pattern in reasons for rejection. Although Karmela's first instinct had been to want to know why Iain had pushed her away, she had pretty soon decided it would be pointless. But what if she had been wrong? What if knowing would actually help her come to terms with it?

She heard Susan and Ellen outside in the courtyard. How could it be breakfast time already? She rushed to the bathroom, picked up her toothpaste and squeezed a neat ball onto the brush. As she leant over the basin, a tear dripped from her nose. It was all very well being logical, but even her body knew she was hurting – pointlessly, she was sure, because the Iain boat had already well and truly sailed. She had to find it in herself to look forwards, not back. They were two thirds of the way through the retreat already, so she needed to refocus. One more push and the end of her first draft would be in sight.

Jo looked at the multi-coloured Post-it notes strewn around her, evidence of a whole morning's work. Each and every one of them contained a scribbled thought or idea about coming clean over who really wrote *Only. Ever. You.*, but she was no closer to working out how to do it. Every direction she turned she found yet another obstacle.

One thing was certain: she was going to divorce Rees. But to be completely free of him, this had to happen first. She clenched her hands into fists then released them. The backlash from readers could be vicious. Let's face it, *would be* vicious. They'd feel cheated, and rightly so. It would be the end of her writing career, but strangely she didn't mind. In fact, the thought was something of a relief. If they sold the house on Wimbledon Common she'd have more than enough to live on while she worked out what to do with the rest of her life.

Already an idea was beginning to form, but if there was too much collateral damage from telling the truth it could be a non-starter. She was coming to realise that what she loved most of all was mentoring new writers. But who would employ her once they knew she wasn't a best-selling novelist? And that she was a total fraudster as well?

FFS, Jo. You're getting nowhere fast.

She typed a quick message to Karmela then walked into her lounge, gazing out of the window over the drying yard and the pistachio fields that rose up the slope. Below her, Lambros was turning the wheel of a horizontal cylindrical drum filled with freshly harvested pistachios, while water trickled from a pipe along the top. Every so often a rattle of de-husked nuts tumbled into the metal tray below, presumably destined to join their fellows on the drying floor.

Hearing footsteps on the stairs, Jo turned away and opened the door.

"I'm sorry if I disturbed your work," she said.

Karmela smiled. "Friends over word count. Every time."

"I'm honestly not sure what I'd have done without you. The more I think about it, the more I realise just how much I owe you. And now I'm asking for even more help."

Karmela beamed. "What can I do?"

"Since I spoke to Mum yesterday, I've been trying to work out what to do now. I know what I want to achieve but have no idea how to get there. Well, I can't say I have no ideas"—she gestured towards the notes scattered across her desk and on the bed in the next room—"I just don't have any that will actually work."

Karmela sat down on the sofa. "Starting with the end result is good. Tell me what you want."

"To leave Rees in such a way that he has no hold over me."

"That is reasonable enough. So to do it, you need to go public about not writing *Only. Ever. You.*"

"You make it sound so simple, but it's really not."

"Legally speaking? With the copyright and whatnot?"

"No. Pam left everything to Mum and she's happy to make the rights over to me anyway. Once I've divorced, of course."

"So tell me exactly what the problems are." She leant forwards, clasping her hands together.

"First and most important is trying to protect Pam's memory, and of course her lover, because she's most likely still alive. I know you'll say that everyone will take the book as a work of fiction, but Rees knows the truth and I'm sure he'd have no compunction in selling his story. Both for the money, and to get his own back."

"I think you are probably right. But if you are worried journalists and the like could uncover Eloise's identity, could we perhaps try to do it first and warn her? How many people in your parliament?"

Jo frowned. "Six, seven hundred?"

"And you know when Pam and her Eloise met?"

"Yes. The year, at least."

"So there will be some politicians from the time without wives, and some whose wives have died since. Others who will not fit the circumstances. We could always contact the rest and…"

"And what?"

Karmela frowned. "We would have to word it carefully, which will need more thought, even once we have found them all. We certainly need time to research it. What is your next biggest concern?"

"It's the whole thing about how people will react, readers in particular. They're going to feel so cheated. Especially the lesbian community because the book's become pretty iconic. I mean, I'd be pissed off if it turned out the author who'd made a name for herself out of one of my favourite books hadn't written it after all."

"To me, it would not matter so much. To be honest, I struggle to remember the titles of some of the books I have read, much less who wrote them. But perhaps I am in the minority. We could ask the rest of the group. And Susan's queer and a total book geek, so she—"

"No!" Jo stood up, then feeling a little foolish, sat down again. "How would I get through the next ten days with them knowing? And what about the damage to the retreat if they demanded their money back? Besides, it would only take one of them to go to the newspapers."

"None of them would. Not Susan; she is too loyal. And Iain ... well, it would not occur to him. Diana is far too nice, and Sophie..."

"What about Sophie? I've always had the impression she doesn't particularly like me."

"I have wondered about that myself once or twice, but have come to the conclusion that she is either a bit moody or up and down with the stress of her husband having dementia. It must be awful, especially when— Jo! Wait a minute. I am sure Diana said he used to be an MP. Sophie must know people. She might even be able to help us."

"I can't, Karmela. I can't..." She put her hand over her mouth, feeling slightly sick. Oh god, if she couldn't tell four more people, how would she ever be able to tell the world? But it was because she cared about what these particular people thought of her, because she valued their good opinion, that it felt so very tough. It wasn't like telling strangers and she just couldn't do it.

"But I could." Karmela thought for a moment. "In a sort of oblique way. Like when you first told me, you said 'What would you think if...', or something like that. I could raise the idea metaphorically. Maybe talk about celebrity books with hidden ghostwriters, and move on from there. Then at least we would have some sort of idea what their reactions might be. Perhaps I could do it over drinks before dinner. You do not even have to be there, if you prefer."

Jo bit her lip. The downside of Karmela's proposal was pretty limited, and at least she'd have some idea of what she'd be dealing with in a wider context. It might just rule some of her ideas out. And if Karmela was right, and the fallout wasn't as bad as she feared, it might rule others in. *If.* A very big *if.* But at least it would move her one step closer to her goal. She looked again at the multi-coloured papers spread across her room like so many flightless butterflies. She had no better idea. Her only option was to trust Karmela, and she absolutely did.

Zina picked up another glass from the washer and began to polish it.

Ekaterini nudged her gently. "You look done-in. I'll finish those if you want to put your feet up for a couple of hours before prepping for dinner."

She shook her head, but the idea was more than tempting. "You have your own work to do."

Ekaterini took the tea towel from her hand. "I'm worried about you, Zina. Bags under your eyes, no spark. You're not"—she made a rounded gesture across her stomach—"*énkyos* are you?"

Zina's eyebrows shot almost to her hairline. "Good god, no." That would be the last thing she needed. "There's just so much to think about at the moment."

"Well, thinking is something you can do sitting in the shade with a cool drink. Off you go, and I don't want to see you again until five o'clock."

"Thank you." Zina turned away quickly so Ekaterini couldn't see the tears in her eyes.

Leaving the kitchen, she paused. Ekaterini was right; her bed was calling, but Mama would be at home and would doubtless want to chat. She would ask her how things were with Lambros, which was something she really couldn't face right now. But perhaps ... perhaps ... instead she should try again to break the impasse. Return to the pistachio field. Right now, before the dregs of her resolve drained away.

His truck was parked almost at the top of the orchard, and she quickened her pace, eager to get this over with. A distant figure emerged, carrying a box of nuts. *Skatá!* It was Iain. What was he doing out here again? Shouldn't he be in his room writing, like the others? Damn the man. How could she speak to Lambros when he was here? She couldn't let him witness her rejection a second time.

A sob escaped her throat, and she stepped further into the shadows while she tried to control it. The trees were barely tall enough to disguise her presence, so she dropped to her haunches, drawing slow circles in the grey dust with her fingers. This was just too awful for words, and she didn't know how to start mending it. The husband she loved with all her heart was becoming a stranger before her very eyes.

Viciously she wiped away a tear, leaving a grainy smear of dirt on her cheek. She was in a proper mess, inside and out. She couldn't risk anyone seeing her like this, but neither could she stay skulking beneath the pistachios. It would only take Jo to look out of her window and she'd be rumbled. With a heavy heart she turned and threaded her way through the orchard towards the farmhouse.

The moment Zina opened the kitchen door, Mama turned off the radio and stormed across the room.

"Zina, how could you?"

Zina stepped back. She'd never seen Mama this mad. Not even close. What the frigging hell?

"What are you talking about?" she asked in a shaky voice.

"You don't know? You don't know! Did you not know it was wrong, or did you think you would not get found out? I expected better of you, my only daughter."

"Found out?" Her words faded to a pathetic echo as she thought of Georgiou. They'd done nothing wrong, but what else could it be? "You think ... me and Georgiou..."

"I don't think. I *know*." Mama's face was inches from hers. "Calandra's daughter saw you at Balos yesterday, cavorting in the sea. I don't think I've ever been more ashamed."

"*Cavorting?*" The word came out somewhere between a squeak and a scream. "If you must know, we were arguing. Because he wanted me to do something I never would. He wanted me to cheat on Lambros."

"Well that wasn't what it looked like."

Zina folded her arms. "That's what it was."

Mama stepped back a fraction. "What were you doing with that man anyway? Chasing after him all the way to Balos beach? I thought it was odd when you said you were going there."

"I wasn't chasing him. I was... I thought... I just thought ... it would be nice to have some company." Oh, that sounded so weak, and Mama was still looking daggers at her. "Some attention, if you must know, with Lambros being—"

"Zina, Zina, don't you ever change?" Her mother wagged her finger. "Why is everything always about you? God, I blame myself, I really do. But with only one child, of course your father and I doted on you. We made you the centre of our world. Made you expect it."

"Expect it? I had to fight to make you notice me, especially when Babá was in the room. And you're just the same with Lambros. You're all over him and you ignore me. No wonder I feel left out. It's just not fair."

Her mother's lips set in a hard line. "Will you stop and listen to yourself? You sound like a six-year-old. I was so proud when you came back here, when you sacrificed so much for your husband. I thought my little girl had finally grown up, but now I can see I was wrong. I'll say it again: not everything is about you."

Zina's head was spinning under the weight of her mother's words. To be attacked like this, by the one person she thought she could rely on to be kind to her. Her very foundations were crumbling.

"I don't have to listen to this—" But her angry words finished in a choked sob.

Mama put her hand on her shoulder. "You do if you want to have any chance of saving your marriage. I've stood back until now. I've tried so hard not to interfere when it's breaking my heart, seeing the two of you hurting so much…"

"Lambros isn't hurting."

"Of course he is, you stupid child. Perhaps I should just bang your heads together and be done with it." Sighing, Mama guided her to the table. "Come on, sit down. Let's talk about this properly."

Zina perched on the edge of the chair, gripping the wooden seat between her fingers. "OK," she said slowly. She supposed she had nothing left to lose, and who knew? Mama might even be able to help.

"All right," said Mama. "Let's start at the beginning. You

said you'd never cheat on Lambros and despite what I was told I believe you. But do you still love him?"

Zina nodded. "Of course I do. I'm ... I'm so lonely without him, but he's built up this wall and I don't know how to get past it."

"You've built up a wall too, Zina, and the longer this goes on, the higher those walls will get. One of you needs to make the first move."

"I did. On Sunday. I went up to the orchard to see if he wanted a cold drink and he was really nasty to me. In front of Iain, as well."

Mama frowned. "That doesn't sound like Lambros."

"I know, I know. I was so frigging hurt. And then I got angry. Then when I went to see Resi on the beach, and Georgiou was there... I promise you, Mama, nothing happened. I didn't encourage him. Not deliberately, but he was paying me so much attention."

"There you go again, Zina. Attention. Let's focus on Lambros for a moment, shall we? The way he's acting seems out of character to me, but almost having a breakdown would change anyone, wouldn't it?"

"He told me he was back to himself now we're here."

"But think, Zina, is he? Has he changed in other ways too?"

Maybe. Subtly. Yes, she was sure he had, but she couldn't really pinpoint how. Oh god, why not? If her marriage was that important... But they'd both been so wrapped up in their work, and if she was honest she knew things hadn't felt right between them for a while. Which had made those flashes of closeness all the more precious when they'd happened.

But now she could see that they hadn't solved anything. All

they'd done was brush this whole thing under the carpet. She put her head in her hands. "It's going to be a long road back, Mama. What's more, he's going to have to want it as much as I do, and I'm not sure he does."

Her mother nodded. "It will most likely be the most difficult thing you've ever done. I think that at the root of it all is you've both had a massive shift in your expectations from life; you both thought you'd be high-flyers in Athens with the world at your feet. But it didn't work out that way for Lambros, which meant you had to give up your dreams too. But you chose to do it for him, Zina. Remember that."

"How could I have not?" Tears filled her eyes again, and Mama wrapped a comforting arm around her shoulder.

"Cry it out, *agápi mou*. Then you can go and freshen up while I phone Calandra and tell her to make sure her daughter stops spreading lies about mine."

"Thanks, Mama," she sniffed. What good would more tears do? She wasn't entirely sure she accepted, or even understood, everything her mother had said. Those painful, painful words. She stood, wiping her eyes. "I think I'll just sit on the terrace for a while and think things through."

Her mother looked up at her. "That sounds like a very good idea to me."

Jo's hand shook as she stood at the carved oak sideboard that served as the honesty bar and poured herself a generous measure of wine. No way could she let Karmela do this alone, but she couldn't do it without a glass in her hand either. While she was wary of letting her wine habit get the better of her again, this was a whole new level – a one-off. She needed that drink to stop her running away.

She almost hadn't made it down here in the first place. Instead she'd clung to the edge of the basin, fighting for air, terrified the panic could descend again at any moment. As she'd breathed slowly in and out she had reminded herself how much she could rely on Karmela because she would make sure nothing went wrong. Yet it would take only one tiny misunderstanding... No. She mustn't think like that. The discussion would be purely hypothetical. This wouldn't come back to haunt her ... until later. When her story came out. Then this little group of people who were becoming dear to her would realise they'd been used and lied to as well.

So much for the trust they were all so proud of, the trust that made sharing their work and their thoughts not terrifying, but a joy. It made the feedback the group gave each other sincere and valuable. How could she expect them to trust each other, when she wasn't prepared to do the same?

She returned the wine bottle to the fridge, then joined the others. They were clustered around two small tables pushed together on the far side of the courtyard, a corner which was both out of the stiff evening breeze and also gave them a view of the glorious pinks, purples and oranges that washed the sky as the sun settled towards the horizon. In front of them were bowls of small black olives and pistachios, which Iain was explaining had been grown by one of Lambros's friends. Susan scooped up a couple of olives and declared them absolutely delicious.

"If I had my way, we'd be eating goat tonight," said Ellen.

"Except the ones here are too darned clever to end up in the roasting dish."

"Why, what happened?" Karmela asked.

"I was working at the edge of the olive grove on my watercolours. There's some sea rocket growing in an old wall there, and it's so delicate it took me a while to capture it, and a number of attempts. I was completely absorbed, then I heard a sort of coughing sound behind me. I jumped out of my skin, and do you know what it was? A goat was eating one of my discarded pictures."

"It must have been pretty realistic to tempt a goat," said Iain, as everyone laughed.

There was a brief silence as he leant down to pat Sybil, who was lying at his feet. Jo held her breath for what felt like forever, then Karmela spoke.

"I was reading a blog online today and it posed an interesting question: how would you feel if it turned out that a book you loved had actually been written by someone other than the author? Some people got quite passionate in the comments, but personally, most of the time I find it hard to remember who wrote the books I read."

"I know what you mean," said Diana, "and the older I get, the worse it is. But going back to the blog, I guess it would depend on the circumstances. If they'd deliberately set out to steal someone else's work, like in *Yellowface*, I think I'd be pretty damn cross."

"But even then, it was not clear cut," said Karmela. "The book was greatly changed by the time it was published so in many ways it had become a joint venture. And the waters were muddied by the whole cultural appropriation debate."

"That book certainly split opinion at the library," said Susan. "On all sorts of levels. But theft aside, I'm never sure about the cultural appropriation thing, because while I do understand the damage misrepresentation can cause, I firmly believe authors' creativity shouldn't be limited by their backgrounds. Why have imaginations otherwise? Why do research? Taken to extremes it would mean we wouldn't have any wonderful historical fiction like Karmela's writing, because it would be outside her lived experience." She picked up another olive and popped it into her mouth.

"And no fantasy novels," added Iain. "Can't say I've come across many hobbits or elves in my everyday life, and I don't suppose Tolkien did either."

"Neither has Rebecca Yarros ever ridden a dragon," said Susan. "At least, not as far as I'm aware."

Oh no, the conversation was drifting from where Jo needed it to go. And as she did need it to go there, she had to push it back on course.

"That's an interesting debate in itself, but we're moving away from Karmela's initial question."

Iain nodded. "On that I agree with Diana. If we're having a discussion about the morals of passing off someone else's book as your own it would depend on the circumstances, but the reality is that it's hardly something I'd lose sleep over, although I'd probably like to see reparations made to the person whose work it was."

Diana nodded. "That's another aspect, isn't it? More often than not, it's not someone's mistake, it's how they put it right. When Sophie and I went for our spa day they served us a truly disgusting lunch – stale bread and salad all dried up – but when we pointed it out they not only brought us fresh plates, but took a good amount off our bill."

"I guess another thing," said Susan, "would be how much I loved the book. If it was a cherished favourite, like *Only. Ever. You.* I'd be gutted."

A lump formed at the top of Jo's chest. She couldn't breathe, couldn't speak.

What now? What the fuck now?

This was a moment like no other she'd ever experienced, a clear fork in the road: ignore it, or do the right thing? She glanced at Karmela, who was opening her mouth to speak, but Jo cut across her.

"Then let's suppose, Susan, it was *Only. Ever. You.*"

Susan's eyes met hers. Only the chatter of the sparrows, roosting in the tree that shaded Karmela's terrace, filled the courtyard, the jasmine-scented air around them cloying and still.

Susan swallowed hard. "Was it?"

"Yes. I … I had a friend who died. It was her book." Jo's eyes dropped to the table. She was frozen in the moment; unable to feel, barely able to breathe, let alone speak. Free falling, free falling again. Except this time it was going on forever. But Karmela released her parachute.

"Jo shared the whole story with me on Monday and it is complicated, as these things often are. Please do not judge her until you have heard everything." She stood and walked around the table, wrapping her arm over Jo's shoulders. "You need a moment, I guess."

She did, but the others deserved an explanation. She

couldn't leave them hanging like this. Her voice breaking, she looked up at Karmela. "Please, tell them."

"How much?"

"Everything."

"OK."

Karmela's words washed over her. Her story. Her life. Pam's sudden death. Her finding the manuscript on Pam's computer and wanting to read it, despite – and perhaps because – she knew how personal it had been to Pam. Her intention to destroy it afterwards, but...

"I knew it!" Sophie burst out. "I knew it from the first moment we read it for book club. You stole it from her! You stole the story from Pam!"

Jo's mouth hung open. God, did that really happen to people? She touched her jaw in something close to wonder. Her thoughts cascaded, flying too fast for her to grasp, failing to crystallise into anything coherent.

Sophie.

Pam.

Sophie. The MP's wife.

"You don't deny it?" Sophie slammed the table with her open palm, setting the glasses jumping.

Jo shook her head, unable to take her eyes off Sophie. So this was where the sniping came from. This was the real reason she was here. This was why Sophie's story and Diana's about their motives for coming to the retreat didn't quite match. "You're ... you're Eloise."

Sophie stood, gripping the edge of the table with both hands. "As if what you've done already isn't bad enough. Nobody knew that. Nobody! Have you any, any idea at all what it's like to read your own story in a book like I had to? I was sick, physically sick."

"I'm sorry, I—"

"Sorry isn't enough and it never can be. You took something precious; something that should have been mine and Pam's alone and you stole it. Made an absolute fortune from it. You … you … you desecrated her memory and I hope you rot in hell!"

Sophie shoved the table so hard that Jo was aware of Iain grabbing it to keep it stable as Sophie stormed away. Her room door slammed, the sound ricocheting around the courtyard like a gunshot.

Karmela was still gripping Jo's shoulders, and for half a moment Jo wondered if it was in case she, too, decided to take flight.

Susan's voice came from a long way off. "You mean, that wonderful story is true?"

Hauling herself together, Jo managed to nod. "Much of it, yes. I honestly had no intention of publishing it, but I told my now husband about it and he … but it really is my fault. I could have stopped it at any time and I didn't." Jo hung her head, unable even to pick up her glass, despite her throat being dry as a desert, leaving it to Karmela to continue the story.

When she finished speaking, Iain filled the silence. "I had the dubious pleasure of meeting Jo's husband a couple of weeks ago and I can vouch that the man's a controlling bully. A young woman mired in grief would have had no chance against him."

"But I still should have…" Jo petered out. She'd said it a

thousand times. It didn't make a jot of difference. She should have, but she hadn't, and that was the end of it.

"Are you all right?" Susan asked and Jo nodded. She wasn't. She couldn't be. But neither could she crumble completely. For the sake of the group, for Zina and her retreat, she had to hold it together.

"Despite all the upset," Susan continued, "I'm glad you did what you did. The happiness the story has given so many people… The courage to be themselves and not have to hide like Anna and Eloise did… The way it put being lesbian centre stage… Whatever the rights and wrongs, *Only. Ever. You.* deserved to see the light of day."

"But it was wrong. I am just so sorry everyone."

Ellen gripped Jo's hands. "Will you stop saying that? You've been brave and dignified this evening. For my money you have nothing to apologise for. You're a victim here too, of your husband's bullying and greed. Domestic abuse stinks, and you've earnt our support."

The others nodded, even Diana, who was looking incredibly pale, raking the pistachio shells within her reach with her fingers and making a small mound of them.

"So what happens now?" Iain asked.

"We carry on with the retreat," Karmela replied. "I cannot say 'as if this never happened', because that is impossible, but I hope we will all come out of it stronger and closer."

"I meant in terms of *Only. Ever. You.*"

"I wanted to make the truth public," said Jo, "the whole truth. But not if it's going to cause Sophie more hurt. Things will just have to stay as they are, so I would very much value your discretion."

"But, Jo—"

"No, Karmela, we went through this when we were wondering if we could track Eloise down. I won't ruin someone else's life just to make mine better."

Zina appeared from the kitchen. "Come on everyone," she called. "Tonight's starter is *kefalotýri saganáki*, and it's not half as nice cold because the cheese goes greasy."

"I'm not sure I can eat," said Jo in a voice that sounded unlike her own.

Diana stood, and reached over to pat her arm. "Me neither, but we should."

"A big glass of wine will help too," added Iain. "And I can tell you all about the time I made the grave mistake of taking Sybil on a Royal Navy yacht. You'll never believe what she did. Ellen's goat has nothing on her."

Jo nodded. Speaking would only unleash a well of tears, but as the little group crossed the courtyard, despite everything, she knew she was among friends, and that would give her the courage to get through the evening. Tomorrow would no doubt be bloody, but for once she would have to let tomorrow take care of itself.

Thursday 21st September

Standing at Karmela's window, Zina watched as Lambros and Yiannis stopped to chat next to Yiannis's car. She'd heard their voices as they rounded the building from the drying yard and now they were directly in her line of vision. Lambros was laughing. Laughing! He clearly wasn't unhappy at all.

Unable to stop her tears, Zina sank onto the sofa. If Mama was wrong and he didn't even care about their estrangement, what could she do? Pack up and go back to Athens and try to find another job? But what about The Retreat House? And what about Lambros? He could only farm here because he was married to her, so should he be the one to leave? But what would happen to him then? This whole thing was such a frigging mess. She buried her head in her hands and sobbed.

"Zina?" She hadn't heard Karmela come in. "Whatever is going on?"

"Oh, I'm sorry. I just need to make the bed. Everything else is done."

"Do not worry about that. What is wrong?"

"Nothing."

"It does not look like nothing to me. And has not for a few days, if I am honest. I have been worried about you, Zina."

Had it really been so obvious? *Skatá!* But as ever, Karmela's eyes were full of kindness and concern. "I've tried so hard to hide it," Zina said, sniffing. "I'm so sorry."

"Stop saying that. You have been faultlessly professional."

"Thank you, but I don't just want to be professional. I want everything to be exceptional, to be the best, and that includes me."

"You *are* the best, Zina. I cannot imagine anyone better at running a retreat, but clearly you are unhappy and I would love to be able to help if I can."

Karmela sat on the sofa next to her, and Zina looked into her dark eyes, the fine lines around them the only feature that gave away her age. She was older than her and had seen so much more of life. Zina was desperate to talk to someone detached from her situation. She needed a friend, and in Karmela she knew she had found one. She should have known before, should have trusted… There could be no holding back, not anymore.

"It's Lambros. We had a row and he doesn't want to make up." That was putting it at its most basic, but it was hard to find the words to explain what she was feeling inside, how lost and confused she was. How stumped for any answer at all. "It's not like him. Normally when we argue it's over and done with quickly, but not this time."

"So when you try to talk to him, what does he say?"

Zina bit her lip. "I've only tried once but he was pretty nasty, and that's not like him either. I've tried to screw up the courage to have another go, but..." It sounded so pathetic to say she'd walked away because Iain was there.

Karmela nodded. "I get it. Nobody likes rejection."

"And he's avoiding me. Deliberately. He's not even sleeping in our bedroom anymore." God, that was a totally humiliating thing to have to admit, but she needed Karmela to know the whole truth so she would understand how desperate the situation was. "I just don't know what to do. Except ... except..." She sniffed. "This is not a battle I can afford to lose."

"*Battle* is an interesting choice of word, especially if you want the disagreement to end." Karmela frowned. "Shall we instead call it a negotiation?"

"I can't negotiate if he won't talk."

"At some point he will have to, and you need to be ready."

Zina nodded. It did make sense.

"As a first step, shall we try to see things from his point of view? Have you given any thought to how your behaviour might appear to him?" Zina's puzzlement must have shown in her face, because Karmela carried on. "To negotiate successfully you will need to understand at least a little of what he is thinking and of what his position might be." She smiled. "If nothing else, try to second guess it. Put yourself in his shoes. Work out what he might want, then you should be able to identify any common ground as a place to start."

This sounded all very well in theory, but... "Common ground?"

"Outcomes that will work for you both. I have undertaken

some dispute resolution at the university, and once people are talking I find it is helpful to make a list of phrases starting with *we* not *me*, as the jargon goes, although obviously, grammatically speaking a phrase should start with *I*. That way the process feels much more collaborative, but of course you also need to know where your own bottom line is. The things that are non-negotiable for you."

"Yes … I do get that." She didn't entirely; she'd need to think about it some more later. The we-not-me bit especially. It sort of chimed with what Mama had been saying yesterday. In a most uncomfortable manner.

"So do you think Lambros sees a busy wife, or one who is avoiding him?"

"I suppose, at first, I was very angry and he knew it, but instead of making up like he always does, he began to avoid me. I'm not sure if I've exactly been avoiding him because I haven't needed to. It's not like we see much of each other anyway, not now the retreat's open. And what with the nut harvest… Oh, Karmela, I don't think I'll ever be able to eat a pistachio again." Her voice rose almost to a wail. She needed to get a grip. She apologised.

"There is no need to say sorry. I can see how much you are hurting. Shall we look at this another way? Obviously you want to sort this out, so what steps do you need to take to make that happen?"

Wasn't that obvious? Even to her. She sighed. "We need to talk."

"Then what is stopping you from making the first move? Apart from the possibility that he might rebuff you again. But you are a determined young woman; you built this marvellous place from scratch and that took some doing."

"Lambros…"

Karmela held up her finger. "No. What is stopping *you*?"

"I want to save my marriage; that's the bottom line. But if I'm honest, this has been rumbling on for a while, even before the row, and—"

She couldn't tell a guest she was less than happy running the retreat, could she? How would that come across? But she'd promised herself, no holds barred, and she trusted Karmela implicitly.

"You won't tell anyone what I'm going to tell you?"

"Of course not."

"I didn't want to come back to Santorini; I did it for Lambros. And for Mama when she was widowed. I loved my job in Athens so much I could hardly bear to leave. The challenge of getting my clients' stories across to a wider audience, making contacts with all the right social media influencers, creating eye-grabbing posts. It was the best thing ever. There was something new every day, and I miss it like hell. But Lambros can't go back to the corporate world. That's something that really isn't negotiable. It's … a health thing."

"So you feel as though you have to make an impossible choice?"

"I love him. Simple as that. But I feel so frustrated here, like I'm wasting my brain. The lack of mental stimulation is driving me nuts." Zina bit her lip. "And, I guess, making me not the easiest of people to live with."

"That I do understand. I would feel the same if I was

spending a good part of my life cleaning and waiting tables. But have you told Lambros any of this?"

Zina shook her head. "Not in so many words. I didn't want him to think I regret coming here."

"You need to be completely honest with him about how you feel, and hope he will be honest with you. Once you know each other's baselines then you can negotiate effectively."

Karmela made it sound so simple, but even before they could get that far a major issue needed resolving.

"What if he won't talk to me?"

"You will have to keep trying until he does. Be so reasonable that he will feel bad if he is not. Starting right now."

Zina nibbled the skin next to her thumbnail. "I suppose I was waiting for the harvest to be over. So he couldn't use it as an excuse."

"It is almost finished though, is it not? Iain said at breakfast he was not needed any longer."

So Lambros would be alone in the orchard. But she wasn't ready—

Karmela interrupted her thoughts. "Clearly you both need to set time aside to have a proper conversation so you can give it the importance it deserves. Do not wait to arrange when that will happen."

"I suppose that makes sense." Much as she knew Karmela was right, Zina felt rather sick.

"Now," said Karmela briskly, "I will make my own bed and you go and find Lambros."

"If he doesn't agree?"

"If that is the case then come straight back here and we can talk about this some more. I really want to help you sort this out, Zina."

So there'd be no wriggling out of this, nor prevaricating either. Karmela was the sort of person who would care enough to make sure she found an opportunity to ask how the conversation had gone. On one level it was entirely wonderful to have a friend like that, but on another…

She thanked Karmela with a heartfelt hug, then made her way along the side of The Retreat House towards the pistachio orchard. Small birds flitted between the trees and cicadas hummed in the tufts of long, dry grass around her. Ahead was Lambros's truck, and she walked slowly towards it, framing and reframing the words she needed to say. Words that needed to focus on *we*, not *me*.

She spotted Lambros working fifty or so metres from the track. Alone, as Karmela had said he would be, his gloved hands grasping a bunch of pistachios, the back of his T-shirt soaking with sweat. Her gut instinct was to return the way she'd come, find an important job in the kitchen and hide. But she couldn't. It wasn't only Karmela, she owed this to herself, and sick as she still felt, she had to do this. Fixing her marriage may be the biggest challenge she'd ever face, but she loved a challenge, didn't she? And Karmela's wise words about negotiation had given her a place to start.

Her husband turned when he saw her, his face expressionless as she approached.

"Lambros, please can we talk? After the harvest, I mean. When we have more time."

He wiped his brow with his forearm, looking only at the

dry earth beneath his feet. "I should finish by the end of the day."

"Then tomorrow. Will you have time tomorrow?"

"Will you?" A muscle twitched in his cheek.

"I will make time. For us."

He nodded. "Fine. We'll do it at three o'clock once I've checked the goats." With that he jammed his sun hat further onto his head and went back to his work.

Lambros had, at least, agreed to talk. Provided he didn't back out. A chill ran through her. What if…? But no, in this thing above all others, failure was not an option. The ultimate challenge. But she could only win if Lambros wanted to as well. *Skatá!* Karmela had been more right than she knew with this we-not-me stuff. It wasn't about winning *against* her husband. It was about winning *with* him.

Karmela typed half a dozen words, then pushed her chair away from her desk. Despite the time she had lost this morning – or maybe because of it – she just could not concentrate. Something she had said to Zina was resonating with her own situation too. Something about listening to and understanding the other person's point of view.

She replayed her conversations with Iain in her head – the jokey ones, the serious ones, the most recent one. The one that had pierced her so much. He had said that he would like to take her out to dinner but… And she had finished the sentence for him. Perhaps he had not intended to do so himself, but if she had left him space, if she had stood silent and waited, he would have been too polite not to fill the void. Then perhaps she would have known what that "but" was. She would have learnt the reason he did not want her.

Would knowing the reason have any bearing at all on her endless machinations about how best to deal with rejection? The thought had half-come to her yesterday, but she'd dismissed it. Had that been wrong? It might be something quite simple, something she could guard against in future. Perhaps something like… Oh, she did not know. Perhaps like not wanting a relationship with someone who lived in a different country. Or it might be something that was really to do with her. It was a frightening thought, but one she needed to face. And what was holding her back from asking him? Just like Zina, it was fear of bloody rejection.

Sranje! She needed to stop prevaricating. She needed to display a fraction of the courage Jo had over the last day or so, and which Zina was doing right now, and confront the problem that was holding her back.

Given Iain was no longer helping Lambros he should be in his room. Karmela hesitated. Nobody had been at their best this morning. It was not surprising, after last night's upset. So perhaps this was not the moment to speak to him after all. Or was she using it as yet another excuse? Either way, they did not have to have the conversation now. She had no desire to ambush him. She just wanted to fix a time to talk.

The late morning heat felt sticky as she crossed the courtyard and the humidity was draining. Ekaterini had already laid the table for lunch under the awning, and the delicious aroma of roasting peppers drifted from the kitchen, but Karmela barely noticed, anxious to get this done.

Her knock on Iain's door was greeted by a cacophony of barking, and with it opened no more than a crack, Sybil squeezed through, jumping up at Karmela as she caught Sybil's paws in her hands to greet her, bending down so the dog could lick her face.

"Oh, hello." It was impossible to tell from his even tone whether Iain was pleased to see her or not, but right now that was not important.

"I will not keep you long," she said. "I only want to fix a time when we can talk. I need to understand why you changed your mind about us. As you know, I am new to dating and I am hoping I can learn from your reasons."

He studied the terracotta tiles beneath their feet. "I doubt it."

"Really?"

"Yes, because I wouldn't mind betting this particular set of circumstances won't ever arise again." Finally he did glance up, a glint of desperation in his eyes. "And it isn't you, honestly."

"So you are not prepared to tell me?" Her request was not unreasonable, surely?

He shrugged. "It won't change anything, because sadly, very sadly, I can't change the past." He tried to look at her, but still could not meet her eyes. "I was an RAF pilot, Karmela. I took part in Operation Deliberate Force. I bombed Sarajevo in the last days of the war. I might even have killed your friend. We don't need to talk about it. It is what it is."

Karmela stepped back so fast her foot almost caught on the bottom of the stairs and she grabbed the newel post to steady herself. This could not be right, surely? This man, standing in front of her, had dropped bombs on a city full of civilians? A city full of children, including Emina?

Iain spoke quietly. "Of course you're shocked. I'm sorry. But you see, the moment I realised, I knew it would come between us, and by the look on your face I was right. Even as friends, I fear it will."

She looked up and stepped away again. Towards the door, this time. "Thank you for telling me. I will go back to my room now and leave you in peace."

Sranje! This hurt almost as much as his rejection itself. An almost doubling-up sort of hurt, like she had been winded. And there was anger. Anger too. But why? Had she not put the war behind her? Had she not been back to Sarajevo and visited Emina's grave with Nejla, exorcising the ghosts?

With no thought as to what she was doing, Karmela walked past her room, heading towards the upper reaches of the gully that split the land in two, her feet finding a path through the low curls of vines. Despite the season some were shooting the tiniest green leaves, fresh and new against the gritty grey soil. Others were no more than frazzled mounds of vegetation, burnt ochre and yellow-brown by the heat of the sun.

Karmela felt frazzled too. Burnt out. Would this wretched war ever go away? Her sensible head told her to remember how much progress she had made. How it was better to allow herself to feel pain, than nothing at all. But this hurt so bloody much it was hard to untangle. Hard to even believe.

Ahead of her was the olive grove with its welcome shade. At this particular point, the gully was less than two metres deep and some animal – most likely a curious goat – had made a track down one side. Her sandals slipped on the soil; she was so not prepared for a hike across open country and she cursed herself. She should be back in her room, writing. But right now she needed the space.

She needed blue sky above, viewed through the branches and silvery leaves of the olives. On the opposite wall of the gully the earth was cream in colour and pockmarked with stones, a thick line of what looked like ash running through it – black pebbles above, but not below. Clear evidence of the eruption that had buried Akrotiri and ripped the island apart.

A trickle of ants trailed from behind a bush that was growing wedged into the gully's side. Had they always been on the island, or had they somehow made it back? A small miracle of nature. Karmela watched as they worked together to haul a fleshy round leaf into their nest. Life went on. Her life went on. Everyone had their journey, even these tiny ants. In and out they went, every day. Only humans stopped to wonder why.

But that wondering why was powerful. It was the reason humans kept learning, kept adapting, kept growing into more fulfilling lives. From the hunter-gatherers who had first roamed the planet, to the citizens of Akrotiri with their wonderful wall paintings and pottery, to where they were today. Human progress never stopped; it was never the finished product, always a work in progress. Like her book. Like ... herself.

Humans learnt from everything, even pain, and she would beat this. She would. She would learn, adapt, change. Like Zina had, coming here from her exciting career in media relations and—

Karmela pulled herself up short. Zina knew about media

relations. Why on earth had she not put two and two together before? How useful could her skill set be to Jo? Karmela clambered back up the slope, then brushed off her shorts. She needed to get her head out of her arse and follow this up.

Time ticked towards noon. High noon, or a whole load of nothing? Would Diana and Sophie turn up together for their one-to-one as usual? Or just Diana? Just Sophie? Or neither of them? Right now, anything was possible. And everything impossible.

Jo had returned to her room early last night, despite Iain trying to convince her to have another glass of wine. The one she'd drunk over dinner had tasted bitter in her mouth as the reality of her situation hit home. She'd been almost within touching distance of being able to leave Rees, and now that chance had been snatched away, leaving a huge empty space where something like hope had grown without her even noticing.

What had really kept her awake though, was what Sophie might do. Ask for her money back from Zina as a bare minimum, she guessed. Which of course Jo would pay. She only wished she could believe Diana's assurances that Sophie wouldn't blow the whole story sky high or find some way to drag her through the courts because she would never want the publicity. But what would happen next? Sophie hadn't shown up for breakfast, or for the morning workshop. Neither had she packed her bags and left. Yet.

She heard footsteps on the stairs, but Jo couldn't work out

whose they were. One set, though. Too slow to be Sophie's; too light to be Diana's. A moment later she heard a tentative knock, followed by Sophie peeping around the door, her fine cheek bones sunken into her face, her eyes red-rimmed. *Oh, god, what had she done? What had she done to the woman Pam had loved?*

Sophie cleared her throat. "Can we ... talk about last night? And about Pam?"

Jo nodded. "Whatever you want. Really." Sophie still hesitated at the doorway. "Come in and sit down."

Sophie took a moment arranging her skirt, smoothing it neatly over her legs. Finally she looked up. "She thought a lot of you, you know. She told me you were the daughter she never had."

Grief welled inside Jo, a cruel twist of wretchedness threatening her, before she managed to muster everything she had to push it away. This was not about her. This was about Sophie.

"That makes it worse, doesn't it?" she said.

"I don't know. I really don't." Sophie sighed. "I didn't come here to hate you, Jo, or to make things difficult. I came here to find out how our story got out there. I had to know, you see. I became obsessed with the idea that Pam had planned it all along, that she had written it secretly and left instructions in her will ... and I felt ... I felt... No, not used, because our love was real. But exposed. Yes, that's it. Exposed."

"It wasn't like that at all."

"I know that now. But last night, as Karmela was talking, and I understood that publication was your choice, not Pam's, all that emotion came ripping through me. Horror, relief and I don't know what, but I couldn't stop it. I had to speak out. And when you told everyone I was Eloise it crystallised into a terrible anger. No one knew about that. No one." She put her head in her hands.

"I'm truly sorry. I was so shocked that it just came out."

Sophie looked up, through red-rimmed eyes. "I should have spoken to you sooner. I know I should. I'd been able to find out so little about Jessica Rose online that it seemed coming to the retreat was my only chance, but when I got here, well, I kept finding reasons not to do it. New ones all the time. First and foremost, it really hit home to me that to say anything at all I would need to reveal my secret self. So I decided to try to gauge what sort of person you were first and whether I could trust you.

"But of course, when you told us your real name I knew exactly who you were. I knew then how you'd got hold of the manuscript, and I knew you and Pam were so close, so I really did think it had been her wish to publish the story. And when you chose the song Pam loved so much for Zina's stupid game, I knew how deeply you cared for her. So I was too frightened to ask, because I was scared of your answer. And besides, there was Diana. She was delighted when I suggested we came here. She's fiddled around writing love stories for years and it's been a joy to see her having such fun. For the first time since Peter died, in fact. It made me reluctant to upset the apple cart."

"You two are such good friends," Jo murmured.

"She's bloody amazing. She sat up with me most of the night, just listening. It must have been a shock to her that I fell in love with a woman, but she didn't let it show. And she didn't know about Lawrence's true nature either. Eventually she told me what Karmela had said about Rees, and I finally understood what had really happened – that he coerced you into publishing *Only. Ever. You.*"

"I still should have stopped it."

"How could you? I could never stand in Lawrence's way when he really wanted something. It's insidious being in a controlling relationship. Sometimes I almost wished he'd come out and hit me so I could have been done with it." She shook her head. "I know that sounds awful, what some women go through, but at least then … I don't know…" She shrugged. "But you don't need me to tell you that. You're still living the nightmare. Diana told me what you planned to do, and you mustn't let me stop you."

"Sophie, that isn't fair."

"It's what Pam would want. And anyway, no one except the people around the table last night need know the book's real."

"I'm afraid Rees does and I'm worried he will milk it for all it's worth, especially if there was money in selling the story."

"Oh." Sophie looked down. "Oh."

"Then we do nothing."

"No, Jo. I don't want to be responsible for keeping you prisoner in your marriage. I could cope with Lawrence and his affairs because I had Pam to love me, to make sure I always believed in myself. And yes, he could be cruel, but we kept up appearances for the sake of the boys and his career. We had a shared goal at least, and that made it just about bearable."

"Your children don't know about Pam, I assume?"

"They know we were friends. They were at boarding school anyway. Lawrence thought it best. The younger one, Paul, he'll be fine with it. He's something of a free spirit, but Sebastian's never liked surprises."

"And finding out his mother's gay would be a very big one."

Sophie frowned. "That's not a label I'm comfortable with. I've watched Susan and Ellen, and lovely as they are, I don't see anything of myself in them. It was simply that the love of my life, my soul mate, happened to be a woman too."

"You said you wanted to talk about Pam," Jo reminded her gently.

"Pam was my angel. She lit up my world from the inside out. When she died I felt as though someone had cut off my right arm, and I had to hide it. I couldn't even grieve as I needed to, because no one knew we were more than casual friends. I never ... never got to say goodbye to her, to mourn her properly. I wasn't brave enough to go to her funeral. I didn't think I'd be able to hold it together."

"I don't think I've grieved properly either. All the guilt over the book, then all its success, the awards, the film... My mum always thought it was because I was the one who found Pam, but that wasn't it at all."

Sophie's eyes met hers. "Was it ... was it peaceful, like in the epilogue?"

"It was, I promise. It was in her sleep and she looked so serene. I knew she was gone, but I sat with her while I waited for the paramedics, and I held her hand."

"Oh, Jo." Sophie started to cry, and the tears that had been prickling Jo's eyes spilled over too. She stood, legs shaking, and moved to the other sofa, where Sophie made space for her. With their arms entwined, they sobbed together for the woman they had both loved, and who had loved them so much in return.

Eventually Sophie reached into the pocket of her skirt for a handkerchief and wiped her eyes. "Pam was a wonderful woman in so many ways. We need to do her and her talent as a writer justice as well. We need to tell the truth."

Jo nodded. "I know. But I don't want to risk you—"

Sophie raised her index finger to silence her. "You need to get out of your marriage. Pam tried to persuade me so many times, even though we wouldn't have been able to be together until she retired. She wanted it for my sake, not hers. In the end she realised the boys were more important. I had to wait until they grew up. But you don't have kids. There's nothing tying you to your husband other than the hold he has over you, which is pretty rich, given he's responsible."

"I could have stopped it."

"You couldn't, and I don't want to hear you saying that again." She smiled at Jo. "Besides, you've done me a favour. You have no idea how wonderful it is to be able to talk about Pam freely; with Diana last night, and especially with you. I have never, ever been able to do it before."

"Any time," said Jo. "Honestly, any time. And I'd like you to meet my mum when we're back in the UK."

"Caroline? Oh, I'd love to." Her eyes were filling again and she tutted. "Look at me, silly old fool that I am."

"You don't seem silly to me."

"I was always a fool for Pam. The happiest fool in the world, when we were together. But seriously, Jo. You need to find a way to get the truth out there."

Jo nodded. "I'll think about it. And you can change your mind at any point, you know."

"I won't." Sophie stood and brushed down her skirt. "Now, I need to wash my face, and then I think I'll have a very large G&T before we eat. I don't suppose you fancy joining me?"

"I would absolutely love to. But just the tonic for me."

When Zina came out of the kitchen to collect the coffee cups after lunch, Karmela was at the table alone.

"Did you find Lambros?" she asked.

"Yes. I came to your room to tell you, but there was no answer."

Karmela's head dipped. "I had to see Iain." She looked up again. "How did it go?"

Zina sat down. "Not great. But at least we've agreed to talk tomorrow afternoon, which is progress."

"So would you have a little time today? I hate to ask when you have so much going on personally, but I think Jo could do with your professional help."

"Professional help?"

"Your media skills."

For the first time in days, Zina's spirits lifted. "Honestly? That would be great. And the timing's perfect. There's nothing more I can do about Lambros until I've heard him out."

"OK, well what I am going to tell you is confidential, but I know I can trust you."

"Go on."

"At the heart of it all is that Jo did not write *Only. Ever. You.*, but of course it is more complicated than that."

Zina rocked back. The last thing she needed was a scandal of these proportions casting a cloud over her first ever retreat. If this came out while Jo was still here, how would that look? It would be an absolute disaster. But then she realised what Karmela was asking; she would be in control of this, so she could make sure it wasn't. She had the skills. And more than anything, she wanted to help Jo as well.

She pulled her chair closer to Karmela's. "Tell me everything."

Zina's head was spinning with the enormity of the task when, half an hour later, she followed Karmela up the stairs to Jo's suite. The Sophie situation complicated matters considerably, but she was sure she could find a way around that as well. It was just the sort of challenge she loved. And exactly what she needed to take her mind off Lambros in the twenty-four-hour wait before their important conversation.

Karmela knocked on the door, walking straight in. "Jo! I am bringing the answer to our prayers. How did we forget that Zina used to work in marketing? And as it happens, she is a media relations expert. Just what we need. So I have explained everything to her, and she is sure she can help."

Jo spun around from her desk. "You can? That would be amazing, but—" Something about her seemed to deflate. "Honestly, I'm not sure what I should do, given Sophie's situation. She's adamant I come clean, bless her, but it's such a risk to her privacy, and her family haven't a clue about her and Pam. It's my actions that have caused this, so it's down to me to minimise any fallout."

"And that's exactly what we're going to do," Zina promised.

Karmela sat in the easy chair in the corner, leaving Zina to perch on the bed. "I am glad you used the words coming clean, because that is most important," she told Jo. "Totally clean. In my experience, whenever there's damage limitation to be done, it's important the whole truth is put out there. Yes, there will be an almighty fuss on social media whatever we do, but it will soon die down if no more scandals come out to keep the story going. People move on surprisingly quickly if there's nothing to see."

"But that's just it. I don't want Sophie dragged through the mud too. It isn't fair on her or her children."

"OK," the cogs that had been unused for so long started to clunk into life. "Rees doesn't know you know who Pam's lover was, does he?"

"No. Only the people around the table last night, and I would trust them all implicitly," said Jo.

"There's no need to mention her name, so we'll have to take the calculated risk that Rees doesn't think it's worth his while to try to find out."

"It's Sophie's risk," said Jo, "and I don't want—"

"Yes, but it is your future," said Karmela softly. "Your thoughtfulness about everyone else is fantastic – it is part of what makes you such a good tutor – but you do not have to take any responsibility that is not yours. Presumably Sophie knew what she was doing when she embarked on an affair."

"But not that the whole thing would be made into a book and a film," Jo snapped.

"Agreed. However, if Sophie thinks the truth needs to come

out then you need to respect that too. I know we can trust Zina to minimise the damage."

Karmela trusted her. As a professional, even after everything she'd told her this morning. Zina's heart sang as she looked from one to the other. Could both these women really be her friends, after all? Could she truly become part of the warmth that obviously flowed between them? The only reasons why not were in her own head and it was more than time to let them go. It was time to roll up her sleeves and give them her all.

"Damage limitation is not only a question of honesty, but of pulling out as many positives as possible. Some sort of public atonement, like a charitable donation, normally helps."

"I can do better than that," Jo replied. "Mum and I have already decided to give any future royalties to charity. That will infuriate Rees even more than Mum claiming them herself, but it can't be helped." She grinned. "And it'll serve him damn well right."

"It's hard to believe a husband would behave as Rees has done," Zina said. It was impossible to imagine Lambros … but then she'd never have expected the last week to pan out the way it had either. She sighed. "But I guess you never know."

"You don't," said Jo. "At first I actually liked Rees making all the decisions. I was such a wet weekend, and completely inexperienced when it came to dating. Then he was brilliantly supportive when I fell apart after Pam died. We were married before I truly realised what was happening. God, I was so naïve back then."

"That's another thing we can bring out. Try to spike his guns."

"What, that he is abusive?" Karmela's eyebrows all but disappeared under her fringe.

"No! No of course not," said Zina. "I meant how supportive he was when Pam died, how he saw to everything. Show how involved he was in what happened, so he can't shirk the responsibility – and so that people can draw their own conclusions. Especially if you pick a domestic abuse charity. But of course you would say, very sweetly, that it was because of Eloise in the book."

"My god, you are good at this," said Karmela, and Zina felt herself glow.

"Say? How will I say?" Jo sounded panicked.

"I'm not a hundred per cent sure yet, but I think the best way is to place an article with a serious newspaper in London. I worked there for a while but my contacts are a bit rusty, so I'll need to have a proper think. Then prime some influencers to be positive on social media. Perhaps your publisher's marketing department could help with that?"

Jo paled visibly. "Oh god. I'm going to have to tell them first, aren't I? And my agent, because of the foreign rights. Not to mention the film people. Thank goodness there are no copyright complications or I could find myself sued to hell as well."

Karmela leant forwards. "Your mum may have to make the rights over to you sooner rather than later. But if you are going to give all future royalties away, then Rees cannot get his hands on them anyway."

"Any idea which charity?" Zina asked. This was so exciting she couldn't wait to get started. She just knew she could make this right for lovely Jo, but it had to be done carefully and properly.

"Perhaps we should ask Sophie to choose?" said Jo, and the others nodded. "Fine. I'll go and fetch her."

As she ran down the stairs, Karmela turned to Zina. "This is a much bigger job than I ever envisaged. You must not let it steal your focus from putting things right with Lambros."

Zina thought for a moment. Undoubtedly it would. Or could, if she let it. The ultimate test of her priorities. She bit her lip, knowing there was only one possible answer she could give.

"I can't let that happen." She looked up, grinning at Karmela. "But hey, I'm a woman. I can multitask, you know."

Friday 22nd September

From behind the safety of her privacy glass, Karmela watched Iain and Sybil set off along the track towards the gully. Although the greyhound was trotting happily at the end of her lead, sniffing the air as she went, her master's head was down. She remembered his use of the word *sadly* yesterday. At the time she had thought it British politeness, but now it looked as though he had meant it.

Was Iain's dejected appearance down to her? Most of the group's energy had returned by the time they had met for the feedback session yesterday afternoon, and not for the first time, Iain had failed to bring anything to read. But neither had he added much to the critiques, which was out of character, and Karmela was sure Jo at least had noticed too.

Their conversation about Sarajevo had shaken her so much that it had most likely shaken him too. Yesterday had proved far too hectic to give it proper headspace, but now, in the quiet calm of the morning, she knew she had to try to unravel it. And she could, safe in the knowledge that Zina was helping Jo in a very practical way, with nothing she could add to the situation at this point.

What had shocked her most was the idea that anything from the war still had the power to hurt. She obviously had not dealt with it as effectively as she had thought. Were the ghosts not sufficiently exorcised by the visits she had paid to Nejla over the last year? But what could she do? Perhaps there always would be a scar. Perhaps erasing it completely was impossible. But recognising it, and learning to live alongside it, that should be achievable, and even the acknowledgement felt like a win.

As should Iain's reason for rejecting her – on one level at least. He was right; these particular circumstances were unlikely to occur again. It was not because of anything she had done. Or how she was. It was not because of the present, it was because of the past, and the fact he believed she would be unable to forgive him.

But who was he to make judgements like that on her behalf? She pondered the thought as she turned from the window to treat herself to a second espresso. It was a rare indulgence, but one which was sorely needed this morning. But perhaps … perhaps … Iain had put those judgements on her because he could not forgive himself.

She pictured herself as a child, looking up at bombers in the sky. Of course it had never happened like that because they had left Sarajevo far too soon for her to have seen them, but she could imagine it. She could imagine herself huddled with Nejla and Emina, gripped by fear as those terrible machines that brought death and destruction rumbled and whined overhead. But they were just machines. With men inside them.

Not even the men who gave the orders. Even further up the chain of command were the men who had decided that bombing her city was a good idea in the first place.

Damn it! Iain had just been a cog in the industrial-scale wheels of war. He could have said no and refused to bomb civilians, but someone else would have taken his place. And then she saw Sarajevo from above, a pilot's eye view. Perhaps it had all been too remote to think of the people at all. Until, years later, when one of them had been given a name.

God, this was some mess. Perhaps, deep inside, Iain was a mess too. She thought of her Dubrovnik neighbour, a teenager when he had fought in that very same war, and for whom it had never really ended. She understood that perfectly; knew it was part of who he was and that sometimes she could help him, and sometimes not. That was the deal and their friendship was worth it. But to have a closer relationship with someone the same? That would be so much harder to cope with. Two sets of scars; his and hers. And not remotely as cute as the sets of embroidered towels and pillowcases in the wedding gift shops in the big department stores.

Espresso cupped between her hands, Karmela began to pace the room. She did not know, she really did not. But she was still drawn to Iain; she still really liked him. And if she could accept what he had done, then the only barrier to them being together was inside his head.

So what was stopping her telling him so? That most basic of human fears: rejection. Back where she had bloody well started, and no further forward at all.

Sighing, Karmela picked up her notebook and pencil, flicking to Jo's wise words on dealing with the subject. As she did so, she remembered the dream she'd had the night she had first considered them; the dream in which her parents had filled the room in that tiny flat in Berlin, leaving no space for her. Squeezing her out. The dream ... the dream ... was not only about rejection, she could see that now, but about memories packed into dusty suitcases, the locks long rusted shut. Those suitcases contained memories which, even over the last year, her mind had refused to access.

Rejection. It had not only been at school, it had been at home as well. She allowed the thought to sink into her. It was not just the dream, it had been real. All too real. Her father hiding in the bottle, her mother in her work. No space for her in either of their lives.

The thought was new, but familiar as well, as though it had been hiding just around the corner of her mind, waiting to pounce. Or to be let in. The real reason, perhaps, that she had been so desperate to get her mother to talk about their shared past. It was not just to make Mama's life better, but to address her own unacknowledged need as well. To understand why she had mattered so little. Why she had not been loved.

Karmela closed her eyes and sat back on the sofa. Outside, the chatter of the birds in the trees celebrated the new day. She remembered walking to school in Berlin beneath linden trees packed with sparrows, her fear increasing with every step. What would they find to taunt her about today? Her mispronunciation of an unfamiliar German word? The button missing from her cardigan?

The worst thing had been the girl who hid her packed lunch. Every single day. Food was so scarce in their household that Karmela had been afraid to tell her parents. Instead, she had hoped against hope that her mother would have some kind of reaction when she said she did not want to take lunch to school anymore. But she had not even noticed. Most likely, she had already left for work and her father had shuffled to the supermarket for a cheap bottle of vodka.

The pain of it all was crawling back as she remembered. Her only shield had been the slow withdrawal of herself from everyone, including her parents, all the while hoping and praying they would notice. She remembered the cold realisation that they had not, and would not. She remembered the intense loneliness she had buried by working so hard on her lessons that by the time the war was over she was top in almost every subject. That was how she had discovered her love of history books, because of the joy in being transported from the present into a place and time where she could not be hurt.

But her past, her past ... it was not neatly dealt with at all. It was... How had she put it to herself while she was watching the ants? A work in progress. Something still festering that was affecting the present and stopping her getting what she now realised she wanted with all her heart.

Sranje! She had to persuade her mother to talk. Her mother was the only one left who shared her memories of the war; her own particular memories. Not mortars, bombs and sudden death, but the grinding bleakness of Berlin for a refugee family – if you could even call what they were a family.

Was that the reason her mother held her at arm's length, both physically and figuratively? Karmela had never seen it quite so clearly before, why their differences still played out in every interaction. The truth of what had happened in Berlin was impossible for Mama to face, because if she did so she would need to accept the harm she had done to her child.

It felt like too much to ask, so should Karmela accept the impasse? Would talking to Mama make things even worse? Could it be better to make peace with the fact her relationship with her mother would never be as good as the ones Jo and Zina had with theirs? Should she accept the comforting thought that her mother had shown she understood enough of her daughter to send her here and encouraged her to write? To follow a new dream?

Or should she, for both their sakes, try one more time to put the past to bed?

Five to three. Zina reluctantly closed her notebook and tucked it into her bag, along with her phone. She'd had a productive half hour in the retreat's dining room after lunch service, checking the current whereabouts of her London contacts and pulling the strands of Jo's story together. Now the time had come to turn her attention to her marriage, and she felt scarily unprepared. But as well as Karmela's advice, in the last twenty-four hours she had begun to realise something important from working with Jo.

Karmela may have talked about understanding the other person's point of view, but Jo had the knack of really feeling it – just look how she was with Sophie. Watching her, it had occurred to Zina what a powerful skill it was. Was it something that she could learn to do? This afternoon would be a very good time to at least try.

Jo's comment about how naïve she'd been when she was younger kept coming back to her as well. Zina had always considered herself streetwise, but that didn't mean she was aware of her flaws. Lying awake last night, she'd realised Mama was right; she did have a chronic need to be the centre of attention. Now she was wondering what else she didn't know about herself. Who did Lambros think she was. Had he not been talking to her because he'd come to hate her for faults she didn't even know she had?

God, that was frightening. What had Karmela said? Be open and honest with him and hope he will be the same with you. But his honesty could prove to be deeply uncomfortable. Or worse.

A chill ran through her. Whatever he said, she'd just have to take it. And resist the temptation to bite back.

As she rounded the corner of the retreat she could see that at least he'd turned up. He was leaning on the fence of the goat enclosure, the one they'd been mending together not so very long ago. Even that simple task had caused some niggles between them. How the hell were they ever going to mend their marriage? She stopped at the thought, forcing down the lump in her throat. They would get there. They had to. Whatever it took.

He didn't turn as she approached, so she joined him at the fence, leaning on it about a metre or so away.

"How did the pistachio harvest go?"

Lambros continued to stare straight ahead. "A good crop. Very little damage. Thank you." Formal. Cold.

"That's great news." Zina forced as much warmth into her voice as she could muster.

"You haven't asked me to come here to talk about pistachios, have you?"

"No, but I've missed hearing about the farm." She expected a smart comeback, something about her never paying attention before, but it didn't happen. After a moment she carried on, "I've missed *you*. We need to sort this out."

"I'm not sure I see the point. You think I'm a failure, that I'm unstable, that I can't stick at anything. Why would you want to stay married to me?" Clipped as his voice was, he couldn't hide the bitterness. Lambros was never bitter. Did he really believe she thought those awful things?

"That's not true!" Well, maybe the not-sticking-at-anything part, but the rest…

Now he did look at her, although his eyes were hidden beneath the brim of his sun hat. "Isn't it? It's what you said."

"I didn't!" She hadn't, had she? Had she? *Putana!* If she had in the heat of their argument, no wonder he was still angry. "When? What did I say?" She was within an iota of putting her hands on her hips, but that wouldn't help. The last thing they needed was another row, and she muttered an apology.

He kicked at the dirt beneath his feet. "Zina, you told me I was unstable. You actually used the word. Twice. But it's not just that; it's the way you behaved towards me, even before the row. It took me a while to see it for what it was, to understand."

"I'm not sure I do. Understand, that is. I came back to Santorini for you. I built up a new business to support you." She said it as gently as she could, despite being tempted to remind him of everything she'd given up. But this so wasn't the moment. She had never, ever, known him to be like this and it was frightening her. She had to suppress her instinct to fight back. Think *we* not *me*. *We* not *me*.

She started to rephrase her words, but he began speaking. "You set up the retreat to rub my nose in it, more like. To prove *you* were the success and *I* was the failure by making a stupid competition out of it all. And I won't live like that, Zina. Not anymore."

What was he saying? That they had no future? Zina's legs were trembling, her fingers gripping the fence. "I ... I just wanted to make it fun," she whispered. "Why didn't you tell me you felt that way?"

"Fun? You thought it was fun?" He looked at her sideways, eyes still hidden by that wretched hat. Then he shrugged. "I guess I never said anything because ... well, I don't really know. I didn't want it, but I didn't know how to stop it either. Perhaps we let a lot of resentments get out of hand."

We. Was that a good sign, or was she overthinking it? Keep it simple, simple. And honest.

"That's what Mama said. That this whole thing wasn't so much about Yiannis and his ATV, but about everything we'd allowed to build up. At first I didn't think ... I couldn't see ... what you had to be resentful about. But now I can. Especially how you've explained it. I'm just so sorry I made you feel that way. I didn't mean to."

Silence. A long one. "Thank you, Zina." That stiff formality again. How was she going to break through? Her instinct was to reach out and touch him, but despite the fact she could see every bead of sweat above his top lip he seemed too far away. Had the wall grown too high after all? Had she left it too late?

Was he going to keep pushing her away, again and again? The lump in her throat was real.

Skatá! Where was her backbone? They were speaking to each other, for the first time in over a week. That had to mean something. Perhaps there was some common ground as well. Just like Karmela had told her to look for.

"How about we talk about those resentments? Work out what we can do to stop them from building up again."

Lambros sighed. "Sensible as that sounds, I'm not totally sure it's a conversation I'm ready for right now. I feel ... I feel..." He stood up straighter. "How's the retreat going?"

"In all honesty? There's been a massive curve ball. It turns out Jo didn't write her bestseller after all."

"Really?"

Zina went on to explain a little of what had happened, while Lambros nodded, asking the occasional question. They were talking. Normal talking. A no-pressure conversation. No pressure was important to Lambros, she knew. Or rather she ought to have known. She'd been too frigging wrapped up in herself again, and it needed to stop. It had to stop. She had to channel her inner Jo, if she could find it. She certainly needed to up her game if she wanted to stay married. Make the biggest possible effort to put herself in Lambros's shoes.

A half-smile played around his lips as she finished talking. "That must be making you happy, being able to do your proper job again."

"It does. But not half as happy as standing here chatting to you."

He sighed and kicked at the dirt again, then looked at her sideways. "Me too. I've missed you as well, Zi. But I don't want to sweep our problems under the carpet or we'll just end up back where we started."

He wanted to try too. He wanted to try! Elation swept through her, but she kept it in check. "Then how about ... how about, every day we come here at three o'clock to talk everything through?"

"And the rest of the time?"

"Be nice to each other? And accept things aren't going to be normal between us straight away. Give each other space to adjust, because the conversations we need to have aren't going to be easy."

He nodded. "I do need time to think and to process that you want to try. I'd geared myself up... I was convinced you'd be asking for a divorce."

She grinned at him. "You must be joking. Have you ever known me give up without a fight?"

Slowly he shook his head. "I don't suppose I have. And this time I'm glad of it. Really I am."

At the end of such an intense week, it felt natural to Jo that the little group would drift apart for the evening. Susan and Ellen had in any case planned to have dinner with their newfound family, accompanied as always by Panora; Iain had said he was taking Sybil for a long walk on Kamari beach; and when Sophie claimed exhaustion, Diana decided to stay at The Retreat House too.

Jo was glad it was just the three of them in the taxi, heading for Zina's favourite winery, which apparently had a terrace overlooking the caldera where they could witness one of Santorini's famous sunsets. Working together this afternoon, Zina had really come into her own. It was hard to pinpoint exactly what had changed; it was almost as though she was being completely true to herself. Although it hadn't been exactly obvious before. It didn't matter; whatever it was, Jo could now see that Zina could become as good a friend as Karmela.

As soon as they arrived, Zina led them through the winery's museum and down a steep flight of steps, then across a tasting room that felt like a cave, and onto the terrace. Jo stopped in her tracks. A stunning view of the caldera unfolded in front of them, the colours of the cliffs exaggerated by the rays of the lowering sun. Every shade of orange and ochre through to rich gold glistened in the last of the light, and below them the sea was the deepest blue she had ever seen.

It was a breathtakingly perfect spot, with tables set out over three terraces on different levels, the winery itself built into the rock behind and below, a stark mixture of local black stone and white-painted walls which all but sparkled. Their vantage point was directly above the harbour, the cliffs around it like a giant pair of encircling arms protecting the quayside hundreds of feet below. Directly ahead were Fira and Firostefani, a muddle of white buildings climbing to the caldera's highest point, and in the distance across the water, Oia, for all the world like a thick layer of icing on top of a cake.

The manager escorted them to a front-row table protected by a large square umbrella. Within moments, three glasses of rosé appeared, along with a dish of olives, some bread and an oval plate of a yellow purée made from fava beans, which he explained were grown by his good friend Yiannis Nomikos, and were the best on the island.

"They won't be when Lambros manages to grow his," said Zina after he'd gone.

Karmela sat back, nursing her drink. "How did it go with him this afternoon?"

"Difficult. Especially at first. But we've made a start. Like you told me, Karmela, we've found some common ground. A starting point we agree on. So we've set aside time to meet every afternoon to talk things through."

Karmela reached across and hugged her. "Go you! I have a feeling that with your tenacity you will be fine."

"Yes, but I need to remind myself to see things from Lambros's point of view as well. Mama tore a strip off me for always wanting to be the centre of attention, but I wasn't ready to listen. Now I can see how right she was. I had a real lightbulb moment when you told me to think *we* not *me*. Not only that, but working with you, Jo, and seeing how empathic you are has really opened my eyes. So many big life lessons. I have so much to thank you both for. At almost thirty I really should know myself much better."

"It is not only you," said Karmela. "I am going through something similar. I thought by facing up to my past last year my life was sorted. Job done." She laughed. "But now I find it is no more than a work in progress."

Calm, competent Karmela, looking so uncertain. After all Karmela had done for her, Jo wanted to help if she could. "Work in progress?"

"Like dealing with rejection. I was so hurt by the girls in my school in Berlin I vowed I would never let that happen again. It was the biggest reason I shut myself off; if I had to be an outsider, it would be my choice. But when you open up to the positives of getting closer to people, there are downsides that come with it too, and rejection is definitely one of them. I'm forty-three and I have had so little practice."

"Is it submitting your manuscript you're worried about?" asked Jo.

Karmela shook her head. "In time I will be, but I am sure the tips you gave us will help. In fact, I am trying to use them in other areas of my life."

Jo frowned. "I'm not sure all of them translate."

"Me neither, but some are a good starting point, like working on the reasons you are being rejected. But perhaps ... perhaps that is where I have made a mistake which will probably affect the group and I am truly sorry."

Zina leant forwards. "Do you want to share?"

Karmela took a sip of her wine, the last rays of light catching the glass and making the liquid shimmer. Across the caldera, the sun was dropping beyond the islands that formed the fragmented far rim, a golden ball in a perfectly orange sky, the sea a greyish bronze below them. Finally she nodded.

"Three heads are better than one, and anyway, I cannot count the times I have almost talked about this with you both over our nightcaps. Almost, but not quite. It is Iain, you see. We were becoming fond of one another, but then he decided it was not what he wanted."

"I knew it," said Zina. "Just seeing you on your morning walks, it was obvious."

"It was?" Karmela looked surprised.

"The way you were together ... your body language, I guess. You just looked like a couple."

"What happened?" Jo asked.

"He gave me no explanation, but the more I thought about it, the more I wanted one. So yesterday I plucked up the courage to ask him. Actually, it was the advice I gave you, Zina. I realised I was not following it myself."

"So what did he say?" Zina sounded breathless, excited almost, to hear the rest of the story, while Jo, aware of her friend's pain, was uneasy about pushing her like this.

"I read a piece in class about growing up in Sarajevo and how one of my best friends was killed in the bombing near the end of the war. It turns out Iain was one of the pilots involved in those raids and he said he knew I would never forgive him. I was so shocked when he told me that I did not disagree."

"And was he right?" Jo asked as gently as she could.

Karmela shook her head. "I do not think so, but there is so much to unpack around this, and it is all very complicated. I need to talk to my mother about what happened during the war too, but that will not be easy either. The trouble is... Oh, I know I can be honest with you both... The problem was not only my classmates, it was Mama too. I need to understand why she behaved towards me as she did, but I am sure that is the last thing she wishes to discuss. I am not close to her, like you both are to your mothers. She will not let me be."

"Oh, Karmela," said Jo. "I am so sad for you. For you both, really."

Karmela shrugged. "I have tried to change things over this last year and although we have made some progress – she sent me here, after all – there is still no real closeness and I am at a loss about what to do next."

Zina reached across and gave Karmela a hug. "If you need to talk through what you might say to your mum, I'm here. I'm not bad with words and especially after all you've done for me, I'd love to be able to help."

"Thank you." Karmela sounded choked.

A hush descended on the terrace as the last rays of the sun disappeared behind the islands, the sky flooding with ochre, pinks and the deepest of purples. Jo held her breath. This was beauty in nature on an altogether epic scale and it made her feel so tiny, so insignificant. If that was the case, perhaps her problems were insignificant too.

The next week would no doubt be one of the toughest of her life, because if Zina's plans came to fruition then her story would come out. Sophie was prepared to take the risk on the basis her name would remain secret for as long as possible, and had agreed it was better done while they were all at the retreat. That way if anything went wrong, they could deal with it together, and at least they were remote from the eyes of the world.

And Jo would have her two new friends beside her. Friends she could absolutely rely on. Friends who had not judged her. Friends who were doing all they could to help. Karmela had said that three minds were better than one, but to Jo they were more like her mum and Pam's three-legged stool: stable and strong. They may be but three small people beneath this incredible sunset, but they were important to each other. Already the bonds felt real.

The ring of Zina's mobile split the silence, and apologising she rushed from the terrace. Jo glanced at Karmela, who was gazing out to sea.

"Aren't we small?" she whispered.

"That is exactly what I was thinking. It puts everything into perspective."

As the last orange-gold rays faded to a glow on the horizon, people around them began to gather their belongings to leave, but a waiter appeared with a bottle of wine that was almost pale orange in colour, and a wooden platter of cold meats and cheese. Zina arrived behind him, rubbing her hands.

"Great, I'm hungry and we certainly have something to celebrate. That call was from a journalist with *The Times* who is prepared to break the story, and they'd like to interview you by video call on Monday morning."

"Interview me?" She knew she shouldn't be so silly. She'd known this was going to happen, but now it was real it was absolutely terrifying. She closed her eyes briefly, Zina's hand snaking into hers.

"Don't worry. We'll prepare a crib sheet and I'll be sitting with you, just off camera, the whole time. You can do this, Jo."

Karmela took her other hand, nodding in the direction of the sunset. Small, insignificant beings. Small, insignificant problems. But a growing friendship that was anything but.

Jo took the deepest of breaths. "Thank you. Thank you both."

Sunday 24th September

It was almost ten o'clock on Sunday morning. Home or away, 10am was the time for Karmela to have coffee with her mother. In front of her on the low table was a decaf Americano and her phone was in her hand. Should she, or should she not, speak to her mother about rejection, and about Berlin? The stakes felt higher now than they had ever been.

But even if she decided to do it, what could she say? How to start this most difficult conversation? She had run it around her head so many times, but not a single decent answer had presented itself. Perhaps it would be better to wait until she was home? But was she only considering that because she was afraid of Mama rejecting her again? The bloody R word. Now she was aware of it, it was everywhere. At least she was having more practice at dealing with it.

The phone in her hand rang, making her jump. She swallowed hard.

"Good morning, Mama."

"Ah, Karmela. Have you had a productive week?"

This was always her mother's main concern, but as she was paying for Karmela to be here she had more than a vested interest. "I am a little behind on word count," she admitted, "but I still have a week to make it up."

"And the quality of the words? It isn't all about the numbers. What does your tutor think?"

"She is very happy with my work. She said it is almost of publication standard already."

"Now that is marvellous," said Mama, with what sounded remarkably like a happy sigh. "I am already looking forward to seeing my daughter's name in the window of the bookshops in town."

"Oh, Mama, it is so very far from a done deal. There is a whole submissions process to get through first, and no doubt rejections before the book is finally accepted." *Sranje!* This was it. This was her opening. If Karmela believed in cosmic intervention, this would surely count as a sign. It may have "proceed with caution" in flashing lights, but it was worth a try.

"I have realised I am not good at coping with rejection."

"Whyever not?" It was the question her mother had been almost guaranteed to ask – and in that brisk tone as well.

"Because I am not used to it. You know that after Berlin I shut myself off from people and things that could hurt me. But by avoiding rejection, I have not learnt to deal with it." Best to keep her mother's part out of the conversation; she would see how the land lay first.

Her mother tutted, and Karmela had a mental picture of her rolling her eyes. "You have a tendency to blame Berlin for everything."

"I am not blaming Berlin. It is the explanation." Karmela took a gulp of coffee. "I need to process it, Mama. To understand, so I can move forwards." Despite herself, she was afraid that how close she was to tears would show in her voice.

"You are blowing this out of all proportion. Very few refugees had a good war, Karmela, and I should know because I spent all my time helping them."

"But not helping me." She swallowed the words back down. Or helping her father. Mama had left them both in their own private hells, but had she acted that way so she could deal with, or avoid, her own? It was a new thought. An intriguing one.

"Sorry," she said. "I know it embarrasses you when I become emotional."

"Don't be so silly. Can't you talk to your tutor about this submission and rejection thing?"

"She's given us some notes."

"Well, there you are."

In for a penny, in for a pound. "But they do not work for every situation. Certainly not in my personal life, as I discovered this week."

"Would you like to tell me what happened?" Had her mother's voice softened just a little, or had she imagined it?

"There is a man here, Iain. I might have mentioned him."

"Yes. The one with the rather delightful-sounding dog."

"That is him. A few weeks ago he asked me on a date, then changed his mind. At the time I thought it was nothing, but I actually realised it was quite hurtful, and that is what made me start to think about rejection. I needed to know why, so I asked him."

"And?"

"He was in the English air force, part of the NATO operation that bombed Sarajevo. He thought I would not forgive him."

"Whyever not?"

"Emina. He might have killed Emina. And before you say anything, yes, it was a long time ago, and for me I am not sure how much it does matter, but it is clearly an issue for him, so it would come between us." Karmela sighed. "And that makes me sad."

"So you really do like him?"

"Yes. He is clever and funny, in that self-deprecating way some British men have, and he is kind as well. I believe he likes me too, especially now I know his reason for stepping back."

"You say he's an intelligent man? Well, of course he likes you. And I can see how a long-distance relationship might be suitable; you are used to living your own life day to day so you would find anything else too claustrophobic." There was a brief pause. "So, the question is, what are we to do about it? You say Emina is the problem?" Stripped back to its most basic elements, she supposed it was, so Karmela agreed. "Let me look in my diaries," her mother continued. "I am fairly sure I recorded her death. And the NATO operation did not kill many civilians, if I remember rightly. They used precision bombing to target the Serb military."

"I did not know you kept diaries."

"Only during the war. We were living through times of international significance and I wanted to make a record. But it will take me a while to find them. They're in a box in the garage somewhere, and I haven't seen them in years."

"If you could try, Mama, that would be wonderful."

"Leave it with me. I'm going out to lunch, but I will start afterwards. What are you doing today?"

"Writing. Then this evening we are all having supper at a taverna on the beach."

"Good. I hope your day is productive. And I will let you know what I find."

After her mother rang off, Karmela sat motionless on the sofa. Diaries. Her mother had kept war diaries. What Karmela would not give to read them. They could hold so many answers… But knowing Mama they would only contain the facts. Her mother's emotions were as locked away as her own had been. And probably always would be. Tears burnt in the back of her eyes again. Oh, she should be used to her mother by now. Used to her being so closed to her. At least she had offered to help in a practical way with the Emina question.

There was nothing more she could, or should expect. Karmela sniffed, walked to the bathroom and grabbed a hunk of toilet roll to wipe her eyes. She needed to let this go. She needed to do what everyone else seemed to: accept rejection and the pain it caused and carry on the best she could. Not try to resolve every little wrinkle. Zina knew she could never have everything she wanted in life so she was focusing on getting the most important part right. And Jo and Sophie were ploughing ahead with revealing the truth about *Only. Ever. You.*, despite the obvious risks. Maybe she, too, needed to accept imperfect solutions. And get on with her bloody book.

As she opened her laptop, Karmela was almost smiling to herself. Even if her relationship with Mama would never improve, she had plenty of friends around her. Friends she cared about, and who cared about her. Friends who accepted her as she truly was. Even with Jo in England and Zina in Greece, even though in some ways they hardly knew each other, she had a feeling they would continue to play important parts in each other's lives.

Perhaps Mama's coolness was not so important after all. It was time to move on, and if the thought did leave a hole in her heart, then so be it. One day she would learn how to heal that as well.

This time, Zina found herself looking forward to her hour with Lambros. The previous afternoon had felt so terribly awkward, especially at first, and had left her wrung-out as a wet rag. She had sensed at one point that Lambros had been close to tears, but most of the time he'd struggled to look at her, his eyes hidden by the brim of that damned sun hat.

He'd been telling her how, in part, he'd prolonged the distance between them because he'd had no idea how he'd cope with what she might say if they spoke. How he'd feared she'd either insist on a divorce, or that they returned to Athens, so he'd have to choose between his marriage and his mental health. How he'd needed to build up the strength to deal with it. Because their row, and what she'd said about him being unstable, had forced him to face the fact that he could never be the man she wanted him to be.

Of course she'd said that wasn't true, but he'd snapped at her, telling her not to lie. Then said gruffly it was her turn to get something off her chest. Which she had. Not about him, but about herself. How Mama had forced her to realise she was an attention junkie, and she was going to do everything she could not to be that way in future, but she would need his help.

Then, like Friday, after more than half an hour of leaning on the fence, he'd suddenly changed the subject, asking her about her night out with the girls. And she'd told him – including how she'd boasted his fava beans would be the best on the island. And he'd replied that he'd been thinking perhaps he might be better growing something else, like white aubergines; that maybe the conditions here weren't right for the beans. By the time the hour was up things had felt a little more normal between them, and they'd walked back to the farmhouse together for a quick drink with Mama on the terrace, before Zina had headed back to work.

Today was Sunday so they had all the time in the world, but would Lambros want it? Would she? The intensity of the conversations they needed to have was so draining. But at least they were having them.

Zina had spent the last hour or so briefing Jo on her interview tomorrow, and when she came down the stairs from her suite, Lambros was waiting for her in the courtyard, cool bag across his shoulder and a picnic rug folded neatly on top of it.

"I thought you might need some refreshment," he said.

She grinned at him. "Great idea."

He smiled back a little shyly, reminding her of when they had first been dating. "And a walk? Maybe a little walk to find a shady spot?"

Zina's heart flipped. His whole demeanour was completely different to the last two days. Maybe the potential to have longer than an hour would take the pressure off. She needed to keep reminding herself how important that was for Lambros. To break up the heavier parts of their conversations with lighter stuff.

"Do you have any plans for later on?" she asked him. "I mean, do you need to rush off anywhere?"

"No. And I'm hoping you don't either. Yesterday was tough and I want today to be more relaxed."

"I have all the time in the world. Look." With a dramatic flourish she took her phone from the pocket of her denim skirt and switched it off.

Lambros nodded. "Good call." Then did the same.

They set off through the vines, the gnarled trunks trained in circles low to the ground in the traditional *kouloúra* manner, leaves drying reddish brown against the dusty grey earth.

"The money came in for the grapes," said Lambros. "And a good price too. Did you see?" She nodded. "These old vines delivered, but there will never be enough to make our own wine."

"I think, perhaps, that we can't make everything. At least not at once. Are you still planning to start your own label with the pistachios?"

They chatted about the farm as they walked across to the dry gully, then up the slope on the other side and between the ragged rows of olive trees. At the top of the rise the sea came into view, sparkling in the afternoon sun. Zina all but gasped; it was so very beautiful – humbling in fact – and she normally took it completely for granted. Had Jo and Karmela talking about how the sunset made them feel small made her notice nature more? Or was it, could it be, to do with being in the here and now with Lambros?

He stopped next to an olive with a thick, knotted trunk, its branches casting an almost perfect circle of shade as the silvery leaves whispered in the breeze. "How about here?"

"It's perfect. It's so easy to forget what a beautiful place this is."

Lambros looked up from spreading the rug. "Too easy to forget everything that's important and get too caught up in the daily grind. We need to promise ourselves not to do that, I think."

Zina sat down next to him. "To make time for us."

She watched as he took off his sun hat, then opened the cool bag and extracted a bottle of her favourite wine. Not local, but a sauvignon blanc from Macedonia she'd discovered in Athens. Oh my god, how thoughtful. How hard he was trying.

He paused, corkscrew in hand. "We talked yesterday about the resentments that built up between us, and afterwards I started to think about how that had happened. Before we'd have a blazing row and be done with it. Everything out in the open. But I think, when I became ill, I didn't have the mental energy and you backed off. Am I right?"

Zina considered his words. "Not consciously, but I suppose I did. Was that wrong?"

"It was kind, beyond kind, like everything you did. I know what you gave up, Zi. And you were right yesterday that I should have been more conscious of how hard it was for you instead of just thinking about myself. I got wrapped up in my recovery, in my own head…"

"Maybe we both got too wrapped up in ourselves and we need to be really aware of that going forwards. But things haven't only changed because of what happened to you; a large part is because we're living with my mother and that's meant we have to keep things in, and it's hard to find the right time to discuss them when we're alone."

Lambros handed her a glass of wine. One of her mama's best glasses, she noticed. If Mama knew she'd have a fit. "And the last thing I wanted was to turn our bedroom into a battleground. Which is really ironic."

"I think that was probably down to me."

It made such a difference seeing his eyes, seeing that slow, easy smile. Reaching across the rug she took his free hand, praying he wouldn't pull away. Instead he folded his fingers over hers, and gave her a squeeze. Just that one touch lit a flame in her very depths. But surely it was too soon? They weren't even sharing a bed, and there was so much more they needed to talk about. She mustn't be impatient. She needed to be in tune with what Lambros wanted too.

They sat in silence, a healing silence, until Lambros sighed.

"This is bliss."

"We have to make more time for us."

"Zi?"

"Yes?"

"You said just now about going forwards. I'd really like to begin to talk about that future. I know it sounds a bit silly, but I need to know what it might look like so I can believe in it."

She looked up at him. "I need to believe in it too. I was so scared when I thought we might not have one."

"Then we agree. But before we start there's one thing I need to make clear. I'm stronger than you think, Zi. Stronger than I thought I was. All the time this has been going on I was waiting to tip back into that dark place again, but it didn't happen. Normal stress, normal anxiety, but not that. So please don't treat me like I'm weak or walk on eggshells around me. Once we're back on an even keel, I think it's healthier for both of us that we row. I'm strong enough to take it."

"Oh, Lambros." Tears filled her eyes. "I don't need a superman." But what did *he* need? "What I mean is, it's wonderful that you're truly better and it's everything I hoped for when we came here. That you would be comfortable in your own skin again and believe in yourself." She looked down and took a sip of her wine. "And the way you've thrown yourself into the farm, how much you've had to learn... How patient and kind you are with Mama. I haven't even told you how proud I am of you for all that. It's one of many things I need to put right."

"*We* need to. It's not all about you, Zina." He winked, squeezing her hand tighter and she thought her heart would burst. There was so much to put right, but as long as they both kept making an effort it would be OK. Better than OK.

"So," Lambros said, "going forward, we need rules."

"Space and time for each other."

He nodded. "Talk about our frustrations."

"No more little contests between us." She glanced sideways at him, "Mind you, I may have to take up basketball again to satisfy my competitive streak."

"As long as it means I don't have to split every sodding invoice between the farm and the retreat. It does my head in."

"One business, two halves."

"And one goal," said Lambros.

"What's that?"

"A home of our own. However long it takes."

"God, yes. I mean … was The Retreat House a mistake, do you think?"

"No. Just look at what you've created. It's a masterpiece; every little detail perfect. I'm every bit as proud of you as you say you are of me."

"You are?"

"Of course I am. And you could look at it as a trial run for designing our own home."

"A home where we can do what we want, when we want. Including arguing. And making up."

Slowly he began to run his thumb up and down her index finger as he held her hand. His touch was electric and she wanted more. So much more. But what did Lambros want? Her eyes met his and his pupils were huge and loaded with passion.

He put down his wine and with his free hand touched her cheek. His Adam's apple bobbed as he spoke. "May I … kiss you?"

Yes, oh yes! She leant into him, nuzzling his cheek, the roughness of his afternoon stubble sending thrills through her skin. After a moment she tilted her head and found his mouth, his kiss every bit as hungry as hers.

Eventually their lips parted, and he took her wine glass gently from her hand, tipping her back onto the rug, her body tingling from head to toe as he leant over to kiss her again, his hand resting on her thigh where her skirt had ridden up. She closed her eyes, wrapping her arms around his shoulders. Like every argument they'd ever had, the making-up would be glorious.

Tuesday 26th September

Half past five. No sense now in even pretending to sleep. The sun wouldn't be up for another hour, but Jo padded into her lounge and opened the window looking out over the pistachio orchard. Pinpricks of stars pierced the blackness above the hillside, and somewhere a lone bird called, *chu-kaar, chu-kaar,* then silence. Soon the day would begin; a day like no other in her life.

She thought back to her wedding day; one which should have been similarly momentous, but somehow hadn't been. She'd been too sick with nerves at the vast number of guests, the reception at The Savoy – Rees's choice of course, where else? If it had been up to her they'd have run away to a tropical beach somewhere. If it had been up to her, would they have married at all?

Impossible to tell. When had any choice been truly hers as far as Rees was concerned? Talking to Sophie, whose experiences were so similar, she'd begun to understand that his behaviour had been predatory right from the start. What was hard to accept was that she'd been too naïve to even half realise it. Maybe if Pam hadn't died, it would have been different. So much would have been. But by far her biggest regret was that Pam and Sophie never had their chance to be together. Just a few more years and they could have had the life they'd always dreamt of.

Today was not a day to look backwards, or deal in what-ifs. Jo knew that. Today, at least, Pam would be recognised as the literary genius she'd been. It would have been pointless to try to hide who the real author of *Only. Ever. You.* was because Rees knew; only Sophie's identity would remain a secret for as long as possible. Hopefully permanently. And Mum, and Sophie, who had known Pam better than anyone, had convinced Jo she was doing the right thing. No way would Pam have wanted Jo's life to continue as it was.

The story would have gone up in the online edition of *The Times* at midnight, and given the time difference, about now bundles of newspapers would be making their way to corner shops, supermarkets and railway stations up and down the UK. Jo had decided she would read it. She had to. Just not yet. Let the secret sleep on for a little longer. It felt strange, having lived with it for so many years. Being without it was like having the shield she'd held against the world ripped away. But she wasn't alone. Zina and Karmela would get her through today, if anyone could.

Reluctantly dragging herself away from the window, Jo headed for the bathroom, stripped off her pyjamas and turned on the shower. Hot, then cold, to chase away the last shadows of the night. But as she carefully applied her make-up no trace of exhaustion remained. Nor had the panic – the thing she feared more than anything – made an appearance. With every minute that passed she was feeling just a little stronger.

A light shone from the kitchen, so she hurried down the stairs and crossed the courtyard. Inside, Zina was smoothing a fresh white cloth over the buffet table.

"Have you seen it?" she asked Jo.

"Not yet. I didn't want to read it alone. Is that a bit crazy?"

Zina hugged her. "Not in the least. But my contact's done us proud. Come into the kitchen and I'll make you a pot of tea."

Jo followed Zina into the long, narrow space. Pots and pans were neatly stacked on shelves down one side and an enormous American-style fridge all but filled the end of one wall. A fan whirred overhead, dissipating at least some of the heat from the oven which emitted the sweet aroma of pastries warming.

A small table stood in an alcove, with a wooden chair on either side, where Zina indicated Jo should sit. "It's not a large space, and I won't trip over you if you're there." She filled the kettle, set it to boil, then opened her phone, shoving it into Jo's hand. "Read."

How strange to see yourself through someone else's eyes. The article began with a physical description of Jo as she'd sat on the sofa for the video call, and named the retreat. She looked up at Zina.

"They've said where I am. Is that a good thing?"

Zina nodded. "It gets the name out there, if nothing else."

Jo carried on reading. Everything was much as she'd said – as Zina had planned. How she'd been unable to resist reading the manuscript she found, how she'd shown it to her boyfriend, who had in turn shown it to a friend in publishing. How fast things had moved. Her regret that she hadn't stopped it. Her plans for any future royalties.

And a final paragraph, one which was the journalist's opinion alone. That whatever the rights and wrongs of what Jessica Rose had done, literature would have been all the poorer if the manuscript had died along with its author. Was that really true? Susan had said something similar, she thought, but her words had become lost in the dreadful misery of that night. Maybe she hadn't been completely wrong to let *Only. Ever. You.* be published after all.

Zina set the teapot and a mug in front of Jo, and she angled the phone towards her. "Do you think that's true?"

"Of course it is," said Zina. "Think of the pleasure the story's given so many people."

"You know what? That alone makes it so much easier to face today."

Zina leant down and hugged her again. Her warmth made it easier too.

It was clear over breakfast that everyone in the group had read the article, and their support wrapped around Jo like a protective blanket. Although they didn't know it, it was something she needed pretty badly for the call she knew she had to make before the morning session.

Back in her room she sat at her desk, phone in hand. It would be quarter to seven in the UK, but Rees would most likely be awake. On the other hand he never ever picked up her calls. It was part of underlining who was in control, Jo now realised. But that was about to end. Although the thought made her even shakier, right now his habit of ignoring her would most likely play to her advantage.

Even so, she was relieved when her call went to voicemail.

"Oh, hi Rees. I was really hoping to speak to you, but I suppose this will have to do. I've come clean about who really wrote *Only. Ever. You.* I've done an interview for *The Times* and it's been published today. Anyway, thought you should know. I'm expecting some social media flak so I'm turning off my phone until it blows itself out." Like hell, she was. But two could play at ignoring calls.

As usual, she left her mobile in her bedside drawer before crossing the landing to the studio. Karmela and Susan were both already there, scribbling away on this morning's prompt: regeneration. Jo could barely believe they had only four more days of the writing retreat left. She'd come to love everything about it: the sharing of her knowledge, the mentoring, the coaxing the best out of everyone, but more than anything, the camaraderie. Life at home would be so very empty.

Home. Curtis. She owed him, at least, an explanation. It was a pretty sad state of affairs that he was the only one, but maybe that could change too. She dashed back to her room and messaged him a link to the article, saying she was sorry if she'd let him down. No missed call from Rees. Maybe he was still in bed. With his girlfriend. She wondered if a boorish middle-aged man with a paunch would be so attractive when his most lucrative source of income dried up.

When she returned to the studio everyone was there, even Iain, stoically plodding away on his keyboard. He was the one member of the group Jo was worried about, especially since Karmela's confession on Friday. Although he was outwardly cheerful, something about his demeanour made her think that the lights had gone out inside and she guessed it had little to do with his struggles with his writing. Once the stress of today was over, was there anything she could do to help? He'd been so very solid in his support of her.

She glanced at the clock on the wall.

"OK everyone, pens down." She smiled at them from her position by the whiteboard. "It's barely believable that we only have a few days to go, so it's high time we tackled the issue of endings. Now, what do you think makes the end of a good book satisfying?"

And with that, Jo's day felt blessedly normal.

It was almost eleven by the time she returned to her room, to find Zina in the last throes of cleaning it.

"I didn't expect you to be doing that today as well," she said.

"Oh, don't worry. I'm keeping my eye on social media and I'm pleased to report it's a very small shitstorm so far, but my guess is there'll be another when the States wakes up. Your not having any profiles is definitely helping. If there's nobody for the trolls to tag with their vitriol they soon move on. It is trending though. Quite a clever hashtag, and I almost wish I'd thought of it: OnlyNeverYours."

Despite herself, Jo burst out laughing. "Oh my goodness, that's so clever. Anything else?"

"Well your phone's been going nuts in your drawer, but I

guess that's to be expected." Zina gave Jo's pillows a final smooth, then straightened.

"Will you stay while I check my messages? There might be something I need your input on."

"Sure."

For once, Jo's lock screen was rammed, so she had to look at her notifications separately. Seven missed calls from Rees, but no voicemail. She'd have to pick up eventually, but she'd let him stew for a while longer. Then a reply from Curtis and a message from her mum, which she'd deal with in a moment. The last was from her agent, so she clicked on it.

She turned to Zina. "*The Bookseller* wants a quote, and a couple of the tabloids have been sniffing around too."

"*The Bookseller* is trade press, right? So we'd best give them something. Do you want to forward the message to me? I'd like to take a look at what the others have said so far, if anything, but I'm minded to just send them the statement we prepared."

"You're happy to handle it?"

Zina grinned at her. "It's my job."

Once Zina had gone, Jo took a carton of peach juice from the fridge and poured herself a glass.

Mum first, or Curtis?

She was a little nervous about what he might have said, but once she'd dealt with it she could relax and chat to her mother. A little nervous? Ha! She'd expected to be an emotional mess today, an out-of-control juggernaut slamming into her with full force, but no, the strange calm of the early morning remained with her. Hopefully it would last a little longer at least.

Tentatively she opened Curtis's message, to be greeted by a

photo of the wild cyclamen they'd planted around the apple tree last year, which was just coming into flower.

Thought you might need a pick me up. Interesting choice of charity. I've been wondering for a while. But now I'm concerned you might not feel safe when you come home.

Bless him; it was so typical of his kindly nature. And perceptive too.

Don't worry, my parents are coming to stay until the worst is over. And thank you for understanding.

If you want me to change the locks, just ask. Anything. Just ask. You need your friends at a time like this.

And he was a friend. A good one. She realised how much she was looking forward to seeing him.

I'm hoping Rees will go quietly.

Divorce is never easy. Take it from me.

She hadn't known he was divorced. He talked about his teenage children a lot, but come to think of it, never a wife. Just went to show, sometimes you needed to listen to what wasn't being said as well.

Thank you, Curtis. I'll see you on Monday. Bring you some baklavá.

As she put down the phone, it rang. Rees. *Get it over with, or not?*

Her finger hovered over the little green icon. No, she'd do this when *she* was ready. *Her* timetable. She would call him. Later. Right now, she was going to settle down for a lovely chat with Mum.

Lunch had taken rather longer than usual, and the wine had flowed a little more freely. Jo, however, had restricted herself to a single glass. She definitely needed her wits about her, even with Zina taking the strain of the media enquiries and seemingly having the time of her life.

It was keeping her busy though, and Panora had been their waitress, telling them all proudly that her daughter's skills were better used elsewhere today. Now, with the table cleared, Zina did appear, joining Karmela and Jo who were lingering over coffee in the courtyard.

"How is it all going?" Karmela asked.

"So far, so good. Obviously with the US waking up there's a bit of fuss on social media, but nothing I didn't expect. A few more interview requests too, but we can go through those later. More importantly, have you spoken to Rees?"

Jo shook her head. "I suppose it is time I bit the bullet. I was waiting until his missed calls got into double figures and they did about half an hour ago." She looked from one of them to the other. "I know it sounds silly, but can you stick around while I phone him? I'll just feel a bit stronger if I have some moral support."

"It is what we do," Karmela grinned, while Zina reached across the table and patted her hand.

There was no backing out now. She'd made the commitment. And then she realised the three of them being together was what she'd been waiting for all along. Learning to stand up to Rees was not going to be easy, however much she wanted to. The habits forged by their years together would die pretty hard.

Jo took a gulp of water. "Then here we go."

It only rang twice before Rees picked up. "What the fuck are you playing at?"

Jo moved the phone a little further from her ear. "Sorry, I didn't quite catch that." Where had that come from? It was almost a clever comeback. Zina put her hand over her mouth to stifle a giggle, and Jo felt her courage grow.

"Of course you did, you brainless cow! What possessed you? You'll never be published again! Your reputation's in tatters. Have you seen the social media?"

"My PR's dealing with all that for me. I'm a little busy teaching."

"So someone's put you up to this, have they? Some money-grubbing little publicist on the make. Not that there'll be any money, not now. You're absolutely mad, Jo. Off your rocker. If you were here, I'd have you fucking sectioned."

Jo took a deep breath. Karmela squeezed her hand.

"Thank you," Jo mouthed, then cleared her throat. "The money won't be a problem, Rees, not once we've sold the house."

"I am certainly not selling that house. What are you thinking?"

"Then you can buy me out as part of the divorce settlement."

"Divorce!" he roared down the phone, making Jo wince. "You can't divorce me."

"Why not? I've plenty of grounds: infidelity, mental cruelty…" On the other side of the table, Zina punched the air.

"You'll never survive without me."

"Actually, Rees, all I've been doing since I married you is surviving, and now I want to live."

"Who is he? That guy with the dog and the dodgy haircut?"

"Grow up, Rees. Why does there have to be anyone?" She was shaking badly now. She'd taken enough. Even with Karmela and Zina beside her, her strength was in tatters. She had to finish the call.

OK, Jo, one last push.

"Message me your lawyer's contact details and we can get the ball rolling."

Jo pressed the end call button, then collapsed onto the table, choking with noisy sobs as the juggernaut of emotion she'd been holding at arm's length all day smashed into her. It was done. It was done, and nothing would ever be the same again.

Zina moved to one side of her, Karmela already on the other, wrapping their arms around her in a protective bubble.

"That was one of the bravest things I have ever heard," said Karmela. "Well done, Jo. We are proud of you."

Jo wept even more.

Wednesday 27th September

After the previous day, and aware she had only a few days of the retreat left, Karmela was determined to complete as much of her novel as possible. She was at an exciting part too, when the women's plans to rescue Agnez the reluctant nun were coming together, their friendship binding them closer with every twist and turn.

It was beyond satisfying, bringing these historical characters to life, although of course she knew nothing of their real personalities. She had made plans for them all before she had started writing, but now she was amazed how they had changed and grown as the story progressed and how much richer they had become on the page. And she especially loved how they surprised her.

Losing herself in their world took some of the dread out of the end of the retreat. Not only would her life go back to normal, but she would miss the others terribly, and she really hoped they would keep in touch in the way she did with her friends in Dubrovnik. But those friends were only an hour's flight away; this group would be scattered all over the world.

And then, of course, there was Iain. An opportunity wasted. She had heard nothing from her mother. It would be unlike Mama to forget, but those diaries must be taking some finding. Time was running out. Probably had run out for any sort of romance. But at least if Mama was right, Karmela might just be able to put his mind at rest about Emina before they parted.

If not exactly on cue, almost an hour later a message flashed on Karmela's screen. It was unlike her mother not to just phone, but here she was asking if it was a good time to talk. Karmela finished the sentence she was writing, saved her document, then called her mother.

"Karmela." No preamble. Her voice sounded strained, her words tumbling over each other in a way they never did. "It's taken me a while. Not to find the diaries, but to read them. It had been so long. And there are things I need to say. But first, what you asked. Emina was not killed in the NATO bombings, but a few days before when Markale market was shelled by the Serbs. Operation Deliberate Force finally put an end to the conflict, so your pilot should be proud."

"He is not *my* pilot."

"But perhaps now... Anyway. There is something else I need to say. Which is that I am sorry."

"Sorry?" This was the last thing Karmela had been expecting. Sorry for what? For not getting back to her for a few days? For—

"Sorry for ... the way I was in Berlin. I had forgotten.

Deliberately perhaps. But when I read my diary for 1995 I realised there was hardly any mention of you at all."

"You were never there." Karmela's heart was jumping in her chest. This longed-for conversation, the one she had reconciled herself to never happening. And now they were having it, with no warning at all. This might be the one and only time her mother spoke of Berlin, and she found herself unprepared.

"I know," said Mama quietly. "But in truth I was shocked. So I looked back over the years. When we first arrived it was all about you: finding a school, finding a tutor to help with your German who would not charge too much, finding an apartment where you could have your own room to study. How worried about you I was because you had changed so much without your friends.

"For weeks your father and I wondered if we had done the right thing, but as the situation in Sarajevo worsened we knew that we had. And other refugees came flooding in and I was asked to help them, and the diaries became more and more about my work.

"Mama, I—" The tears running down her cheeks left salt on her lips, her throat almost too full to speak.

"No, let me finish. This is hard enough without interruptions. I thought you were settled and had made new friends. And your father … his drinking… I closed my eyes to that too. Closed my eyes and lost myself in my work. Because there I could help people, and I could not help him. He would not be helped. And instead of being a proper mother, I turned my back on you both. You may be prepared to forgive your pilot, Karmela, but I do not know how you will ever forgive me."

Oh god, oh my god. Poor Mama. Karmela stifled a sob. "There is no need for forgiveness. War damages each of us differently, and we all find our own way of coping. That is something I learnt, and part of what I have been trying to tell you, but never mind. The important thing is to recognise it, then you can move on."

There was silence on the other end of the phone, then a sigh. "I am too old to move on, as you put it, Karmela."

"No, Mama, you are never too old. We can do this together."

"As you have been nagging me to do for the last year."

"Something like that." Karmela found herself smiling.

"You never give up, do you?"

This was it. Time for the big one. If ever there was a moment to say it, it was now. "Because I love you, Mama."

What did she expect in response? Nothing. For her poor, damaged mother to use the word right now would be a step too far. And yet, for the first time since she was a child, Karmela did feel loved. Mama may not be able to say it, but she had shown it – in sending Karmela here, in reading her diaries to find out about Emina, and more than anything, in talking about the war.

Her mother cleared her throat. "Thank you, Karmela. Now go and find your pilot and tell him the good news."

"Mama, before you go, will you be willing to talk about this some more when I get home?"

Another sigh. "I thought you would say that. And truthfully, I do not know. I need to get used to the idea, but if it will help you ... what you said about rejection ... then I owe you at least that. I will not reject you again, my daughter."

With a soft click her mother put down the phone. Karmela flopped back on the sofa. Had that conversation really happened? She ran through it in her head, remembering and cherishing every word. Her guess that her mother had been avoiding her own pain through her work had been right, and now she realised perhaps, despite what she had said, something might change. Even if it did not, there was a new understanding between them, a new closeness. A tear trickled down Karmela's cheek. If they never spoke of Berlin again, today had been enough.

Now she had her part of the bargain to fulfil. She had to finish her book. Then maybe, just maybe, her next one would be about mothers and daughters. Perhaps the most precious relationship of all.

It was just after three when Zina jogged down the track from The Retreat House to find Lambros leaning on the fence.

"Sorry I'm late."

He kissed her on the nose. "No worries, I've being doing a bit of goat meditation. Just look at them – half a dozen pallets and they're happy as anything."

"Getting their mental stimulation?" she teased.

He winced. "Don't go there, Zi. I can't believe I was so crass ... but I think I might have found a way to make up for it."

She snuggled closer to him, and he wrapped a strong arm

around her shoulder. "I like the sound of that." She ran her fingers under his shirt.

"*Kyría* Sideris! You have a one-track mind. And this is a serious idea."

"Then tell me."

"What you're doing now for Jo. It's going really well, isn't it?"

"Yes. She's been a joy to work with on a project like this; she's so honest and open. Only one of the British newspapers was nasty. They made a comment about her hiding away in Greece for the announcement, but I was able to counter that by giving an exclusive on the retreat she's been running to one of their rivals."

He pulled away. "You're positively glowing."

"It's been great. I'll be sorry when it's over."

"But that's my point. It doesn't have to be, does it? You being on Santorini has proved absolutely no barrier to you doing the job you love. You can do it from anywhere."

"The clients, though. They like to meet you. And you need to be seen to have contacts."

"For ongoing work, I get that. But for one-off projects, crisis management, freelancing for other agencies… Come on, Zi. Surely it's worth a try?"

He was right. He had to be right. And he'd thought of it before she had, damn the man. But no, no … bless the man. Bless her husband for seeing what she could not. A way of making her life here so much better. It would never be the bright lights and social whirl of Athens, but perhaps Athens wasn't the issue after all. She gripped his hand.

"There are ... possibilities." And challenges. Challenges galore.

"Of course there are. And if it makes you happy, that's all that matters." He looked serious for a moment. "But I also know you can't work any more hours. It's just not possible. So how about we employ someone to do the cleaning. It's not exactly your favourite job, is it?"

"But how could we afford to?"

"Easily, I would guess, once you start earning. I imagine you could charge quite a high hourly rate. In the meantime though, while you build it up, maybe we could get someone in part-time. I've worked it out; the money we earnt for the grapes would cover a couple of mornings a week between now and Christmas, and I could always do some labouring work when construction gets going again at the end of the season."

"But what about your projects, Lambros? What about the dairy for the goats?"

He screwed up his face. "They don't have to have kids next spring. I'm not sure they're ready for motherhood anyway – they're idiots."

"They're goats."

They watched as three of them tried to climb on a particularly rocky pallet at the same time, before the small nanny with the white face head-butted one of the others off. Zina leant into Lambros again, the late summer sun warming their backs, her mind buzzing with possibilities. To have this, *and* to have all the excitement and promise of her career. Sure, there'd be obstacles to overcome, and more compromises, but they could make it happen. They really could.

She'd just have to ensure that not all the compromises were

Lambros's; that however busy she became, she still made their time together a priority. *We* not *me*. She would be forever thankful to Karmela for telling her that. Not only in terms of her marriage, but it would make the growing friendship between herself, Karmela and Jo so much more enduring and rewarding too. Friends for all time, instead of just for a good time, as her friends in Athens had sadly proved to be. But perhaps she'd been too wrapped up in herself to be more than a good-time friend too.

Well, not anymore.

The scrabble of Sybil's paws on the stairs heralded Iain's arrival for his last one-to-one, and still Jo was unsure whether she'd be brave enough to put her plan into action. She'd done quite a lot of brave things recently, so there was no reason she couldn't, but whether she should was another question entirely. How far should the boundaries of being a writing mentor stretch? On the other hand, how far would she go for a friend? She had taken so much from Karmela and now it was definitely time to give.

"Hi, Jo. Am I late?"

She checked the time on her phone, although she didn't need to. "Two minutes to, as ever. Honestly, Iain, I can set my clock by you."

"I'm nothing if not predictable." But the laugh in his voice sounded forced.

"Sit down, anyway."

Once in the room, Sybil greeted Jo by nudging her nose

against her legs, then stretched across the rug close to Iain's feet. Even she seemed subdued, but dogs were percipient creatures. This one more than most.

"I'm sorry I've been a disappointment on this retreat, Jo. You've brought everyone else on so much, but I haven't exactly been a credit to your teaching. Far from it."

"Unlike the others, you came here not knowing if writing was for you."

"At least I've answered one question."

"Well, I don't think you're ever going to want to finish your novel, but this Greek mythology sketch you gave me to look at ... it's really very clever and laugh-out-loud funny."

For the first time he looked up, meeting her eyes with his startling green ones. "It is?"

"The way you've made Apollo sound somewhere between a naughty schoolboy and some sort of seedy sex symbol. Where did you get the idea?"

"I picked up a mythology book when I went to Kamari to walk Sybil and it inspired me. He came over as so up himself I wondered if I could take him down a peg or two. I know it's not the most polished..."

"I don't think it needs to be. Not all creative fiction does. If you take nothing else from the retreat it's that you have a real knack for comic pieces, so please don't give up writing them."

Iain nodded. "Thank you. But how anyone fathoms stories straight from their heads, then writes it all down in a way that makes you forget yourself, is beyond me. When I listen to the others read during the feedback sessions, I'm in awe."

"I don't think the way you perceive your writing prowess is the only reason you've been unhappy recently though, is it?"

He almost jumped in his seat. "Unhappy?"

"Don't get me wrong, you've hidden it well. You've joined in with everything and still told your funny stories when the conversation flags at dinner, but your spark's been lacking, Iain, and if I'm not being too personal here, it worries me."

He bent down and fondled Sybil's ears. "In part it's … I don't know … everyone's beginning to talk about going back to their lives. Ellen has an exhibition to set up for November, Diana can't wait to see her grandchildren, Karmela has her lecturing. And I have no clue at all about what I'm going to do. I hoped that while I was here I'd work something out."

It would be no consolation to him that Jo was equally lost, so she held her counsel. But he hadn't mentioned Karmela. Well, only in passing. But what had she expected? If he was nursing what he believed to be an unrequited passion for her, then he probably wouldn't come right out and say it. What man would? She'd been a fool to think she could get him to open up to her. And she needed to reply to what he'd said.

"Is there any rush?"

"There's no urgency as such, but I will need to start earning again early next year. A former fellow officer has a flight simulation business he's looking to expand and he's asked if I'm interested, but I'm really not. I'd rather do something completely different. But the problem is I won't have the necessary skills or experience. Whatever they may turn out to be."

"I couldn't help noticing that you enjoyed working with Lambros on the farm. Or was that just to escape from having to write anything?"

This time his laugh sounded more genuine. "At first, for

sure. But I really loved it. Even to the point of wondering whether I could afford to buy a smallholding, but looking at the economics it would have to be somewhere fairly remote and I'm not sure I'd be that comfortable with my own company."

One final attempt. Jo fingered the hem of her tunic. "There's no one special in your life?"

"Not for a long time. A very long time." He looked thoughtful. "There almost was, but the same thing came between us. How other men in the forces manage, I do not know."

"And what was that thing? If you don't mind me asking."

He sat up straight. "No, actually, I don't. It would be good to get a woman's view. An impartial one. It's the fact that I killed people for a living."

He was definitely talking about Karmela. "It isn't inevitable that a woman would see your job like that. Flying missions must have been a tiny proportion of your time. And it's not as if the decision to end anyone's life was yours; you were carrying out orders."

"Does that make it better or worse?"

"That you were doing your job?"

He looked down, fondling Sybil's ears, as the dog gazed up at him. "The thing is, when you join up as a youngster, like I did, you don't even think about it. I just wanted to fly, and I'd been in the air cadets since I was thirteen. Back then, the girls rather liked it." He smiled briefly. "But grown-up women don't."

"You said there was someone recently. Have you actually discussed it with her?"

He shook his head. "This time was personal. And the look on her face. I'll never forget it."

OK, Jo. Bite the bullet. Oh god, was that even an appropriate phrase? "Karmela? And Sarajevo?"

"Yes." His clipped voice was very much the RAF officer. He'd closed her down.

But Jo had one more thing to say. "Iain, talk to her properly. What do you have to lose? If you're right, then after Saturday you'll never see her again. But if you're wrong…"

Those green eyes bored into hers, unflinching. Silence. A long silence.

"Sorry if I've overstepped the mark," she said.

He stood, Sybil scrambling to her feet next to him. "You're only trying to be kind to me, I get that. And it's fine. Really it is. See you for the feedback session."

He was a couple of steps down the stairs when she called after him. "Not just kind to you, Iain, kind to both of you." Perhaps that, if nothing else, would make him think.

Thursday 28th September

Waiting in the lobby of her room, Karmela was alert to the click of the massive oak door in the corner of the courtyard as it opened, followed by the tinkle of Sybil's name tag against her lead. Now was the moment. She had no wish to run after Iain today.

She stepped outside, causing him to start, and Sybil to leap in her direction, barking.

"Quiet!" Iain hissed, as Karmela crouched down to fuss the dog, rendering her silent in seconds.

She looked up at him, grinning. "Her? Or me?"

"Both of you," he whispered furiously. "It's hard to put all the blame on the dog." He paused. "She's pleased to see you."

But was he pleased to see her as well? From his guarded expression, she thought perhaps not.

"Do you mind if I join you?" she asked, betting he would not be rude enough to refuse.

"Sybil would never forgive me if I said no."

She stood. "Then we must not disappoint her."

Together they left the courtyard and strolled down the track, the soft glow of dawn rendering the russet leaves on the vines even more vibrant. In the distance the pops of hunters' guns punctured the silence as on the neighbour's land they chased down rabbit for the pot.

For a while, neither of them spoke, Karmela searching for the words to begin.

"This time next week I will be walking through the city to work, with traffic thundering past. I am going to miss the peace and quiet. How about you?"

"I'm not really sure. My house in Bristol's let out and the tenants don't leave for a couple of weeks, so rather than stretching my sister's hospitality to its limits I thought I might take the slow way home. I might head across from Athens to the Adriatic and work my way up the coast."

"Oh, you will see such wonderful places. Kotor, Dubrovnik of course, Split, Pula…"

"I can't miss Dubrovnik. I feel as though I've already been there, courtesy of the extracts you've read to us from your book."

"You are very kind, but that is the city of five hundred years ago, although in truth certain parts of the old town would still be recognisable to the Ragusans. They did a very good job of rebuilding it after the shelling and mortar attacks in the war."

They were coming to the top of the gully where the shadows were long, despite the rapidly lightening sky. Iain released Sybil from her lead and the dog pranced hopefully around Karmela's legs. Having laid the foundation, Karmela had to say her piece.

"Talking of the war, Emina was killed before Operation Deliberate Force started. I asked my mother to check, so you are off the hook." She tried to meet his gaze, but he was looking at Sybil. "That is, if you want to be."

With that she clicked her fingers and ran down the valley, Sybil overtaking her within seconds. Back and forth they went as she made playful attempts to catch her as she zoomed past, skidded to a halt, then started all over again.

As she ran, she hoped and prayed that Iain would join in, but he stayed where he was, and Karmela's thumping heart sank. Just as well they would never see each other after Saturday. She was sure she could survive the embarrassment until then, but the walk back to the retreat might be excruciating, so she played with Sybil until she could barely breathe. Finally she had to stop, resting her hands on her knees, then looked up at Iain from a distance of about twenty metres.

"Your turn I think."

He walked slowly towards her. "And what about you?" he asked. "Does knowing when Emina died make a difference to you?"

Karmela unbent her body, trying to ignore the stitch in her chest. So he did want the conversation, after all. "I don't think it ever did. Not in itself."

"But your reaction when I told you! Karmela, I know I didn't imagine it."

"That was shock, and I am sorry. But the man you are now has not changed for me. I do not know what you carry from the missions you have flown, from the job you had to do, and perhaps I never will. Perhaps you have moved beyond it. We could just accept that we both have scars, or we could decide to explore them together. They might matter and they might not. But there is only one way to find out."

It was a far, far, longer speech than Karmela had set out to make, but she felt completely calm now everything was out in the open. She could say no more. It was up to him. And if his answer was no she could move on without regret.

"You really want to try?" Now he was looking at her. A long look from those stunning green eyes, just like the one on the ferry, that very first day of the retreat.

"Yes."

"Then OK."

She burst out laughing. "OK? OK? How is that meant to make a woman feel?"

"I told you I'm out of practice."

"Even so, that sounded particularly grudging."

He smiled, his whole face lighting up from the inside out. "Far, far from it. More like I'm stunned. I cannot believe my luck."

"Then would you like to have another go? Maybe show some enthusiasm, this time?"

"It's the very least you deserve."

To her intense surprise and joy, and accompanied by a cacophony of barking from Sybil, he picked her up and swung her around, before kissing her firmly on the lips.

Oh god, oh my god. How good did this feel? How exciting, how exhilarating. How new and shiny and…

He put her down, clutching his back. "You ask a lot from a middle-aged man, you know. Especially before breakfast."

Karmela dissolved into a fit of giggles. "You mean we are not worth it?"

"I didn't say that."

"Well then," said Karmela, tucking her arm into his, the glow from his warmth spreading through her. "Well then." That amazing feeling of oneness was back, and she did not think she would ever tire of it. This time she would grab it with both hands and she would not take no for an answer.

When Jo walked into the studio, the group was gathered around the table for the final feedback session of the retreat. This time tomorrow they would all be packing their cases and preparing for the farewell dinner; it was barely possible to believe the retreat was almost over. Just one more day, then on Saturday they'd be gone, never to be together again. The support she'd had from these people, through one of the most tumultuous periods of her life, she would never forget.

Sophie had been truly amazing. Their shared experience of bullying husbands had drawn them together, and it was to Sophie she'd taken Rees's increasingly threatening messages.

"Ignore them but keep them all," she'd advised. "And get yourself a divorce lawyer sooner rather than later. But if he's never been physically violent towards you before now then I very much doubt he'll start. He's just flailing around, trying to find another way of controlling you."

Much as Jo had come to understand Sophie, Diana was probably the person she knew the least, but she recognised her as the glue that held the group together with her unfailing kindness and tact. She also knew how to write a romance, and had in the end admitted that most of the work on their novel had been hers. When Jo told her she very much hoped she'd carry on writing with a view to publication, she'd asked if Jo would continue to mentor her. As a paid assignment, of course.

Jo had been about to say she didn't need the money, but it struck her that she probably did. Not immediately, and not for a while, but she certainly had no plans to write another book, and she didn't know if, given all the fuss, the magazines would take Jessica Rose's short stories anymore. Whether anyone else would employ her as a mentor, she doubted too. Except Zina, who had bravely asked her back next year. Which she had of course declined until they were absolutely sure how her reputation stood.

She sat down on the chair the group had left for her at the far end, setting her notebook on the table. "So here we are," she said. "The last feedback session. Iain, I think you're going to kick off with the piece we discussed at your one-to-one."

He grinned at her. "Actually, I'm not. I am going to read first, but something different. We wanted this afternoon to be a tribute to our wonderful teacher, but Karmela was adamant you'd be embarrassed if our pieces were about you, so we decided to each write something on your undoubted qualities and I've chosen courage."

Jo raised her hands to her burning cheeks. "Oh my goodness, I didn't expect this." What an absolutely wonderful thing. Her throat constricted.

Bugger. Not now, Jo.

But would it matter if she let her emotions show? These amazing people were her friends, after all.

"Well don't expect too much. Not from me anyway. You know how much I struggle to words get even in the order right."

Diana giggled, while Karmela groaned theatrically, holding her head in her hands.

Iain certainly had his spark back, and Jo was pretty sure she knew why. She had seen him and Karmela return from their walk this morning, so close they were all but touching, and when he'd glanced up at her window and spotted her, she was sure he'd winked. Karmela had had her head down writing today, but Jo would try to get a quiet moment with her later to find out what had happened. As if her friend's relaxed demeanour didn't already tell her.

Clearing his throat, Iain began to read.

"You must be brave.

"If I had a pound for every time someone told me that I wouldn't need to work again. Perhaps it is brave, flying at speeds in excess of a thousand miles an hour. Brave sounds a lot like bravado.

"Perhaps you can learn bravery, but true courage comes from within. Not from creating fears, but from facing them down. Not from flying high, but from hauling yourself out of the low. From grasping life with both hands.

"That is perhaps the scariest thing of all."

Iain stopped and grimaced.

"Susan challenged me to write it in fifty words, but windbag that I am, I went a bit over. Sorry."

"I think it was still fairly succinct," said Susan. "In fact, I would have liked the ideas explored a little more. They were so interesting."

Everyone in the group had been on some sort of journey, and Susan's was one of the most heart-warming. To have found her family – and so quickly, too, thanks to Panora – must feel like some sort of miracle, and instead of writing a history she'd had the bright idea of creating what she called a scrapbook of words – short stories, poems, flash fiction – all relating to her own feelings and what she was learning about her Greek relatives and their lives. Jo admired her for taking such an innovative approach and had loved working with her on the pieces she'd completed so far.

"Yes, I would have liked more too," Jo agreed. "Now I'm over the embarrassment of your choice of topic."

"But you are brave," said Diana, "and you're not the only one." She looked at Sophie, who shook her head slowly.

"Only by proxy. Anyway, I've written about empathy."

Jo struggled to control her emotions as Sophie read, not just because of her words, but because of the way the group had chosen to show their appreciation. Everyone had tried their best and pulled together to make this happen. By the time the last reader, Diana, had finished, Jo could barely stop her voice from shaking.

"I can't tell you how proud I am of you all," she said. "I was terrified when I came here but you have been a joy to work with, and I thank you from the bottom of my heart." Should she say more? Probably, but she felt too choked. Clearing her throat, she carried on. "Now don't forget that tomorrow morning I will need your feedback on the retreat, then there is just one final day for you to carry on with your work. Or head for the beach, or go shopping or sightseeing. It's up to you."

"I can't believe it's almost over," whispered Susan, her voice every bit as emotional as Jo's as she wiped her misting glasses.

"We came as strangers and leave as friends." Diana, of course.

"And there's plenty of room in my house if anyone wants to come to London," added Sophie.

Iain stood. "It's been a pleasure, and an honour, to listen to your work unfold, even if I haven't written anything much myself. Now, a little bird tells me that Zina has some of that excellent Santorini sparkling wine in the fridge, and it would be a shame to waste it."

"Something to celebrate?" Jo asked.

"Of course." He winked at her. "The most important things: friendship, honesty, courage and laughter."

Friday 29th September

Zina was setting small jars of gypsophila, rosemary and some very expensive rosebuds along the centre of the table when her mother's car pulled up next to the courtyard. Susan and Ellen spilled out, laden with boxes.

"How are we going to get all this home?" asked Ellen. "I'm not even sure we're allowed to take some of this stuff in."

Panora appeared from the driver's side. "Yes, but you could not refuse your family's gifts. Anyway, Ekaterini has grandchildren who like biscuits and cakes."

Susan flung her arms around her. "I don't know what we would have done without you. You've been amazing."

"I've loved every minute of it." Mama's face was glowing in a way Zina hadn't seen for a good long while, enhanced by the subtle make-up she had recently taken to wearing. She'd even had her hair cut and dyed, and was sporting a new chunky bead necklace which toned perfectly with her terracotta-coloured top. She had come out of herself so much that it made Zina worry how her mother would fare once her new friends had gone home. No doubt she'd miss them as much as Zina would, and she would have to find some way of filling the void for her.

"And just you remember what we said," Ellen told her. "Think about it. Seriously."

Panora watched them head to their room.

"What was that about?" Zina asked. It couldn't be Mama visiting them in the States; they'd already been talking about that for at least a week.

"They think, and to be honest, I have been thinking too, that I should start a business helping Americans with Greek heritage to find their families. Do you think it could work?"

"It's pretty niche, but I don't see why not." Her mother's face dropped. *Skatá!* She hadn't meant to sound less than enthusiastic ... she'd just been thinking. She gripped both her hands. "We'll make a plan. I'll find out how we can reach these people so they know about you, then I'm sure it will fly."

"There's quite a community in Detroit, apparently, where Susan comes from originally. It would be a place to start." Mama hugged her. "If you can promote it for me, it will be successful, I know. Now, I must go and pick the herbs Ekaterini wants for the garnishes tonight."

Zina hoped that her mother's confidence in her was not misplaced, but she was buoyed by the job she'd done for Jo. It was only a few days since they'd broken the story and the fuss had all but died down already. A famous tree on Hadrian's Wall had been vandalised and the media had all moved on to that. Thankfully. Well, not for the tree, but for Jo it had worked a treat.

And just as good was that while liaising with the publicity

team at Jo's publishers, Zina had been able to drop into the conversation that she was available for freelance projects, and they had asked for more information. Next week she would sound out some of her Athens contacts to see what the chances were of some work from them. She didn't need to be greedy; just enough to keep her brain busy. So she wouldn't have pent-up frustrations to vent on Lambros.

The table dressed to her satisfaction, she took some photos for her Instagram then headed for the kitchen. Tonight Ekaterini was preparing a Santorini feast, using as many local products as she could. The canapés included tiny *tomatokeftédes*, cubes of *chloró* cheese, and thin slices of *apóchti*, local pork cured with cinnamon and herbs. Then the starter would be fava with octopus, followed by Ekaterini's vegetable moussaka, which had been baking in the oven since early this morning.

For Zina the most exciting course would be dessert: honey-rich *melitinía* tarts served with ice cream made from Lambros's pistachios. Not only was it a chance to showcase one of his products to the retreat's guests, but Jo had begged Zina, Lambros, Panora and Ekaterini to join them for this special treat and to enjoy a little time together.

Zina did not like to think of the goodbyes that would follow. She had never considered that over the course of a month her guests would become friends. Some more than others, of course, and she felt a deep affinity for Karmela and Jo in particular, who had listened to her and understood. They had helped her to find a way through her problems, and been such wonderful examples of personal awareness. Her biggest lightbulb moment had been not when she'd realised it was a skill she was sorely lacking, but that it was one she could learn.

She would miss their presence more than she could say, but knew they would keep in touch. They had already made tentative plans for a weekend at Frankfurt's famous Christmas market – somewhere they could all reach relatively easily – and Zina just hoped she'd be able to afford it.

It seemed such an extravagance, but Lambros had told her she would easily earn the money with one or two freelance projects. Zina was determined that he would have a treat too, and if they couldn't afford a ticket for him to watch his beloved Olympiacos play in Athens the same weekend, then she wasn't going anywhere.

He hurried into the courtyard now, dressed in black jeans and a white linen shirt.

"Will this do?" he asked anxiously. "It's an age since I've dressed up."

She wrapped her arms around his neck and kissed him. "You look awesome."

"But do I look like a wine waiter?"

"An extremely sexy one. But come inside. We don't have much time and I need to show you where everything is."

A few minutes later Zina heard the oak door at the bottom of the staircase open, and she peeped out of the bar to see Iain emerge. He stopped in his tracks, gesticulating wildly at the table.

"Oh shit, shit! Zina, where's Lambros?"

They raced outside to find the smallest white-faced goat with her hooves on the end of the table, nibbling delicately at the rosebuds in a flower arrangement.

"*Bástardos zóo!*" Lambros yelled, diving around one side of the table, while Iain ran towards the other. Thankfully the shouting was enough to scare the goat off, as well as bring Susan and Ellen rushing from their room and Ekaterini from the kitchen.

Zina watched as Lambros turned to Iain, his face pale. "Oh god, she's going to kill me! Kill me!"

Not one, but two goats peeped around the corner of the building, and Lambros lunged, arms waving like a human windmill, before chasing after them, followed by Iain. They looked so ridiculous, so comical, and within moments both Zina and Ekaterini were bent double laughing, Ellen and Susan joining in.

Once she recovered herself, Zina checked the table. "I think we need a clean cloth," she said, looking at the hoof-shaped marks.

Susan appeared at her shoulder, then flicked the worst of the dusty soil away. "Oh no. And leave the flowers half-eaten too. We're going to have to tell the others about this; it was just so funny."

Ellen proffered her phone. "I managed to get a video too. It's a bit blurry though – Lambros moved so fast."

Susan giggled. "Perhaps I'll write a *flash* fiction about the goat who came to dinner."

They started to laugh again. "You do that," Zina told her, "and I'll give it to Lambros for his birthday."

Mama rounded the corner, clutching a bunch of herbs. "I think you'd better go and tell Lambros he's not in disgrace. He and Iain are skulking just down the track."

How ridiculous. Of course he wasn't. Why would he even think—? But Zina knew. This time she knew.

"Mama, can you start serving the drinks? We won't be a moment."

Lambros and Iain were about a hundred metres away, not exactly returning to the courtyard with any enthusiasm or speed. A couple of weeks ago she would have been angry, but now she recognised this was her fault. How absolutely mortifying she'd got herself into a place where her husband feared her reactions.

When she reached them, Lambros could barely look at her. "Zina, I'm so sorry."

She smiled and lifted his face in her hands. "You have nothing to apologise for. In fact, it was really funny."

The tension dropped from his shoulders. "Straight up?"

"Straight as you like. And I'm the one who's sorry, because I became such a miserable, humourless bitch you thought I'd go off on one. If only I could have seen it at the time ... but I'm changing, Lambros, I swear."

"And I shouldn't have overreacted." He brushed some hair that had come loose from her ponytail away from her face, and tucked it behind her ear, as Iain melted into the dusk behind them. "I guess the truth of it is, although we've made great progress we're still a little uncertain of each other's reactions. The things that could be flashpoints are going to feel clunky for a while."

"Misunderstandings will happen. We're married after all."

"We just need to learn to handle them better."

"And we will."

"And not forget we need to work as hard on our marriage as we do everything else."

He was right, so right. But at this moment they had a job to do for their guests. Zina put a finger on his lips. "Listen to us, Lambros. The way we're talking. That in itself means we're going to be fine."

He kissed the top of her head, then tucked her under his arm as they returned to The Retreat House as one.

Saturday 30th September

In the moment of waking, before even opening her eyes, Karmela was able to sense every subtle difference. The slight slope of the mattress away from her, the touch of the sheets on her naked skin, the warm breath in her ear. So this was what it was like to share a bed with someone. She felt safe. Cocooned. A frisson ran through her as she remembered the night before.

After dinner she had accompanied Iain on his last walk of the day with Sybil – a brief foray into the pistachio orchard, where they had kissed under the stars, like characters in Diana and Sophie's romantic novel. And when they returned to the courtyard, instead of saying goodnight, she had taken his hand and led him into her room. Nothing ventured, nothing gained. And she was so very glad she had ventured.

There had been a gentleness to his passion that had taken her breath away. No clumsy fumble, this; every touch showed how much he cared, and she hoped she had made him feel the same. The ultimate oneness. The ultimate cliché too. She really did feel that in their love-making they had become one, and it had awakened something inside her that she now knew had been missing. Quite what it was, she could not tell. She would come to it in time, she was sure.

Afterwards they had lain face to face and talked for hours – of places visited, of books, of childhood memories. The good ones, with no fear of mentioning Emina's name, and yet he had held her to him when she did. But now, as the birds began to sing outside, she realised they had spoken only of the past. The future was what they had been avoiding; even the immediate one of today's goodbye.

Iain stirred beside her, and she turned to him. Aware of the movement, Sybil jumped off the sofa, stretched, then padded over to place her nose on the edge of the bed.

"She's asking to come up," he murmured, his voice thick with sleep. "Not very romantic."

"Does she usually?"

"I'm afraid so. It's our little routine. I make coffee, then come back to bed while she curls at my feet and falls asleep again."

"Well you know where the machine is."

His laugh was early morning throaty. "Fair enough."

Iain swung his legs from the bed, tousling Sybil's ears and saying, "Up you come." The dog needed no second invitation and settled with her head on Karmela's thigh. Karmela switched on the bedside lamp, watching as Iain walked to the coffee machine. His body was in good shape: broad shoulders, sturdy thighs with a definite tan line halfway up them, and just the tiniest of love handles above his hips. She wondered for a moment how he viewed her scrawniness, but dismissed the thought. She could change nothing about it, and nor would she expect him – or any man – to change anything for her.

The machine had warmed up and he held a pod in his hand. "This one?"

"Yes. Espresso please."

"Because it was a long night?"

"Because I always drink it first thing."

He nodded and slotted in the pod then pressed the button. "I guess we have a lot to learn about each other. If we can work out how we go forward."

Karmela wriggled up the bed. "Perhaps we do not run before we can walk? Or maybe that is not the right English expression." She frowned.

"Are you thinking ... take it one step at a time?"

"That is it. Yes."

"Do you have any bright ideas for step two?" He walked across, handing her her coffee, before retreating to make his own.

"Are you still planning to drive up the Adriatic coast?"

"Yes, but my plans can be changed."

"No. It is fine. Perfect, in fact. I was thinking ... I could fly to Dubrovnik next weekend. We could meet there."

"You'd do that for me?" He sat on the edge of the bed, cradling his cup.

"It is only an hour, and it is one of my favourite places, and where most of my dearest friends live. You ask so much!" She laughed. "And besides, there is one particular friend you might find it interesting to meet. He fought on the ground in the war that you helped to finish from the sky. He was nineteen when it started and it changed him forever. If

Operation Deliberate Force stopped just one more teenager going through what he did, then you might see it differently."

"In truth I try not to see it at all. I've flown missions not only in Bosnia, but in Iraq, Afghanistan ... but it was never my country, never my family in the firing line. My weak spot is the men I lost; and as I got older, they got younger. Sometimes I see their faces and those times are dark. But it doesn't last long and I made my peace with it years ago. They paid the ultimate price while I was lucky, and I had a career I loved."

"Thank you for explaining. As you say, we have so much to learn about each other."

"Starting next weekend. But I don't want this to stop, Karmela. Last night was"—he looked down and cleared his throat—"very special. And I hope it was for you too."

She grasped his hand. "You made it special."

"We made it special."

So there was a we, that sense of oneness she had craved without really knowing it since the early days of holding hands on their morning walks. It felt like an adventure, and even the knowledge they would have to part in a matter of hours took nothing away from the feeling. A feeling of belonging. Not to a group of people, but to one other person.

Karmela put her cup on the bedside table and reached up to kiss him. After a few moments he slid beneath the sheets, pushing a reluctant Sybil out of the way. His skin on her skin, his taste in her mouth. One chapter of her life ending, and another beginning.

~

The courtyard was silent, the goodbyes that had punctuated the morning finally over. Jo had struggled from her bed at six to bid farewell to Susan and Ellen, then straight after breakfast Iain had taken Karmela to the airport, before going on to catch the mid-morning ferry. Finally, just minutes ago, Zina's car had disappeared up the track with Sophie and Diana on board. Her first writing retreat was over.

Jo's cases were already in her hire car, but she had half an hour yet before needing to leave. She stood for a moment, the lemon muskiness of the brightly coloured pots of geraniums tickling her nose. The dining table where they'd eaten such delicious food and talked the evenings away looked forlorn, stripped bare to the polished wood and not a crumb to be seen.

Her footsteps echoed as she ran up the stairs to her room. Of course it was hard to say goodbye because so much had happened here; her life had changed in one short month. Would she ever come back? It was far too soon to know. Plans were beginning to whirl around her head and if one in particular came to fruition, this time next year she would be starting a post-graduate certificate in teaching creative writing. If she was properly qualified, the fact she had once been Jessica Rose would cease to matter. In fact, no one need ever know.

Jo didn't want to have to spend the future hiding things. But common sense told her she should see where her reputation was in a month's time. In six months. Yesterday afternoon she'd given an interview to *The Washington Post*, and the female journalist had focused almost exclusively on the domestic abuse angle, one minute exploring it as it played out in the book, the next trying to get Jo to admit she was a victim too.

Doing so felt like a step too far. She had no desire to call Rees out in public. Her divorce would be bloody enough as it was, and the thought of going home had made her feel sick inside for most of yesterday … until she'd received a message from Curtis, telling her Rees had just left with three large suitcases. With any luck he wasn't planning to come back.

Jo couldn't blame him for everything, though. Not only because she still believed she could have stopped *Only. Ever. You.* being published, but also because there were things about herself she needed to change. Only so much could be put down to grief. She had made mistakes, and she damn well needed to learn from them.

She knew that deep inside she was still the painfully shy girl she'd always been. Yet at the same time, the Jo who had been so terrified she'd almost backed out of the retreat was a distant memory. Something had shifted. Something this month had forever changed.

Was it that she'd found her true skill? Teaching writers their craft, mentoring them as they honed it? She'd never be quite good enough as a novelist herself, and now she knew that instinctive knowledge had eroded her already fragile confidence too. But with work, and the courage to overcome her shyness, she could be a pretty good teacher, she was sure.

As Jo gazed over the courtyard towards the russet-coloured vines and olive grove beyond, she knew that finding enough courage would be the hardest part. She wrapped her arms around her rib cage, biting down on her lip. But with Karmela beside her she had conquered her biggest fear and told her mother the truth. Karmela was naturally brave, and it seemed it was contagious, because

Zina had found the inner grit to act decisively to save her marriage.

Jo knew that in the coming weeks and months, their little WhatsApp group would prove a tower of strength, both given and received. They were all going to need it, and they all had plenty to share. Already she couldn't wait for their visit to Frankfurt at Christmas, and as soon as the dust had settled at home she would book their tickets and hotel as a thank-you for everything these amazing women had done for her. She had a feeling theirs was a friendship that would endure.

With a final look around, Jo picked up her laptop bag, which had been leaning against the bookcase. On the day she arrived she'd noticed the copies of *Only. Ever. You.* on the shelf. The original paperback in English, plus the version with the movie poster cover. Translations in German and Greek. She'd been studiously ignoring them, but now she removed the books one by one, took her pen from her bag and wrote in each.

A novel by Pamela Collins, published as Jessica Rose.

If she'd come here weighed down by lies, she was leaving in the stark light of the truth. The next few months would be far from easy, but there was no going back. Only forwards. Starting right now.

~

Zina and Lambros walked down the track towards the farmhouse hand in hand. She'd come back from taking Diana and Sophie to the airport to find him hard at work cleaning Karmela's bathroom, having already stripped the bedding from all the rooms.

Now, three hours later, every inch of The Retreat House was shining, ready to receive new guests tomorrow. It was the first of a series of four week-long yoga retreats which would take them to the end of Santorini's main tourist season. After that she had little in the diary until March, except for a Christmas crafting week at the beginning of December and a handful of corporate getaways.

She had enquiries to follow up that might generate more, but nothing from Georgiou's HR director. If she even existed. God, she'd been such a fool and her toes curled with embarrassment inside her trainers. But if nothing else, the experience had helped to show her how precious her marriage was.

As they approached the house, they could see Mama outside, pegging washing to the line.

Lambros sighed. "I wondered if she'd be out. All those freshly made beds at the retreat looked mighty inviting."

"If we weren't running on the absolute minimum of linen changes."

"We won't always be so hand-to-mouth."

She shrugged. "I could always sell some of my work clothes on eBay."

"Not now you might need them. And besides, you always look so sexy in high heels."

"Lambros Sideris, what are you like?" She grinned at him.

"Just making up for lost time. And with a lull in the work on the farm, I even have a bit of energy."

"I had noticed." Zina gave him a quick kiss. "We need to start working on how to get our own home in the quickest possible time." She gazed up at the rusting iron rods sticking up from the farmhouse roof. "I did wonder if we could build up, like Babá always planned to, then divide the building between us."

"I think we could still find ourselves on top of each other, and not just literally. There's plenty of space elsewhere on the farm, but of course it'll be more expensive starting from scratch and we'd need the right permissions. But that way we'd get exactly what we want."

She leant into him, picturing a modern house of sleek lines and glass, and the latest eco technology. "It sounds like heaven. Maybe at the top of the olive grove, with a view of the sea."

"Maybe somewhere a bit nearer the existing water and electricity?"

"That's right, bring me crashing back down to earth," she said.

"Tell you what, let's pick a couple of sites and compare the costs. We'll have to budget, so we know how much we need to save. And of course, we'll only be able to build during the winter months so it will take an age anyway."

"Can't we just ... you know ... dream a little first?"

He hugged her tight. "Without dreams, we'd never be able to make them come true."

By the time they reached the farmhouse, Mama was back in the kitchen. "There are some beers in the fridge, and I've made *riganáda* in case you're hungry."

Lambros flopped down. "You're a lifesaver, Panora. Cleaning rooms is hard work." He picked up a slice of the toasted bread and tomato juice ran down his wrist.

"Tell me about it." Zina kissed her mother on the cheek. "Thanks, Mama."

Her mother sat at the table next to Lambros, while Zina fetched the beers. "One for you?" she asked.

"No, I'm going out, to see Eleni and Savvas. Look, you might as well know. One of his staff is leaving next month and he's offered me a part-time job."

"But what about your business idea?"

"I can do both. This job is in the bakery itself, so it's an early start and I'd finish by about eleven. I know I would be busy, but that's what I want, Zina. I need to move on with my life. I'm sure your babá would wish it."

"I'm sure he would too. You're still young, after all."

Mama nodded. "When I realised I'm only a few years older than Susan and Ellen and I felt like their aged auntie, I knew things had to change."

"Never," said Lambros gallantly.

Mama raised her eyes to the ceiling. "The point is that I am relatively young, and sad as it makes me, I can't have my old life back, so I need a new one. I need a change. A total change. In this house, my Petros is everywhere. At first it was a comfort, but now... The job Savvas is offering, because of the hours, the flat above the shop goes with it." She looked from one to the other of them. "You need your own space. I've seen that more and more these last weeks. It isn't fair on you, the way we've been living."

Zina was stunned into silence. This was the answer to their prayers, but was it really the right thing for Mama?

"Are you sure we're not pushing you out of your home?" asked Lambros finally.

"In truth I'm not sure about anything, but if there's one thing this last month has shown me, I can't waste the rest of my life getting old before my time. And if it doesn't work out, then I'll have to come back."

Zina took both her hands. "You really want to do this for yourself? Not just for us?"

"I do. I want to get out into the world again. Working for family is a pretty low-risk first step. And I'll be able to save for my trip to America."

Zina's eyes filled with tears. This was not about her, or even Lambros. It was about Mama, her mama who'd come so far from her navy and black widow's uniform that she was wearing a rich turquoise silk shirt over her jeans. It was frigging wonderful. "I can't tell you how proud of you I am. But please, please, never think you can't come back."

"One day, we want to build our own home anyway," said Lambros. "This will always be yours. But thank you. Thank you for giving us the space when we need it most."

Mama picked up her handbag. "I must go, or I will be late."

They followed her out to the car, watching as she bumped up the track.

Zina turned to Lambros. "I had no idea…"

"Me neither. It goes to show that you live with someone, think you know them, and then they surprise you like this."

Was there anything behind his comment, or was it as casual as it sounded? "Do I surprise you, Lambros?" she asked.

"This last week, in more ways than you can imagine. Wonderful ways. I feel like I'm getting to know you all over again. And yet, you're the same girl I married." He shook his head slowly. "I'm a lucky, lucky, man."

"*We*'re lucky, Lambros. I was terrified we were growing apart, but now we have the chance to grow even closer. Our thirties could be our best decade yet."

She put her head on his shoulder as he held her tight. Up the valley the domed roofs of The Retreat House glowed in the sun, the breeze carrying the scent of wild thyme from the fringes of the abandoned fava field. And Zina realised, for the first time since they'd returned to Santorini, it felt like home.

Acknowledgments

With love from Santorini

It's October as I write this, and our last full day on Santorini. I always prefer to do my research trips once the first draft of a book is finished, so I can focus on the places that come to matter to my characters and the details of life in a foreign country. For this book, at first I felt very much alone, because unlike my Croatian novels, I didn't have a friend to help me.

A little over four months ago, this book did not exist. I had a vague idea in my mind that when Karmela returned to Zagreb from her sabbatical in Dubrovnik, where she joined The Dubrovnik Book Club, she would find a writers' group. Then that group would be led by an author with a secret and a controlling husband. It was only during a snatched lunch with my then editor Bonnie Macleod that the setting became a writing retreat. And we agreed it would be somewhere other than Croatia.

By the end of a very long train journey back to Cornwall I had sketches for a cast of characters. Bonnie and I loved them all, and after she left One More Chapter for pastures new, Charlotte Ledger helped me to knock them into shape and suggested the ideal location for the retreat was Santorini. And could I write it by Christmas because she wanted it for next year.

Like Zina, I'm normally up for a challenge, and I knew this one was just about do-able, especially with editor Laura McCallen on board, and my word count buddies from the Cariad chapter of the RNA urging me on – not to mention providing me with their best ways of dealing with rejection for Jo to give to her class.

So last Monday, when I arrived on Santorini, I had a completed first draft to work on. I knew exactly which of the wonderful destinations on the island my characters would be visiting, so I had the onerous task of going to them too.

I always prefer to show something of the traditional life in my locations, so I decided to set the retreat in a beautiful rural area, far away from the caldera rim. Farming on the island is becoming eroded by buildings relating to the tourist trade and the sad fact is that much of the middle belt of Santorini is low-rise urban sprawl. But to the south, in particular, a slower pace of life can still be found.

I am hugely indebted to Yiannis Nomikos and Yianna Nikolopoulou of Nomikos Estates for introducing me to Santorini's traditional crops and how they are grown, processed and turned into delicious deli products. The morning spent with Yiannis was the best of our trip; he gave his time and enthusiasm so generously – not to mention the wonderful goody bag of products we came home with. You can find out more about this wonderful enterprise – and perhaps visit yourself – here: https://nomikosestate.com/

Another foodie treat – and I do appreciate how much my readers love local food – was a visit to Venetsanos winery with its fabulous caldera views. The location features in the book and again is a place well worth visiting, with knowledgeable staff and wonderful wines, which can be served with local specialities like the ones Ekaterini chooses for dinner on the last night.

We stayed near Megalochori, and for a village holiday less on the beaten track (well, less for Santorini) I really recommend it, because it hasn't lost its heart. Our base was the gorgeous Caldera's Dolphin Suites (https://www.calderas-dolphin.com/) and my thanks go to manager Kyriakos Dasouras in particular for answering my questions about island life in such detail and with such patience.

Not being a dog owner myself, I put out a call on Facebook for funny dog stories. Thank you to everyone who answered, especially Jen Gilroy and Sophie Ide whose waggy tales made it into the book. Also to Sue and Gordon Kind at Finca el Cerrillo who graciously allowed me to name Sybil after their dog, and to use the jukebox game, which we play every year.

Some personal thank yous to end with, and in many ways these are the most important. To Rosanna Ley and the friends I have made on her writing retreats at Finca el Cerrillo in Spain, for getting thoroughly behind the book. To fellow novelists Jan Baynham and Kitty Wilson for their beta reading, and all the other writer friends who keep me sane. To Helen Williams, newly arrived at One More Chapter, for picking up the baton and running with it with such wisdom and enthusiasm. But most of all to Jim, my husband and constant companion on all life's journeys. Including research trips to beautiful islands.

If you would like to keep in touch with news about my books, it would be great if you would sign up to my newsletter (https://mailchi.mp/99543ad90bea/sign-up), or join my Facebook community (https://www.facebook.com/EvaGlynAuthor), or follow me on Bookbub for news of deals (https://www.bookbub.com/profile/eva-glyn). Do let me know what you think of *The Santorini Writing Retreat*. I'd love to hear from you.

Escape to Croatia and join a new book club with friends, favourite reads and a mystery to unravel...

In a tiny bookshop in Dubrovnik's historic Old Town, a book club begins...

Newly arrived on the sun-drenched shores of Croatia, Claire Thomson's life is about to change forever when she starts working at a local bookshop. With her cousin Vedran, employee Luna and Karmela, a professor, they form an unlikely book club.

But when their first book club pick – an engrossing cosy crime – inspires them to embark upon an investigation that is close to the group's heart, they quickly learn the value of keeping their new-found friends close as lives and stories begin to entwine...

Available now in paperback, eBook and audio!

The author and One More Chapter would like to thank everyone who contributed to the publication of this story...

Analytics
James Brackin
Abigail Fryer

Audio
Fionnuala Barrett
Ciara Briggs

Contracts
Laura Amos
Laura Evans

Design
Lucy Bennett
Fiona Greenway
Liane Payne
Dean Russell

Digital Sales
Laura Daley
Lydia Grainge
Hannah Lismore

eCommerce
Laura Carpenter
Madeline ODonovan
Charlotte Stevens
Christina Storey
Jo Surman
Rachel Ward

Editorial
Janet Marie Adkins
Kara Daniel
Charlotte Ledger
Lydia Mason
Laura McCallen
Ajebowale Roberts
Jennie Rothwell
Helen Williams

Harper360
Jennifer Dee
Emily Gerbner
Ariana Juarez
Jean Marie Kelly
emma sullivan
Sophia Wilhelm

International Sales
Peter Borcsok
Ruth Burrow
Colleen Simpson
Ben Wright

Inventory
Sarah Callaghan
Kirsty Norman

Marketing & Publicity
Chloe Cummings
Grace Edwards
Emma Petfield

Operations
Melissa Okusanya
Hannah Stamp

Production
Denis Manson
Simon Moore
Francesca Tuzzeo

Rights
Helena Font Brillas
Ashton Mucha
Zoe Shine
Aisling Smyth
Lucy Vanderbilt

Trade Marketing
Ben Hurd
Eleanor Slater

The HarperCollins Distribution Team

The HarperCollins Finance & Royalties Team

The HarperCollins Legal Team

The HarperCollins Technology Team

UK Sales
Isabel Coburn
Jay Cochrane
Sabina Lewis
Holly Martin
Harriet Williams
Leah Woods

And every other essential link in the chain from delivery drivers to booksellers to librarians and beyond!

One More Chapter is an award-winning global division of HarperCollins.

Subscribe to our newsletter to get our latest eBook deals and stay up to date with all our new releases!

signup.harpercollins.co.uk/join/signup-omc

Meet the team at
www.onemorechapter.com

Follow us!
@OneMoreChapter_
@onemorechapterhc
@onemorechapterhc
@onemorechapterhc

Do you write unputdownable fiction? We love to hear from new voices. Find out how to submit your novel at
www.onemorechapter.com/submissions